ALEXANDRE DUMAS

GEORGES

A new translation by Tina A. Kover

Edited, with an Introduction and notes, by
Werner Sollors

Foreword by Jamaica Kincaid

THE MODERN LIBRARY

NEW YORK

Frontispiece: *Alexandre Dumas* (1829),
from a lithograph by Achille Devéria, with Dumas's signature

GEORGES

ALEX · DVMAS ·

ALEXANDRE DUMAS

Alexandre Dumas, who lived a life as dramatic as any depicted in his more than three hundred volumes of plays, novels, travel books, and memoirs, was born on July 24, 1802, in the town of Villers-Cotterêts, some fifty miles from Paris. He was the third child of Thomas-Alexandre Davy de la Pailleterie (who took the name of Dumas), a nobleman who distinguished himself as one of Napoleon's most brilliant generals, and Marie-Louise-Elisabeth Labouret. Following General Dumas's death in 1806 the family faced precarious financial circumstances, yet Mme Dumas scrimped to pay for her son's private schooling. Unfortunately he proved an indifferent student who excelled in but one subject: penmanship. In 1816, at the age of fourteen, Dumas found employment as a clerk with a local notary to help support the family. A growing interest in theater brought him to Paris in 1822, where he met François-Joseph Talma, the great French tragedian, and resolved to become a playwright. Meanwhile the passionate Dumas fell in love with Catherine Labay, a seamstress by whom he had a son. (Though he had numerous mistresses in his lifetime Dumas married only once, but the union did not last.) While working as a scribe for the duc d'Orléans (later King Louis-Philippe), Dumas collaborated on a one-act vaudeville, *La Chasse at l'amour* (*The Chase and Love*, 1825). But it was not until 1827, after attending a British performance of *Hamlet*, that Dumas discovered a direction for his dramas. "For the first time in the theater I was seeing true passions motivating men and women of flesh and blood," he recalled. "From this time on, but only then, did I have an idea of what the theater could be."

Dumas achieved instant fame on February 11, 1829, with the triumphant opening of *Henri III et sa cour* (*Henry III and His Court*). An innovative and influential play generally regarded as the first French drama of the Romantic movement, it broke with the staid precepts of Neoclassicism that had been imposed on the Paris stage for more than a century. Briefly involved as a republican partisan in the July Revolution of 1830, Dumas soon resumed playwriting and over the next decade turned out a number of historical melodramas that electrified audiences. Two of these works—*Antony* (1831) and *La Tour de Nesle* (*The Tower of Nesle*, 1832)—stand out as milestones in the history of nineteenth-century French theater. In disfavor with the new monarch, Louis-Philippe, because of his republican sympathies, Dumas left France for a time. In 1832 he set out on a tour of Switzerland, chronicling his adventures in *Impressions de voyage: En Suisse* (*Travels in Switzerland*, 1834–1837); over the years he produced many travelogues about subsequent journeys through France, Italy, Russia, and other countries.

Around 1840 Dumas embarked upon a series of historical romances inspired by both his love of French history and the novels of Sir Walter Scott. In collaboration with Auguste Maquet, he serialized *Le Chevalier d'Harmental* in the newspaper *Le Siècle* in 1842. Part history, intrigue, adventure, and romance, it is widely regarded as the first of Dumas's great novels. The two subsequently worked together on a steady stream of books, most of which were published serially in Parisian tabloids and eagerly read by the public. In 1843, *Georges* appeared, the only novel in which Dumas represented racial prejudice toward people of color. He is best known for the celebrated d'Artagnan trilogy—*Les trois mousquetaires* (*The Three Musketeers*, 1844), *Vingt ans après* (*Twenty Years After*, 1845), and *Dix ans plus tard ou le Vicomte de Bragelonne* (*Ten Years Later; or, The Viscount of Bragelonne*, 1848–1850)—

and the so-called Valois romances—*La Reine Margot* (*Queen Margot*, 1845), *La Dame de Monsoreau* (*The Lady of Monsoreau*, 1846), and *Les Quarante-cinq* (*The Forty-Five Guardsmen*, 1848). Yet perhaps his greatest success was *Le Comte de Monte-Cristo* (*The Count of Monte Cristo*), which appeared in installments in *Le Journal des débats* from 1844 to 1845. *Le Chevalier du Maison-Rouge* (*The Knight of Maison-Rouge*, 1845–1846) was also a collaborative effort. A final tetralogy marked the end of their partnership: *Mémoires d'un médecin: Joseph Balsamo* (*Memoirs of a Physician*, 1846–1848), *Le Collier de la reine* (*The Queen's Necklace*, 1849–1850), *Ange Pitou* (*Taking the Bastille*, 1853), and *La Comtesse de Charny* (*The Countess de Charny*, 1852–1855).

In 1847, at the height of his fame, Dumas assumed the role of impresario. Hoping to reap huge profits, he inaugurated the new Théâtre Historique as a vehicle for staging dramatizations of his historical novels. The same year he completed construction of a lavish residence in the quiet hamlet of Marly-le-Roi. Called le Château de Monte Cristo, it was home to a menagerie of exotic pets and a parade of freeloaders until 1850, when Dumas's theater failed and he faced bankruptcy. Fleeing temporarily to Belgium in order to avoid creditors, Dumas returned to Paris in 1853, shortly after the appearance of the initial volumes of *Mes Mémoires* (*My Memoirs*, 1852). Over the next years he founded the newspaper *Le Mousquetaire,* for which he wrote much of the copy, as well as the literary weekly *Le Monte Cristo,* but his finances never recovered. In 1858 he traveled to Russia, eventually publishing two new episodes of *Impressions de voyage: Le Caucase* (*Adventures in the Caucasus,* 1859) and *En Russie* (*Travels in Russia,* 1865).

The final decade of Dumas's life began with customary high adventure. In 1860 he met Garibaldi and was swept up into the cause of Italian independence. After four years in Naples publishing the bilingual paper *L'Indépendant/L'Indipendente,* Dumas returned to Paris in 1864. In 1867 he began a flamboyant liaison with Ada Menken, a young American actress who dubbed him "the king of romance." The same year marked the appearance of a last novel, *La Terreur Prussiene* (*The Prussian Terror*). Dumas's final play, *Les Blancs et les Bleus* (*The Whites and the Blues*), opened in Paris in 1869.

Alexandre Dumas died penniless but cheerful on December 5,

1870, saying of death: "I shall tell her a story, and she will be kind to me." One hundred years later his biographer André Maurois paid him this tribute: "Dumas was a hero out of Dumas. As strong as Porthos, as adroit as d'Artagnan, as generous as Edmond Dantès, this superb giant strode across the nineteenth century breaking down doors with his shoulder, sweeping women away in his arms, and earning fortunes only to squander them promptly in dissipation. For forty years he filled the newspapers with his prose, the stage with his dramas, the world with his clamor. Never did he know a moment of doubt or an instant of despair. He turned his own existence into the finest of his novels."

CONTENTS

FOREWORD

Jamaica Kincaid

Georges: Yes, it is a great joy to read this new translation of Alexandre Dumas's long lost and forgotten novel, for it is fantastic, picturesque, almost believable, romantic, suspenseful, violent (as is to be expected when Africans, enslaved or not, are involved), sexy, naïve, and many more things besides.

And why do I think so? Here is an explanation: My mother, in an attempt to distract my young interest in her, taught me to read, and by the time I was three and a half years old, I could do so. This caused such a sensation among everyone, including and especially me. I then had very little to read: there was the tin of Ovaltine, the tin of butter from New Zealand, a book my mother owned which described the human body and the known tropical diseases that could destroy it, the King James version of the Bible. I read the writing on the tins over and over, each time as if they were new, each time as if I had never read them before; I read the book on the body and the tropical diseases that could kill it over and over because it was illustrated and the illustrations were described and the descriptions were fabulous, and better still, not understood by me; I read the King James version of the Bible because it was all of the above as it was also many things apart from all of the above. I soon came to think of reading as "sweet" and by that I was not referring to any relationship to the five senses (I knew then there were five of them), I was thinking of something that did include them but also something that I had no real way of putting into words. At that time I could read but I was also learning to read; at that time the sensation that is reading became known to me.

Georges would have been so welcome to me then, for I would have approached it with complete freshness (reading was new, and the novel before me, *Georges,* was not imaginable; I was innocent of the intricate workings of the world in which I lived), taking it as it presented itself, a romance and all that comes with romance; a tale of adventure and all that comes with that; a narrative of the virtues and the virtuous explicated and exalted and then made shoddy and questionable and full of suspicion and then renounced and abandoned.

The world of *Georges* is an island, and that island is Eden before it was despoiled by European conquests and afterwards the only thing left of it was, well, the vegetation, especially the vegetation. The landscape of Eden is the perfect landscape for this kind of situation: it offers the best sunsets against which murderous grudges take a short rest; the unprecedented hurricane will interrupt the outcome of the most successfully planned revolt; the trees are always overbearing in fruit and the enslaved escapee may be lost among their thick trunks but will never die of hunger; that thing called Time is not the same thing that is familiar through a wristwatch. Such is the physical world of *Georges.* Like Eden, too, this island is a source of contests of will, only not God and Lucifer, just England or France.

Georges himself (the hero, all of this novel comes from him, is about him) is not Adam (in any case Adam is not a hero of that story), he is not an original man, he is not the first of his kind, but he has the vanity to think himself so. As a child, he suffered an insult and this insult is new, unlike any insult visited on any child before; all life from then on is experienced and interpreted through this initial childhood event. Georges is not a slave but he is descended from slaves; Georges is not white but he could pass for white; Georges is not an entirely free man (he is partly descended from the enslaved) but his manners in every way are so correct that really free men (European) cede him a place in their presence and even their society.

In the world in which I was growing up, in St. John's, Antigua, the landscape of *Georges* was an everyday reality; the people inhabiting that landscape were familiar but not in real time; they were from yesterday, but as if yesterday were one hundred years ago before today.

This is, for me, the glory of *Georges:* I am reminded of an early pleasure and it so vividly portrays a long-ago recent past. The two are intertwined to such an extent that they are one: early, long ago, recent, past! It has been six hundred years now since Christopher Columbus left the coast of Spain and set off on a journey to find a new world, or was it to prove that the world was round, or was it to prove that people everywhere found a confounding and unrewarding curiosity in other people and places far removed from anything they knew. Within Dumas himself all of these things were true: he was a French man, and he was descended from Africans and Europeans, and he was a writer.

Writers need someone to read them, no matter what age they are writing in. More important, readers, budding or otherwise, need something to read. *Georges* was written over one hundred years before I was born and later learned to read. I am reading it now, and at my age it should be an old story, but an old story becomes a classic because it manages to bring up something new, something that it seems you have never heard of before.

———

JAMAICA KINCAID is the acclaimed author of many books, including *Annie John, A Small Place,* and *Lucy.* She lives in Vermont.

INTRODUCTION

Werner Sollors

A glaringly visual and truly suspenseful novel, *Georges* is a little-known gem among Alexandre Dumas's more than three hundred volumes of fiction, drama, travel literature, and autobiography. First published in 1843, a particularly fruitful year in Dumas's adventurous life, *Georges* preceded by only one year the appearance of the *Les Trois Mousquetaires* (*The Three Musketeers*) and the beginning serialization of *Le Comte de Monte-Cristo* (*The Count of Monte Cristo*)—the two novels for which Dumas was to become most famous. In fact, in his hero-genius Georges Munier, Dumas anticipated certain aspects of his best-known protagonists, d'Artagnan and Edmond Dantès, as Scott Robert Russell has shown; Georges also undergoes a long period of self-steeling preparation in which he has to learn to exert self-control and to dominate his passions in order to gain heroic stature, and he experiences injustice at the hand of lifelong enemies—in his case a father–son pair of biased, small-minded, and vindictive villains whom he later has to confront.

In the mid–nineteenth century, Romantic-Realist French fiction dominated the imagination of the Western world perhaps as much as American popular culture ruled the globe at the end of the twentieth century; *Georges* gives the reader all the melodramatic pleasures of that genre, as it offers vivid, truly spectacular scenes of sea battles and festivals, of a slave conspiracy and a wild pursuit, of a grand ball and a hurricane, of a horse race and a pig chase, of a duel and of gambling, of imprisonment and escape, and of a beautiful bathing maiden saved at the last second from the jaws of a vicious shark. *Georges* appeals to our wish for hair-raising suspense and swashbuckling adventure and surprises us with a dramatic rescue at the last moment by a pirate in disguise. It rewards our sentimental expectations with the love story between Georges and Sara de Malmédie as well as with the tenderly drawn bonds among the three men in the Munier family. With its richly rendered setting on the île de France, it gratifies exotic-picturesque fantasies of a romantic island by presenting a bird's-eye view of verdant mountains under clear and starry skies, and by letting the reader almost literally feel the sea breezes redolent with floral perfume that are drifting through bamboo blinds. An aviary bustles with turtledoves, fondijalas, and flycatchers; the flora is a mix of Parisian and tropical flowers: tuberoses, Chinese carnations, Spanish jasmine, anemones, Indian roses, and the colorful Cape amaranth as well as francopenny and tamarind trees.

The teeming mass of humanity populating the novel includes heroes and villains, virgins and courtesans, allies and enemies, governors and captains, masters and slaves, brave hearts as well as cowards and traitors; the cast of major and minor figures comes from a broad spectrum of the world's population. Among the Africans are Yoloffs and Mozambicans, Malgaches and Lascars; Laïza and Nazim are Anjouans from the Comoros Islands; there is the Chinese trader Miko-Miko, happy to find out that Georges, who was raised by a Chinese nursemaid, can speak his language; among Europeans, there are French and English characters as well as a seemingly Dutch captain. Georges goes to France and Italy, and because travels to the Orient were at that time "all the rage," he also visits Greece, Turkey, Asia Minor, Syria, and Egypt and meets Muhammad Ali just before Ibrahim Pasha quelled the Wahhabite rebellion in the Arabian peninsula. In the particularly colorful section on the Yamsé festival on île de France the narrator also explains the division between Shiites and Sunnis that lies behind the very name of that feast. Dumas's novel thus offers a broad and, one could even say, global perspective of a small place, and with his knowledge of French, English, Arabic, and Chinese, Georges embodies the virtues of the cosmopolitan hero that such a world would seem to require. Dumas's broad topographic reach should not mislead the reader to assume that all of the novel's place-names are real: Googling Antonio the Malay's supposed birthplace, "Tingoram," for example, yields only references to Dumas's *Georges*.

The novel also gives a precise sense of history and embeds its plot in the transformation of the island, connecting it with the larger historical changes that have taken place from the period of the Revolution and Napoleon to around 1824, the time in which the bulk of the novel is set. Île de France was first colonized by the Dutch, then became French, and changed its name back to Mauritius after the sea battle of 1810 (the subject of chapter 2) that brought the island first into British hands. The beginning of the novel is thus set thirty-three years before its date of publication, and Dumas partakes in the vogue of historical fiction to which he explicitly alludes when he mentions Sir Walter Scott. Like other participants in the new postrevolutionary vogue of the historical novel, Dumas mixed historical personages (Captain Willoughby, for example) with imaginary ones (Lord Murray) and was eager to trace the changes that divided a "then" from a "now." The way in which the novel twice identifies the island's capital, "Port Louis, formerly Port Napoleon," thus alerts the reader to a past that has given way to a different present, a present that in turn is destined to become past. The French defeat at Mauritius is a step toward Napoleon's abdication, yet Napoleon remains a touchstone not only for the dramatic changes Dumas's world had undergone since 1789 but also for the inspiring role played by the self-crowned emperor-genius who spread the ideals of the French Revolution around the world. It is thus no coincidence that Georges attends the Collège Napoleon in Paris.

The reference to Scott is not the only literary allusion, for *Georges* is deeply steeped in broad readings going back to ancient authors and myths. Without disturbing the pace and flow of the narrative, Dumas tells his nineteenth-century story in a rich web of literary allusions that anchored the new tale he was telling in the storehouse of stories familiar to the reader, from Venus, Diana, and the hetæra Lais of Corinth to Jupiter, Helios, and Enceladus. These references also serve to enhance the sense of the novel's intelligence, a sensibility that includes narrator as well as hero. The very choice of the bird's-eye view of the island with which chapter 1 opens is thus revealed as a technique Dumas adopted from Alain-René Le Sage's *Le Diable boiteux* (*The Limping Devil*), in which the title character, the devil Asmodée, takes the student Don Cléofas above Madrid and lets him see through rooftops and walls. Dumas's narrator thus plays the part of the devil. As Dumas makes explicit in two references and an allusion, his choice of the île de France as a setting is also an acknowledgment of Bernardin de Saint-Pierre's immensely popular island love story *Paul et Virginie:* The narrator states at the beginning that the reader may have guessed that the tomb he describes at the Church of Pamplemousses is that of Bernardin de Saint-Pierre's star-crossed lovers whose sad poetic memory is evoked when Georges returns to the island in chapter 4; and *Paul et Virginie* is also the book Georges reads when he awaits his execution—not, as the priest expected, the Bible. Georges and Sara's story may have grown in part out of *Paul et Virginie,* but *Georges* rewrites the sad love story as one that does not end with the faithful lovers' tender union in death at Cape Malheureux. Instead, Dumas suggests that there is a future on earth for his romantic couple.

Other references are made to characters, works, and scenes such as Adamastor from Camoens's *Lusiads,* Cervantes's *Don Quixote,* Samuel Richardson's *Clarissa,* Lord Byron's *Cain,* and the witches' night scene at the Brocken in Goethe's *Faust.* Such allusions, common in novels of the period, also amount to a pact with the reader who, a century and a half ago, would have been expected to catch most of them, whereas the modern reader will need annotations for many. The novel's multiple noteworthy allusions to Satan and to various devils from literature—Asmodée, Mephistopheles, Lucifer—are part of the work's Romantic spirit.

Is *Georges* then a genre piece? Is this novel that must have circulated widely in the nineteenth century, that was translated (often freely) into English, German, Spanish, Italian, Dutch, Norwegian, and Swedish, and was adapted for the stage in Paris, nothing but a representative (though perhaps particularly vivid) work of a line of fiction that one could call the French Hollywood of its time? This is, of course, a rhetorical question, even though *Georges* could still be turned into an exciting Hollywood film today. The negative answer my question calls for is given by the fact that Georges is not only a hero like d'Artagnan and Dantès, but also a man of color, a mulatto—and the word *mulâtre* appears more than fifty times in the French text of the novel. Like Dantès, Georges reappears in his original world as a new, "transfigured" man, but Georges's disguise is that he is often taken for white; and like d'Artagnan he has to face his eternal antagonists, but in Georges's case the antagonists he confronts are also the embodiment of color prejudice. This makes *Georges* exceptional in Alexandre Dumas's own œuvre, for it is the only novel in which Dumas—the celebrated, though at times also reviled, man of color—focuses on the color complex.

Léon-François Hoffmann, a most careful critic of Dumas's *Georges* who ranks it among Dumas's best, yet too-little-known works, focused on this aspect of the novel. He found that in *Georges,* Dumas employed, but did not get carried away by, melodramatic plot machinations and that he instead wrote a complex novel in the "noble" sense of the word. Was this the case because of his serious theme: that of the struggle against the vulgar yet common color prejudice of M. de Malmédie and his son Henri, similar to that which Dumas—as Hoffmann amply documents—was also exposed to? Georges Munier is, in this context, a particularly intriguing and strong character, a fully formed mixed-race hero, whose psychological development from age twelve to twenty-six, from sensitive and vulnerable childhood to self-possessed maturity, is well drawn in the novel against the background of the racial pressures he experiences. What distinguishes *Georges,* then, is that it is a *problem novel,* in addition to everything else that it takes on so well; and the problem of color prejudice that it examines is one that has not gone away and seems particularly relevant in our own days.

The political dialogue between the demagogic Antonio who plays the race card and the idealistic rebel Laïza who invokes the principle of liberty is as strong an indication of the novel's timeliness as is Georges's quip in defense against Antonio's hypocritical attempt to subvert his leadership by stressing indignantly that Georges "loves a white woman!" Georges responds that "there is another victory for men of color, for the white woman loves me, too." (*Et c'est un triomphe de plus pour nous autres hommes de couleur . . . car la fille blanche m'aime.*) Dumas's narrative position is clear, for Antonio who plays up the issue of racial loyalty is, in fact, the traitor in this book; and Georges, who has given his slaves freedom and four piastres each, has only the noblest of motives. It deserves mention in this context that *Georges* was published eight years after slaves had been freed in the British colony of Mauritius and five years before France would free slaves in its own colonies.

What informs the novel is not only the conflict over African slavery, first abolished in France in 1794, but then reinstated in 1802 (by Napoleon!) and ended only in 1848. Neither is it prejudice against *all* nonwhites that *Georges* excoriates or an attack against all forms of bias that the novel exemplifies: one only has to remember the hardly flattering description of the Chinese whom the narrator twice calls "the Jews of the colony," or the account of the many blacks who, unlike the idealistic Georges who is ready to lead them, do not participate in the slave revolt because they find the barrels of rum the governor sets out for them more enticing. It is telling that Georges's brother, Jacques, whose sarcasm in this matter seems vindicated by the plot, has been making his living as a slave trader.

The book's central tension is between rich white Creoles and equally rich though discriminated-against mulattoes on île de France. The question is how the bigoted and aggressive men in the white Creole Malmédie family can be restrained by the mixed-race Muniers who are also rich and hold slaves. In fact, Georges is a multimillionaire who can afford to free his slaves. *Georges* is not so much an abolitionist or a black novel then, but, as Hoffmann has argued, a "mulatto novel." And it is in this aspect that the author's autobiographical investment in the novel has been sought, for Georges Munier is a man of color who was imagined by Alexandre Dumas, France's most famous nineteenth-century man of color. Dumas would seem to invite such a reading when he connects his hero Georges with the Chevalier de Saint-Georges, a Guadeloupe-born mixed-race composer and military leader in whose American legion of mulattoes the novelist's father, Thomas-Alexandre Dumas-Davy de la Pailleterie, once served.

There was, however, no biographical connection between Dumas and Mauritius; in fact, Dumas had never been on the île de France when he wrote *Georges* and he would also never visit the island later on. Yet he rendered his setting so vividly in the novel that one is surprised to realize that he did so only with the help of secondary sources, among them accounts by his friend Félicien Malleville, a Mauritian. Perhaps Dumas's île de France was a symbolic stand-in for another island to which the writer traced his own roots, the American island that he lets Laïza mention, "Saint-Domingue, now called Haiti" (a distinct echo to "Port Louis, formerly Port Napoleon"), forever associated with the revolution undertaken by people of color in the name of liberty.

If Dumas's île de France carries the legacy of his ancestral Haiti, the island of a successful rebellion, it is also very much the island of love. Dumas may have been inspired to tell an interracial love story against a revolutionary island background by a then still-young tradition of French fiction about race, romance, and revolution, often informed by tales coming out of Haiti and in which mulattoes played important roles. Victor Hugo's *Bug-Jargal* (1826) was an early milestone in that tradition. Alexis de Tocqueville's travel companion Gustave Beaumont wrote the novel *Marie* (1835), which features a rebellious mulatto named Georges. The New Orleans expatriate and free man of color Victor Séjour published "Le Mulâtre" in the *Revue des Colonies* (1837), the Parisian organ of a radical society of People of Color and edited by Martinican Cyrille Charles Auguste Bissette. It is the story of a mulatto named Georges who becomes a rebel against his own white father, and it begins in Saint-Marc, "a little town of Saint-Domingue, these days the Republic of Haiti." Dumas, who later on helped the Louisianan in his career as a dramatist in Paris, may have known him as early as the 1830s. In any event, Séjour's "Mulâtre" was published in the very journal to which, one year later, Dumas sent an open letter against a maliciously circulated rumor suggesting that Dumas would be contributing poetry to the pro-slavery *Revue coloniale.* In that letter Dumas stated that his sympathies were for the opposite party, as was well known among all whom he counted as "frères de race et des amis de couleur" (race brothers and colored friends).

Dumas may have also read "Les Épaves" by Fanny Reybaud, a popular novella of 1838 with a heroic, Paris-educated mulatto genius who is enslaved by a vicious and jealous white Creole, but then dramatically freed by and married to a white aristocratic heiress at the very end; the Danish fairy-tale writer Hans Christian Andersen adapted Reybaud's tale in his romantic play *Mulatten* (1840). The tradition of which *Georges* was a part continued after Dumas. In his novel *O Mulato* (*Mulatto*, 1881), the Brazilian anti-slavery novelist Aluízio Azevedo, for example, represented the well-educated and handsome mixed-race protagonist Raimundo, whose love for the beautiful and white Ana Rosa is vehemently opposed by her father.

It is not surprising that even though *Georges* remains relatively unknown today, Dumas has been a fairly constant reference point for African American intellectuals, as Michel Fabre has shown. Thus when the runaway slave William Wells Brown went to the 1849 Peace Congress in Paris as one of twelve delegates from Massachusetts, he desired to meet Dumas. This was still before Brown became the first African American to write a novel in English. He had a letter of introduction, but the connection did not work out. Yet one night at the opera, Brown noticed "a light-complexioned mulatto, apparently about fifty years of age,—curly hair, full face, dressed in a black coat, white vest, white kids,—who seemed to be the centre of attraction not only in his own circle but in others. Those in the pit looked up, those in the gallery looked down, while curtains were drawn aside at other boxes and stalls to get a sight at the colored man. So recently from America where caste was injurious to my race, I began to think that it was the wooly head that attracted attention when I was informed that the mulatto before me was no less a person than Alexandre Dumas. Every move, look and gesture of the celebrated romancer were watched in the closest manner by the audience." Frank J. Webb signaled that he was writing suspenseful fiction in Dumas's vein by letting his gory thriller "Two Wolves and a Lamb" (1870) end on the île Ste-Marguerite—an island famous as the setting of *L'Homme au masque*

de fer (*The Man with the Iron Mask*), the last volume of Dumas's Musketeers series.

Brown saw Dumas in person, and Webb was his contemporary and
may have also met him in Paris, but later African American authors
who did not would invoke Dumas together with Pushkin as writers to
be held in high esteem as a source of racial pride and as implicitly
supporting a critique of the American racial scene. This is true, for example, for a character in Frances Harper's novel *Iola Leroy* (1892) who
proclaims that "Alexander Dumas was not forced to conceal his origin
to succeed as a novelist." In Charles Chesnutt's often ironic short-
story collection *The Wife of His Youth* (1899) the narrator says about
Solomon Sadler who makes it his business to know everything about
colored men of distinction: "He could give the pedigree of Alexander
Pushkin" and "the titles of scores of Dumas's novels (even Sadler had
not the time to learn them all)." In 1914 Chesnutt also devoted a lively
address to Dumas, in which he reviewed Dumas's family history and
literary career and offered a critical assessment of the writer whom
"one reads solely for the story" and whose "invention was kaleido-
scopic in its variety and spontaneity." Chesnutt found that Dumas's
"heroes are men of blood and iron, who know what they want and proceed to take it, by artifice at times but preferably by the strong hand."
Addressing the question of whether Dumas's race mattered, Chesnutt
surmised: "There was . . . about him a certain naïveté, an abounding
good-nature, and a verve or swing which is almost as well punctuated
as ragtime; and these, as well as his robust physical vigor, his brown
complexion and his curly hair, may perhaps be safely attributed to his
dark blood. He was not ashamed of it, often mentioned it with not the
least self-consciousness—it was of no social or business disadvantage
for him in France, where talent has always been recognized and rewarded in absolute disregard of race or color—and he wrote one
novel, *Georges, the Planter of the Isle of France,* of which the race problem
in one of its aspects formed the motive."

In the Harlem Renaissance, Gwendolyn Bennett published the
poem "Lines Written on the Grave of Alexandre Dumas" in the pages
of *Opportunity,* opening with the address, "Thou, great spirit, wouldst

shiver in thy granite shroud / Should idle mirth or empty talk / Disturb thy tranquil sleeping." Langston Hughes viewed Dumas's successful career as a sign that freedom for colored writers was far greater in France than in the United States. Thus Hughes reported that his father responded to young Hughes's admiration for Dumas with the brief comment, "Yes, but he was in Paris where they don't care about color." Later Hughes wrote in his poem "Prelude to Our Age": "In other lands Dumas and Pushkin wrote / But we, / Who could not write, made songs: *Swing low, sweet chariot.…*" In 1936 John F. Matheus and W. Napoleon Rivers prepared an annotated school edition of Dumas's *Georges* in French that was reprinted in 1970. And in *White Man, Listen!* (1957), Richard Wright held up an at first unidentified passage from *The Count of Monte Cristo* and commented: "Did a Negro write that? It does not sound Negroid." Dumas was, Wright emphasized, "a Negro according to American racial codes," yet "his being a Negro was the least important thing about him." This was so because "he could attend any school he wanted to; . . . he could engage in any profession he wanted to; he could live where he wanted to; he could marry whom he wanted to; and if he had the mind and talent, he could win fame if he wanted to. He did win fame. He was at one with the culture in which he lived, and he wrote out of the commonly shared hopes and expectations of his age." Wright's conclusion about Dumas is in implicit contrast to the situation of African American writers who were not fully at one with America: "We can say that Dumas was integrated with the culture of France and was a Frenchman."

Still, while Alexandre Dumas has been a favored writer among African American writers and intellectuals, *Georges* seems not yet to have enjoyed a wide readership among them. Not even Langston Hughes, with his long-standing interest in writing about mulatto themes in poetry, drama, and fiction, or Richard Wright, whose long years of Parisian exile made him more deeply aware of the French literary tradition, appear to have known *Georges*. The same also seems true for Frederick Douglass, who was exceptional among African American intellectuals in angrily criticizing Dumas for having "never said one word for his race" (as one of his contemporaries reported).

This, a pretty clear suggestion that Douglass had not read *Georges*, did not prevent Douglass from taking his second wife to see the Château d'If, the setting of *The Count of Monte Cristo*, "because the genius of the Negro writer had woven around it such a network of enchantment." Frederick Douglass may have been reluctant to think of Dumas as a race hero, but he did want to see Gustave Doré's statue of the famous writer in Paris.

That statue is not the only indication of Dumas's public reputation in France. The high esteem in which Alexandre Dumas is held in that nation can be measured by the fact that in November 2002 Jacques Chirac's government transferred Dumas's ashes to the Panthéon. Dumas is the first author of color to receive this, the highest honor in France. At the ceremony, there were readings from the *Les Trois Mousquetaires* and *Le Comte de Monte-Cristo*. Let us hope that soon *Georges* will also be read with renewed interest in France and, in this lively new translation by Tina Kover, in the English-speaking world.

GEORGES

I

L'ÎLE DE FRANCE

Have you ever, on a long, cold, melancholy winter night—alone with your thoughts and the wind whistling through the hallways, the rain pounding against the windows—have you ever leaned your forehead against the mantel, absently watching sparks dance on the hearth, and longed to flee our wet and muddy Paris for some enchanted oasis? Somewhere fresh and carpeted in green, where you could lie in the shade of a riverside palm tree and doze off without a care in the world?

Well, the paradise of your dreams exists! Eden awaits you; the water flows clear and bright there, falling and surging up in bright dust; the palm fronds wave gently in the soft sea breeze like feathers in a genie's cap. The jambosa trees, laden with iridescent fruit, stand ready to offer you their sweetly scented shade. Come, follow me now.

Let us make for Brest, warlike sister of bustling Marseille, standing sentinel over the waves. Choose a vessel from the hundreds anchored in its port—perhaps a brigantine, long-masted, lean, and light-sailed, fit even for the hardy pirates dreamed up by Walter Scott, that romantic poet of the waves. It's early September, the perfect time to begin a long voyage. Let us board our chosen ship and leave sum-

mer behind in our quest for spring! Adieu, Brest, Nantes, Bayonne—
adieu, France!

See there, on our right, that granite peak towering ten thousand
feet into the clouds? Look, in such transparent water even its mighty
roots are visible. It is Tenerife, the ancient Nivaria, rendezvous point
for the eagles that swoop and glide around its crest, looking as small as
doves from this great distance. This, however, is not our destination;
it's simply a stray bit of Spain, and I've promised you the garden of the
world.

Look, on the left—that barren rock, burning in the tropical sun?
Our modern Prometheus spent six years chained there. England
chose that wasted islet to erect a monument to its own shame, to the
stake where Joan of Arc burned and the scaffold where Mary Stuart
died. It is a political Golgotha, and for eighteen years it was the pious
rendezvous point where all ships converged. But—enough of the
regicide St. Helena, we will have nothing more to do with her, now
that the martyr is gone.

We've reached the Cape of Storms now. See the towering peak in
front of us, its summit lost in the mists? This is the giant Adamastor,
who appeared to the author of *The Lusiads*. It marks the very end of
the earth—the prow of that great green vessel on which we are all
passengers. How the waves crash with furious impotence against its
rocky face! It is impervious, invincible, forever anchored here in the
port of eternity with God himself as captain. Let us keep on. Beyond
these verdant mountains lies nothing but barren stone and sun-
scorched desert. I promised you pure water, gentle shade, succulent
fruit, and radiant blooms, did I not?

Ah, the westerly wind has finally brought us to our destination—
the Indian Ocean, theater of the *Arabian Nights*! There is grim Mont
Bourbon, with its sulfurous, eternally flaming volcano. Spare a glance
at its fiery maw and smell its fumes. Just a few knots more now; we pass
between île Plate and Coin-de-Mire and round pointe aux Cannon-
iers, and we drop anchor at last. Our trusty brigantine has earned a
rest. We have arrived! This is the blessed island itself, hidden away in
this far-flung corner of the world like some virginal maiden whose
mother jealously guards her beauty from covetous suitors' eyes. This

is the Promised Land—the pearl of the Indian Ocean. This is île de France.

Now, chaste daughter of the seas, twin sister of Bourbon, blessed rival of Ceylon, let me raise a corner of your veil so that I may introduce you to a foreign friend, my fellow traveler here. Let me just loosen your sash—there! Ah, beautiful captive! We are two poor pilgrims from France—France, who will, perhaps, arrive one day to reclaim you at last, rich daughter of India, for the bride-price of some poor European realm...

As for you, dear readers, who have followed our eyes and our thoughts this far, let me bid you a very hearty welcome to this land of fertile fields, bountiful harvests, and endless springs and summers bursting with flowers and fruit. Let me wax poetic for a moment and tell you of the wonders of this place. It is a veritable Aphrodite, born of sea foam to reign over a celestial empire, her toes in the sea and her head in the clouds, crowned with golden days and crystalline nights, eternal jewels gifted by God himself—which the English have never yet managed to take from her. Come, then—air travel doesn't bother you any more than sea travel, does it? Good! Grab hold of my coat-tails, then, you new Cléofas, and fly with me to the peak of Pieterboot, almost the highest mountain on the island. We can see everything from there!

The sky is always clear, as you see, and thickly clustered with stars; it is a blue carpet where God left behind gold dust in each of his footsteps, and where each atom is a world in itself. The whole island is laid out at our feet like an enormous map, 145 leagues around. Its sixty rivers look like silver threads winding their way to the sea, and its thirty mountains are thickly forested with takamaka, palm, and basket trees. See, among all those rivers, the great waterfalls of le Réduit and la Fontaine, rushing wildly from deep in the woods to crash thunderously into the ocean below—the mighty ocean that, calm or stormy, will always defeat the fury of the cascades. There, too, is the mighty rivière Noire, flowing majestically, shaping everything in its path and showing how time and tranquility always conquer unbridled rage. Gloomy Brabant stands among the other peaks like a giant sentinel keeping watch for enemy attacks. There is the crest of Trois-

Mamelles, around whose base curl the Tamarin and Rempart rivers, as if the Indian goddess Isis wished to leave her mark. Gaze, finally, at the towering summit of le Pouce, near Pieterboot, for it is the highest point on the island; it seems to touch the very heavens, reminding us of the celestial court that will eventually render judgment on us all.

Before us is Port Louis, formerly Port Napoleon, the island's capital city, protected from invaders by île des Tonneliers. See its many wooden houses and the two rivers running among them, which turn into veritable torrents after every storm. Its population holds a sample of every race of Earth. There are Creoles being carried about in palanquins, so indolent that their slaves are trained to respond to gestures rather than words; then there are the blacks, for whom the sun rises and sets by the lash of a whip. Falling somewhere between these two extremes are the Lascars, faces tanned under their green and red turbans. There are the Yoloffs of Senegambia, tall and handsome, with skin dark as ebony, sparkling eyes, and teeth like pearls; there are the short Chinese, flat-chested and wide-shouldered, with their bare heads and drooping mustaches. No one understands their language, yet they are masters of trade; there is no profession they do not practice; no merchandise they do not sell; no service they will not provide. They are the Jews of the colony. Gaze at the Malays, small, cunning, copper-skinned, and vindictive, who will forget a kindness in the blink of an eye but bear a grudge forever; the gentle giants of Mozambique; the Malgaches, slim, ruddy, and clever; the tall, proud Namaquois, trained to hunt tigers and elephants from earliest childhood. And there, in the midst of this teeming mass of humanity, are the English officers stationed on the island or in the port, proud in their scarlet jackets, black helmets, and white trousers. They look around them with supreme disdain, dismissing Creole and mulatto, master and slave, native and colonist with equal scorn; they speak only of London, of dear old England, and of themselves.

Behind us bustles Grand Port, formerly Port Imperial, established originally by the Dutch and then abandoned, for the same strong breezes that bring vessels so easily into the harbor too often prevent them from leaving as well. After years of neglect and decay, it is only today that houses are beginning to rise anew from the old ruins—a town once more, with a bay in which schooners seek refuge from pirates against a backdrop of green-forested hills where slaves hide from their tyrannical masters. Just behind those emerald peaks, almost under our very feet, you will find the region of Moka, lying on the slopes that face away from the port, perfumed with the scents of aloe, pomegranates, and cassis. It is a garden within a garden, the garden of the world; always festive and beautiful, the most breathtaking spot on the island.

Let's face Madagascar again. To our left, beyond le Réduit, are the beautiful plains of Williams and Saint-Pierre, then Moka, the loveliest part of the island, divided by the rounded bulk of Mont Corps-de-Garde, shaped like a horse's rump. Farther on, past the Great Woods, is the savanna, with its winding rivers called Citronniers, Bain-de-Négresses, and l'Arcade, and its well-defended port, so perfectly protected by steep hills that only friends may enter. Its pastures are as fertile as those of the Saint-Pierre Plains, its soil as virgin and untouched as that of the American wilderness. Farther inland there is an enormous lake filled with moray eels large and savage enough to devour live deer and even runaway slaves foolish enough to attempt a swim.

Finally, we turn to our right. Here is the Rempart district, dominated by the peak of Mont Découverte, beyond whose summit the ships' masts rise like so many delicate willow branches. There are Cape Malheureux, the Bay of Tombeaux, and the Church of Pamplemousses. Here, too, are the two side-by-side huts of Madame de la Tour and Marguerite. It was at Cape Malheureux where the *Saint-Géran* sank, and in the Bay of Tombeaux that the corpse of a young woman was found, a torn portrait clutched in her hand. She was laid to rest in the Church of Pamplemousses, and just two months later a boy of the same age was buried beside her. You may have already guessed it: They were the tragic young Paul and Virginie, star-crossed tropical lovers buried in a single crypt, whose deaths are still mourned in the sighing rise and fall of the waves as a tigress might mourn the cubs she herself destroyed in a momentary fit of rage or jealousy.

So! Now that I have acquainted you with our fair island, with her inlets and shores, her rivers and hills, you may go wherever you like,

day or night—to the île de la passe de Descorne in the southwest, or
to Mahebourg on Petit-Malabar; along the coasts or deep in the interior; you may swim the rivers or climb the mountains, or watch the
blazing disk of the setting sun light up the plains as if they were afire
or the moon cast her melancholy light on the peaks, and if you are
lulled by the afternoon heat, the Chinese rose water, or the Spanish
jasmine, if you feel as lazy as if you had taken opium, you may stretch
yourself on the soft green grass and abandon yourself without fear to
the voluptous pleasures of sleep. If you are wakened, though, by a
gentle rustle of leaves, be assured that it's no Jamaican beast nor Bengal tiger; there are no reptilian hisses to be heard on île de France, nor
the nocturnal roars of any predatory animals. No; it is only a bright-
eyed young black girl gazing curiously through the bamboo stalks at
this new European visitor. Simply smile at her and she will gather you
a feast of ripe bananas, mangoes, and tamarinds. Say but one word to
her, and she will reply, in her low and wistful voice, "I slave; I do what
you want." Shining with pride and satisfaction at your kind looks or
tolerant words, she will refuse all pay and offer to lead you to her master's house. Follow her down a tree-lined avenue to a pretty home
with a flower-filled garden. Here lives the planter—he may be a
benevolent father to his slaves or he may be a tyrant, but then, that has
nothing to do with you. Enter and sit at the family table, and you—the
honored guest—will be served from dishes of fine china and goblets of
clearest crystal, endlessly refilled with the island's best ale. Hunt in
your host's fields as much as you like; fish in his rivers; dine on his fat-
test calf. Here, the arrival of a guest is cause for celebration, like the
return of a prodigal son to Paradise.

The English have long coveted this beloved daughter of France.
They have hovered around her, attempting to seduce her first with
rich gifts, then threats, and finally by force. She met every approach
with supreme disdain, this lovely Creole of ours; she acquitted herself
so well, in fact, that the men who desired her were so anxious to possess her that she had to be guarded as one might keep watch over a
fragile Spanish nun. For a time it seemed that she would be left in
peace, that she would be able to fend off any aggressors—but England

launched a final, impassioned attack, and one morning île de France learned the terrible news that her sister island Bourbon had been taken. Sharpening their knives and polishing their guns, the defenders waited for the enemy to appear—and on August 23, 1810, accompanied by the deafening thunder of cannon fire, they came.

Lions and Leopards

It began at five o'clock in the evening. Half the inhabitants of île de France gathered on the hillsides around Grand Port, transfixed by the spectacle unfolding below them, just as the ancient Romans once watched gladiators fight to the death. The vast harbor, walled by reefs and shoals, served as the arena; the combatants were French and English ships.

On the morning of the twentieth, five French ships coming from Madagascar neared île de France, led by Captain Duperré of the *Bellone*. They had recently engaged in a string of skirmishes; they had won battles, but these had left them damaged, and Duperré hoped to refit his battered fleet at Grand Port. At that time, the region was entirely French, and the tricolor fluttered from both the fort at île de la Passe and the schooner anchored below it—so, naturally, the brave captain believed himself among friends. Accordingly, he ordered the rest of the fleet to bypass île de la Passe and make directly for Grand Port. The corvette *Victor* struck out in front, followed by the *Minerva*, the *Ceylon*, and the *Bellone*, with the *Windham* bringing up the rear.

As the *Victor* passed the anchored schooner, the latter signaled that English ships had been sighted off île de la Passe. Captain Duperré replied that he was perfectly aware of it; there were four English vessels, to be sure—the *Magician*, the *Nereid*, the *Sirius*, and the *Iphigenia*, commanded by Commodore Lambert—but since Captain Hamelin was also near the island with a second French fleet consisting of the *Entreprenant*, the *Manche*, and the *Astrée*, he felt sure that the enemy would be considerably outgunned if hostilities were to erupt.

A moment later Captain Bouvet, second in the convoy, was surprised to see signs of suspicious activity aboard the schooner. Studying the other ship with a seaman's unfailing eye for detail, he saw that it was missing the marks normally distinguishable on a French vessel. He immediately shared his observations with Captain Duperré, who told Bouvet to take precautions and that he would do likewise—but, alas, they could not warn the *Victor;* she was too far ahead. It was a horrific shock for her crew, then, when cannon fire erupted from both the schooner and the fort, ripping through the corvette's sails and shattering her decks! English flags speedily replaced the tricolors. It was a trap!

Rather than retreating, the wounded *Victor* returned the English schooner's fire—but weakly. Captain Duperré, aboard the *Bellone*, signaled the *Windham* to go for reinforcements and ordered the *Minerva* and the *Ceylon* to follow him. The three ships advanced in the thick silence that often precedes a raging storm. The *Minerva* was soon exchanging artillery fire with the enemy. The *Ceylon*, a swift and lovely brigantine recently captured from the English, wasted no time in joining the fray. Meanwhile the *Bellone* dropped anchor between île aux Singes and pointe de la Colonie. Captain Duperré, receiving word that île Bourbon had been taken, sent word to Governor-General Decaen that he and his fleet had been engaged at Grand Port. By noon on the twenty-first, Decaen had infantrymen en route to assist the defenders.

The *Windham* had been taken by the English frigate *Sirius* in the early hours of the twenty-first as she attempted to drop anchor in the rivière Noire. The frigate's commander, Captain Pym, then made for Grand Port, flanked by the *Magician* and the *Iphigenia*. The second French fleet—the *Entreprenant*, the *Manche*, and the *Astrée*—pursued them hotly, but they could not overtake the English ships before they reached the harbor.

At midday on August 22, the *Sirius* reached Grand Port and joined the schooner—now known to be the *Nereid*, under the command of Captain Willoughby. The two ships advanced on the French, intent on destruction—but the *Sirius* caught bottom, and her crew was occupied for the rest of the day in setting her afloat once more. The reinforcements arrived that night, giving the French a total of fourteen hundred men and 142 guns.

At two o'clock the following afternoon, the English frigates *Magician* and *Iphigenia* arrived in the harbor. The enemy forces were now seventeen hundred men and two hundred cannons strong.

A terrible silence prevailed as the ten thousand mountainside spectators watched the four enemy frigates advance with grim confidence, sails lowered, toward the French defenders. It would be a battle between lions and leopards, a fight to the death.

Our sailors fired the first shot. A burning hail of bullets and cannonballs soon engulfed both groups of combatants. The skirmish was fierce—at first it seemed that the enemy might prevail, for the English quickly crippled both the *Minerva* and the *Ceylon*. The *Bellone*, captained by the courageous Duperré, faced all four foes at once, spewing fire like an erupting volcano for better than two hours while her sister ships repaired their damage enough to reenter the fray.

The *Nereid* was the first to tire, and the French forces concentrated their fury on her. For more than an hour she was bombarded with shot, but the white flag of surrender did not appear. Her masts splintered and fell; great holes gaped in her hull; finally she lapsed into immobility.

A moment later Captain Duperré was hit as he turned to give an order to his lieutenant. Knowing himself to be seriously—perhaps mortally—wounded, he turned command of the *Bellone* over to Captain Bouvet with the order that the French ships should be destroyed rather than surrendered. Night had fallen, and combat ceased until one o'clock the next morning, when the moon illuminated the battle-ground with its pale rays.

Captain Bouvet, on the *Bellone*, instructed Lieutenant Roussin to take the helm of the *Victor* in its wounded commander's stead and ensure that the *Nereid* was completely out of commission. Only an occasional musket shot still echoed now and then from the battered English ship, but Roussin followed Bouvet's orders to the letter and fired on the *Nereid* until she was silent as a tomb. Still the white flag did not appear. Suddenly cries of *"Vive l'empereur!"* were heard among the ruins, and seventeen French prisoners taken at île de la Passe emerged from belowdecks. The British standard was lowered and the tricolor of France hoisted. Roussin gave the order to board the crippled ship, but at that moment the English turned their own guns on the lost prize, and in the end the *Victor* simply collected the French refugees and left the devastated hulk of the *Nereid* to float.

The French fleet now concentrated its fire on the *Magician*. Captain Bouvet was resolved to destroy the enemy frigates one by one, and the bombardment did not cease even as the English ship, battered and listing, was abandoned by her few surviving crew members. The lifeboats, too, were soon downed; wounded men could be seen in the water, struggling to reach the two remaining frigates—but plumes of smoke issued from the *Magician*'s portholes, and in an instant the entire ship was engulfed in flames. Scant moments later there was a frightful explosion, like a volcano erupting, and the vessel was no more. Nothing was left: no debris, no wounded men, not even any floating corpses. Only a large empty space between the *Nereid* and the *Iphigenia* indicated the place where the *Magician* had been.

As if exhausted, both the French and English fleets left off their fire. The rest of the night passed in repose. The next morning, however, combat began anew. The *Sirius* was chosen as France's next victim. After two hours the English ship was in ruins; her masts had been completely obliterated, and her hull was in tatters. She could do nothing but sink. Her remaining crew rigged her with bombs before they abandoned ship—the captain, of course, was the last to leave—and, at eleven o'clock in the morning, like the *Magician* before her, she exploded and was gone to keep her rendezvous with Saint Barbara.

The *Iphigenia*'s fate was now sealed. Alone against four defenders, she raised her sails, pulled up anchor, and made a break for the mouth of the harbor—better to escape with damage than to meet the same fate as her sister ships—but it was not to be. Captain Bouvet ordered the *Minerva* and the *Bellone* to give chase. Not a single Englishman would survive to report the defeat—after all, there were Trafalgar and Aboukir to avenge!

The two noble French frigates, battered as they were, hoisted their sails and followed the *Iphigenia*. Shouts rose from the island, urging them on. For a time it seemed as if the English vessel might escape; she was too far ahead of her pursuers, and their bullets fell uselessly into the water, far short of their target. But then all of a sudden—three more ships appeared at the mouth of the harbor, the tricolor fluttering atop their masts! It was Captain Hamelin, arrived from Port Louis with the *Entreprenant,* the *Manche,* and the *Astrée*! Needless to say, the *Iphigenia* was easily, and utterly, obliterated. The French did not take a single prisoner.

Meanwhile the *Victor* approached the wrecked carcass of the *Nereid.* Fearing some surprise attack, the French sailors boarded her with great caution—but the silence that prevailed was indeed a deathly one. The decks were strewn with bodies, the blood ankle-deep. One Englishman, mortally wounded, managed to tell them that the command to raise the white flag had been given no less than six times— but every time, French gunfire had killed the men attempting to execute the order. The captain had retreated into his quarters, and no one had seen him after that.

Lieutenant Roussin, entering the cabin, found Captain Willoughby at a table still laid with a bottle of rum and three glasses. One of his arms and one leg had been shot away. His first mate lay near him, dead of a bullet wound to the chest. Willoughby's nephew William Murray sprawled insensible—but alive—at his uncle's feet, bleeding from his side.

Captain Willoughby, with his remaining hand, made a feeble attempt to offer Roussin his sword; the lieutenant refused it, and instead saluted the dying Englishman. "Sir," he said, "when an officer has fought as courageously as you have, he need offer his saber only to God himself."

Roussin ordered that Willoughby should receive all possible medical attention—but the noble commander of the *Nereid* died the next day. The French were pleased, however, that William Murray had been taken alive. We will see him again as our story unfolds.

III

Three Children

As might be expected, the English did not allow the loss of four warships to put them off their conquest of île de France; instead they now sought to both win a new victory and avenge an old defeat. Barely three months after the events I have just described, a second battle occurred at Port Louis, opposite where the first battle had raged, quite as ferocious as the first one but with a very different result.

Instead of four warships and eighteen hundred men, twelve frigates, eight corvettes, and fifty transports bearing twenty or twenty-five thousand men now landed on the coast and advanced rapidly toward Port Louis, which, as I have said, was then called Port Napoleon. The island's capital presented an almost indescribable spectacle as it braced itself for the attack. Excited crowds milled in the streets, ignorant of the true danger they faced; even the most outrageous rumors found widespread belief as they passed from ear to ear. An aide-de-camp of the commanding general appeared periodically among the multitudes, carrying orders and scattering pamphlets written specifically to arouse patriotism and anti-English sentiment among the locals. Their fervor increasing by the moment, men thrust their hats onto the points of their bayonets and waved them vigorously, crying

"Vive l'empereur!" and vowing to fight to the death if they must. The crowd fairly vibrated with enthusiasm; the rapidity of their transition from uneasy calm to imminent action had incited their hunger for battle.

The real hub of activity was the place d'Armes in the city center. Here thronged caissons drawn by small Timor and Pégu horses in full gallop, cannons painfully dragged by groups of artillerymen, teenage boys with smooth, powder-blackened cheeks. Civil guards in full uniform could be seen hurrying toward the square alongside volunteers in every sort of attire, who had added bayonets to their hunting rifles, and alongside blacks clad in tattered military dress, carrying every type of firearm and saber. This motley crowd shouted and jostled one another, adding to the general hubbub that rattled the city and made it hum like a vast beehive.

Once they had arrived at the place d'Armes the men calmed down a bit. Half of the island's garrison was already there, composed of enlisted troops: fifteen, perhaps eighteen hundred men, drawn up in ranks and waiting for the order to march against the enemy. Their attitude, at once proud and unworried, seemed to silently reprove the noise and tumult that characterized their brave but untrained civilian comrades who were less familiar with this sort of combat, even while they admired the civilians' bravery and willingness to go into battle. The blacks crowded to one side of the square, while the national volunteers attempted to imitate the soldiers' military discipline by drawing near to them and trying unsuccessfully to arrange themselves in identical lines.

The man who appeared—through his own strenuous efforts, truth be told—to be the leader of the volunteers was forty or forty-five years of age and wore a field officer's epaulets. He was unremarkable in appearance, with impassive features devoid of what an artist might refer to as character. He was coiffed, shaven, and decked out as if for a parade; every few moments he unbuttoned his military coat a bit farther to reveal the brocade vest, ruffled shirt, and embroidered cravat beneath. A comely boy of twelve years of age stood near him, discreetly attended by a black servant and luxuriantly dressed in vest and white trousers, frilled shirt, green jacket with silver buttons, and feathered gray beaver cap. He displayed the arrogant sort of ease that often accompanies wealth; a scabbard hung from his belt, and he clutched a small sword in his right hand, imitating the officer—whom he loudly and pointedly addressed as "Father"—as closely as he could manage. The battalion leader seemed as proud of this appellation as he was of the eminent post to which the trust of his fellow citizens had elevated him in the national militia.

A short distance away from this splendid father and son stood another family group, humbler in appearance but certainly just as notable, made up of a man in his middle forties and two boys, twelve and fourteen years of age. The man was tall, spare, and slightly stooped, not by age, but by the consciousness of his inferior position. His coppery skin and frizzy hair marked him out immediately as a mulatto, one of those unfortunate colonial beings who cannot be forgiven for their color, no matter how much success or wealth—and this is often quite substantial—they may attain. He was dressed with elegant simplicity and armed with a gold-inlaid, short-barreled musket topped by a long, sharp bayonet. A cuirassier's saber hung easily from one side of his tall frame, and his pouch and pockets bulged with spare cartridges.

The older of the two boys who accompanied this man was a tall youth with skin bronzed more by outdoor sport than by his African blood. He was as sturdy and robust as a lad of eighteen; consequently, his father had allowed him to participate in the action that was about to begin. He was armed with the double-barreled shotgun he normally used for hunting, and he had a reputation for skill with the weapon that was envied by older men. His youth was more evident than usual at the moment: He had placed his gun on the ground and was wrestling playfully with an enormous Malgache dog someone had brought along in case the English were accompanied by bulldogs.

The younger brother was a small, delicate child who seemed an unlikely member of the physically impressive family I am attempting to describe. Unlike Jacques—for so the older brother was named—Georges looked at least two years younger than he really was; he was skinny and fragile, with slender limbs, long black hair, and a melancholy face of a paleness not often found in the colonies. He lacked both the tall stature of his father and the powerful body of his brother, who seemed to have taken all the strength intended for both boys. On the other hand, his gaze was so penetrating, so troubled, and so deeply intelligent that it, along with the frown that was already ever-present on his forehead, gave him an air so virile and a will so determined that everyone who met him was astonished that such weakness and such power could reside together in the same individual.

Georges was unarmed and kept close to his father's side, tightly clutching the barrel of the latter's inlaid musket and watching both his father and the field officer with interest. How was it, he seemed to wonder, that his father—so much richer, braver, stronger than the other man—did not also wear ornate military finery, laden with medals— why had he never been awarded any particular distinction?

A black man, clad in blue linen vest and culottes, stood by like the attendant of the boy in the frilled shirt, waiting for the men to march into battle. He would care for young Georges when his father and brother went off to fight.

The booming of cannons had been audible since early morning, when General Vandermaesen, with half of the garrison, had marched against the enemy to check its progress at Mont Longue and at the confluence of the Pont Rouge and Lataniers rivers. He had held them back bravely since then, but as the day wore on he began to fear that he might lose all of his men at one stroke, and to suspect that he might have been fighting a dummy force and that the main body of the English forces might take another route to the capital, which was now defended only by the remaining half of the garrison and the national volunteers. As it turned out, his courageous band of only eight hundred, bravely holding off four thousand British and two thousand Sepoys, was forced to retreat little by little toward the city, taking note of every detail of the land that might give them an advantage, but always pushed back farther and farther.

The sounds of their approach, the booming of artillery, the shouts of the men, and the rattling noise of musket fire, could be clearly heard in the place d'Armes, growing louder by the moment. Rather than being intimidated, though, the defenders of Port Louis became even more impatient for action. They had been condemned to inaction on the orders of the general and stationed in the square, and it had only served to increase their courage. The regulars bit their lips and muttered curses through their bushy mustaches, while the volunteers fidgeted and exclaimed aloud that if they had to wait much longer, they would be obliged to break ranks and rush to meet the enemy in any manner they could.

Just then they heard the general returning. At the same moment drums pounded a call to arms and a mounted aide-de-camp galloped past the square, waving his hat and crying out, "To your posts, men! The enemy approaches!" He disappeared as suddenly as he had come, and to the rattle and crash of the military tambourine the soldiers fell into line with the speed and precision born of long-standing habit, filing rapidly out of the square. Despite their best efforts at imitation, the volunteers could not match this military efficiency, and it took them several moments to form ranks. A further delay occurred when some of the men began marching on the right foot and some on the left, causing the entire group to halt in confusion. The tall man with the inlaid rifle, seeing an empty place open up in the middle of the third line of volunteers, kissed his younger son, handed the boy over to the blue-clad black servant, and hurried with Jacques to slip into the vacant spot.

As the father and son approached, the men on either side of them drew back so that they found themselves alone at the center of an ever-widening circle, much like the one caused when a falling stone ripples the surface of a pond. The fat man in epaulets, who had finally succeeded in bringing the first line of volunteers to order, noticed the disruption in the third. Raising himself on his toes, he called: "To your ranks, men! To your ranks!"

Despite the officer's commanding tone, an objection rang out. "We want no mulattoes among us!" The cry was taken up by more voices and repeated like an unrelenting echo by the entire battalion.

The field officer saw the mulatto standing alone at the center of the empty space, and the older boy, red with anger, who had already moved back a few steps to put a bit of distance between himself and the hostile faces surrounding him. The officer pushed through the first two lines of volunteers, who parted to let him pass, and marched straight up to this man of color who'd had the insolence to join a group of white soldiers. He looked the mulatto up and down with flagrant disdain, while the other man stood upright as a post.

"Monsieur Pierre Munier, isn't it?" the field officer asked at length. "Do I really need to tell you that you're not wanted here?"

Pierre Munier could have knocked the rotund little man to the ground with one blow, but he remained silent. He met the officer's gaze and then averted his eyes humbly, increasing both the other man's arrogance and his anger.

"What are you doing here?" The small man spat out the words, giving the mulatto a shove with the flat of his hand.

Pierre Munier spoke at last. "Monsieur de Malmédie," he said, "I had hoped that differences in color would not matter on a day as dangerous as this one."

The fat man sneered. "You had hoped! What gave you reason to hope?"

"My wish to die defending our island, if I must."

"*Our* island," muttered the field officer. "*They* own plantations as we do, so they think the island is theirs!"

"Of course I realize the island isn't really ours, any more than it is yours; of course I know that, sir," Munier said hastily. "But if we argue over semantics instead of marching against the enemy, soon it won't belong to either of us."

"Enough!" The field officer cut him off, stamping his foot on the ground. "Is your name listed among the national guards?"

"It is not, sir—as you well know," Munier replied. "You refused me when I tried to enroll."

"Well then, what do you want?"

"To fight with you, as a volunteer."

"Impossible!" said the fat man.

"But why? Monsieur de Malmédie, I implore you—"

"Impossible," the field officer said again, drawing himself up. "My men want no mulattoes in their company."

"No mulattoes!" the soldiers cried out again.

Pierre Munier's shoulders drooped, and he looked on the verge of tears. "You will not let me fight?"

"Gather a corps of colored men and lead them yourself, then. Or join the black detachment," the little man said dismissively.

"But—"

"I order you to leave this battalion!" Monsieur de Malmédie shouted angrily.

A small voice piped up, trembling with fury. "Come away, Father, from these people who insult you." A hand pulled forcefully at Pierre Munier.

"Yes, Jacques, I'm coming," he said absently.

"It isn't Jacques, Father—it's Georges."

Pierre Munier turned in surprise. It was indeed his younger son, who had escaped from the Negro attendant to teach his father this lesson in dignity. Munier bowed his head and sighed deeply. The soldiers resumed their ranks and filed out of the square, de Malmédie at their head. Pierre Munier was left alone between his children, one of whom was red as fire and the other pale as death. He cringed before the double reproach of Jacques's flushed face and Georges's white one. "What would you have me do?" he asked his sons. "You see how it is."

Jacques was a lighthearted, philosophical child at heart, and he hurried to console himself after the initial stab of pain. "Bah!" he exclaimed to his father, snapping his fingers dismissively. "Why should it matter to us if that fat man scorns us? We're richer than he is, aren't we?" He threw a glance at the boy in the frilled shirt. "If I catch his brat Henri anywhere near me, I'll give him a thrashing he won't soon forget."

"Dear Jacques!" Pierre Munier, grateful for his older son's attempt to assuage his father's shame with insouciance, gazed at his older son fondly, then turned to Georges, hoping that he would be able to shrug off the slight as easily as his brother had. The boy's face was stony but for a nearly indiscernible smirk playing around his lips. It was an expression of such disdain, such pity, that Pierre Munier responded to it as if his son had actually spoken. "What would you have me do?" he repeated helplessly. "For heaven's sake, what would you have me do?"

He waited uneasily for the boy's reply, dreading the cold accuracy with which he knew Georges had gauged the situation. The child said nothing at first, gazing at the far end of the square. "Father," he said at last. "Look at those black men over there—they need someone to lead them."

"You're right, Georges!" Jacques exclaimed cheerfully, his humiliation already forgotten. Confident in his own strength, he took comfort in Caesar's maxim: "Better to be commander of these, than to be commanded by those."

Inspired by the younger boy's words and the elder's attitude, Pierre Munier approached the group of mulattoes. They recognized him immediately as one of the most respected men of color on the island—almost a father figure—and crowded around him, asking eagerly for orders and imploring him to lead them into battle.

Almost at once an extraordinary transformation took place in Pierre Munier. The sense of inferiority that he could never quite shake off in the presence of whites vanished, to be replaced by an appreciation of his own worth. He straightened to his full height, and his eyes—which had been kept humbly lowered before M. de Malmédie—flashed with energy. His voice grew firm and commanding where it had trembled a moment before. Slinging his gun gracefully over his shoulder, he drew his saber and, motioning in the direction of the enemy, cried, "Forward!"

He glanced once more at his younger son, now safe under the watchful eye of the blue-clad black and clapping with pride for his father, and proceeded with the mulatto corps down the same road previously taken by the regulars and the national guard. "Télémaque, take care of my son!" were his departing words to the Negro man in blue.

———

The line of defenders had broken into three parts. To the left, the Fanfaron bastion faced out to sea, armed with eighteen cannons. The entrenchment proper stood at the center with twenty-four guns, and the Dumas battery—protected by only six guns—was on the right. The vanquishing enemy, likewise divided into three columns, soon abandoned the first two points in order to focus on the third and weakest, which was defended only by members of the national guard. Instead of being intimidated by the sight of the compact but mighty force advancing on them with the terrible regular discipline of the English military, the brave young men of the Dumas dashed eagerly to their posts and fought with the skill and accuracy of seasoned veterans. The English troops, though surprised by such resistance, doubled their efforts to conquer the unexpected strength of the foe. The little battery then managed a feat worthy of a juggler astonishing his audience with trick upon trick, each more dazzling than the last, by increasing its volleys still further, firing with such rapidity that the meticulously arranged British ranks began to show signs of disorder. The enemy having now come within the range of light weaponry, musket shot began to fly. Stunned to see their numbers dropping so precipitously, besieged from all sides, the enemy began to retreat.

The regulars and the national guard battalion, acting on the captain-general's orders, had come to the aid of the Dumas battery. They charged, bayonets raised, attacking the enemy's flanks while the battery's cannon fire continued to thunder overhead. The regulars executed the maneuver with their customary precision, cutting through the right side of the English ranks and adding to their confusion—but the national guard battalion, commanded by M. de Malmédie, made a critical error. Instead of acting in tandem with the regulars and advancing on the left flank, they attacked from the front, forcing the Dumas to stop its cannon fire. The British took advantage of the lull to turn on the national guard. They stood their ground courageously at first, but they were vastly outnumbered and lost so many men that they were soon forced to give way. The English troops moved forward on the nationals' right; their superior numbers and experience easily overwhelmed the defenders. The enemy was advancing like a rising tide, seemingly unstoppable, when all at once the cry of *"France! France!"* rang out behind them. A deafening fusillade of musket fire burst out and was followed by profound silence.

A rumble of movement had begun in the enemy's rear lines and spread quickly forward. The British fell like ripe wheat before an onrush of bayonets. They were surrounded, besieged from all sides, and in less than ten minutes the new attackers had hacked a bloody path through their ranks to free the unfortunate battalion. The reinforcements then wheeled around to the left and attacked the enemy's flank. M. de Malmédie ordered his men to act in conjunction with their rescuers and they, too, moved rapidly against the British. The Dumas battery, now free to resume firing, lost no time in joining the triple barrage and showered the enemy anew with shot. The French victory was secure.

M. de Malmédie threw a relieved glance at the liberators and then cringed, loath to owe his safety to such men. Indeed, it was the black corps, commanded by Pierre Munier. Seeing the British rear flank exposed, he had immediately ordered his three hundred men to attack. Pierre Munier had executed the maneuver with the skill of a general and the bravery of a soldier and was now fighting at the very front of the action, his tall figure drawn up to its full height, his head bare, eyes flashing and hair whipped by the wind. He was fearless—daring—superb! His voice rang out above the mêlée, crying, "Forward! Forward! Take the flag!" His men followed him unhesitatingly as he plunged into the midst of the disordered English troops. He disappeared from view, reappeared, vanished again—and finally rose, uniform disheveled and face bloody, but holding the British flag aloft.

The general, fearing that some trap might still befall the French troops, gave orders to sound the retreat. The regulars, leading the English prisoners, were the first to depart. The national guard followed them bearing the bodies of the dead, and the corps of blacks, with the captured flag, brought up the rear.

The entire population of Port Louis had heard of the victory by then. They swarmed to the port in droves to welcome the combatants. Naïvely imagining that the English had been beaten so soundly that they would not return, they cheered deliriously for the returning troops. The triumph was so unexpected and so fantastic that they were nearly drunk with happiness and pride. Everyone was triumphant; everyone was victorious. They had been prepared to fight, but not to win so gloriously. Old and young, men, women, and children all vowed that they would always fight to the death to defend their island—excellent promises made in good faith, no doubt, but promises that would not have been worth much if another English regiment had shown up just then!

In the midst of the general approbation, special attention was paid to the English flag and its captor. Exclamations of praise and applause were lavished on Pierre Munier, whose men crowed and boasted in response while their leader, resuming the role of humble mulatto, shyly answered the many questions hurled at him. Jacques watched proudly, his gun with its bloodstained bayonet resting beside him, while Georges—who had escaped from Télémaque's vigilant gaze—clutched his father's hand and tried to hold back tears of joy.

M. de Malmédie stood a few paces away from the blacks, his once fine clothing tattered and dusty. He, too, was surrounded by his family, but their congratulations were for escaping with his life, not for his brilliant military feats. Flushing with embarrassment, he loudly demanded what had become of his son Henri and the black attendant, Bijou. They pushed through the crowd to meet him; the boy threw himself into his father's arms, while the servant heaped compliments on his master.

Just then someone approached to tell Pierre Munier that a Negro who had fought under him and been seriously wounded was at the point of death, and had asked to see his leader. Pierre Munier looked around for Jacques, hoping that the boy would hold the flag for him—but Jacques had found the Malgache dog again, and he was absorbed in a game with the animal. Georges followed his father's gaze, then held out his hand. "Give me the flag, Father," he said. "I'll keep it for you."

Pierre Munier smiled and embraced his son affectionately, kissing him on the forehead and pressing the flag into his hands. Georges held it upright with difficulty, bracing it against his thin chest, and Munier hurried away to comfort his brave comrade at the moment of death. Georges remained alone with the flag, basking in the remembrance of his father's glory. His wandering gaze came to rest on the child with the frilled collar, and disdain replaced the pride in his eyes. The other boy stared back at Georges with envy, wondering how it was that his own father had not also managed to capture a flag. Concluding that the only way to obtain such a trophy was to take someone else's, he moved menacingly toward Georges. The young mulatto sensed his intention immediately, but stood his ground.

"Give that to me," said Henri.

"What?"

"The flag."

"It isn't yours," retorted Georges. "It belongs to my father."

"So what? I want it."

"You can't have it."

The boy with the frilled collar reached out to seize the flag. Georges turned even paler than usual and took a step backward. His opponent, with the arrogance of a spoiled child used to being given everything he desires, lunged forward and grabbed hold of the flagpole. "I want it, I tell you!" he cried shrilly.

"And *I* tell *you* that you can't have it," Georges repeated, pushing the other boy with one hand and clutching the flag in the other.

"How dare you touch me, you dirty mulatto!" Henri shrieked. "I'll show you!" He drew his little sword and gashed Georges in the forehead before the other boy could defend himself. Blood trickled down the child's face. He stared at Henri coldly.

"Coward," was all he said.

Enraged, Henri was about to lash out again when Jacques sprang to his brother's aid. He struck the tormentor a blow that sent him sprawling to the ground. Seizing the sword, Jacques broke it into pieces and spat on the fragments before tossing them dismissively at the other boy. It was now Henri's turn to flush with humiliation, his pride wounded as deeply by Jacques's fist as Georges's brow had been by the sword.

The entire scene passed so quickly that neither M. de Malmédie nor Pierre Munier could prevent it. They noticed the altercation at the same moment and came running, Pierre Munier breathless and trembling, M. de Malmédie red with affronted rage. "Did you see what just happened?" the field officer choked out.

"Alas, yes, Monsieur de Malmédie," said Pierre Munier. "Believe me, I would have prevented it if I had been here."

"In your absence, your son has laid hands on mine!" de Malmédie shouted. "A mulatto's son—daring to strike a white child!"

"I'm truly sorry, monsieur," stammered Pierre Munier. "I beg your pardon for the offense."

The little man puffed himself up. "Your apologies are insufficient, sir."

"But—what more can I do?"

"What can you do?" M. de Malmédie repeated. "I'll tell you—you can have the rascal flogged who dared to touch my Henri!"

"Have me flogged, eh?" Jacques picked up his gun, once more appearing older than his years. "Come on and try, Monsieur de Malmédie!"

"Jacques, hush!" hissed Pierre Munier.

"I'm sorry, Father, but I was right," Jacques said stoutly. "M'sieur Henri attacked my brother with a saber when Georges had done nothing to him! That's when I struck M'sieur Henri."

"What? Attacked my Georges with a saber? Son, are you hurt?" Pierre Munier leaned anxiously toward the boy.

"It's nothing, Father," said Georges.

"It is *not* nothing," cried Pierre Munier. "Your forehead is bleeding!" He looked up at M. de Malmédie. "Look; Jacques is telling the truth! Your son nearly killed my Georges!"

Faced with such incontrovertible evidence, M. de Malmédie turned to his son. "Well, Henri," he said. "How did this happen?"

"It wasn't my fault, Papa," Henri protested. "I wanted the flag so I could give it to you, and the fool wouldn't let me have it."

M. de Malmédie turned on Georges. "And why did you refuse to give Henri the flag, you rascal?"

"It doesn't belong to him, or to you," Georges said calmly. "It is my father's."

M. de Malmédie heaved an exasperated sigh and turned back to his son. "And what happened next, Henri?"

"He wouldn't give me the flag, so I tried to take it. That's when this great beast ran up and hit me in the face."

"That's how it happened, eh?" said M. de Malmédie.

"Yes, Father."

"He's lying!" Jacques exclaimed. "I only touched him when I saw that my brother was bleeding! I wouldn't have done it otherwise."

"Silence, you good-for-nothing boy!" roared M. de Malmédie. He took a step toward Georges. "Give the flag to me." The child retreated, clutching the flag more tightly. "Give me that flag," repeated M. de Malmédie in a more threatening tone.

"Sir, it was I who captured that flag from the British," murmured Pierre Munier.

"I'm aware of that—but I won't have it known that a mulatto dared argue with me. Give me the flag, boy."

"Sir—"

"I'm ordering you. Obey your commander."

Pierre Munier felt the urge to reply, *You are* not *my commander; you refused to let me fight under you,* but the words died on his lips. His timidity once again overcame his courage, and he sighed. His heart swelling with mute indignation, he gently took the flag from Georges's hands. The boy did not resist as Pierre Munier handed the flag to M. de Malmédie; the fat man turned and walked away without another word.

It was truly painful to see a man of such deep and noble character yield to so vulgar a bully, but so it was. Even worse, his actions surprised no one. The same sort of thing occurs every day in the colonies. Brought up from infancy to regard white men as a superior breed, Pierre Munier had allowed his proud spirit to be crushed without even attempting to resist. He was fearless under a hail of musket shot, but cowered when faced with the prejudices of the whites. It is as they say: The lion may attack a man, but will flee in terror at the cock's crow.

Georges had remained stoic as his own blood ran down his cheek, but now he burst into tears, standing empty-handed before his father, who watched with inexpressible sadness. Jacques clenched his fists with fury and swore that someday he would get his revenge—on Henri, on M. de Malmédie, on all white men.

Just then a dust-covered messenger galloped past them on horseback, shouting that the British were descending from the Williams Plains and the Petite-Rivière, ten thousand strong. The watchtower at the summit of la Découverte signaled the arrival of yet another British squadron of five thousand, which had just dropped anchor in Grande-Rivière Bay. Finally the news came that the remnants of the army corps defeated that morning had now regrouped along the rivière des Lataniers and were ready to march again on Port Napoleon in tandem with the troops coming from Courtois Bay and le Réduit. The colonists knew it would be folly to resist such an overwhelming force, and the captain-general gave the order for the national guard and the volunteers to disband. He had the full authority of His Majesty, the Emperor Napoleon, he declared, and he would negotiate the city's surrender with the British. The enemy was twenty-five thousand men strong, and the island had barely four thousand defenders. The men retreated reluctantly to their homes, leaving only the regulars to patrol the empty streets.

———

The surrender was accepted and signed early on the morning of December 3. At five o'clock, the paper changed hands. The British occupied the stockade that same day, and took possession of the city and its harbor the following morning.

Eight days later the French squadron departed the port at full sail but in captivity, taking with it the entire garrison. It was reminiscent of nothing so much as a father ousting his wayward sons from the family home. The islanders remained on the quay, watching sorrowfully until the last rippling flag was out of sight. Then a heavy silence fell over them. One by one they sighed and returned home—save for two men: Pierre Munier and his black slave Télémaque, who stood alone on the shore.

"M'sieur Munier," ventured the black at last, "we ought to climb that hill. We should still be able to see little m'sieurs Jacques and Georges from there."

"You're right, Télémaque—we can at least watch the ship a little longer, even if we can't see *them*." Pierre Munier climbed la Découverte with the eager agility of a young man, and watched the disappearing *Bellone* until darkness fell. He could not see his sons, of course—the distance, as he had predicted, was too great for that—but he could at least watch the ship that was carrying them away from him.

For it was true—Pierre Munier, at great emotional cost to himself, had broken up his family and sent his children to France under the protection of the brave General Decaen. They were bound for Paris, carrying letters of introduction to two or three of their father's long-time business associates. Pierre Munier claimed that he was sending his boys to finish their education abroad, but in reality he had done it for fear of the violent hatred M. de Malmédie now bore against his family. The father was terrified for his sons; they might fall victim to the little man at any moment. It caused him great pain to part with his boys, but he could not bear the idea of their falling victim to the spite and venom of such a powerful man.

As for Henri de Malmédie, his mother was far too fond of him to allow such a separation. In any event, he needed no further education; he already knew the most important thing: Colored men, *all* colored men, were born to respect him, and to obey.

IV

FOURTEEN YEARS LATER

It was a happy day on île de France whenever a European ship was sighted in its harbor. Nearly everyone in the colony would turn out to greet the arriving vessel, hoping for news of distant relatives or friends—a letter, a portrait, even a loved one in the flesh, come home at last. These ships were the bridge, the ephemeral chain linking Europe and Africa, and the news of their approach inevitably spread around the island like wildfire, the cry "There is a ship in view!" echoing from the peak of Mont Découverte.

I speak of the peak of Mont Découverte because incoming vessels, seeking a westerly wind, were nearly always forced to pass Grand Port, skirting the coast a distance of two or three leagues, passing Quatre-Cocos, dodging between île Plate and Coin-de-Mire, circling the island to drop anchor in Port Louis after several hours, where waiting crowds pressed close on the quays. Since I have already told you of the anxiety with which everyone in île de France awaited news from Europe, it will not surprise you at all to hear of the excitement when, on a bright morning in late February 1824 around eleven o'clock, the *Leicester,* a pretty thirty-six-gun frigate, dropped anchor in Port Louis after first signaling its arrival at two o'clock the previous afternoon. Let us now make—or renew, rather—the acquaintance of two gentlemen on deck.

One was a fair, regular-featured man with blond hair and blue eyes, a little taller than average, who looked considerably younger than his forty years. At first glance he seemed a perfectly ordinary, agreeable fellow. His hands and feet were small and well formed, a trait thought to indicate good breeding, especially among the English; his voice carefully modulated, perhaps a bit flat in tone. His gaze seemed to wander aimlessly; from time to time he squinted and parted his lips to reveal two rows of pearly white teeth—an expression that might be taken for a nervous tic, but upon closer examination served instead as an opportunity for him to unobtrusively size up his surroundings. Upon first meeting him, shallow men tended to dismiss him out of hand, and he took pleasure in allowing them to do so—for he was, in fact, a man of great depth, intensely conscious of his own superiority, and his veiled demeanor was like a thousand-foot drop concealed by two inches of snow. He delighted in remaining silent when heated debate raged around him—that is, unless someone expressed an opinion different from his own. If that occurred, and if he believed he had found a worthy opponent, he attacked with lightning speed, eyes suddenly blazing, voice rising passionately as he argued point after point with clarity and eloquence. Otherwise he was content to keep quietly in the background. It was not that he lacked confidence—his pride in some things ran to excess—but he always, *always* conducted himself with rigid self-control. Though the effort often cost him dearly, his ironclad discipline never wavered. Every time a pointless suggestion, or a wrong idea, or an example of misguided vanity presented itself, the extreme refinement of his character quickly stifled any urge to utter a sarcastic remark or flash a mocking smile. Even when he could not entirely repress his irritation, he concealed the emotion with the habitual flicker of his eyes. He knew well that the best way to see and hear all that went on around him was to appear blind and deaf. He might even have wished to appear paralyzed in the manner of Sixtus Quintus, but this had proven too difficult even for him, and he had abandoned the effort.

The other young man was pale, with long, dark hair and large, deep brown eyes that bespoke a sensitive, ever-preoccupied mind and a firmness of character that immediately struck everyone who met him. It seemed as if his entire being was directed not by physical instinct but by moral strength—a rarity indeed. His gaze shone with some fire within, darting rays of light that seemed to come from the very depths of his soul. His features were pure, if slightly irregular; the smoothness of his forehead was marked by a faint scar, barely perceptible except when his face flushed red. A fine black mustache shadowed firm lips and even white teeth. The gravity of his character was unmistakable; it showed in his perpetually knitted brows and serious expression— here, undoubtedly, was a man of deep introspection and unshakable resolve. In contrast with his companion, who was forty years old but looked a decade younger, he, at twenty-five, looked closer to thirty. He was of average height, but well proportioned; his limbs were a bit on the slender side, perhaps, but it was clear that he could move with speed and agility when roused by emotion. He gave the impression of barely controlled nervous tension rather than great strength; it was obvious to those who beheld him that nature had given him quickness and coordination but refused him true vigor. He was dressed with elegant simplicity in a perfectly cut frock coat and trousers made by one of the best tailors in Paris, and the ribbons of Charles III and the Légion d'honneur were hung with careless grace from his lapel.

The former had boarded the *Leicester* at Portsmouth, the latter at Cadiz. They had immediately recognized each other from various meetings in the salons of London and Paris, and had greeted each other as old acquaintances. Though they had never been introduced, the sea air, the unvarying scenery, and the close confines of the ship dissolved their aristocratic reserve and made conventional formalities unnecessary. They exchanged only pleasantries at first, then spoke at greater length, and at the end of two days each viewed the other as a man of great worth and congratulated himself on discovering such a companion for the long journey. It was a voyage of three months, and they developed the sort of friendship that, lacking history, serves as a temporary distraction rather than holding any promise for the future. During long equatorial evenings spent discussing science, politics, and art, matching intellects as if they were sparring partners, they came to know each other well, and to consider themselves equals.

On one occasion, though, the first man gained an advantage over the second. A sudden squall had overtaken the *Leicester* just after she rounded the Cape of Good Hope. The ship's captain, struck by a falling spar, had been carried to his cabin unconscious; the first mate was seriously ill and could not leave his hammock. The blond passenger, seizing a bullhorn, issued a series of orders with the forcefulness of a man used to command and the knowledge of a seasoned sailor. The frigate was thus able to outmaneuver the worst of the storm. The danger past, the blond man's face lost the resplendent pride that had blazed there for an instant, as it does when any man fights the powers of God, and reassumed its habitual, somewhat bland expression. The timbre of his voice, which a moment before had rung louder than thunder, became low and smooth once again. With a gesture as casual as his actions of a moment before had been poetic, he handed the bullhorn to a nearby lieutenant.

Throughout this startling episode, the dark-haired passenger had watched his friend's every move with rapt attention. His face remained inscrutable, but in his eyes there shone the envy of one suddenly conscious of his own inferiority to a man he had previously believed to be his equal. When they stood together at the rail once more, he ventured a single comment: "You have captained a vessel, then, milord?"

"Yes," returned the blond man simply, giving no sign that he had noticed the honorific. "I even reached the rank of commodore, but six years ago I became a diplomat. I suppose I just remembered my former occupation a moment ago, that's all."

The two men did not speak further of the incident, but from then on it was clear that the younger stood a little in awe of the elder. During the three months of their voyage together they had never questioned the affinity they felt for each other; they knew each other to be men of intelligence, and both were en route to île de France, and that was enough. The subject of social standing never arose. When their destination was finally sighted the dark-haired man was at the rail; the always rousing cry of *"Land, ho!"* from the crow's nest quickly brought his blond companion on deck as well.

"We seem to have arrived, milord," remarked the younger man. "I must admit, though, that much as I strain my eyes I can't see any land—just a sort of mist on the water."

"Hmm, yes," the other man replied. "It takes a sailor's eye to spot true land in the midst of sea, sky, and clouds. Old sea dog that I am, I can see our island quite well."

"Here is more proof, milord, that you are a more accomplished man than I! I can hardly believe you; it seems impossible."

"Here, then," said the blond man, handing his companion a spyglass. "Look, and I will describe what you see using only my naked eye. Will you believe me then?"

"Milord," was the incredulous response, "I know you are a man among men in every way; you need do nothing to prove yourself to me. I will accept the spyglass, but to satisfy my heart's desire of seeing home rather than my curiosity about your claim."

"Come, come!" The blond man laughed. "I see that the island air is already affecting you; you're turning into a flatterer!"

"Me, flatter you?" The dark-haired young man shook his head. "The *Leicester* will round the globe before I ever stoop to flattery! I simply want to thank you, milord, for the kindness you have shown me during our long journey—for the friendship, I might even presume to call it, that you have graciously bestowed on a poor stranger."

"My dear companion," the Englishman replied, taking the other man's hand, "I hope that for you, as for me, there can be no strangers in this world except brigands, thieves, and drunks; all men of worth are relatives of a sort, and we recognize one another wherever we may meet. Now, enough of your compliments, my young friend! Take this glass and look, for we will soon be too close to the island to make my little demonstration of any use."

The younger man obliged and held the spyglass to his eye.

"Can you see?" his companion inquired.

"Perfectly."

"Île Ronde is there on the extreme right, is it not?"

"Indeed it is."

"And now we are approaching île Plate—there is a brigantine at its foot that looks, curiously enough, like a warship to me just now. Tonight we'll be where she is, and tomorrow we'll follow in her wake."

The dark-haired man lowered the glass and squinted at the horizon, but he could see nothing. "Miraculous!" He shook his companion's hand, laughing, and raised the glass again.

"Do you see Coin-de-Mire," continued the blond man, "nearly indistinguishable from Cape Malheureux, that place of such sad and lyrical memory? And the crag of Bambou, just in front of Mont Faience? And there, the mountain of Grand Port, and Mont Créole to its left?"

"Yes—yes, I see it all, and I remember everything well, from my childhood. I've guarded my memories like the most precious treasures, Lord knows. And you"—he closed the spyglass in his palm with a snap and turned to the other man—"you remember it, too, don't you? This is not your first time here. Your descriptions are based on remembrance as much as on the sharpness of your vision."

"True," the Englishman conceded with a smile. "I see that there's no chance of hoodwinking you, my friend! But," he continued, "I imagine that my memories of this place are less sweet than yours. I came here first at a time when you and I were most likely enemies—it is fourteen years ago now."

"But—that is just when I left île de France!" the dark-haired man exclaimed.

"Were you still there for the naval battle at Grand Port—which, for the sake of national pride, I shouldn't even mention, considering how badly we were beaten?"

"Oh, feel free to speak of it, milord!" returned the younger man. "You English have taken your revenge on us so many times that even your defeat holds a sort of pride."

"I was here for that battle," the blond man said. "I was serving in the navy then."

"As a cadet?"

"As lieutenant on a frigate."

"Forgive me for saying so, milord, but you can't have been much more than a child fourteen years ago!"

The blond man smiled. "How old would you say I am?"

"Close to my own age, I should think. Thirty, perhaps?"

"I am near forty," the Englishman replied. "I told you this was your day for flattery."

The younger man, astonished, looked closely at his companion. There, at the corners of his eyes and mouth, were the faint lines that betrayed his true age. He nodded slowly. "I do remember that battle," he said quietly, "and another one, too, that took place on the opposite side of the island. Do you know Port Louis, milord?"

"No—I only know this part of the shoreline. I was seriously wounded in combat at Grand Port and taken back to Europe as a prisoner of war. This is my first visit back to the Indian Ocean, and it will probably be a very long one indeed."

As if the exchange had awakened unpleasant memories in both men, they moved mechanically away from each other and leaned upon the rails in silence.

The *Leicester* made her entry into Port Louis the next day, passing île d'Ambre and reaching the foot of île Plate to be greeted with all the excitement I described at the beginning of this chapter, which habitually met every ship arriving from Europe. It was welcomed with even more than the usual fanfare, because the colony was expecting its future governor. That individual had come on deck as the ship approached the harbor, impressively attired in a general's uniform. It was only then that the dark-haired man knew the identity of his traveling companion. The blue-eyed Englishman was none other than William Murray, former sailor and erstwhile ambassador, who had just been named governor of île de France by His Majesty the king of England.

Remember, dear reader, the young lieutenant who was wounded aboard the *Nereid*, nephew of the ill-fated Captain Willoughby and sole survivor of the battle of Grand Port? He has reappeared as promised, and will play a very important role in our story.

As the new governor prepared to disembark, he turned to his traveling companion. "In three days I am giving a grand dinner for île de France's dignitaries," he said. "I hope you will do me the honor of being my guest."

"With the greatest pleasure, milord," the young man responded. "But before I accept, I should tell you that I am—"

Lord Murray waved his hand. "Just have yourself announced at the door, my dear sir, and then I will learn your name. I know your worth already; that is all that matters."

With a smile and a salute, the blond man moved to join the *Leicester*'s captain in a dinghy that sped for land, rowed by ten vigorous men. A full complement of soldiers stood at attention on the shore, and the cannons fired in a royal salute as the little boat reached Chien-de-Plomb. Cries of "*Vive* Lord Murray!" greeted the new governor as he disembarked. Bells rang out, and the guns of both the fort and the frigate boomed out, to be answered by those of the other ships in the harbor. He responded graciously, waving and inclining his head to the crowd; then, accompanied by the city's officials, he disappeared in the direction of the official residence.

The very islanders who cheered the arrival of their new governor were the same who had wept at the departure of the French fourteen years before—but that is a long time, to be sure, and most of the older generation was gone. No one now guarded the memory of things past like an ancient family tree. Fourteen years had been enough to dim the memories of destruction and of the deaths of close friends, and to make the people forget their vows to defeat the enemy at any cost. Time, it seems, is all it takes to destroy a great man, or a great nation.

V

THE PRODIGAL SON

All eyes followed Lord Murray until the doors of the governor's residence closed behind him, then returned curiously to the deck of the
vessel, where the dark-haired man was just descending the gangplank.
The crowd had seen Murray address this stranger graciously and
shake his hand; they decided that he must be some young French or
English nobleman—a suspicion that was only reinforced when they
noticed the double ribbon affixed to his lapel; one of these ribbons was
a bit less common then than it is today. He gave the spectators ample
opportunity to watch him, first scanning the crowd as if he expected to
find a friend or relative among them, then standing at the water's edge
as first the governor's horses, then his own, were brought off the ship.
That task completed, he spoke a few words in an unknown language to
his tanned equerry, who was dressed in the costume of an African
Moor, and, taking their two horses—trapped in the Arabian fashion—
by the bridle, since the animals' travel-swollen legs would not yet
allow them to bear riders, the two men departed, the dark-haired
stranger still glancing around as if he yet hoped to see a familiar face
appear suddenly in the milling crowd.

Among the islanders grouped on that particular dock, which was generally known as Pointe-aux-Blagueurs, was a rotund man of fifty or fifty-five with graying hair, coarse-featured and loud-voiced with a perpetually downturned mouth, and a handsome youth in his mid-twenties. The older man was dressed in a frock coat of burgundy merino wool with a lace cravat at his throat. The younger man, whose bearing and expression seemed modeled on his companion's though his features were sharper, wore a gray hat and silk scarf with his white waistcoat and trousers. There was no mistaking the fact that the two were closely related.

"I say, there's a handsome fellow," the fat man remarked as the dark-haired stranger passed them. "We'd best keep a close eye on our wives and daughters if he stays on the island for long."

"Fine horse, too," the young man agreed, observing the animal through a lorgnette. "Pureblood Arabian, unless I miss my guess."

"Anyone you know, Henri?"

"No, Father, but if he wants to sell that horse, I know someone who'd be glad to pay a thousand piastres for it."

"And that someone would be Henri de Malmédie, wouldn't it, my boy?" The older man chuckled. "Well, buy it, if it pleases you. You're certainly rich enough."

The dark stranger must have overheard Henri de Malmédie's offer and his father's approval of it as he passed, for he stopped to fix a disdainful—even threatening—eye on each of them in turn. His lip curled with scorn and he turned away dismissively, but as he continued on his way he could be heard to mutter softly: "Them again! Always them!"

"Why, what quarrel could a newcomer possibly have with us?" M. de Malmédie exclaimed.

"I've no idea, Father," said Henri, "but if he looks at us in that way the next time we see him, you can be sure I'll ask."

"Now, Henri," said the father in a tone that clearly indicated pity for the stranger's ignorance, "he doesn't know who we are."

Henri's face was grim. "Then I'll teach him."

———

The stranger whose dismissive glance had provoked Henri de Malmédie into threatening him made his way toward the ramparts, seemingly unaffected by the impression he had made and with no evident desire to return and gauge its effect. As he approached the gardens belonging to the island's garrison, his attention was caught by a group gathered on a small bridge linking the gardens to the courtyard of a stately house. At the center of the group stood a lovely girl, perhaps fifteen or sixteen years old. The stranger, obviously a cultured young man and thus naturally drawn to beauty of any sort, was instantly captivated. He paused to gaze at his leisure.

She was at the doorstep of the mansion now; she belonged, no doubt, to one of the wealthiest families on the island. There was a governess with her, whose long blond hair and translucent complexion marked her out as an Englishwoman. An old black man stood nearby as well, dressed in white pantaloons and waistcoat, ready to obey the girl's slightest command.

The girl's beauty was further enhanced in comparison with the ugliness of the man standing silent and immobile before her, with whom she was vainly attempting to negotiate the purchase of a charming carved-ivory fan, as transparent and fragile as lace. The seller was a bony, yellow-skinned individual with almond eyes and a long braid hanging down his back from beneath his large straw hat. A bamboo pole rested on the ground at his feet; baskets affixed to each end of it overflowed with the kind of feminine baubles that, whether in the outdoor markets of the tropics or the elegant shops of Alphonse Giroux and of Susse, were sure to turn the heads of young girls as well as their mothers. The lovely Creole girl stood amid the bric-a-brac, her attention focused on the fan—a delicate ivory thing, etched with fantastic representations of palaces, pagodas, and exotic beasts and birds existing only in the imaginations of the craftsmen of Canton and Peking.

She had simply asked the price of the fan—but this proved to be the difficulty. The Chinese man, on île de France for only a few days, spoke neither French, nor English, nor Italian, and had stood in silent confusion when the girl repeated her question in each of those languages. The ignorance of the man from the banks of the Yellow River was already so well known around the colony that the inhabitants of Port Louis called him by the same single name—*Miko-Miko.* This was what the merchant repeated endlessly as he hawked his wares around the city; it meant nothing more than "Buy, buy." Miko-Miko had managed to communicate via hand gestures until now, but as the girl had never had the chance to study the sign language of the Abbot de l'Épée, she was unable to understand him or make him understand her. It was at this opportune moment that the stranger approached her.

"I beg your pardon, mademoiselle," he said. "I couldn't help but notice your predicament. Might I be of some service? I would be glad to act as your interpreter."

"Oh, sir!" exclaimed the governess, while the girl blushed prettily. "You see us at our wits' end! Mademoiselle Sara and I have tried for ten minutes together to make this man understand us. We have spoken to him in French, English, Italian, but he comprehends nothing!"

"Perhaps this gentleman can speak another language he might understand, dear Henriette," interjected the girl. "If he can find out the price of this fan, he will have done me a great service—I simply long to have it, you know."

"But it is impossible," said dear Henriette. "This man doesn't seem to speak any language at all!"

"He speaks the language of his home country, surely," said the stranger.

"Yes, of course, but he is from China—and who on earth speaks Chinese?"

The stranger smiled. Turning to the merchant, he spoke several words unintelligible to the women. It would be impossible to describe the expression of astonishment that spread across poor Miko-Miko's face when he heard the beloved accents of his far-off mother country, resonating like the echoes of distant music in his ears. He let the fan drop from his grasp and, seizing the strange newcomer's hand, kissed it again and again. The dark-haired man repeated his question, and Miko-Miko answered it in tones of rapture and wonder a bit ill suited to such practical subject matter as the price of a fan.

"It's twenty pounds sterling, mademoiselle," the stranger said, turning back to the young woman. "Around ninety piastres."

"Oh, I *do* thank you, monsieur," said Sara, blushing again. "Isn't it lucky, dear Henriette," she continued in English, turning to her governess, "that monsieur speaks this man's language?"

"Quite astonishing," dear Henriette agreed.

"There is a simple explanation," the young man assured them, switching to English as well. "My mother died when I was just three months old, and I was nursed by a poor woman from the island of Formosa who was in service to our family. Her language was the first one I learned to speak, and even though I rarely have occasion to use it, I still remember a few words of it—an ability for which I am quite thankful indeed, since it has allowed me to do you this small service today." He pressed a Spanish doubloon into Miko-Miko's hand; then, signaling the servant to follow him, he gave the two women an easy salute and departed.

Following the Moka road, the stranger had just arrived at the path leading to the Pailles at the foot of Mont Découverte when he stopped short and stared at a point halfway up the hill, where an old man sat on a wooden bench with hands folded and eyes fixed on the sea. The stranger stood frozen for a moment as if he could not believe his eyes, and then all doubt seemed to vanish. "It *is* him," he murmured. "My God! How he has changed!"

Taking care not to be seen, the stranger made his way up the slope. Two or three times he stopped and pressed his hand to his heart, as if trying to repress some emotion that threatened to overwhelm him. The old man did not move at the newcomer's approach, but he was obviously aware of it; he turned his head when the young man sat down next to him, and with a timid salute stood and took several steps back.

"Oh, pray, do not disturb yourself on my account, monsieur!" said the stranger.

The other man sat down again, but this time at the farthest edge of the bench. A lengthy silence passed, during which the old man continued to gaze at the sea and the stranger, at his companion.

Finally the young man ventured to speak. "Monsieur," he said, "were you here, about an hour and a half ago, when the *Leicester* dropped anchor in the port?"

"Why—yes, I was, monsieur," the old man replied humbly, surprise evident in his voice.

"The arrival of ships from Europe does not interest you?"

"But why do you ask me such a thing, monsieur?"

"Surely," said the young man, "if you were interested, you would have gone to the dock like everyone else."

"You are wrong, monsieur," the old man answered, shaking his gray head sadly. "Very wrong, indeed. No one is more interested in the arrival of European ships than I. For fourteen years I have come to this hillside every time such a vessel arrives, no matter its country of origin, in the hope that it might bear letters from my children—or even my children themselves. It tires me to stand for very long, though, so I come and sit here, in the same place I watched them sail away so long ago."

"And why do you not go down to the port yourself?" inquired the stranger.

"I did, for the first few years," the old man replied. "But the disappointment became too much to bear. Eventually I sent my Negro Télémaque in my place. Waiting for him here allows me to hope a little longer. If he returns quickly, I imagine that he is bringing word that my children are here at last; if he is delayed, I tell myself he is collecting a letter. Usually, though, he comes back empty-handed, and I go home alone and weep, always telling myself that the next ship will surely bring happier tidings."

"Poor Father," the stranger murmured.

The old man looked astonished. "You pity me, monsieur?"

"I do, most sincerely."

"But—don't you know who I am?"

"You're a man, and you suffer," the stranger said simply.

The old man's voice trembled. "I am a mulatto," he said in a low, embarrassed voice.

The young man's face flushed red. "And so am I."

"You, a mulatto?" cried the old man.

"Yes."

"*You*, a mulatto!" the old man repeated, as if he could not believe it. He stared at the red-and-blue ribbon on the stranger's lapel. "Ah! Now I understand your pity. I took you for a white at first, but I know now that we are friends—brothers."

"Yes," murmured the stranger, taking the old man's hands in his. There was an expression of infinite tenderness on his face. "Perhaps even more than that."

The old man seemed not to have heard him. "Well," he said. "I feel I can tell you everything now! It will do my heart good to speak of my troubles. I have two sons, monsieur—or perhaps I should say I *had* two sons, for God only knows if they are both still alive! I loved both of them as much as any father could. I must confess, though, that one of them—the younger—held a special place in my heart." The stranger seemed to tremble, and drew a little nearer his companion. "It might shock you," the old man continued, "that a father can love one child more than the other. It is wrong, I know; but my younger boy was the weaker of the two. There; that is my only excuse."

Here the old man paused and looked away, as if ashamed at the confession he had just made. The stranger quickly dashed a tear from his cheek.

"You would understand if you had known them, monsieur," the old man said, turning back to his listener. "It wasn't that Georges—that was my younger boy's name—was the handsomer of the two. On the contrary; his brother, Jacques, was much better looking. But Georges's frail body housed a mind of such strength and intelligence that if I had put him in school here in Port Louis, I'm certain he would have been the star pupil, though he was only twelve years old." The old man's eyes shone with pride and enthusiasm for an instant, but his expression quickly dimmed again. "I couldn't send him to school here, of course. It was a white school, and we are only mulattoes."

The stranger's eyes flared, and a look of mingled fury and disdain flashed across his face. The old man appeared to take no notice. "That was why I sent them both to France," he continued. "I hoped that a proper education might calm Jacques down a bit—cure him of his vagabond tendencies—and also, perhaps, teach Georges not to be so stubborn." He sighed. "But it seems that God did not approve of my plan. Jacques shipped out on a privateer during a trip to Brest, and I have heard from him only three times since then—always from somewhere on the other side of the globe. Georges, on the other hand, has written to me often, from England, Spain, Egypt; I fear, though, that his obstinacy has only increased with age. His letters are beautiful, but I have never shown them to anyone."

"Neither of them has ever written to you of returning home, then?"

"Never, and who knows if I will ever see either of them again? It would make me the happiest man on earth to be reunited with my sons, but I have never asked them to come home. If they have chosen to remain there, it is because they are happier in Europe than they would be here, and if they do not feel the need to see their old father again, it is because they have found people in Europe whom they love better. So be it. I wish only for their happiness—though, I confess, Georges's absence has been most painful for me, and so has the fact that he has never spoken of returning to île de France."

"Perhaps he hopes to surprise you, monsieur," said the stranger in a voice quivering with emotion.

"Would that it were so!" The old man sighed, clasping his hands and raising his eyes heavenward.

"He might wish to come to you unrecognized," the stranger continued tremulously, "so that he might bask in your presence, in your love and benediction."

The old man shook his head. "Impossible! I should always recognize my Georges."

"And yet," the young man burst out, unable to restrain himself any longer, "yet you have *not* recognized me, dear Father!"

"You—*you!*" the old man cried, trembling violently. He searched the stranger's face. "No—you cannot be Georges. There is some resemblance, but—you are so tall, so handsome! He is only a child, and you are a man!"

"It is indeed I, Father! You must know me!" Georges cried. "Do not forget that fourteen years have gone by since you last saw my face—I am nearly twenty-six now! Here—if you doubt me still, look at the scar on my forehead. It is the mark of a saber cut given to me by Henri de Malmédie, that day you so bravely captured the English flag. Open your arms, dearest Father, and press me to your heart, and you will know that I am your son!"

With these words, the stranger flung himself on the old man's breast, repeating again and again that he was, truly, Georges. Pierre

Munier, hardly daring to believe in so much happiness, clasped the young man hesitantly, then tightly, in his arms. Just then Télémaque appeared at the foot of the hill, shoulders slumped and face sorrowful, reluctantly bringing the news that there was still no word from either of his master's beloved sons.

VI

TRANSFIGURATION

Let us leave the father and son to their joyful reunion now, and journey back in time to retrace the physical and mental transformation experienced by the hero of our story during the last fourteen years—years that changed him from a boy to a man.

I meant, at first, simply to repeat the story exactly as Georges told it to his father—but since this is a tale made up of intimate thoughts and secret sensations, we may be justifiably skeptical that a man of Georges's character will tell the entire truth—especially when he is speaking about himself! So I will tell it in my own way. I am quite familiar with every detail of it, and you may be assured that I am completely impartial. I will conceal no feeling, be it good or bad, nor any thought—honorable or otherwise.

I will begin just where Georges did: aboard the *Bellone*, sailing away from île de France.

Pierre Munier, whom we have already gotten to know a little, had from his earliest entry into active manhood adopted a line of conduct toward whites from which he never deviated. Lacking the strength of will to fight such overwhelming prejudice, he had resolved to disarm the whites with continual submission and humility. He had neither the strength nor the will to challenge any white man to a duel, no matter how offensive the man's prejudice might be to him; despite his wealth and intelligence, he spent his life apologizing for his very existence. He never sought public or administrative office; he strove only to remain lost in the crowd.

The same attitude that kept him from public life governed his private actions as well. Generous and magnanimous by nature, he yet lived so simply as to be almost monastic. His home contained abundance but no luxury, the two hundred slaves he owned—worth a fortune in themselves—notwithstanding. He did not own a palanquin until age and sorrow induced him to give up his habit of traveling everywhere on horseback; even then, he chose the plainest equipage he could find. Always careful to avoid the slightest quarrel, invariably polite and submissive, he never displayed even the barest hint of dislike or resentment. Indeed, he would rather lose ten arpents of land than open or even support a court case that would have won him twenty. One could always be sure of finding a coffee or manioc plant or some sugarcane at the plantation of Pierre Munier, who invariably thanked the seeker for coming to him instead of someone else, and at the best price, too. His generosity, born of his excellent heart, to be sure, but also of his timid character, had earned the friendship of his neighbors, but it was rather passive in nature. No one ever thought of returning the favors he granted them; they simply tried to avoid hurting him. Even so, there were always those who, despite his immense wealth, his many slaves, and his spotless reputation, wished him ill on account of his skin color. M. de Malmédie and his son, Henri, were among this number.

Georges, who was born into the same circumstances as his father but whose weaker constitution had denied him the pleasures of physical exercise, had focused all his energies inward. Like many a sickly child he was mature beyond his years, and instinctively discerned the reasons for his father's behavior. Even then, though, the man's pride that surged in the child's chest prevented him from acting likewise. He hated the whites who despised him and scorned the mulattoes who allowed themselves to be so despised. Very early on, he resolved to conduct himself in a manner completely opposite from his father's. He would face such absurd and unreasonable oppression head-on and, as soon as he was strong enough, crush it, man by man, strangling it like a youthful Antaeus. The child Hannibal, spurred onward by his father, had declared war on an entire nation; young Georges, *despite* his father, would fight prejudice to the death with the same ferocity.

Georges left the colony after the battle described earlier in our narrative and arrived safely in France. Along with his brother, Jacques, he enrolled in the Collège Napoleon where, placed in the lowest grade, he immediately resolved to rise to the head of his class. For him, superiority could be gained solely through meticulous organization; he learned quickly and well. Initial success only stoked the fire; the more he achieved, the more he desired to achieve. True, such intense intellectual focus did not improve his physique; he remained small and frail. God, however, had provided a support to this slim young sapling. Thanks to the protection of his brother, the laziest yet strongest boy in class, Georges—the hardest worker, but the weakest body—was able to pursue his studies unmolested.

Unfortunately, this tranquil state of affairs did not last long. Two years after their arrival in France, Jacques and Georges spent a holiday in Brest with a merchant acquaintance of their father's. Jacques—who had long heard the siren call of the sea—took the opportunity to escape their prison, as he called the school, and ship out aboard a privateer, which he described in a letter to Pierre Munier as a French military vessel. Upon returning to school, Georges immediately suffered the cruel consequences of his brother's absence. Utterly defenseless in the face of the jealous resentment and even hatred aroused in his classmates by his academic prowess, he was shunned, beaten, and ill treated all around. Every boy seemed to have a favorite way of tormenting him. It was a trial indeed, but Georges bore it courageously.

Reflecting more seriously than ever on his position, Georges realized that moral superiority mattered little without physical strength to match. Until he possessed the latter, he would never be respected for the former. He must combine the two if he wished to be complete as a man. From that moment onward, he was altered. He exchanged shyness, isolation, and inactivity for sport, exuberance, and roughhousing; he spent only enough time at his books to maintain the intellectual preeminence he had attained during the preceding years. Clumsy and awkward at first, he was mocked by his peers—the shame of which only made him strive harder. Georges was not sanguine by nature; rather, his was a bilious courage, and he was inclined to avoid danger rather than actively seeking it out. He could act bravely only after reflection, and though this sort of courage is all the more admirable for being morally justified, in his private thoughts he feared he was a coward.

He fought for himself at each quarrel—or rather, he was engaged to fight—and was beaten many times, but he invariably returned to the ring, again and again, until he won. Victory eventually came, not because he was stronger than his opponents, but because he was fiercer. Even during the most heated fray, he kept his cool, watching for the slightest hint of weakness in his adversary and then using it against him. He began to earn the respect of his peers; once they recognized his unfailing determination, they thought twice before goading him. However weak an enemy might be, a man will hesitate to fight him if he knows the enemy's determination is greater than his own.

Naturally, the ardor with which Georges pursued his new lifestyle produced physical results. Little by little, he gained strength and muscularity. Encouraged by his initial tries, he decided to put that year's school holidays to good use. Not once did he crack a book that summer; instead, he learned to swim, fence, and ride. He was exhausted, always exhausted—sometimes he was so tired he became feverish—but eventually he grew accustomed to it. Again and again he pushed his body to its limits and beyond, building endurance and stamina. He augmented sport with manual labor, digging and carrying for hours on end. When night fell he shunned his warm bed, choosing instead to wrap himself in his coat and fling himself onto a bearskin on the ground. Georges was no fool; he was well aware that he might be endangering his health, even his life, by living so harshly—but after all, what would his life be worth without superiority of strength and prowess? In the end determination triumphed over nature. Weakness fled like an incompetent servant banished by his master. In three short months Georges changed so much as to be nearly unrecognized by his classmates. Now it was he who challenged and defeated those who had bullied him in the past; now it was he who was feared and, being feared, was respected.

As for the rest, in the natural way of things his face gained beauty as his body gained strength. He had always had wonderful eyes and perfect teeth; now he let his unruly black hair grow long and tamed it so that it curled romantically about his collar. His sickly pallor vanished, and healthy color came into his cheeks, giving him a poetic air of melancholy and distinction. Just as the youth had worked to become strong, so the man worked to become handsome.

When Georges finally earned his diploma and left Collège Napoleon, he was an attractive youth of about five feet four inches, slender but well formed. He knew nearly all that a young man about to enter the world should know; but of course this was not enough for him, and in this, as in everything else, he wanted to be superior to all other men. The continuing studies he set for himself became easy; freed from the strict routine of his school days and master of his own time, he soon developed a rigid schedule of his own. He rode at six o'clock every morning, went shooting at eight, and fenced from ten o'clock to noon. Between noon and two o'clock he took classes at the Sorbonne. From three to five he painted or drew in one studio or another, and his evenings were spent at the theater or at some fashionable soirée, to which his polished manners and easy grace, more than his fortune, afforded him easy access.

Thus Georges immersed himself in the world of Parisian artists, intellectuals, and aristocrats. Well versed as he was in art, science, and fashion, he soon gained a reputation as one of the most intelligent minds, the most logical thinkers, and the most distinguished gentlemen in the city.

He had almost attained his goal, but there was still one more trial to undergo. Georges did not doubt his superiority to other men, but he was yet unsure of the degree to which he had mastered his own self-control. He decided to put himself to the test.

Georges had always shied away from gambling, fearing he would become addicted to the game. Now, however, he went to Frascati's with his pockets full of gold. He had told himself he would play three times, for three hours each time, and that his limit at each session would be ten thousand francs. Win or lose, when those three times were finished, he would play no more.

The first day Georges lost his ten thousand francs in less than an hour and a half. He spent the remaining ninety minutes watching the other men play. His purse still held the twenty thousand louis he had allotted for the second and third tries, but he kept his resolve and did not spend them that day.

On the second day he won twenty-five thousand francs, but instead of stopping while he was ahead, he forced himself to continue playing until the requisite three hours were up—and lost every cent of his spoils.

On the third day he fared badly at first and was down to his last banknote when the tide suddenly turned. He had only forty-five minutes left to play, but during that short time he had the sort of luck that, as the superstitious old crones might say, could only be ascribed to a pact with the devil. An invisible sprite seemed to be perched on his shoulder, whispering in advance which color would hit and which card would win. Gold and banknotes piled up before him, to the astonishment of his audience. Georges himself could hardly think anymore; he laid a great pile of money on the table and told the croupier to stake all of it anywhere he liked. A random choice was duly made— and Georges won.

Two professional gamblers, who had been following Georges's run of luck and had also won a great deal that night, chose that moment to take a different approach to the game; they bet against him in the next round. Fortune, however, continued to smile on Georges: The men lost all they had won, then everything they had with them; they ended by borrowing—and losing—fifty thousand francs from the banker. Georges seemed to take no notice of them; he watched the pile of money growing before him and cast occasional, impassive glances at the clock, to see if the three hours he had allotted himself had elapsed. When the predetermined hour arrived he stood, gave his winnings to a waiting servant, and departed with the same sangfroid he had displayed at the gaming table; the same tranquility he had invariably shown, win or lose.

Arriving home, he simply threw the bills and coins into a drawer, and would not allow himself to open it for a full week. When he did finally count the money, it amounted to 230,000 francs. His return to the gaming house was awaited anxiously, but in vain. Georges was satisfied. He had mastered a passion.

In addition to his many virtues, Georges possessed the hot-blooded nature of a man born in the tropics. One night after a drunken binge, several of his friends took him to the home of a Parisian courtesan famed for her beauty and charm. That night, though, Georges was to produce in this modern Lais a reemergence of virtue. The entire night was spent talking to her of moral philosophy. One would have thought the mistress of the house aspired to win the Montyon Prize! Still, the young woman listened with an expression of desire in her eyes that belied the clinical tone of the conversation. For his part, Georges found the woman utterly enticing. Thoughts of this lovely Astarte haunted his virginal mind for three days after the encounter. On the fourth day he returned to her lodgings and climbed the stairs to the front door, his heart hammering in his chest. Ringing the doorbell with an almost convulsive motion and unconsciously keeping the bell cord clenched in his hand, he heard the footsteps of the housemaid. He commanded his heart to be still and his face to be impassive, and in a completely emotionless voice he asked the maid to conduct him to her mistress.

But the girl had already heard his voice from her boudoir, and she appeared on the staircase with a joyful countenance. This brooding, reserved gentleman had made a profound impression on her, and she hoped fervently that love—or at least desire—had brought him back to call on her.

She was mistaken. Georges was testing himself yet again. He had come to see if he would be able to resist the fire in his blood. He stayed for two hours talking calmly with the girl, wagering himself that he would be able to remain cool, and struggling against the torrent of desire aroused in him by her caresses. Finally, victorious once more, confident that he could control even his most primal desires, he took his leave.

As I have said, our hero did not possess the kind of bravery that led him to rush headlong into danger, but he certainly had the courage to face trouble when he could not avoid it. Still, the fear that he was a coward continued to plague him. He could not be sure of how he might react if true danger was imminent. Would he stay, or would he run? The idea tormented him strangely, and he resolved to take the next opportunity that came along to expose himself to real peril—and that opportunity did arrive, under very strange circumstances indeed.

One day Georges and a friend went to Lepage's shooting gallery. As they waited for a free booth, Georges busied himself watching one of the gallery's regulars—a man who, like himself, was known as one of the best marksmen in Paris. This paragon was firing off shot after brilliant shot, every one a bull's-eye, each shot piercing the exact same spot as the bullet before it, with the sort of ease that is traditionally attributed to the Chevalier de Saint-Georges, and that drives neophytes to despair. He displayed his prowess in a hundred different ways, once slicing a bullet in half on the blade of a knife, and followed this feat with many others of the same sort. He was, it must be said, quite as impressed with himself—perhaps more so—than any of his spectators, and Georges's presence only served to further excite his ego. He continued firing, self-consciously displaying his skills to their utmost. His consternation may be imagined when, instead of receiving the praise he expected from his rival, he overheard Georges remark, "He's a good shot, certainly, but it's a very different thing to aim at a man instead of a target."

The man was astonished and then angry at such a dismissal of his prowess as a duelist. He finally turned to Georges when the other man expressed a negative opinion of him for the third time and, with an air half mocking, half threatening, said: "I beg your pardon, monsieur. You appear to be questioning my abilities in a way I find most insulting. Would you be so good as to explain yourself?"

"I don't think my words require any explanation, monsieur," Georges returned.

"Well, then, may I at least ask you to have the goodness to repeat yourself—so that I may understand the meaning of your words, and the intention with which you uttered them?"

"I said," replied Georges with perfect calm, "that, having watched you fire one bull's-eye after another, I believe you would not be so sure of your hand, or your eye, were you firing at a man's breast instead of a target."

His rival's eyes narrowed. "And why not, pray?"

"Because," Georges said, "it seems to me that every man must feel something, some emotion, when he pulls the trigger to shoot another man—enough to throw off his aim at least a little."

"You have fought in many duels, monsieur?"

"No, not a one."

"Ah! Then it doesn't surprise me that you imagine one might feel fear, at such a moment," the man said, with a slightly ironic smile.

Georges shook his head. "I beg your pardon, but I think you have misunderstood me. There are emotions other than fear that may make a man tremble, when he kills another man."

"*I* never tremble, monsieur."

"Very possible," Georges said coolly. "But I maintain that at twenty-five paces—the same distance at which you are able to fire so many consecutive bull's-eyes—you would—"

"Twenty-five paces, monsieur?"

"—you would miss a living target," finished Georges.

The other man flushed. "I assure you, that is not the case."

"You will forgive me," said Georges, "if I do not take your word for it."

"Are you calling me a liar, monsieur?"

"No; I am simply stating a fact."

The man's lip curled. "I don't suppose you would care to prove this 'fact' through experimentation?"

Georges met his sneering gaze squarely. "I wouldn't mind."

"Surely, though, you want to use someone else as the test subject."

"Myself, or someone else; it doesn't matter," Georges said dismissively.

"I warn you, monsieur, you are taking a great risk."

"I think not," said Georges with a faint smile.

The other man looked furious. "Really, sir, this is too much. You insult me deliberately."

Georges shrugged. "You're free to think what you like."

"Very well," his rival said grimly. "Choose your hour."

"Now, if you like."

"And the place?"

"The bois de Boulogne is very near."

"And your weapon, monsieur?"

"My weapon! The pistol, of course. We aren't fighting a duel, after all, merely conducting an experiment."

The man bowed to Georges. "I am at your service, monsieur."

"On the contrary; it is I who am at yours."

The two young men, each with a friend, proceeded to the bois de Boulogne. Their seconds tried to dissuade them from the confrontation, but to no avail. Georges's adversary insisted on an apology, while Georges argued that he would only be obliged to give one if the other man killed or wounded him, thereby proving that he had been wrong. Once they arrived at the woods, their friends attempted to place them thirty paces apart, but Georges refused, saying that it would only be a fair experiment if he, the target, was twenty-five paces from the marksman as they had agreed. The twenty-five steps were duly measured out.

Thus thwarted after a futile quarter of an hour, the seconds finally suggested they toss a coin to see who would fire first, but Georges refused this, too. By rights, he insisted, the other man must shoot first. His adversary, his honor wounded yet again, argued that it would give him an unfair—and, certainly, unneeded—advantage if either of two such powerful men gave the other the courtesy of shooting first. Georges held firm, however, and his rival was obliged to cede the point.

A man from the shooting club loaded each man's pistol with the same amount of powder and the same number of bullets they had used before. Indeed, they were the exact same ones each man had used at the gallery. Georges had insisted upon that point.

The two men duly moved twenty-five paces apart and took their pistols from the seconds. The seconds then withdrew, leaving the combatants to fire on each other in the order they had agreed on.

Georges took none of the precautions usually observed by duelists: He did not try to shield any part of his body with the pistol; his hand rested at his side, giving his rival a clear shot at his chest. The other man did not quite know what to make of such conduct. He had participated in many duels, but he had never been confronted with such cool bravery. He began to doubt himself. Twice he raised the pistol, and twice he lowered it again. This was in complete violation of dueling etiquette, but Georges remained unfazed. "Take your time, sir," was all he said.

On the third attempt, the other man fired. There was a moment of terrible suspense for the spectators; then Georges turned and bowed to each witness to show that he was unhurt. "Well, monsieur," he said, "it seems you have proven me right. It is indeed true that when a man fires upon another man rather than at a target, he is less sure of his grip."

His rival inclined his head in acknowledgment. "Yes," he said. "I was wrong. And now you may fire in your turn."

"I, fire at you?" Georges picked up his hat and handed the pistol to his second. "Why should I do that?"

The other man looked astonished. "It is your right, monsieur, and I insist upon it. I confess that I'm curious as to whether your aim will be better than mine."

Georges shook his head. "I'm afraid you have misunderstood me," he said, unruffled as ever. "I never said I could hit you; I simply said that you couldn't hit me, and you did not. I have proven myself correct. As far as I'm concerned, the experiment is over." Ignoring the other man's protests that he must shoot in his turn, he stepped into his coach and took the road to the barrière de l'Étoile, remarking to his companion: "Well! Didn't I tell you that there would be a difference between shooting at a target and shooting at a man?" His satisfaction was complete; he had passed the final test. Never again would he doubt his own courage.

———

The three adventures I have just related caused a good deal of talk around Paris, and our hero became even more admired. Two or three coquettes made it a point of honor to vanquish the resistance of this modern Cato, and since he no longer had any reason to reject them he was soon quite a fashionable young man indeed. He did not allow himself to be completely captivated by the whirl of society, however; and one bright day he bid farewell to Paris and to his charming mistresses, and set out for London.

There Georges was well received everywhere he went. He kept horses and dogs; rode, hunted, and shot; gambled and won and lost large sums with aristocratic insouciance. He also made the nodding acquaintance of Lord Murray during this time, but as we have seen, they did not then form any real friendship. By the end of the year he was able to leave London, as he had left Paris, with a reputation as a well-bred and charming gentleman-about-town.

That was the era when travels to the Orient were becoming all the rage. Georges visited Greece, Turkey, Asia Minor, Syria, and Egypt. He was presented to the great Muhammad Ali just before Ibrahim Pasha began his invasion of Arabia; he accompanied the viceroy's son into battle, and received a sword of honor and two fine Arabian horses as a reward for his bravery.

En route back to France, Georges passed through Italy, where preparations for the Spanish campaign were under way. Hastening to Paris, he volunteered to join the ranks of the first battalion. Unfortunately, against all expectations, the Spanish forces were quickly broken. The campaign, which everyone had expected to be so momentous, was not much more than a military exercise in the end. At Trocadéro, however, things were a bit different. It was soon evident that this last bastion of the peninsular revolution would have to be taken by force.

The regiment to which Georges belonged was not chosen for the assault, so he changed regiments directly and became a grenadier. When the signal was given, Georges threw himself head-on at the opposing forces, and was the third to enter the fort. His name was listed with honor in the dispatches, and he received from the hands of the duke d'Angoulême the croix de la Légion d'honneur and, from those of Ferdinand VII, that of Charles III. He had enlisted in the army with the sole aim of achieving one such military distinction, and now he had received two. He was overwhelmed with joy and pride.

At last Georges felt that the time had come to return to île de France. He had accomplished everything he hoped to, and more; his wildest dreams had come to pass. There was nothing left to do for him in Europe. He had battled civilization, and conquered it; now it was time to take on barbarism. His was a proud and enthusiastic soul, one that could never be satisfied by living in European luxury, wasting the strength he had so painstakingly built so that he might wage war on his home soil. Everything he had done in the last ten years, he had done with the sole aim of becoming such a superior man that he would be able to destroy the prejudice no colored man had yet dared oppose. He cared nothing for France's 33 million men, nor for any of the 150 million people of Europe. The offices of deputy and minister held no attraction for him; the distinction between republic and kingdom was of no consequence to him. The chief place in his heart was occupied by a tiny green island tucked far away in the southern seas like a nearly invisible grain of sand at the bottom of the vast ocean. There, Georges believed, existed the only problem worth solving. He was haunted by the memory of his subjugation, and going home was his only hope of throwing off that yoke forever.

When the *Leicester* docked at Cadiz on her way to île de France, Georges requested permission to board the vessel. It was quickly granted, both because he was highly recommended by French and Spanish authorities and because another passenger, Lord Murray, learning that the young man was a native son of their destination, was anxious to learn as much as he could about the island he was to govern from the mouth of one who had been born and raised there. This young man, the Englishman reasoned, would surely be able to tell him much of the thousand tiny political and moral details of the place that it is so important for a governor to amass before setting foot on the territory over which he is to preside.

We have already seen how they renewed and expanded their acquaintance during the voyage to Port Louis, and how they had reached the point of real friendship by the time of their arrival.

We have also seen how Georges, though devoted to his father, did not reveal his identity to Pierre Munier until after yet another long, painful test of his own self-control. The old man's joy was increased tenfold by the utter unexpectedness of it, and also by the fact that the man he now beheld was so vastly changed and improved from the boy he had missed for so many years. As they walked together down the road to Moka, the father gazed rapturously at his son, often stopping to clasp him in an embrace so loving that it brought tears to the young man's eyes despite the stalwart manner he had cultivated so carefully.

After walking for some three hours, they reached the outer edge of the plantation. Télémaque hastened ahead of them to alert the servants, so that everyone had gathered in the courtyard by the time they arrived. Georges and his father found themselves surrounded by Negroes in a state of mingled joy and fear—after all, they had not seen this new young master since he was a child. What sort of a man had he become? What kind of master would he be? Any worries were quickly put to rest, however, when Georges decreed three days of rest for the entire household.

Anxious to see the extent of the Munier landholdings, Georges scarcely sat down long enough to dine before going out with his father to view the estate. A series of fortunate speculations, as well as years of skilled management, had made it one of the most beautiful properties on the island. Its central point was the residence, a simple and spacious building surrounded by banana, mango, and tamarind trees. A wide, tree-lined avenue led to the main road, the lush border concealing perfumed hedges covered with enormous flowers that swayed gently in the breeze, which caressed the orange and banana trees, dipping and rising like a bee caught between two succulent blooms, or a heart that hesitates to choose between two desires. Behind the house was a large and verdant garden containing more fruit trees, and beyond that, immense fields of corn and sugarcane so heavily laden with their bounty that they seemed to beg for the kind services of the harvester.

Then, too, there were the slave quarters, which indeed no great plantation was without.

The center of this area was occupied by a large structure that served as a barn in the winter and a dance hall in the summer. Sounds of merriment issued from the building now: laughter, drums, tambourines, and Malgache harps. The blacks had wasted no time in beginning their three days' holiday. Primitive and uninhibited by nature, they worked and played with equal fervor, and often danced until they dropped from exhaustion. They were startled, however, by the unexpected arrival of the master and his son. They hurried to arrange themselves in rows, each seeking his proper place, like soldiers surprised by their captain. After a moment of silence, they burst into heartfelt applause and hurrahs of joy. They were well fed, well clothed, and fairly treated, and they adored Pierre Munier as the best mulatto in the colony; a man who was humble with the whites and never cruel to the blacks. Georges's return, as I have said, had caused great fear among the slaves. As if he could sense the effect of his presence, he raised his hand to signal that he wished to speak. Instantly a profound silence fell. The Negroes listened raptly to the words I will momentarily recount, words that fell from the young man's lips as slowly as a promise and as solemnly as a vow:

"My friends," he began, "I am deeply touched by the welcome you have shown me. It gratifies me to see you so content, and to know that my father is the source of that contentment. He obviously treats you well, and I thank him for it. It is my duty, as it has always been his, to ensure the happiness of those I hope will serve me obediently and well. You are three hundred strong, with only ninety huts among you; my father tells me it is his wish to build sixty more, one for each husband and wife. Each hut will have a small garden where you may grow potatoes, tobacco, and yams, and raise chickens and pigs. Any man who wishes to may go and sell his produce at the Sunday market in Port Louis; any money you earn will be your own. Thievery will be severely punished, but if any of you are treated unjustly by the overseer, you have only to report it and justice will be served. As for the subject of runaways, I cannot imagine that any of you would commit such an act; let me simply say that I hope you are, and will continue to be, too content here to think of leaving us."

Cries of approval greeted this little speech. It will doubtless appear quite alien to those sixty million Europeans whose happy fortune it is to live in constitutional freedom, but it was the first charter of its kind ever bestowed in that colony.

VII

THE BERLOQUE

The next evening, which, as I have said, was a Saturday, in another barn located at the foot of Mont Trois-Mamelles, a different and more serious group of blacks sat around a large fire, occupied in what the colonies call a berloque; that is, everyone busied himself with a variety of tasks according to his needs, his temperament, or his character. Some worked at handicrafts destined for sale at the Sunday market; others cooked rice, manioc, or bananas. One man smoked a pipe of tobacco that was not entirely indigenous but had been grown in his own garden, while another simply chatted in a low voice to his neighbor. Women and children came and went ceaselessly among the groups, tending the fire. Despite the industrious atmosphere and the fact that it was a Saturday, though, the gathering had a decidedly gloomy air. The source of this unhappiness was not, as one might expect, the master of the plantation; rather, it was the mulatto overseer. For this building was located on the lower part of the Williams Plains, at the foot of Mont Trois-Mamelles, an area that formed part of the property of our old acquaintance M. de Malmédie.

Surprisingly, M. de Malmédie was not a bad master, as we understand the word in France; this rotund little man was not given to hatred or vengeance. He was simply puffed up with pride in his own civil and political importance, and in the purity of the blood that flowed through his veins. He had a healthy share of native pride, and his was the sort of prejudice that, on île de France, still plagued men of color at that time. His slaves were not worse off than anyone else's; nor were they better off. Still, they shared the unhappiness common to slaves everywhere. M. de Malmédie saw Negroes not as men, but as machines, made for labor. If one of these machines did not function satisfactorily due to laziness or fatigue, it must simply be wound up again—with a whip, if necessary; this was precisely what M. de Malmédie had instructed his overseer to do.

As for Henri de Malmédie: He was the exact portrait of his father—but twenty years younger, and possessed of an even stronger dose of pride.

The moral and material situations of the Williams Plains slaves and those of the Moka quarter were vastly different, as we have seen. Gaiety came naturally at the Munier berloques; elsewhere, it was forced. A song, an acrobatic feat, or a tale of fantasy was needed to excite M. de Malmédie's slaves; happily, there was one man among them who habitually took this task upon himself. In the tropics just as in our country, in the Negro quarters just as in the soldiers' barracks, there is always a man who assumes the exhausting duty of making his fellows laugh. He is recognized and thanked in a thousand different ways, though it is true that if his comrades forget to honor his efforts, as sometimes happens, the buffoon suddenly realizes that he is the creditor, and that his audience owes him. In this case, the name of the man who filled the position occupied by Triboulet and Angeli at the court of the kings Francis I and Louis XIII was Antonio; most people called him Antonio the Malay to distinguish him from the other Antonios on the island, who undoubtedly would have been offended by the misidentification. He had been born at Tingoram. He was a small man, with a block-like torso supported by a pair of impossibly spindly legs. His feet were enormous; his arms, so long that he resembled an orangutan and looked as if he could pick up an object from the ground without bending over. The whites found him grotesque, but among the less partisan and beauty-loving blacks he was noted for his humor, energy, and wit—even though, from time to time, he seemed to bare a tiger's teeth from beneath his monkey skin.

The berloque was decidedly gloomy, as I have said, until Antonio slipped unseen behind one of the barn's large wooden pillars. Peeking from his hiding place, he hissed in perfect imitation of a cobra, one of the most terrifying reptiles to be found on the island of Malay. This sound, so common on the plains of Tenasserim, in the marshes of Java, and on the sands of Quiloa, would have frozen most people with terror—but île de France holds no such dangerous reptiles, other than the sharks that swim in schools along the coastline, and here the effect was quite different than the wide-open eyes and mouths the Malay might have hoped for. Laughter and cries of: "It is Antonio the Malay! *Viva* Antonio!" erupted from the gathering. Only those who were Malgaches, Yoloffs, or natives of Zanzibar, who remembered the cobra's hiss from their youth, were momentarily afraid. One man, a beautiful youth who might have passed for white had his fine features been a shade or two paler, half rose to his feet. He, too, murmured "Antonio the Malay," but his voice held a note of disdain quite absent from those of his neighbors.

With three bounds of his long legs, Antonio moved to the center of the circle and sat down tailor-fashion on the ground near the hearth. "Sing to us, Antonio!" his audience clamored. Unlike some virtuoso sure of the effect he will produce, Antonio did not wait to be asked twice. Twanging a few preliminary notes on a mouth organ, he danced about crazily as he sang the following song:

> I live in a little hut
> I must duck down to enter;
> My head touches the ceiling
> While my feet touch the floor.
> I have no need of light
> At night, when I want to sleep;
> Because I have the moon
> And many holes to see it through, thank God!

My bed is a little Madagascan mat,
My pillow a piece of white wood,
My water jug is an old calbasse
And I drink rum from it on New Year's Day.
When my wife keeps house
On Saturdays, for supper
She cooks for me, in my little hut,
A banana, roasted in the ashes.

My trunk has no hinges,
And never do I close it
In a bamboo box like that with no lock
Who would want my loincloth?
But on Sunday, if I am given the day
I buy a bit of tobacco,
And all week I smoke it
In my big Carouba pipe.

The effect this somewhat crude song had on the listeners cannot be understood without having lived among this race of simple and primitive men, for whom everything is a matter of sensation. Despite the song's weak rhymes and simple ideas, the slaves were transported. The first and second verses were greeted with laughter and applause; the third, with shouts of approval and hurrahs. Only the young Negro who had greeted Antonio's arrival with scorn shrugged, an expression of disgust on his face.

Strangely, rather than basking in the attention he was receiving, Antonio slumped forward with his head in his hands. Since he was the sole source of gaiety among the slaves, they began to be sad again, and begged him to sing another song or tell another story—but he turned a deaf ear, remaining incomprehensibly immobile and silent. One of his friends clapped him on the shoulder. "What's wrong with you, Malay?" he demanded. "Are you dead?"

"No," Antonio said. "I'm quite alive."

"Well, what are you doing?"

"Thinking."

"About what, for heaven's sake?"

"I'm thinking about the berloque," Antonio said. "It should be a happy occasion. Every man is able to work for himself—though there are some lazy good-for-nothings who idle the time away smoking, like you, Toukal; or cooking bananas like Cambeba there. Look how industrious Castor is, making chairs! Bonhomme carves wooden spoons! Nazim is the laziest of all; he does nothing."

"I do what I please," scowled the fine-featured and disdainful young black. "I am the Stag of Anjouan, just as Laïza is the Lion. The affairs of stags and lions are of no concern to snakes."

Nazim's words seemed to echo in the large barn. After a moment of silence, Antonio continued. "As I said, the berloque is a time for pleasure, but it seems to me that to keep your work from overtiring you, Castor, and to make your tobacco taste even sweeter, Toukal, and to keep you from falling asleep while your banana cooks, Cambeba, there must be someone here to tell you stories and sing you songs."

"Well, yes, but that's what you are for, Antonio," said Castor. "You know many fantastic stories and wonderful songs."

"But," said Antonio, "if I were not here, then who would sing songs and tell stories? You would be so tired from the week's work that you would all fall asleep! Then there would be no berloque! You would make no more bamboo chairs, Castor—nor you any more wooden spoons, Bonhomme! Your pipe would go out, Toukal—and Cambeba, the banana you are roasting would surely burn! Isn't this true?"

"True, true," the crowd murmured. Only Nazim remained silent and disdainful.

"So it seems to me that you should be grateful to me, for keeping you awake and making you laugh!"

"Yes, thank you, Antonio! Thank you!" the crowd cried.

"Who can tell tales to keep you awake, and sing songs to make you laugh?"

"Laïza; Laïza also knows many stories!"

Antonio frowned. "Yes, but his stories make you tremble with fear, do they not?"

"True," murmured the Negroes again.

"Who else can sing songs for you, but Antonio?"

"Nazim—he knows many beautiful songs."

"Yes," said Antonio. "But his songs always make you cry."

"Yes," agreed the crowd.

"So it is only Antonio who knows funny stories and songs!"

"Yes, it is true," the Negroes said.

"Who sang you a song just four days ago?"

"You, Malay."

"Who told you a story just three days ago?"

"You, Malay."

"Who sang you a song the day before yesterday?"

"You, Malay."

"Who told you a story only yesterday?"

"You, Malay."

"And who has already sung you one song today, and will soon tell you a story?"

"You, Malay. It is always you."

Antonio puffed out his chest. "Well, since I am so important and do so much for you while you work and smoke and cook your bananas, since I sacrifice myself for you so much that I can't do anything for myself, isn't it fair that I receive something from you in return?"

The justice of this observation struck everyone in the crowd—but my historian's conscience must admit to you that only a few actually raised their voices to reply in the affirmative.

"For example," the Malay continued, "I think Toukal should give me a little of his tobacco for my pipe. Don't you think, Cambeba?"

"Yes!" Cambeba cried eagerly, thrilled that he had not been the one asked to contribute. So Toukal was forced to share his tobacco with Antonio.

"Now," continued the Malay, "just the other day I lost my wooden spoon. I have no money to buy another one, because instead of working I have spent my time singing songs and telling stories for you. Don't you think, Toukal, that Bonhomme should give me a wooden spoon to eat my soup with?"

"Of course!" Toukal exclaimed, glad that he was not the only one imposed on by the Malay.

Antonio extended his hand to Bonhomme, who handed him the wooden spoon he had just finished whittling.

"Now," Antonio said, "I have tobacco for my pipe and a spoon to eat my soup with, but I have no money to buy what I need to make the soup. It is only fair that Castor give me the pretty little footstool he has been working on, so I can sell it in the market and buy a little piece of beef. Isn't that right, Toukal? Bonhomme; Cambeba; don't you agree?"

"Yes, Cambeba, it's only fair!" shouted Toukal, Bonhomme, and Cambeba.

And Antonio, half genial and half threatening, seized from Castor's hands the stool to which the latter had just attached the very last peg of bamboo.

"Now," Antonio said, "I am already tired from singing for you, and I will be even more tired after I tell you a story. I must regain my strength by eating something. Right, Toukal? Right, Bonhomme? Right, Castor?"

"Yes!" the three men affirmed.

A terrible thought occurred just then to Cambeba.

"But," said Antonio, showing a double row of glimmering white teeth like a wolf's, "I have nothing to put in my mouth."

Cambeba felt his hair stand on end, and he instinctively reached his hand toward the hearth.

"It is only right," continued Antonio, "that Cambeba give me a bit of his banana. Don't you all think it would be fair?"

"Yes, yes, it is only fair!" Toukal, Bonhomme, and Castor cried with one voice. "Yes! It's only right! Banana, Cambeba! Banana, Cambeba!"

All the other voices picked up the cry. "Banana, Cambeba! Banana, Cambeba!"

Poor Cambeba cast a panicked glance around the room, then launched himself at the hearth to rescue his banana—but Antonio stopped him halfway, grabbing him with surprising strength. He passed one end of the rope used for hoisting sacks of corn to the barn's loft through Cambeba's belt and motioned Toukal to pull on the other end; the unfortunate Cambeba was ten feet in the air before he knew what was happening. The crowd hooted with laughter as he dangled helplessly, his hands still scrabbling toward the hearth.

"Bravo, Antonio!" the audience cheered, roaring with mirth. Antonio now strode to the hearth, where he plucked the smoking banana out of the ashes.

"My banana, my banana!" howled Cambeba in tones of deep despair.

"Yes, here it is!" Antonio said nonchalantly, waving it at his victim.

"I can' reach him," Cambeba whined.

"What? You don't want it?" said Antonio, feigning confusion.

"I up too high; can' reach him!" said Cambeba again, pitifully.

"Well, then," Antonio said, imitating Cambeba's accent, "I eat him myself, so he not go to waste." He began to peel the banana, exaggerating his movements so that the watching blacks erupted in fresh gales of laughter.

"Banana not for me, Antonio," pleaded Cambeba. "He for my wife; she sick, can' eat nothing else. I steal banana for her because I need him so much; please give him back!"

Antonio sighed theatrically. "Crime does not pay."

"Poor Narina, my poor Narina; she have nothing to eat, she be so hungry," Cambeba moaned.

"Have pity on this man." It was Nazim, the handsome young black from Anjouan, who had remained silent during Cambeba's ordeal, his face troubled.

"Keep quiet," Antonio shot back.

"Lower him," Nazim said with dignity that would have impressed a king. Toukal, who still held the end of the rope from which Cambeba was suspended, looked uncertainly from Nazim to Antonio, who ignored him.

"I said to keep quiet," Antonio repeated, glaring at Nazim, "but you keep talking."

"I do not take orders from dogs," Nazim said, his voice dripping with scorn.

"Watch yourself, Nazim," Antonio growled. "Laïza isn't here, and you can't do much without your brother."

"I said you are a dog, Antonio," Nazim repeated, rising to his feet.

The watching blacks broke into groups on either side of Nazim and Antonio, so that the handsome Negro from Anjouan and the grotesque Malay were directly facing each other, not ten steps apart. Antonio bared his teeth angrily. "You keep a safe distance when you say such things, Nazim."

"I'll say it again now, and nearer!" cried Nazim. With one great stride, he shortened the distance between them to two paces. "You are a dog," he repeated, his nostrils flaring and his gaze boring into the Malay's.

A white man, in such a situation, would have flung himself at his enemy with no further delay. Instead Antonio retreated a few steps, crouched like a reptile about to attack its prey, and drew a knife from his pocket, snapping it open. Nazim saw this and knew immediately what the Malay meant to do, but he showed no flicker of fear. He stood, erect and silent as a Nubian god, waiting for Antonio to make his move. The Malay glared venomously. "Laïza isn't here," he said again, and lunged. "Woe to you, Nazim!"

"Laïza *is* here," contradicted a deep and sonorous voice.

The man who had spoken these words had done so in a neutral tone; he had not gestured or made a signal of any kind. Nonetheless Antonio froze; the knife, a scant two inches from Nazim's breast, fell to the ground. Welcoming shouts of "Laïza!" rose from the crowd of Negroes; they turned as one to the newcomer, immediately assuming an air of obedience.

Laïza, whose mere presence inspired such respect, was a man of medium height with impressively muscular limbs. He stood straight and motionless, arms folded across his chest and glittering eyes half closed, resembling nothing so much as a lion at rest. To see so many blacks waiting in respectful silence for his slightest word or gesture, one might have thought he was a king about to decree war or peace to an African horde; yet he was, as they were, merely a slave.

After a few moments of sculpture-like immobility, Laïza raised one arm and pointed at Cambeba, who was still helplessly suspended ten feet in the air, silent like the others, watching the scene below him. Toukal hastily let the end of the rope drop, and Cambeba—to his great satisfaction—found his feet on the ground once more. His first action was, naturally, to look around for his banana; unfortunately, it had disappeared during the commotion just past.

Laïza, meanwhile, stepped out of the barn and returned a moment later with a wild hog slung across his shoulders. "Here, children," he said, letting the animal fall to the hearth. "You see, I have thought of you. Take care you divide it fairly." The blacks, their hearts and stomachs touched by such generosity, gathered admiringly around the carcass.

"We have good supper tonight," said a Malabar happily.

"He as black as a man from Mozambique," said a Malgache.

"He as fat as a Malgache," said a man from Mozambique.

It will not surprise the reader that admiration soon gave way to hunger among the spectators. In the blink of an eye the hog was butchered. A portion was reserved for the next day; the rest sliced thinly for immediate cooking or cut into joints for roasting. The blacks sat down again, smiling in anticipation of the meal to come. Only Cambeba remained standing, leaning dejectedly against the wall in a corner of the barn. "What is the matter, Cambeba?" Laïza asked, noticing him. "What are you doing over there?"

"Nothing, Papa Laïza." *Papa* is a title of honor and affection among Negroes, and the slaves of the Malmédie plantation, young and old, had unanimously agreed to bestow it upon Laïza.

"Are you in pain from being hung by the waist for so long?"

"No, Papa! I not so soft as that!"

"Well, then, are you unhappy?" Cambeba nodded. "Why?" Laïza prodded.

"Antonio take my banana, and I have nothing for my poor sick wife to eat," said Cambeba mournfully.

"You can take some of this good meat to her."

"No, Papa, she too sick to eat meat."

"Holà!" Laïza exclaimed to the crowd. "Who among you will give me a banana?" As if by magic, a dozen bananas were snatched from the hearth and proffered to Laïza. Selecting the most tempting of them, he gave it to Cambeba, who took it and dashed from the barn without even thanking his benefactor. Laïza turned to Bonhomme, the banana's previous owner. "Don't worry, Bonhomme; you have lost nothing. In return for your banana, you shall have Antonio's share of the meat."

"What will I eat, then?" Antonio demanded.

"You can eat the banana you stole from Cambeba," said Laïza.

"But—it is lost!" whined Antonio.

Laïza shrugged. "That is no concern of mine," he said, turning away.

"Bravo!" cheered the crowd. "Crime does not pay!"

The Malay got to his feet, glaring at the taunting, jeering faces of those who, moments before, had applauded his torment of poor Cambeba. He left the barn without another word.

"Be careful, my brother," Nazim said to Laïza. "I know Antonio. He will try to get revenge on you."

"I think it's you who had better take care," Laïza returned, "for he would never dare attack me."

"We will watch out for each other," said Nazim. "But we can speak of that another time. We have something else to discuss, you and I."

"Yes—but not here."

"Let us leave, then," said Nazim.

Laïza shook his head. "Not now. Wait until the others are busy with supper." With that, the two men raised their voices and chatted about inconsequential trifles until the meal was ready. Then, with the crowd's attention thus pleasantly occupied, they slipped out of the barn unobserved.

THE TOILETTE OF THE RUNAWAY SLAVE

It was now almost ten o'clock. The sky, though moonless, sparkled with stars; it was beautiful as only a late-summer night in the tropics can be. The constellations we have all known since childhood—the Little Bear, the Archer, Orion, and the Pleiades—were clearly visible in the heavens, but in positions so different from the ones we are used to seeing that a European might have had trouble recognizing them. In the midst of the familiar constellations was an unfamiliar one, the Southern Cross, which is never seen in our boreal hemisphere. The night was utterly quiet except for the noise of the tenrecs that throng the banks of the rivière Noire and the songs of blue jays and fondi-jalas, the nightingales of Madagascar, and the soft crunch of drying grass beneath the brothers' feet. They walked in silence, casting occa-sional, anxious glances around and pausing often to make sure they were alone. Finally they reached a dense, secluded grove of bamboo trees and sat down together on the ground, each gazing at the other and waiting for him to speak. Without doubt this latest investigation had proven more reassuring than those before it, for they looked at each other with expressions that implied they felt safe, and leaned back against the trunk of a wild banana tree whose large leaves drooped over them like a magnificent canopy in the middle of the withered rose leaves surrounding it.

"Well, my brother?" Nazim said, with the same touch of impatience he had shown earlier in the barn, when Laïza had cautioned him not to ask any questions in front of the other blacks.

Laïza sighed. "You're still determined, eh?"

"More than ever. It would kill me to stay here, don't you see? I've worked long enough. We are the sons of a chief! This wretched life is not for me. If I don't return to Anjouan soon, I will die."

"It is a long way from here."

"So?"

"It is the stormy season."

Nazim shrugged. "The wind will only carry us faster."

"And if our boat sinks?" Laïza pressed.

"Then we will swim as long as we're able, and when we tire we'll look one last time at the heavens, where the Great Spirit awaits us, and sink beneath the waves."

"Alas!" murmured Laïza.

"I prefer death to slavery," Nazim said stoutly.

"You've made up your mind, then, to leave île de France?"

"I have."

"Even if it means risking your life?"

"Yes."

"You've only got perhaps one chance in ten of making it to Anjouan," warned Laïza.

"At least I have a chance."

Laïza sighed again. "As you wish, my brother. Just be sure that you have thought it through."

"I have been thinking it through for two years," Nazim said. "I've been sure of it ever since I was captured in battle by the chief of the Mongallos and sold into slavery, like you before me. When they chained me, I tried to strangle myself with the chains. When they tied me down in the hold, I tried to dash my brains out against the wall. I tried to starve myself, but they forced me to eat and drink. They sold me quickly at half price, because I was so willful, so obviously determined to kill myself as soon as I found a way—and I would have, my brother, if I had not been so unexpectedly reunited with you. When I heard your voice again, when I felt my heart and my lips against yours, I was so happy I thought I could live again. Your love reignited the spark of life in me for a year, but then—forgive me—even that was not enough. I cannot forget our island, or our father and Zirna. It has become too heavy a load for me to bear. It became more humiliating by the day, until finally it was impossible. It was then that I told you of my desire to flee, to return to Anjouan; to see Zirna again, and my father, and our island. You said to me, 'Rest, Nazim. You are weak, and I will do your share of the work, because I am strong.' So you have gone out every night for the past four days, and done my work while I rested. Haven't you, Laïza?"

"Yes, my brother," said Laïza. "But listen to me! Only wait a little longer. It will be worth it, I promise you. We are slaves today, but in a month—in three months—in a year—*we* might be the masters!"

"Yes, yes, Laïza," Nazim nodded. "I know you are planning, hoping."

"Yes, and you must imagine how it will be when the whites are humiliated in their turn!" Laïza's voice filled with intensity. "They will work for us, ten or twelve hours every day—and if they are lazy, we will punish them with their own whips, beat them with their own clubs! There are eighty thousand of us, and only twelve thousand of them. It's only a matter of time."

"As you said to me, there is only one chance in ten of success—if that."

"And as you said to me, there is still a chance. Please, stay."

Nazim shook his head. "I cannot wait any longer, Laïza. I cannot. My mother's spirit has come to me and told me to return home."

Laïza looked astonished. "You have seen her?"

"Every night for two weeks I have been visited by the same nightingale that used to sing at her tomb in Anjouan. It has crossed the ocean on its little wings and found me here. I recognize its song. Look; here it is now."

Indeed, at that very moment a Madagascar nightingale, perched on the highest branch of the tree under which the brothers sat, broke into melodious song. As they listened in pensive silence, the bird stopped singing to fly a short distance in the direction of their homeland, then began warbling again. Once, twice, it repeated this action until the two exiles could no longer catch the distant echoes of its plaintive song, which reminded them so painfully of home.

"It has returned to Anjouan," said Nazim. "It will come back, again and again, until I return home."

"Then you must go," said Laïza softly.

Nazim looked at his brother. "Now?"

Laïza nodded. "Everything is ready. I have hollowed the trunk of the largest tree I could find into a canoe, but I feared that someone would notice the stump, so instead of chopping it down I merely sawed above and beneath it, so that one good push will topple it. I made a set of oars out of branches, as well. Go and find it, alongside the rivière Noire, and you can leave this very night. The current is strong; it should carry you swiftly downstream."

"You will not come with me?"

"No. I am staying."

Nazim looked dismayed. "What keeps you here? What can possibly prevent you from returning with me to the home of our fathers?"

"I told you: We have been planning for more than a year to revolt. We are nearly ready now, and I have been chosen to lead the insurrection. I would be betraying everyone if I left now."

Nazim shook his head. "No—there is something else; I know it."

"What do you think is holding me back, then?"

Nazim looked his brother squarely in the eye. "The Rose of the rivière Noire."

Laïza started, and for a moment he could not speak. "It is true," he said at length. "I love her."

"My poor brother!" murmured Nazim. "What will you do?"

"Nothing. I must be content to gaze at her from afar, as I did yesterday and today, and as I will do tomorrow."

"Does she even know you exist?"

"I doubt it."

"Has she ever spoken to you?"

"Never."

"Well, then, why not think of our homeland instead?" Nazim urged.

Laïza shook his head. "I've forgotten it."

"And what of Nessali?"

"I've forgotten her as well."

"And our father?" pressed Nazim.

Laïza heaved a great sigh and buried his face in his hands. "Listen," he said finally, looking up at his brother. "You cannot convince me to leave, any more than I can convince you to stay. I must be near her, don't you understand? I must breathe the same air she does. She is everything for me—family as well as country. I must see her if I am to live. Each of us must follow our destiny, Nazim. You will return to Anjouan, and I will remain here."

"What will I say to our father, when he asks me why you haven't returned?"

"Tell him . . ." Laïza's voice was strangled. "Tell him I am dead."

"He will never believe me," Nazim said, aghast.

"Why not?"

" 'I have not been visited by his spirit,' he will say."

"Then you must tell him I have fallen in love with a white woman," said Laïza roughly. "Then he will curse me, no doubt. But I cannot leave île de France as long as she is here."

Nazim rose to his feet, defeated. "I must trust that the Great Spirit knows what is best. Lead me to the canoe, my brother."

"In just a moment," Laïza said. He, too, rose and withdrew a shard of glass and a gourd filled with coconut oil from a hollow in the tree beneath which they had been sitting.

"What is that?" demanded Nazim.

Laïza turned to him. "If you're lucky, you might reach Madagascar, or even the mainland, within eight or ten days," he said. "But what if a sudden squall capsizes the canoe? Tomorrow, or the day after tomorrow, you might be driven back to this coast. Your description will spread like wildfire, and you will be hunted as a runaway. You will have to hide behind trees and rocks."

Nazim started to protest. "My brother, I am the Stag of Anjouan, just as you are the Lion."

"Yes, but, like a stag, you may fall into a trap. You must be able to slip easily from a captor's grasp. Here is glass to cut your hair, and coconut oil to put on your body. We will oil your limbs, and shear off your hair. It is the toilette of the runaway slave."

Nazim and Laïza went to a clearing, and by starlight Laïza began, with the aid of his glass shard, to cut his brother's hair off as quickly and completely as if he were a skilled barber using the finest razor. This done, Nazim disrobed and his brother poured a portion of the coconut oil from the gourd onto his shoulders. The handsome black from Anjouan smeared it over every bit of his body. Thus anointed and shorn, the young man looked like a Grecian athlete prepared for competition.

Laïza would not rest easy until they had put their precautions to the test. Once, like Alcidamas, he had grabbed a horse by its back feet, and the horse had not been able to escape. Like Milo of Croton, he had taken a bull by the horns and tossed it over his shoulders and kicked it with his feet. He was incredibly strong, and if Nazim could escape his grip, he could escape anyone's. Bracing himself, Laïza grabbed at his brother with all his strength—but Nazim's arm slipped out of his iron grasp like a wriggling eel through a fisherman's fingers. Laïza caught him again by the shoulder, this time bringing the other man tightly against his chest as Hercules did to Antaeus—but again, Nazim got away with ease, like a snake sliding between a lion's fangs. Laïza knew his brother could run like the wind—once Nazim had raced the very animal from which he took his nickname, and had beaten it—and now he knew he could not be taken by surprise. He was satisfied.

Laïza pressed the three-quarters-full gourd of oil into Nazim's hands, making him promise to guard it carefully, along with the manioc roots that would feed him and the water that would quench his thirst. Nazim attached the gourd firmly to his belt.

Then the two brothers looked at the sky. Judging by the position of the stars, it was past midnight. They took to the road leading to the rivière Noire and disappeared into the dark woods at the base of Trois-Mamelles. Behind them, around twenty feet from the bamboo grove they had just left and where all their secret conversation had taken place, the shadowy figure of a man who had heretofore been utterly still, so that he might have been taken for another of the tree trunks among which he hid, rose like a ghost from the underbrush, paused for an instant, threw a threatening gesture after the two brothers, and, as soon as they were out of sight, darted away in the direction of Port Louis.

It was Antonio the Malay, who had that very evening sworn to take revenge on both Laïza and Nazim. He would keep his word.

And now, as Antonio runs like the wind on his long legs, if my readers permit it, I will proceed ahead of him to the capital of île de France.

THE ROSE OF THE RIVIÈRE NOIRE

After paying Miko-Miko for the Chinese fan whose price Georges had told her to her utter astonishment, the young woman we have so recently met standing at the threshold of her home was, while her Negro servant helped the Chinese merchant replace his wares in the bamboo baskets, proceeding inside, accompanied as always by her governess, and thrilled with the day's purchase, which would inevitably be forgotten tomorrow.

Moving with the nonchalant, languid grace peculiar to Creole women, she settled herself upon a comfortable chaise longue in her boudoir that served as both bed and seat. This was placed in the center of a charming bedroom filled with rare and costly porcelains from China and Japan, and the tapestries covering the walls, which île de France natives referred to as patna, had been imported from India's Coromandel coast. The tables and chairs were built of the cane so plentiful in warm climates, and the room's two opposing windows opened upon a tree-filled courtyard and a vast shipyard, respectively. Sea breezes, redolent with floral perfume, drifted through the bamboo blinds.

As the girl reclined on the settee, a plump green parakeet as big as a sparrow that was her especial pet fluttered onto her shoulder and nibbled curiously at the newly acquired ivory fan. She opened and closed the fan distractedly, gazing absently into space. Since it was obvious that it was not her fan—charming as it was—that occupied her thoughts, we know that some new desire did. Her eyes, seemingly fixed on some point in the room where there was no object remarkable enough to attract her attention, appeared to see instead some inner dream. What is more, this dream doubtlessly held for her the aura of reality; from time to time a small smile crossed her face and her lips moved, responding silently to a silent memory.

Such preoccupation was so alien to the usual habits of the young girl that her governess noticed it immediately and, after watching her charge's mobile face for a moment, asked: "Why, Sara, what *is* the matter with you today?"

The girl started as if she had been wakened from a dream. "Oh! Nothing, dear Henriette. I was just—just amusing myself, as you see, with my parakeet and my new fan."

"Yes, I see you doing that," the governess said, smiling. "But I also see that you are thinking about something else entirely."

"No, I—"

"Now, Sara," the governess interrupted, but kindly. "You've never lied to me. Why begin today?"

The girl's cheeks flushed scarlet. "You're right," she admitted. "I was thinking of something quite different. The young man who was so helpful to us today—I was wondering who he is, and where he came from. I've never seen him before today—he must have arrived aboard the governor's ship." She hesitated. "Is it wrong for me to be curious about him?"

"Of course not," said Henriette. "It would only have been wrong to tell a falsehood about it."

"I'm sorry, dear Henriette," said Sara sweetly, and offered her cheek for the governess to kiss. The two women remained in a somewhat awkward silence for a moment; then both started to speak at the same time. Both sought to find another topic of conversation, and each kept stopping to let the other speak. There was another moment of silence; then the girl spoke again. "What did you want to say, dear Henriette?"

"What were *you* saying, Sara?"

"I was going to say that I would like to know if our new governor is a young man."

"Would it please you if he were?"

"Oh, yes! For then he would give dinners, and parties, and balls! That would make dull old Port Louis a bit more lively. I would give anything for a ball!"

"You love to dance, don't you, my child?"

"Oh, so much!" cried Sara. Henriette smiled again, and the girl's face fell. "Oh, dear—have I said something wrong again? There's no harm in dancing, is there?"

"Not exactly," said Henriette, "but you must learn to restrain yourself a bit. You are too passionate for your own good."

Sara smiled with immense—and well-practiced—charm. "What would you have me do? It is my nature, dear Henriette. I love and I hate, and I can hide neither. You've told me yourself that dishonesty is worse than anything else."

"Yes, I know—but there is a large difference between experiencing feelings and abandoning oneself constantly to one's desires, or even one's instincts, Sara," Henriette replied seriously. The hasty reasoning of her charge was almost as troubling as the outbursts of her primitive nature, and these worried the governess more than she cared to admit.

Sara tossed her head coquettishly. "Oh, I know that European ladies—those who are called ladies, at least—are fashionably diplomatic—neither honest nor dishonest, finding safety in remaining silent and unmoving—but you must not expect such restraint from me, dearest Henriette! I am not a civilized lady! I'm a little savage, brought up among wild forests and raging rivers! If I see something I like, I must have it, then and there. Everyone has spoiled me a bit, you see— even you! If I'm not given anything I desire, I take it for myself, and I'm always forgiven for it. I'm afraid I'm quite used to having my way."

Henriette raised her eyebrows. "And just how will you manage this charming nature of yours when you are married to Monsieur Henri?"

"Oh, that's all settled," said Sara innocently. "Henri's a good sort of fellow. I shall let him do whatever he pleases, and he'll do the same for me. Isn't that right, Henri?" She turned toward the door as she spoke, for just at that moment M. de Malmédie and his son had come into the room.

"What's that, my dear?" Henri inquired, stepping to Sara's side and kissing her hand.

"Isn't it true that, when we are married, you'll never deny me a thing?"

"Good heavens!" exclaimed M. de Malmédie. "Is the little wife-to-be making demands already?"

"You said you would take me to balls if I wished it," continued Sara, "and let me stay as long as I liked—didn't you? You won't be one of those disagreeable husbands who insists on leaving after the seventh quadrille! And I may sing as much as I like, and go fishing, too, and you'll buy me lovely hats from Paris, and shawls from India, and perhaps even an English or Arabian stallion."

"Certainly, certainly," said Henri, smiling. "Odd that you should mention Arabian horses—we saw a handsome pair of them today. Probably for sale, too. Now that I think of it, it's just as well you weren't there, Sara. You might have asked for them, and I wouldn't have been able to get them for you."

"I saw them, too!" Sara cried. "They belong to a stranger, do they not? A dark young foreigner, about twenty-five years old, with beautiful hair and superb eyes?"

Henri chuckled. "Paid more attention to the man than the horses, did you?"

"Of course not, Henri. The young man approached and spoke to me—I only saw the horses from a distance, and they didn't even whinny."

Henri frowned, and so did his father. "He spoke to you? The rascal! On what pretext, Sara?"

"He isn't a rascal, Henri," protested Sara. "Henriette was with me, and she can vouch for him, too. There was really nothing improper in his speaking to me. Lord, it couldn't have been simpler! I had just come from church, you see, and there was a Chinaman waiting for me at the door, with baskets full of the sweetest trinkets—fans and purses and all sorts of other lovely things! I simply *had* to have this fan—isn't it a pretty one, Henri?"

"Look here," interrupted M. de Malmédie, "this doesn't explain how the young man came to speak to you."

"I'm getting to that, Uncle," said Sara. "I asked the price of the fan, but the man spoke only Chinese. We were very embarrassed, Henriette and I. We asked around among the other people who had gathered to see the pretty wares, in case any of them spoke Chinese and could act as an interpreter. Dear Henriette and I were quite at a loss—but then the young stranger happened upon us, and he was able to speak to the merchant in his own language! The fan was only eighty piastres; a good price, wasn't it, Uncle?"

M. de Malmédie snorted. "That was the going rate for a Negro, before the English put a stop to the slave trade."

"Wait, Sara," interjected Henri, "am I to understand that the foreigner speaks Chinese?" The girl nodded, and he turned to M. de Malmédie with a laugh. "Well, what do you think of that, Father?"

"What's so funny about that?" Sara inquired.

"Nothing, nothing," Henri replied, still chuckling. "An impressive skill, indeed. The fellow can chat with—oh, let me see—teacups and lacquered screens!"

"Not much else to be done with a language as rare as that," agreed M. de Malmédie.

"Yes, a *very* well-educated chap—a regular Mandarin," Henri laughed sarcastically, for the memory of the dark stranger's haughty glance still rankled.

"If he is a Mandarin, he's an educated one," said Sara. "He spoke Chinese to the merchant, then French to me, and finally English to dear Henriette!"

"Well, now," said M. de Malmédie. "He speaks all those languages, does he? I could use a fellow like that, as a clerk in my countinghouse."

"Alas, Uncle," said Sara, shaking her head. "I believe he must already have a much more exciting position."

"With whom, pray?"

"Why, with the king of France!" Sara exclaimed. "Didn't you notice the ribbon of the Légion d'honneur in his buttonhole?"

"Bah! These days, one needn't even be in the military to receive such a decoration," said M. de Malmédie.

"Still, he must be distinguished in some way," Sara persisted, feeling compelled to defend the stranger's honor without knowing exactly why.

"Probably got the ribbon because he speaks Chinese," said Henri dismissively.

"In any case, we'll soon know more about him," said M. de Malmédie, ignoring Sara's frown and Henri's piqued expression. "He arrived aboard the governor's ship, and I'm sure he'll remain on île de France for some time. No doubt we'll have the opportunity to see him again soon."

Just then a servant knocked and entered the room, bearing a letter sealed with the governor's signet. It was an invitation from William Murray to Sara and both of the Malmédies announcing dinner and a ball, to be held the following Monday. Sara was delighted; she had just taken delivery of some charming new artificial flowers from Paris with which to trim her gowns, and nothing seemed more pleasant than the prospect of spending a whole evening dancing and showing off her new finery.

Henri, despite the outward coolness with which he greeted the news, was pleased as well; he rightly considered himself one of the handsomest men in the colony, and such social gatherings always afforded the opportunity to meet attractive women. His marriage to his cousin had long been a foregone conclusion, but as the event had not yet actually taken place, and Sara had never manifested even the slightest bit of jealousy, he felt quite free to flirt with whomever he chose.

As for M. de Malmédie, he nearly burst with pride at the sight of his name on the invitation. He read it three times over, reveling in his own importance. The governor had not been on île de France more than three hours, and already he had invited the Malmédies to dine with him! The plump little man's view of himself as one of the most illustrious personages on the island was most agreeably reinforced.

Of course, some of the family's plans had to be altered. Henri had invited about a dozen of his friends for a stag hunt on the following Sunday and Monday, to begin at a charming country house he owned on the banks of the rivière Noire, one of the most picturesque areas of the island, and continue over an unpopulated, game-filled stretch of savanna that made up part of M. de Malmédie's property. Now, since one of the days planned for the hunt was now occupied by the governor's ball, the sport would have to take place on Saturday and Sunday instead—not only because the Malmédies were now otherwise engaged, but because some of their invited guests had, naturally, also been asked to accept the honor of dining with the governor. Accordingly, Henri hurried to his room to dash off a dozen notes, which the Negro Bijou was then charged with delivering to their respective addressees.

M. de Malmédie took his leave of Sara as well, saying he had business to attend to but, in reality, anxious to tell his neighbors that in three days he would be able to give them his opinion of the new governor, since he had been invited to dine with him the following Monday.

As for Sara, she declared that in such unexpected and important circumstances, she had too much to do to leave with the men on Saturday morning, and that she would rejoin them Saturday night or early on Sunday. The rest of that day and all the next were spent—as Sara had said—making preparations for the soirée. Thanks to the unwavering calm of dear Henriette in making the arrangements, Sara was indeed ready to leave on Sunday morning as she had promised her uncle. The gown had been tried on and the seamstress, a skilled woman, had promised that it would be ready for Sara to wear by the next morning. The girl was quite content with this; if there were any corrections to be made, they would still have part of the day to make them.

The girl finally made her departure in the most joyous of moods. Next to a ball, Sara loved the countryside above anything else. There she could follow her own desires. In the country she could frolic to her passionate heart's content, something she could never do in town. She recognized no authority at these times—not even dear Henriette's, and the governess had more power over her than anyone else. If she felt languid, she could choose a bed of grass and lie for hours in the shade of the jambosa and grapefruit trees. At these moments she lived the life of a flower, drinking in the scents, the air and sunshine, through every pore, listening to the songs of the bluejays and the fondijalas and watching the monkeys swing among the branches and the green-spotted and red-striped lizards that were so common on île de France—one step could send three or four of them darting away in all directions—scurry through the verdant grass. She would stay there for hours, communing with nature, listening to its thousand sounds and soaking in its thousand harmonies. She often felt that she was no longer a young woman at all during these sojourns; rather, in her spirit she became a gazelle, a bird, a butterfly; fording rivers in pursuit of sparkling ruby-headed dragonflies, leaning over precipices to gather leaf-cups in which drops of dew trembled like living silver, and darting like a nymph beneath waterfalls whose sparkling curtains of spray concealed her form like so many veils of gauze.

When she was thus lost in voluptuous daydreams, Sara's cheeks would flush deeply and vividly pink. Her blooming face, so different from the pale and expressionless visages of the other Creole women, led the nickname-loving Negroes of île de France to call her—with typical poetry—the Rose of the rivière Noire.

Sara was gloriously happy that Sunday. The hours to come held the promise of the two things she loved best in the world: an afternoon spent outdoors in the countryside, and a glittering ball the following night.

X

THE BATH

At that time the island was not, as it is today, crisscrossed by roads that permit easy travel to the different parts of the colony. The only means of transport were the horse and the palanquin. Whenever Sara went into the countryside with M. de Malmédie or Henri it was invariably on horseback, for she was an experienced and skillful rider, and extremely fond of that form of exercise; Henriette, however, preferred the palanquin, so this was how Sara traveled when she was with her staid English governess. That Sunday, the two women set out in side-by-side palanquins, each borne by four well-built blacks and followed by four more. They were carried near enough to each other that they could converse easily through the curtains, while their attendants, secure in the promise of a sizable gratuity, sang loudly, thus announcing to passersby the generosity of their young mistress.

Sara and Henriette were a study in contrasts, both physical and moral. We have already become acquainted with the former: black-haired, black-eyed, and capricious, with teeth like pearls, delicate hands and feet, and a figure sylph-like in its grace. As for the latter, permit me now to say a few words about her.

She had been born in London as Henriette Smith, daughter of a professor who, intending her to be a teacher as well, had carefully instructed her in French and Italian from early childhood so that she spoke them with the ease of a native. Her father, like many members of his profession, had died in poverty, leaving Henriette, then twenty-five, talented but so poor that she had little hope of attracting a husband. A musician friend who was aware of her talent for languages suggested that they combine their skills to open a school for young women—but though each of them lavished attention and care on the endeavor, it proved unsuccessful, and the two were forced to dissolve their partnership.

Soon afterward, the wealthy father of one of Henriette's erstwhile pupils received a letter from Monsieur de Malmédie of île de France, with whom he often conducted business. M. de Malmédie was looking for a governess for his young niece and wondered if his London friend might know anyone suitable. He promised a handsome salary in light of the fact that whoever accepted the position would have to leave Europe, and Henriette, poor and with no one and nothing keeping her in England, and facing the prospect of starving if she stayed, looked on the offer as a gift from heaven. She boarded the very next ship to île de France armed with letters extolling her virtue and talent, and M. de Malmédie, receiving her graciously, immediately put her in charge of the care and education of his niece Sara, aged nine.

Naturally, Henriette asked M. de Malmédie how he would like his young niece to be educated. He replied that it was entirely up to her—in fact, it was precisely because he didn't wish to be bothered with such matters that he had hired a governess. She was an intelligent woman, he said; she should simply teach Sara what she knew. There was only one thing he required. The girl was irrevocably destined to become the wife of her cousin Henri, and it was very important that she never become attracted to any other man. M. de Malmédie desired the union for reasons other than his affection for both his son and his niece—more financial than familial. Sara was heiress to a vast sum that would more than double during her minority in the care of her uncle.

At first little Sara had been terrified of this new governess who had come from far across the sea. Henriette's appearance was not, in truth, very reassuring. She was a tall, thin woman around thirty years of age, with a rather prim and spinsterish way of dressing. Cool-eyed, pale-skinned, and thin-lipped, she had ashy blond hair that did little to warm the overall effect. She was always immaculately dressed and coiffed; Sara had never once seen her in a nightgown, and she used to imagine that instead of sleeping in a bed like a mere mortal, Henriette spent her nights in the closet like a doll, emerging fully dressed each morning. For a long time these fears had the effect of prompting Sara to obey her governess to the letter. She learned some English and Italian, played the piano, the guitar, and the Malgache harp—her favorite over all other instruments, from which she drew sounds that enchanted the most famous Madagascar-born virtuosos on the island—with skill, and sang like a nightingale.

Even as Sara's education proceeded, though, she retained everything that made her character unique—and so did Henriette, who did not alter from what God and her education had made her. Thus the two women, so different from each other, lived side by side, together yet separate. Despite this, they grew very fond of each other as the years passed. Each possessed excellent qualities, and Henriette developed a profound attachment to her young pupil, a sentiment that Sara returned fully. The governess often called the girl "my child," while Sara, finding the terms *miss* and *mademoiselle* too cold for the affection she bore her governess, used the nickname *ma mie*—dear—Henriette.

There was one area in which Henriette's tutelage was decidedly lacking. Her own education had focused exclusively on the intellect, and she had neither the taste nor the ability for physical exercise. Despite Sara's repeated entreaties, the governess refused to take up riding; even Berloque, the quiet little garden pony, intimidated her. The narrow cliff roads, bordering sharp drops, made Henriette so nervous that she often went two or three leagues out of her way to avoid them. Boats, too, caused her nerves to jangle with anxiety. She was extremely prone to seasickness, and claimed that she had not been well a single day of the voyage from Portsmouth to Port Louis, which had taken a full four months. You will probably not be surprised, then, when I tell you that she existed in a constant state of worry about young Sara. The girl rode like an Amazon, bounded about the rocky hillsides like a gazelle, and swam like a mermaid, often disappearing momentarily into the cool depths—and as Henriette's poor heart fluttered in terror, she resembled nothing so much as an unfortunate chicken who has adopted a swan and must now watch as her charge swims for the first time while she stays on the riverbank, uncomprehending, clucking in disapproval at such willful risk taking.

At the moment, Henriette was being carried in a comfortable and very safe palanquin—but even then she was preoccupied with worry, whereas Sara chattered rapturously about the pleasures of the ball to come. It was a magnificent May morning, spring for us but autumn in île de France, when nature prepares itself to be flooded with rain and bids a fond good-bye to the sun, and as the women progressed the landscape grew ever wilder and more lush. Crossing the bridges fording both the source of the rivière du Rempart and the waterfalls of the rivière du Tamarin, whose fragility made Henriette shiver, they wound around the foot of Trois-Mamelles. Told that Sara's uncle and Henri were out hunting with friends between the Great Basin and the Plains of Saint-Pierre, they crossed the small rivière du Boucaut and passed the rushing rivière Noire. Finally, there was the country house of M. de Malmédie.

Sara ran to say hello to the house staff, whom she had not seen in a fortnight, and to visit her aviary, an immense wrought-iron enclosure filled with Guida turtledoves, fig trees, fondijalas, and flycatchers. Her next stop was the garden, which boasted a multitude of flowers originally brought from Paris: tuberoses, Chinese carnations, anemones, Indian roses—and that tropical jewel, the immortal Cape amaranth. The garden was enclosed by hedges of frangipane and Chinese rosebushes, which flowered all year long. This was Sara's kingdom; here she was queen.

As long as her charge remained in the gardens, Henriette could relax and stroll along the smoothly graveled paths—but her repose was short-lived. Sara spoke to the old mulatto woman who had nursed her as a baby and now lived in dignified retirement at the country house, kissed her favorite turtledove, laced a few flowers into her dark hair, and then declared it time to go out. Thus poor Henriette's anxieties began all over again.

When Sara was younger, Henriette had tried mightily to curb the girl's restless, independent spirit and introduce her to life's more sedate pleasures—but in vain. Sara always managed to escape, and if the governess refused to accompany her on one of her rambles, she simply went alone. Eventually Henriette's desire to watch over her charge had triumphed over her personal uneasiness. She usually contented herself with sitting where she could watch Sara as the girl climbed up and down the hills, and as long as the two were within earshot, Henriette was relatively content. Today the two women set out as usual— the elder with a book and a resigned sigh, and the younger with a flush of excitement on her blooming cheek.

However, it was not a walk that Sara had in mind. Today she wanted to go swimming in the beautifully calm and clear bay of the rivière Noire, where one could see twenty feet down in the depths and watch the madrapores burrowing in the sand and the various crustaceans walking among the waving sea plants. Sara had been careful, as usual, to tell dear Henriette nothing of her plan—but the old mulatto nurse had been told, and she waited with the girl's bathing costume at the indicated spot.

Sara and Henriette made their way down along the banks of the river, which widened until the bay appeared before them, shimmering like an enormous mirror. Dense clusters of tall trees bordered each side of the water like so many columns holding up the vast blue canopy of the sky through which only an occasional ray of sunlight penetrated, their roots twining serpent-like around the rocks. Where the riverbed grew wider, the trees on the two banks leaned forward, taking advantage of the space created by the water, and formed a sort of gigantic tent. The whole place held an air of dark mystery; the only sounds to be heard were the rasping squawks of the gray-headed parrots; the only animals to be seen were a few of those reddish monkeys called aigrettes that were so plentiful on the island that numerous attempts to destroy the population had failed, and an occasional bright-green kingfisher that shot up, frightened by the women's footfalls, to disappear again into the foliage on the other side of the river. Mangrove vines stretched across the water like arrow shafts, brilliant as emeralds, to disappear among the tangled vines on the other bank.

Sara loved places like this; their harmony of tree and rock and river, and their savage beauty and profound solitude, made her heart sing. She understood this primitive scenery in some deep corner of her soul. No paintbrush or pen could possibly reproduce such a landscape, but it was reflected in Sara's mind and in her heart.

Even Henriette was not immune to such a magnificent spectacle; she viewed it with admiration, but her principal thoughts were always of the girl who was her charge.

They reached the summit of a small hill, and Henriette seated herself here to keep an eye on Sara, who leapt like a wagtail from rock to rock toward the water. With a sigh, she pulled the tenth volume of *Clarissa Harlowe*—her favorite novel—from her pocket, and began to reread it for perhaps the twentieth time.

Meanwhile Sara made for the clump of bamboo trees where the mulatto nurse waited for her. Having retrieved her bathing costume, she stepped to the water's edge and looked around with the shyness of a classical nymph. Eventually, having ascertained to her satisfaction that there was no one else around, she took off her garments and draped herself in a tunic of white linen that fell to her knees, leaving her arms and legs bare and unencumbered. She was the very image of the goddess Diana as she stood on the riverbank, preparing to enter her bath.

Climbing onto a rock that overhung a deep spot in the bay, Sara dove into the water and swam a few yards before resurfacing. She headed toward a large boulder that marked a very deep spot, confident in her own strength and mastery of the element in which—rather like Venus—she had, after a fashion, been born. She plunged and resurfaced, moving away from the place where she had entered the water. A moment later, on the riverbank, Henriette raised her head as she heard someone call her name once, then twice. It was Sara, and the governess, resisting what she knew would be a futile urge to call the girl back to shore, stood and stepped to the water's edge so that she might see her more clearly. The lovely mermaid, treading water, gestured toward the woods excitedly, and Henriette was soon able to make out the howling of a distant pack of hounds, which grew louder every second. All at once, about two hundred feet above the place where

Henriette was standing, a majestic stag burst from the underbrush, springing across the river in a single bound and disappearing among the trees on the opposite bank. The dogs followed an instant later, splashing through the water and into the woods after their prey.

Sara, in the bay, had watched the spectacle with the excitement and delight of a true huntress. She let out a cry of joy—but the next instant her cry was answered with a heartrending shriek of terror. Henriette turned in alarm to see the old mulatto woman standing silent as the statue of Horror, pointing mutely at a gigantic shark about sixty feet away from the girl, its dorsal fin clearly visible above the water as it swam lazily toward her. Too horrified even to scream, Henriette sank to her knees on the grassy bank.

Sara had turned at the mulatto nurse's cry and seen the danger that threatened her. With admirable calm, she struck out for the nearest shore, but it was at least forty feet away. She was a strong swimmer, but her chances of reaching the bank before the shark overtook her were slim indeed.

Just then, another cry rang out. A Negro, clenching a long knife between his teeth, appeared from among the trees and dove between the tangled mangrove roots into the bay. With strong, sure strokes he swam nearly a third of the bay in an instant, in an attempt to intercept the path of the shark, which was now only a short distance away from its intended prey and was swimming frighteningly fast, with easy flips of its tail, toward Sara. She stared at it and at her would-be rescuer as they both raced toward her.

Henriette and the mulatto nurse, waiting together on the riverbank, were breathless and frozen with fear and suspense. Their position on a high rock allowed them an all-too-perfect view of the terrible scene below them. Their arms were extended toward the girl they loved, but they both knew they were powerless to save her and cried out with alternating fear and hope. Fear soon won out. Despite the efforts of Sara's rescuer, the shark now appeared to be closing in on her; there were only a few feet between them now; the Negro was still twenty feet behind the monster. The girl, pale as death, could hear the beast's tail as it lashed the water, bringing it ever nearer. She shot a last, desperate glance at the shore; there was no way she would reach it in time. Raising her eyes heavenward, she gasped a brief prayer. Only God could save her now.

Just as the shark opened its great jaws to tear into the girl, there was a sound like an explosion, and the animal rolled over in the water, its white belly gleaming. Henriette, who had squeezed her eyes shut in dread of the horrible spectacle about to take place, opened them as a second blast cracked the air. The governess heard a sonorous voice behind her utter two calm words: "Good shot."

Turning, she saw a young man grasping the branch of a cinnamon tree in one hand and a still-smoking rifle in the other. He stared past her, watching the shark as it convulsed in the water and then turned to attack the nearest victim—Sara's erstwhile rescuer. The Negro dove at the beast's approach, disappearing under the waves with the animal in single-minded pursuit. The surface of the water, churning, turned red with blood. It was obvious that a struggle to the death was raging in the depths.

Meanwhile, Henriette ran to the river's edge and slid down the rocks to extend her hand to the exhausted Sara. Scarcely able to believe that she had escaped death, the girl had no sooner emerged from the water than she sank to her knees, the governess at her side in a near-faint of shock and relief. When the two women had recovered sufficiently to raise their heads, the first thing they saw was Laïza, standing on the shore, his arms and legs lacerated and bloody. The carcass of the shark floated in the bay. Sara and Henriette then looked up to the crag of rock where their rescuing angel had appeared, but he was gone. It didn't matter; they had both seen his face and recognized him at once. It was the young stranger so recently arrived in Port Louis.

Sara now turned to the black man who had shown such great proof of his devotion to her. But after silently gazing at her for an instant, he vanished in his turn among the trees. Sara looked around for him, but in vain. He had disappeared, just as the stranger had.

XI

THE PRICE OF NEGROES

At the same instant M. de Malmédie and Henri rushed up to the women, followed by their fellow hunters. It was only then that Sara remembered she was half naked; blushing, she wrapped herself in a loose peignoir provided by the mulatto nurse and moved shakily, leaning on Henriette's arm, her heart still hammering, to join her uncle and cousin.

The two men had been following their prey to the riverbank when they heard the two shots from Georges's gun; thinking at first that it was one of their companions firing at a deer, they had looked in the direction from which the sounds had come—only to witness, vaguely and from a great distance, the final moments of the terrible scene I have just described.

Sara and Henriette now found themselves the center of attention. Asked what had happened, the governess found herself still too upset to speak; it was the girl who recounted her entire ordeal.

There is a substantial difference between actually seeing a horrible event and simply hearing it described, but here the rifle smoke still lingered in the air and the shark's bloodied body still floated in the water, and Sara, the victim herself, told her story to great effect. The hunters gallantly assured her that they would have hastened to save her, and regretted that they had not reached the scene a few moments earlier; they could swim just as fast and shoot just as straight as the two saviors, no doubt. Sara listened politely, but a secret voice inside her insisted that no one could have rescued her except the two men who had.

Just then the barking of the dogs alerted the group that the stag had been brought to bay. Satisfied that Sara was safe, the hunters turned their attention back to the prey they had been pursuing all morning. First two or three men stole away from the outer edge of the group; then Henri, feeling that it would be impolite not to accompany them, departed, as well. Within ten minutes Sara and her governess were left alone with M. de Malmédie. The three returned to the house, where a feast had been laid out for the hunting party. The rest of the men joined them in short order, and Henri took great pride in presenting Sara with one of the stag's hooves, which he had cut off himself. She thanked him graciously while he observed with satisfaction that all the pretty color had returned to her cheeks, and the dinner proceeded on a happy note. Henriette, still shaken by her charge's ordeal, had asked to be excused from the party—but Sara, with the resilience of youth, presided over the table with her usual grace.

During dessert, several toasts were drunk to Sara's escape from death. None of them, however, mentioned the unknown Negro or the strange hunter who had actually rescued her. All credit for the miracle was carefully ascribed not to Laïza and Georges, but to Providence, which had intervened to save M. de Malmédie's beloved niece and Henri's betrothed. The men then drank to their own bravery— and Sara, charmingly straight-faced, praised each of them for his courage in the hunt. At the end of the meal, M. de Malmédie's overseer came in to tell his master that an escaped Negro had been caught and returned to the plantation. This was by no means an uncommon event, and M. de Malmédie merely nodded and said that the usual punishment should be administered.

"The usual punishment, Uncle?" Sara enquired. "And what is that?"

"Nothing, nothing, my child," M. de Malmédie assured her, and turned back to his guests. Ten minutes later the men were informed that their horses were ready. Lord Murray's soirée was scheduled for the following evening, and the party had agreed to return to Port Louis so that they might have an entire day to prepare themselves. Sara went to Henriette's room to find her governess in good health, but still so upset that the girl told her to remain at the country house awhile longer to recover. It was no bother, insisted Sara; she could return to town on horseback quite easily, leaving the palanquin for Henriette.

As the group started out for Port Louis, Sara saw three or four blacks busily cutting up the carcass of the shark. The old mulatto nurse had told them where to find it, and they had hurried to retrieve this valuable source of oil. The rest of the plantation's Negroes were assembled near Trois-Mamelles; as the party approached them they realized that the crowd was being forced to witness the punishment of a recaptured slave, as was customary in those days.

The victim in this case proved to be a young man around seventeen years of age who stood, bound with ropes, near the ladder on which he was to be stretched. As the riding party drew near, another black who had been sitting near the bound man and tending to a wound on his head stood up and moved toward M. de Malmédie—only to be restrained by the overseer.

"Here, what's this?" M. de Malmédie asked.

"Monsieur, it is the slave Nazim you see bound and awaiting punishment," the overseer replied. "He will receive the standard one hundred and fifty lashes."

"And why has he been condemned to receive one hundred and fifty lashes?" demanded Sara.

"He ran away, mademoiselle. This is the man we caught earlier."

"How did you get him?" inquired Henri.

"Oh, it was simple! I waited on the riverbank until he was quite far from shore, and then I went after him in a skiff with eight strong rowers. We followed him around the southwest cape; there were probably two leagues of ocean between us. He only had two arms, and we had sixteen; and he was in a miserable little canoe that was no match for our well-made boat. We overtook him without too much difficulty. He dove out of his boat like a porpoise and swam for shore, but he tired himself out pretty quickly and I struck him a good one on the head with an oar when he came up for air. He fainted straightaway—in truth, at first I thought I might have killed him—and we hauled him into our boat and tied him up. He didn't come to until we had reached Brabant, but as you see, he's on his feet now."

"You might have seriously hurt him," put in Sara, anxiously.

"Just a scratch, mademoiselle," the overseer assured her. "These black devils have heads like rocks."

"Why have you waited so long to administer the punishment?" demanded M. de Malmédie, severely. "It should have been done as soon as I gave the order."

"Yes, sir," said the overseer hastily. "But, you see, his brother—who is one of our best workers—said he had something important to tell you before the punishment was carried out. I knew you would be passing by shortly on your way back to Port Louis, so I allowed the delay."

"It's good that you did," Sara assured the overseer. "But where is he, the brother of this unfortunate fellow?"

"I am here," announced Laïza, coming forward. Sara uttered a little cry of surprise. She knew him immediately: He was the man who had so bravely risked his life that morning, attempting to save hers. Strangely, he gave no sign that he even recognized her. His eyes remained fixed on M. de Malmédie. Sara saw, as he came near her, that his arms and legs were still raw and bloody.

"Well, what do you want?" M. de Malmédie demanded.

"To beg a favor from you," replied Laïza, keeping his voice low so that Nazim, who was not twenty paces away, would not hear him.

"What favor?"

"My brother, Nazim, is only a boy," said Laïza. "He has lost a great deal of blood from the wound in his head. He might be too weak to survive the punishment you have decreed for him. If the lash kills him, you will have lost a Negro worth at least two hundred piastres."

"What are you saying?" asked M. de Malmédie.

"I propose an exchange."

"What sort of exchange?"

"Let me take the hundred and fifty lashes, instead of Nazim. I'm strong enough to bear it; I'll work tomorrow as usual. My brother is only a child—a hundred and fifty lashes would kill him."

"I can't allow that," said M. de Malmédie while Sara gazed at the slave in silent astonishment.

"Why not?"

"It would be an injustice. You've done nothing wrong."

"But I have," Laïza said. "It was I who persuaded Nazim to run away. I made the canoe he used to escape; I shaved his head myself, with a bit of broken glass, and anointed him with coconut oil. So, you see, it is really I who deserve to be punished, and not my brother."

Now Henri joined the conversation. "You should *both* be punished," he put in. "Him for running away, and you for helping him do it."

"Then give me three hundred lashes, and be done with it," said Laïza steadfastly.

M. de Malmédie turned to the overseer. "A hundred and fifty lashes to each of these rascals."

"Wait, Uncle!" Sara cried. "Please—I ask you to pardon both of these men!"

M. de Malmédie turned to his niece, astonished. "Why on earth should I do that?"

"Because this is the man who jumped into the river this morning to save me from the shark! He deserves to be rewarded, not punished."

"She recognizes me!" murmured Laïza, as if to himself. Then, louder, to M. de Malmédie: "The only reward I ask is that my brother Nazim be spared."

"Not so fast, you devil," said M. de Malmédie. "Did you, or did you not, rescue my niece?"

"I did not," replied Laïza. "She would have been lost, if it had not been for that young marksman."

"But he did everything he could to save me, Uncle!" insisted Sara. "He fought the shark—look, his wounds are still bleeding!"

"I did fight the shark, but only to save myself," said Laïza. "I had to kill it, to preserve my own life."

"Please," Sara pleaded, turning to her uncle. "Surely you won't refuse me their pardon?"

"I'm afraid I must," said M. de Malmédie. "If there was even one example of mercy granted on an occasion like this, they would all try to escape, the devils—hoping there would be another pretty mouth like yours there to intercede on their behalf."

"But—"

M. de Malmédie shook his head. "Just ask these fellows," he said, gesturing to Henri's hunting companions. The group assured Sara that a show of mercy could only lead to disastrous consequences. He turned back to his niece. "So you see, it's impossible."

The girl persisted. "A man who has risked his life for me shouldn't be whipped on the very same day! He may have earned punishment from you, but he certainly deserves to be rewarded by me!"

"Well then, let each of us act as we must. You may reward him—after I have punished him," said M. de Malmédie.

But Sara would not give up. "Uncle, please! After all, what wrong have they actually committed? Their escape plan did not succeed!"

"What they have done, my dear, is reduce their own value. A Negro who has tried to run away loses one hundred percent of his value, you see. Yesterday I might have gotten eight hundred piastres for this pair, five hundred for this one and three for that one over there; but today, if I asked six hundred, nobody would pay me that much."

"Indeed, I wouldn't give you that much," agreed one of the hunters.

A man's deep voice spoke up then, one that made Sara tremble. "Well then, monsieur, I'll be more generous than you have been. I will pay a thousand."

Turning, the girl saw the stranger from Port Louis, the man who had saved her life that morning. He stood nearby, dressed simply but elegantly in a hunting costume, leaning casually on a double-barreled rifle. He had obviously overheard the entire discussion.

"Ah!" said M. de Malmédie. "It is you, monsieur!" Henri did not speak, but a feeling he could not quite name caused the blood to mount to his face. "Let me thank you, sir," his father continued, "for rescuing my niece—she has told me she owes her life to you. If I'd known where to find you, I would have come to you directly—not to make excuses for myself, but to express my sincere gratitude."

The stranger did not reply, but bowed with an air that somehow combined both modesty and disdain—which did not go unnoticed by Sara. "Yes, monsieur," she said, "we can certainly never repay you for your bravery. Please be assured, though, that I will never forget it was you who saved my life."

"I hardly think two bullets and a bit of gunpowder warrant such thanks, mademoiselle," said the stranger gallantly. "For my part, I would be quite content if Monsieur de Malmédie's gratitude extends so far as to sell me these two slaves. I have much need of them, you see."

M. de Malmédie turned to his son. "Henri," he said in a low voice, "didn't we hear someone say yesterday that a slave ship had been sighted near the island?"

"Yes, Father."

"Ah! Then we can easily replace these ne'er-do-wells."

"I await your reply, monsieur," said the stranger.

"Yes," said M. de Malmédie. "Ahem! I will turn them over to you, monsieur, with the greatest pleasure. You may take them, though they're both a bit battered, as you see, and might not be able to work for a day or two. If I were you, seeing as neither of them has done a bit of work in three or four days, I would give them the correction they deserve, this very day."

"That, monsieur, is my business now," said the stranger, smiling. "I will send one thousand piastres to your house this very evening."

"Wait, monsieur," interrupted Henri. "I believe you have misunderstood my father's meaning. He means to give you these slaves as a gift. Their miserable lives are worthless in comparison with my fair cousin's. But let us at least offer you that which we have, and which you seem to desire."

M. de Malmédie grimaced at his son. The stranger drew himself up. "I beg your pardon, sir," he said with dignity, "but that was not our agreement."

"Then let me suggest a slight change to the agreement," interposed Sara hastily. "Please accept these two slaves for the love of her whose life you saved, as a token of my especial gratitude."

The stranger bowed. "I can hardly refuse such a gracious offer," he said gallantly. "Now it is I who am in your debt." He took a step backward to let the party move on. He exchanged salutations with the men as they passed; his eyes met Sara's in a brief glance. He stared after them as they departed, a frown creasing his forehead as it always did when he was preoccupied with some bitter thought, then shook himself and turned to M. de Malmédie's overseer. "Unbind this man," he said, gesturing to Nazim. "He and his brother belong to me now." The overseer, who had overheard the conversation between M. de Malmédie and this stranger, hastened to obey.

When this was done, and the two blacks stood beside their new owner, Georges pulled a bag, heavy with gold, from his pocket, and addressed the rest of M. de Malmédie's slaves. "Since I have received a gift from your master," he said, "it is only right that I make you a present in return. Take this purse, and divide its contents among you." He placed the bag in the hands of the slave nearest him. Then he turned to Laïza and Nazim, who awaited his orders in respectful silence. "As for the two of you," he said, "from this moment on you may do what you please. You are free."

Cries of astonishment and joy erupted from the brothers. They were unable to believe that a man for whom they had done nothing could be so generous—but Georges repeated his words, and they fell to their knees, kissing his hands again and again.

It was growing late. Georges donned his broad-brimmed straw hat and, throwing his rifle over his shoulder, walked alone down the road to Moka.

THE BALL

Port Louis was buzzing in anticipation of the dinner and ball to be given by Lord Murray at the governor's palace on Monday night.

For one who has not lived in the colonies, especially île de France, it is difficult to imagine the luxury that reigns below the twentieth meridian. Besides the marvelous Parisian finery that crosses the ocean to grace the forms of wealthy Creole ladies, there are diamonds from Visapour, pearls from Ophir, cashmeres from Siam, and muslins from Calcutta. Every ship en route to Europe from the land of *1001 Arabian Nights* stops at Port Louis to leave a portion of her cargo of treasures there. Even a man accustomed to Parisian elegance or English abundance cannot help but be dazzled by the brilliant spectacle of a party on île de France.

In his three short days on the island, the fashionable and comfort-loving Lord Murray had entirely redecorated the governor's palace so that it resembled the finest apartments to be found on the rue du Mont-Blanc or in Regent Street. The colony's elite began arriving there at four o'clock in the afternoon, the men dressed impeccably in the latest fashions and the ladies shimmering with diamonds and pearls, their soft and luscious delicacy—unique to Creole women—

the only trait distinguishing them from their European counterparts. Each entrance was greeted with smiles and murmurs of recognition. As usual, the women tried to outdo one another in the richness of their gowns and jewels; the blond loveliness of the English ladies contrasted strikingly with the dark hair and eyes of the tropical beauties. Port Louis is a small place, and its upper classes are well known to one another; the only curiosity generally expressed would be which new dress this lady had lately bought, of what material it was made, and which ornaments she had chosen to wear. The Creole ladies were especially curious about what the female English guests would wear, since coquetry is the theater of île de France, and the native women strive eternally to outdo foreigners in loveliness and finery. The murmur that swept through the group at each new arrival was, in general, louder and more prolonged when the valet announced a European name whose sound jarred with that of the islanders'; this was especially evident when comparing the fresh brunettes of the tropics with the pale, blond daughters of the North.

As the newcomers entered the foyer, Lord Murray rose to greet them with the impeccable manners of a true English high-society gentleman. He offered his arm to the ladies and guided them to their seats with gallant compliments; he extended cordial handshakes and kind words to the men. Everyone was completely charmed by the new governor.

The arrival of the messieurs de Malmédie and Sara was awaited with particular interest, both because M. de Malmédie was one of the richest and most distinguished men in the colony and because Sara was known as an heiress of remarkable elegance and beauty. When they were finally announced, every head turned to watch Lord Murray as he went to greet her; surely it was this lovely girl's toilette that had delayed her family's arrival.

No. In contrast with the other Creole women and against all expectations Sara was dressed, with startling simplicity, in a ravishing gown of Indian muslin so light and filmy that Juvenal called the gauzy material "woven air." The dress bore neither embroidery, nor diamonds, nor pearls, and she wore no jewelry—only a crown of wild roses in her hair and a posy of the same flowers at her waist. No bracelet was on her wrist to emphasize the rosy tint of her skin. Her raven hair tumbled to her shoulders in silky ringlets, and she carried the ivory fan purchased two days earlier from Miko-Miko.

Since île de France's elite was rather small, as I have said, and everyone was acquainted with everyone else, the memorable entrance of the Malmédie family was assumed to be the last noteworthy arrival of the evening. The guests milled about the room and mingled among themselves, but it seemed as if Lord Murray was still waiting for someone to appear. This puzzling behavior was explained within ten minutes, as the doors were thrown open once again and the chamberlain announced in a loud voice:

"Monsieur Georges Munier!"

If a thunderbolt had crashed down in the midst of the assembly, it would not have caused a greater stir than the pronouncement of that single name. All heads turned, wondering who was about to enter; although the surname was a well-known one on île de France, Georges had been away for so long that most people had forgotten he even existed.

Now he made his entrance.

The young mulatto was dressed simply but stylishly in a beautifully cut black coat, his medals dangling from a gold chain attached to the lapel. His close-fitting trousers showed off his trim, well-shaped legs, and another fine gold chain hung from the pocket of his white waistcoat. He wore a cravat of black silk, knotted with careless elegance, and the paleness of his handsome face was accentuated by his jet-black mustache and long, dark hair.

Lord Murray was obviously delighted to see him. He went to him immediately and took him by the hand, presenting him first to the English officers and ladies in the room as a gentleman he had had the good fortune to meet on the voyage to île de France, whose company had made the trip a most agreeable one. He then turned to the rest of the guests. "Ladies and gentlemen," he said, "I'm sure I need not introduce Monsieur Georges Munier to you. He is one of your fellow countrymen, and the return of such a distinguished compatriot to île de France is cause for celebration indeed."

Georges inclined his head, a gesture that was met with silence and a few murmurs, but Lord Murray appeared not to notice the uncomfortable atmosphere in the room. One of his servants announced dinner, and he took Sara's arm and led the way in to the banquet table.

Knowing Georges as we do, it is perhaps not surprising that he had chosen to be the last guest to arrive. Preparing to battle the prejudice he was so firmly resolved to conquer, he had wanted to meet all of his enemies face-to-face. His announcement and introduction had produced exactly the effect he desired.

Indeed, no one had been more affected by Georges's appearance than Sara. Hoping to see the young hunter from the rivière Noire at the dinner party, and knowing he had arrived at Port Louis in the company of Lord Murray, she had chosen her ensemble carefully— eschewing the exaggerated luxury often found in the colonies for the lovely simplicity we have found so pleasing—and waited eagerly for the European stranger to arrive. As soon as she and her family arrived at the ball she had looked for his dark eyes everywhere but had not seen them; she could only hope he was delayed and that she would soon know more about him.

Drawn into a circle of other ladies while Henri and M. de Malmédie went off to mingle with the men, Sara was finally rewarded with the announcement of M. Georges Munier. She shivered with a sort of premonitory thrill at finally hearing his name—a name well known on the island, indeed, but hardly expected at such a gathering. She could not keep her eyes off him; his manly bearing, noble brow, and cool smile drew her gaze like a magnet. He seemed to her even more dashing and handsome than he had been the other times she had encountered him. Her heart pounded when Lord Murray introduced Georges to the crowd, and ached when cold, bigoted silence greeted his words. Her eyes, when they met his just before Lord Murray took her arm, were filled with tears. She lowered her head to hide her blushes, fearful that others might notice them—but she needn't have worried. No one except M. de Malmédie and Henri knew of the events that had so recently brought the two young people together; no one else would have thought to link Sara de Malmédie and Georges Munier in any way.

Sara was seated on the new governor's right; on his left was the wife of île de France's garrison commander. The commander himself sat opposite her, placed between two of the most distinguished Creole ladies on the island, who in turn sat beside M. de Malmédie and Henri, respectively. Georges, either by chance or the good intentions of Lord Murray, sat between two English belles. Sara breathed a sigh of relief. She knew foreigners did not share the island prejudices that must have dogged Georges all his life, and that these visitors had not been in île de France for nearly the time required to absorb such negative racial feelings. Georges's conversation with his fair neighbors was gallant and convivial. The women were obviously enchanted by him; he spoke their language as if he had been born to it. Glancing around, Sara saw that Henri's eyes were fixed on her. She knew exactly what was going through his mind. Blushing furiously, she lowered her eyes to her plate.

Lord Murray was a gentleman in every sense of the word, born to play the role of gracious host—so difficult to learn if one is not taught from infancy to assume it. He conversed with his guests easily, moving smoothly from one topic to another, speaking to the English officers of famous battles won and to the Creole merchants of promising business prospects. Now and then he chatted to Georges in a way that showed the two men to be so well educated as to be comfortable discussing any and every subject they wished. And so the dinner passed pleasantly. Georges, with a charming combination of intelligence and modesty, impressed the officers with his experience on the battlefield and the merchants with his knowledge of international commerce. Sprinkled familiarly throughout his conversation were the names of prominent French, English, and Spanish artists, aristocrats, and statesmen, indicating that this young man was very well connected indeed.

Much of what Georges said passed well above the heads of most of the dinner guests, but there were a few among them knowledgeable enough to recognize the young man's superior intellect. Their astonishment, and even envy, increased—but so did their repulsion at his mulatto birth. Henri de Malmédie, feeling that Sara had paid Georges more attention than was proper for a white woman, and an engaged one at that, did not trouble to hide his bitterness. The name of Munier brought with it unpleasant childhood memories; Henri recalled the day when he had tried to wrench the captured English flag from Georges's hands, and Jacques Munier had struck him violently in the face. This long-ago humiliation lay, smoldering, in his heart, and the idea that Sara's life had been saved the day before by a man he despised so much only increased Henri's hatred.

As for the elder M. de Malmédie, he had spent the majority of the evening engaged in a lively discussion with his neighbor about the latest method for refining sugar; if employed, it would increase his estate's revenue by a full one-third. After his initial surprise at finding out that Georges Munier was his niece's rescuer and the new governor's intimate friend, he thought no more about the matter.

Needless to say, this was not the case with Henri. He listened to every word that passed between Lord Murray and Georges; he had to admit that the mulatto was the more intelligent of the two. Studying the firm steadiness in Georges's face, he realized that the sickly child he remembered was no more. Here was a dangerous opponent, ready, willing, and able to challenge him.

If only, thought Henri, Georges had returned to île de France and resumed the submissive role his blood dictated in the eyes of the whites. If he had been content to settle into the obscurity of his boyhood once more, Henri would not have given him a second thought; their childhood altercation of fourteen years before, as well as Henri's grudge against the mulatto, would have remained buried deep in his memory. But the man, with insufferable pride, had paraded himself around as a gentleman—had entered the governor's house as if he were an aristocrat—had, by doing a service to Sara, involved himself with the Malmédie family! He had presumed to sit at the same table as Henri himself, acting as if they were equals in rank! This was too much; it was more than Henri could bear. From now on, he thought, he and Georges Munier were at war.

As the guests left the table to mingle in the gardens, Henri looked for Sara. She was seated with several other ladies in a bower near which a group of gentlemen was taking coffee. She seemed to shiver a bit at his approach, as if fearing what her cousin might have to say to her.

"Well, my fair cousin," said Henri, leaning over the back of her bamboo chair, "what did you think of the dinner?"

"I assume you're not speaking of the food," replied Sara, smiling.

"No, indeed—though for those of us who do not live on dewdrops and floral perfumes as you do it was a magnificent feast indeed. No, my question tends in a more . . . social direction, as it were."

"Oh—I thought it in very good taste. Lord Murray is an admirable host, and everyone seemed quite at ease."

"Certainly, certainly; that makes it even more astonishing that a gentleman of such high breeding would be guilty of the sort of impropriety he has imposed on us."

"What do you mean?" Sara asked, though she knew perfectly well what her cousin was trying to say. Her heart beat strongly in her chest, and she looked steadfastly into Henri's eyes with a strength even she did not understand.

Henri ignored both the expression on Sara's face and the nagging voice of his own conscience. "Why, he allowed Monsieur Georges Munier to sit at the same table with us."

Sara turned pale. "I find it much more shocking, cousin, that you would make such an observation—especially to me."

"And why shouldn't I?"

"Because if it hadn't been for Monsieur Georges Munier, whose presence here tonight is so distasteful to you, I would be dead—and you and my uncle would have spent today mourning me, rather than feasting at the governor's table."

"Ahem—yes, yes, of course," said Henri, coloring. "Yes. I am quite aware of the debt of gratitude we owe Monsieur Georges for saving a life so precious to us. You must remember yesterday, when he offered to buy those two Negroes from my father and I insisted on giving them to him instead."

"Ah!" cried Sara, her eyes narrowing. "And with the gift of two Negroes, you feel your debt to be entirely acquitted? Let me thank you then, my dear cousin, for placing the value of my life at a thousand piastres!"

"*Mon Dieu*, my dear Sara, but you are interpreting things strangely today! Do you really think I would, for an instant, put a price on a life I value more than my own? I only meant to suggest that any white woman would be in an awkward position indeed if Monsieur Georges Munier were to ask her to dance!"

"Am I to assume that you think this woman ought to refuse him?"

"Yes, most assuredly."

"Even though, in refusing a man who has never given her the slightest offense—who has done her service on more than one occasion—she would be insulting him in such a serious manner that he would be justified in seeking an explanation from her father, or brother, or husband."

"I presume that in such a case, Monsieur Georges would remember who he is, and do us the justice of recognizing that a white woman does not lower herself to the level of a mulatto."

Sara's eyes blazed. "Well!" she said. "I *do* beg your pardon, cousin, for daring to express my opinion on such a matter—perhaps I do not know Monsieur Georges very well—but it seems to me that if he sought to avenge his honor, a man such as he, who wears two croix de guerre on his chest, would hardly be cowed by the feeling of humiliation you are saying he must possess—quite without reason, I might add."

Henri's face flushed with anger. "In any case, my dear Sara," he said coldly, "I trust that the fear of exposing me or my father to the wrath of Monsieur Georges Munier will restrain you from dancing with him, even if he should have the temerity to ask you."

"I will dance with no one, monsieur," said Sara icily. Rising, she walked away from him and sat down near a female friend who occupied a table beside Georges's.

Henri stood still for a moment, stunned by Sara's behavior, then moved to seek out a group of Creole gentlemen he knew who would, in all likelihood, have more sympathy for his views than his cousin had. An hour passed, during which Sara and Henri remained pointedly distant from each other and Georges remained at the center of an admiring circle of English officers and businessmen who obviously harbored little or none of the prejudice found in his own countrymen. Eventually the doors were thrown open again, revealing the reception room now bare of furniture and blazing with light. The orchestra struck up a lively melody to signal the first dance. The ball had begun.

It was a sore trial for Sara to sit quietly while her friends enjoyed the ball, for as we know, dancing was one of her favorite pastimes. She blamed the situation entirely on Henri and thought of him with bitterness, while her emotions regarding Georges tended in another direction entirely. She began to experience feelings for him that were deeper and more tender than any she had ever known. It is one of the noblest qualities possessed by women to feel compassion for the oppressed, as well as admiration for those who resist this oppression.

Just then Henri, hoping that his cousin would be unable to resist the temptation of the music, asked her to dance the first with him, as usual. Sara looked at him coolly, and repeated that she had no intention of dancing that evening. Henri bit his lip until it bled and instinctively looked around the room for Georges, who was dancing with the young Englishwoman he had earlier escorted in to dinner.

For reasons entirely different from her cousin's, Sara's eyes also sought out Georges. When she saw him, her heart twisted in her chest. He was dancing with another woman! Perhaps he was not thinking at all of Sara, who had made such a sacrifice that evening by refusing to dance for his sake—an act of selflessness that, until that night, she would never have believed herself capable of. The remaining moments of the dance were among the most painful that Sara had ever known.

The music finally ended, and Sara could not tear her gaze away from Georges as he conducted his dancing partner to her seat and then went to stand next to Lord Murray. The two men exchanged a few words, and then both moved in Sara's direction! All the blood in her body seemed to rush to her heart.

"Mademoiselle," said Lord Murray, "here is my friend and traveling companion who, with perhaps too much attention to European etiquette, will not ask you to dance until he has been properly introduced to you. Allow me to present Monsieur Georges Munier, one of the most distinguished gentlemen it is my pleasure to know."

Sara fought to keep her voice steady, to appear almost calm. "Monsieur Georges and I are already old acquaintances, milord. He did me a small service on the day of his arrival, and later he did me a greater service still—he saved my life."

"What! Monsieur Georges was the young hunter who rescued you by shooting the shark that attacked you while you were bathing?"

"None other, milord," answered Sara, blushing deeply, for it had only just now occurred to her that Georges had seen her in her bathing costume. "I'm glad you've mentioned it, since yesterday I was too upset to thank Monsieur Georges as ardently as I would have wished to, and now I can say truly that it is to his skill and nerve that I owe the pleasure of my attendance at your ball tonight."

"Yes, let us add our thanks as well," said Henri, who had joined the little group unseen. "We were also quite shaken—hardly able to express our thanks to Monsieur Georges at all."

Georges had not yet said a word. His penetrating gaze seemed to reach the depths of Sara's soul. He bowed to her in acknowledgment, but ignored Henri completely. "In that case," said Lord Murray, "I believe Monsieur Georges may make his request without fear of refusal. Go ahead, my friend."

Georges bowed again. "I hope Mademoiselle de Malmédie will grant me the honor of dancing the next with me."

"Oh! I am truly sorry, monsieur—I hope you will excuse me—but I have just refused my cousin the same request, as I don't mean to dance tonight."

Georges gave Sara a smile that said he understood her perfectly. Drawing himself up to his full height, he gave Henri a glance of utter disdain, one returned by the younger M. de Malmédie, which left Lord Murray in no doubt as to the pure hatred that existed between the two men. The Englishman kept silent, however, and merely said to Sara: "I hope it isn't yesterday's fright, mademoiselle, that keeps you from dancing tonight."

"I'm afraid so, milord," Sara said. "In fact, I feel so unwell that I was just about to ask Henri to find my uncle and tell him I wish to go home."

Henri hurried off straightaway in search of M. de Malmédie, and Georges took the opportunity to lean close to Sara and murmur, in a voice audible only to her: "You have a noble heart, mademoiselle. I thank you."

Just then Lord Murray took Sara's arm, and she could only meet

Georges's eyes briefly, trembling. "Are you really determined to leave us, mademoiselle?" asked the governor.

"I'm sorry, yes," said Sara. "I'd like to stay—but I really do feel quite ill."

"In that case," said Lord Murray gallantly, "allow me to call for one of my own carriages to conduct you home." He moved away to speak to one of his servants, and Georges and Sara were left standing alone.

"Sara," said Georges, his voice low. "When I left Europe to return to île de France, I could only hope I would find a heart like yours—but I hardly dared believe such happiness could truly exist."

Sara felt as if she might faint. "Monsieur," she murmured, "I—don't know what you mean."

"I mean, dear mademoiselle, that since I first saw you I have been living in a sort of dream that, if it ever comes true, will make me the happiest of men." At that moment, M. de Malmédie and Henri came hurrying toward them. Georges bowed and walked away without another word.

Lord Murray joined the family a few minutes later to tell them that the carriage was ready, and offered Sara his arm. As they reached the door, she cast a single glance of regret over her shoulder. She had had such high hopes for the evening, and it was ending in such a way! For the briefest instant her gaze again met that of Georges. He seemed to be following her with his eyes.

The governor saw the Malmédies safely off in his carriage, then returned to the entry hall. Georges was there, preparing to leave in his turn. "What, are you going, too?" Lord Murray exclaimed.

"Yes, milord—it is eight leagues to Moka, and I have a long ride ahead of me. I'm fortunate to have a horse like Antrim; that is sure."

"If I may ask," said Lord Murray, "is there some particular quarrel between you and Monsieur Henri de Malmédie?"

"Not yet," said Georges, with a faint smile, "but it is very likely that there soon will be."

"Perhaps I am mistaken, but it seems to me that your enmity with that family is not new," observed Lord Murray.

"Childhood grudges, milord, which have grown into very adult feelings of hatred. Needle pricks, but ones that have festered into deep wounds."

"And is there no way of settling this quarrel peacefully?"

"I did hope so, milord. I thought fourteen years under English rule might have killed the prejudice I have come back to fight, but I was wrong. Now it remains only for the athlete to anoint himself with oil, and to step into the arena."

"My dear Don Quixote! Are you not encountering more windmills than giants?"

"Judge for yourself," said Georges, smiling again. "Yesterday I saved the life of Mademoiselle Sara de Malmédie. Do you know how her cousin thanked me tonight? By forbidding her to dance with me, that's how."

"What? Impossible!"

Georges shook his head. "It's quite true, milord."

"Why, in heaven's name?"

"Because I am mulatto."

"Well, what is your plan?"

"Plan, milord?"

Lord Murray grinned. "Come now, we are old friends! Tell me what you plan to do, and I'll tell you whether I approve."

Georges smiled again. "I admit, I do have a plan—one that came to me this very night."

"And what is it?"

"It is that, within three months, I am going to make Mademoiselle Sara de Malmédie my bride."

With that, Georges saluted his friend and departed. His servant waited at the door with his two magnificent horses. Georges swung into Antrim's saddle and took off at a gallop down the Moka road. Upon arriving at the plantation, he asked after his father—only to be told that the elder Munier had gone out at seven o'clock that evening, and had not yet returned home.

THE SLAVE SHIP

The next morning Pierre Munier knocked on his son's door. Since his return to île de France, Georges had paid a great deal of attention to his father's magnificent estate, and his knowledge of European industry had inspired him with several ideas for expansion. Pierre Munier, with his practical mind, was all for the project, but it required more manpower than they currently possessed, and since the abolition of public slave trading, Negroes had become so much more expensive that the Muniers did not have the means to buy the fifty or sixty blacks they needed without enormous sacrifice.

Consequently, on the night of the ball Pierre Munier had been happy to learn that a slave ship was in view just off the coast, and he had, in accordance with the habits of colonists and dealers in black flesh, gone down to the shore to exchange signals with the ship indicating his desire to do business. The slaver had responded favorably, and the elder Munier was eager to give Georges the good tidings. The father and son decided that they would go at around nine o'clock that evening to Pointe-aux-Caves, below Petit-Malabar. Pierre Munier then left for his daily inspection of the estate, while Georges took his rifle and sought the peace and solitude of the woods.

Georges paced among the trees, lost in thought. What he had said to Lord Murray the night before had been no joke, but a firm resolution. All his life the young mulatto had been preparing for what was to come. He had always excelled at anything he attempted; his achievements, added to his wealth, assured him a distinguished position in French or English society; he had the money to live comfortably in Paris or London—but he was not satisfied with this. Eager to fight for his beliefs, he had always known he must come home to île de France and conquer the prejudices that reigned there. He had remained incognito as long as possible, in order to study his enemy from the safety of anonymity; he had kept himself ready to seize the opportunity to fight, whenever it might come. He was poised to begin the struggle in which either the man or the idea would end by perishing.

Upon setting foot in Port Louis and seeing again the same men he had always seen before his departure, Georges realized a truth he had often doubted while in Europe: Everything was exactly the same as it always had been in his homeland—despite the fourteen years that had passed; despite the fact that the island was now English instead of French; and despite its being called Mauritius now, rather than île de France. From that day onward he had been on guard, always prepared for the moral duel he had come to fight, just as another man might prepare for a physical duel. Sword in hand, he had waited for the time when he would be able to face his adversary and strike the first blow.

However, like Cesare Borgia, who had readied himself for the conquest of Italy on his father's death, and who had then died himself, Georges now found himself involved in a situation he had not anticipated—and at the worst possible moment. On the very day of his arrival in Port Louis, he had met a beautiful girl—and thoughts of her had haunted him ever since. Then Providence had placed him just where he needed to be to save the life of the girl he had been dreaming of, and finally Fate had reunited them the previous evening. One look into her eyes had told him that she loved him, just as he loved her. From then on, Georges knew he must fight not only for pride, but for love as well. There was only one problem: His coolness and self-possession had deserted him. Now he burned with a passion that threatened to overwhelm him.

If a heart as well protected as Georges's had been so smitten by the mere sight of Sara, imagine how much stronger the effect of his handsome face and the circumstances in which she had encountered him had been on the juvenile existence and virginal soul of Sara! Orphaned young and raised in the home of M. de Malmédie, destined to double her fortune when she reached her majority, Sara had grown up assuming that she would one day be the wife of his son, Henri. It had not been an unpleasant prospect; after all, Henri was a handsome fellow, and one of the richest men on the island. None of his friends had ever tempted her; she had grown up with them, and these young hunters and dancers were so much like brothers to her that it would never have occurred to her to distinguish one from another. She had been perfectly content when she met Georges—but in any young girl's life, the appearance of a handsome young stranger, distinguished and elegant of form, would be an event indeed—even more so, as you may imagine, in île de France.

The young stranger's bearing, the timbre of his voice, the words he uttered—all had remained in Sara's memory without her understanding exactly why, like a song one hears only once, and then repeats again and again in the mind. If she had met him under ordinary circumstances, she would probably have forgotten him within a few days; even after a second encounter, she might have wished him farther away rather than closer. But this was not to be. God had decided that Georges and Sara would see each other again at a supreme moment, and thus the scene at the rivière Noire had taken place. To the curiosity Sara had felt at their first encounter was joined the poetry and recognition of the second. In an instant Georges had been transformed in the young woman's eyes from a stranger into a liberating angel. He had saved her from a painful death, saved her from being denied the happy future of a sixteen-year-old girl.

Nor could Sara help comparing the conduct of Henri, who was to be her husband, with that of Georges, of whom she knew nothing. On the very day she had first encountered Georges, Henri's crude jokes about the stranger had made her feel defensive and uncomfortable. His eagerness to rush away and bring down the stag so soon after her brush with death had wounded her to the quick, and his arrogance on the night of Lord Murray's ball had dealt a blow to her pride. Indeed, he had asked her to insult Georges in a way she would not have done to any man. That night, which might have held so much happiness— but which Henri had made solitary and sad—had caused her to face her true feelings, perhaps for the first time. She had known, then, that she did not love her cousin—that she loved another man instead.

As so often happens, one revelation led to another. She thought about her uncle: Would he have cared for her, an orphaned child, so tenderly if she had not been the heiress to a million and a half francs—more than twice as rich as Henri in her own right? She saw him then, clearly, for what he was—a single-minded and calculating father, seeking an advantageous marriage for his son. The adoption had not, she realized, been based on love. Her trust and affection crumbled, and the gratitude she had always felt toward M. de Malmédie vanished, leaving only pain, harsh judgment, and anger in its wake, as is often the case when the heart is wounded.

Georges had foreseen all of this; indeed, he had counted on it to help him best his rival for Sara's affections. Now, though he told himself to do nothing that day, deep in his heart he felt unbearably impatient to see Sara. He had his rifle on his shoulder, hoping for a good hunt—his favorite pastime, and a distraction that would help occupy him for the rest of the day—but he could not deny himself. His love for Sara was already stronger than any other feeling. So around four o'clock, unable to resist his desire any longer—not to see the young girl, for he could never present himself at her house, but simply to be near her—he saddled Antrim and, holding the Arabian steed's reins lightly, rode to the island's capital in less than an hour.

He had come to Port Louis with a single hope, but as I have said, that hope was entirely dependent on chance. Unfortunately, chance was not in his favor today. He rode all the streets surrounding the Malmédie house; he crossed the jardin de la Compagnie, which was the usual haunt of the city's inhabitants, no less than twice. He rounded champ de Mars, where everything was being prepared for the upcoming races, three times. But nowhere, even in the far distance, did he see anyone who resembled the girl he was searching for.

By seven o'clock he had lost all hope. Heavyhearted and exhausted, he took to the Grande-Rivière road—but this time he held tight to his horse's reins as he went farther away from Sara, who doubtless had no idea that Georges had passed through the rue de la Comédie and the rue du Gouvernement ten times; or that he had been barely one hundred steps away from her. As he and his horse, who was puzzled by the unaccustomed restraint, passed by the free Negro camp just outside Port Louis, a man darted from one of the wooden huts lining the road and grabbed his hand. It was Miko-Miko, the Chinese merchant who had sold Sara the carved-ivory fan. An idea came into Georges's head almost at once. This peddler, whose trade permitted him to enter any house on the island and whose ignorance of French protected him from suspicion, might be of great use to him. He dismounted and accompanied Miko-Miko into his shop. The Chinese man insisted on showing him everything in the place, gratitude evident in every gesture. Miko-Miko was lonely; the only others in île de France who spoke Chinese were two or three rival merchants, so he never talked with them. He begged Georges for some way, any way, to be of service to him.

There *was* something he could do, said Georges; a mere trifle, really. He needed a plan of the inside of M. de Malmédie's town house—specifically, he wanted to know the exact location of Sara's rooms. Miko-Miko understood immediately—as I have said, the Chinese were the Jews of île de France. Georges then wrote, on the back of one of his calling cards, the prices of various items he knew would be most likely to tempt the girl. No one must see this card, he told Miko-Miko, except Sara herself. Giving the Chinese man a few coins, he told him to come to the Munier plantation in Moka at three o'clock the next day. Miko-Miko promised he would be there, and that he would do everything Georges had asked.

It was now eight o'clock, and Georges had agreed to meet his father and the servant Télémaque at Pointe-aux-Caves at nine. He remounted his horse with a lighter heart, as it takes little to change the color of the horizon when one is in love, and took the road to the Petite-Rivière, reaching the rendezvous point at dusk. Pierre Munier, with his habitual punctuality, had been there for ten minutes. At nine thirty the moon rose large and bright in the sky; it was the moment

they had been waiting for. Looking at a spot halfway between île Bourbon and île de Sable, they saw a light flash once—twice—three times;
it was moonlight, glancing off a mirror. At this well-known signal,
Télémaque built a small bonfire on the sand and let it burn for precisely five minutes before extinguishing it.

Half an hour passed. Then Georges and his father saw a faint black
shape appear upon the waves, growing more distinct as it neared the
shore. It proved to be a large galley, its oars dipping noiselessly into
the water. Finally the ship's keel grated on the sandy beach, and as the
Muniers approached it a man stepped ashore, followed by a dozen
sailors armed with muskets and hatchets who set about unloading the
galley's cargo of blacks. There were about thirty of them, and more
were on the way aboard a second ship.

The man who had first disembarked, the ship's captain, now came
up to Pierre Munier and his son and spoke a few words that revealed
him to be extremely knowledgeable about his trade. He seemed
strangely familiar to both of them; he was around thirty years of age,
tall and broad-shouldered. His hair was curly and very black, and he
had a bushy mustache and beard of the same hue. His face and hands
were bronzed by the tropical sun so that he looked like an Indian from
Timor or Pégu, and he was dressed in a vest and trousers of blue linen
and a broad-brimmed straw hat. A rifle was slung casually over one
shoulder, and a saber that was like the Arabian ones, but larger, with a
hilt like a Scottish claymore, hung from a scabbard at his belt.

If the slaver's captain had been the object of close scrutiny by the
two men from Moka, they, no less, had been carefully observed by
him. The slave trader's eyes went from one man to the other with
equal curiosity; indeed, it seemed as if he could not tear his eyes away.
Georges and his father, though, were unaware of the examination to
which they were being subjected. They began inspecting the blacks
one by one; almost all of them were from far-distant Senegambia
and Guinea on the east coast of Africa, which was a desirable quality
since, unlike slaves from Madagascar, Mozambique, or the Plains of
Cafres, they were too far from home to harbor any hope of returning
there, and thus almost never tried to escape. Despite the value of his
wares, the captain named prices that were quite reasonable, and the

father and son purchased the first boatload of slaves before the second had even touched shore.

The second transaction went much like the first; the captain had an admirable assortment of blacks from which to choose, and seemed extremely knowledgeable—indeed, a true connoisseur of the commodity in which he dealt. Île de France had proven a lucky destination for him; it was his first time doing business there, as he had up to that point done business mostly in the Antilles.

When the sale was completed Télémaque, himself a native of the Congo, approached the newly acquired slaves and spoke to them in their native language about the pleasant conditions of life on the Munier plantation. They were extremely lucky to be owned by messieurs Pierre and Georges, he said, who were the fairest and best masters on the island. They were fortunate they had not been purchased by any of the other planters. The slaves dropped to their knees in the sand and, using Télémaque as an interpreter, pledged themselves to the two mulattoes, promising that they would work faithfully and well.

Upon hearing the names of Pierre and Georges Munier the slave captain, who had been listening to Télémaque's speech with an attention that showed he had made an especial study of the different dialects of Africa, gave a great start. He gazed at the two men with even more intensity than before. Still, they seemed to take no notice of this. The moment had come to complete the transaction, and Georges asked whether the captain wished to be paid in gold or bills. They were prepared for either answer; Pierre Munier's saddlebags were full of gold, and his wallet was stuffed with bills. The captain said that he preferred gold. Georges gave him the 150,000 francs, and the money was loaded onto the second dinghy for immediate transport to the ship. The crew departed next, but to the astonishment of Georges and his father, the captain did not accompany them. On his orders the galley pushed off, leaving him standing on the shore with the two Muniers.

The captain watched his ship until it was lost beyond the horizon, then turned toward Georges and Pierre Munier. Stretching out his hands, he said simply: "Hello, Father! Hello, brother!" They stared at him, frozen. "Well now!" he said. "Don't you remember your Jacques?"

There were rapturous cries of shock and elation. Jacques embraced first his father, then his brother, and extended his hand to Télémaque, who took it—though not without a slight shiver at touching a man who traded in slaves.

By a strange coincidence, Fate had reunited the family made up of a man who had spent his entire life suffering from prejudice against color, a man who made his living by exploiting it, and a man who was ready to die fighting it.

The Slave Trader's Philosophy

It was indeed Jacques Munier, whom his father had not seen in fourteen years, nor his brother in twelve. Let us acquaint ourselves with the tale of his long absence.

Jacques, as I have said, had shipped out aboard one of those corsairs that, armed with French authorization papers, in that era often swooped suddenly from our ports like eagles to wreak havoc on English ships. It had been a difficult initiation, perhaps, but far easier than what he would have undergone in the Imperial Navy, which at that time was blockaded in our ports and spent as much time at anchor as this "other" navy—lively, carefree, and independent—spent roaming the seas. Every day there was some new combat; not because our privateers actively sought battle with warships but because, fond as they were of Chinese and Indian merchandise, they could not resist pouncing on the heavily laden merchant vessels as they trundled homeward from Calcutta, Buenos Aires, or Veracruz. If these ships were unprotected, it was a simple matter to overtake and despoil them—it usually took only two or three hours, in fact; but if they were themselves armed, escorted by an English frigate or two with fangs and claws, it was a different matter entirely. Great amounts of gunfire would be exchanged, many men and blacks killed, and copious damage done to masts and spars. After bombarding each other from a distance the privateers and frigates would draw near enough to fight broadside-to-broadside and then aboard one ship's deck, and the merchant ship would flee to the haven of some English port (if it did not, like the fabled donkey, fall prey to another privateer) to be greeted with sighs of relief from the East India Company and promises of a generous reward for the defending frigate's surviving crew. That was the way of things at the time.

Privateers usually spent the better part of their time engaged in battle; of the thirty or thirty-one days that make up each month, twenty or twenty-five were spent in combat. On the days they did not fight, the ships were generally blasted by storms. In such an environment as this, I say again, young sailors learned quickly. The high casualty rate and lack of conscription meant that ships were almost never fully crewed, but because every sailor aboard was there by his own will, quality, fortunately, usually replaced quantity. Whether waging a battle or weathering a storm, no man had a set duty. Everyone could perform any task with skill.

Obedience to the captain or, in his absence, his second-in-command was the ironclad rule. In the six years Jacques served aboard the *Ca-lypso*, two men—one from Normandy and one from Gascony—had attempted mutiny. The captain had split the first man's head open with an ax; his lieutenant had shot the second through the heart. Both bodies had then been summarily dumped over the side of the ship—it would have been bad for morale to keep them on board. Since that time the control exercised by both Captain Bertrand and the first mate, Lieutenant Rébard, had been absolute.

Jacques had always had a taste for the sea. As a child he had spent countless hours climbing the riggings and exploring the decks of the ships that docked in Port Louis to do business with his father and other men of île de France. The good-natured captains had been happy to indulge him, explaining how things worked and allowing him to roam freely on their decks and climb high into their crow's nests. By the age of ten Jacques, for whom any ship was a fighting ship, was constantly at the docks waiting for the incoming vessels to arrive, and carving masts from the trees and ropes from the reeds. By the age of twelve he could be counted a true authority. He could name every part of a ship and describe endless maneuvers in exact detail. If his father had allowed it, any commander would have been glad to take him on board as a midshipman first-class.

But as we have seen, Pierre Munier, anxious for his son to have a good education, had enrolled him at the Collège Napoleon in Paris instead of the Collège d'Angoulême, where he would have been able to study what he loved most. The result only confirmed the old saying, "Man asks, and God grants." Jacques, after spending two years drawing frigates in his composition books and launching toy frigates in the Luxembourg lake, took advantage of the first opportunity that came his way to turn theory into practice. On holiday in Brest, visiting the frigate *Calypso,* he told his brother, who had accompanied him, that he could return to shore alone. As for himself, Jacques said, he had decided to become a sailor.

Both brothers did as Jacques had suggested, and Georges returned alone, as I have said, to the Collège Napoleon.

Jacques's manly bearing, sturdy physique, and good-natured countenance won the approval of Captain Bertrand, who quickly promoted him to the rank of able seaman—a mark of favor that caused much grumbling among his shipmates. Jacques was unperturbed; he held strict notions of fairness and unfairness, and those who doubted his worth were simply ignorant of it. It was only natural that they resent him, an untried novice. He had a golden opportunity to prove himself soon enough, when a storm hit the ship and he braved the topmost rigging to cut loose a poorly knotted sail. Later, during his first battle aboard the *Calypso,* he sprang aboard the enemy vessel before his captain had done so; the breach of sailor's etiquette earned him a thumping that laid him low for three entire days. Still, Bertrand could not help but admire his bravery, and forgave him in short order. From then on it was Jacques's privilege to board third, behind only the captain and first mate. After that the rest of the crew never said another word against Jacques. In fact, the old sailors came to him and were the first to shake his hand.

This satisfying state of affairs lasted until 1815. I mention 1815 because Captain Bertrand, who was a true skeptic, had never taken the fall of Napoleon seriously. Perhaps this was why, having nothing else to do, he made two voyages to the island of Elba and, on one occasion, had the honor of being received by the ex-ruler of the world himself. The emperor and the pirate had a conversation that seemed to afford Bertrand great inward pleasure, though he never revealed what had been said. When he stepped back aboard the *Calypso*, though, he was heard humming the following verse:

> Ran tan plan tirelire,
> Comme nous allons rire!

On his return to Brest he began to prepare the *Calypso* for active service, loading her with powder and bullets and recruiting the remaining men he needed to complete his crew. Those who knew the captain knew that he would never have acted in such a way if he was not absolutely certain that something momentous was about to happen. Sure enough, six weeks after the *Calypso*'s last voyage to Porto-Ferrajo, Napoleon landed at the Gulf of Juan, and three weeks after that he made his entry into Paris. Captain Bertrand set out from Brest Harbor a mere three days later, sails hoisted and the tricolor fluttering proudly from the mast. Barely eight days had passed before he returned in triumph, towing a magnificent three-masted English vessel he had taken, laden with choice Indian spices. The money gained from the sale of the ship and her cargo was distributed evenly among the *Calypso*'s crew, and Bertrand and his men set out immediately in search of another prize.

As we know, however, one does not always find precisely what he is looking for. After nearly a year of stifling boredom, the *Calypso* and her crew found themselves face-to-face with another English vessel. As Fate would have it, this was the *Leicester*, the very ship that would later carry Lord William Murray and Georges Munier to île de France.

The *Leicester* had ten cannons and sixty men more than the *Calypso*, and instead of cinnamon, sugar, or coffee, she was loaded with shot and shells. At her first sight of the privateer she dispensed with formalities by letting fly a thirty-six-pound ball that buried itself neatly in the *Calypso*'s hull.

The *Calypso*, unlike her sister Galatea, who clamored to be seen, would have gladly become invisible and fled at that moment. Captain Bertrand was no fool; he knew immediately that here was nothing to be gained, and everything to be lost. The *Leicester*'s commander was none other than William Murray himself, who at that time had not yet retired from active service and was known far and wide as one of the most fearful sea wolves to be found between the Straits of Magellan and Baffin Bay. Accordingly, Bertrand shifted the *Calypso*'s two largest guns to stern and fled as fast as he could.

The privateer was a long and narrow brigantine, built for speed, but it soon became evident that, like a sea swallow facing an eagle, she could not outrun the *Leicester*. The frigate pursued her relentlessly, firing at intervals in a clear demand for surrender to which the *Calypso*'s only reply was a hail of gunfire.

Jacques had been carefully studying the *Leicester*'s spars, which seemed to him a weak point on the English frigate. Changes might be made in the rigging, he thought, that would be to the advantage of ships like the *Calypso*. He made a remark to this effect to Lieutenant Rébard, who was next to him on deck, but received no answer. Turning, he saw the reason—Rébard had just been cut in two by a cannonball.

The situation was becoming dire. The two ships would be side by side in less than half an hour, and the *Leicester*'s crew outnumbered the *Calypso*'s by a third. Jacques stooped to confer with one of the gunners, but at that moment the man's knees buckled and he slumped forward against the breech of his gun. Jacques took hold of the man's collar and hauled him impatiently to his feet—only to find that the poor fellow had swallowed a bullet—death by heartburn, as it were.

Almost without thinking, Jacques shoved the man's body to one side and bent over the gun. He sighted—aimed—cried "Fire!"—and let fly with a burst of shot! Then he leapt onto the bulwark to see what he had done. The effect on the *Leicester* was immediate and catastrophic. The enemy ship's mizzenmast snapped like a willow branch and crashed to the deck below, carrying sails, sheets, spars, and a portion of the starboard bulwark with it.

Shouts of joy echoed from the decks of the *Calypso*. She had won the battle with barely a scratch and was free to pursue her course, untroubled by the crippled English frigate. The captain's first action was to appoint Jacques lieutenant in Rébard's place—an action that was greeted with universal acclaim by the crew. That evening a mass was held for the dead. Most of the bodies had been thrown overboard during the skirmish, but Rébard's had been kept so that he might be given the honors due a man of his rank. The corpse was sewn up in a hammock with a thirty-six-pound cannonball at each end—to prevent unseemly floating—and solemnly consigned to the depths.

When night fell Captain Bertrand took advantage of the darkness to return to Brest, sending the *Leicester,* which had quickly repaired the damage to her mast, on a wild-goose chase to Cape Verde. This misadventure did much to ruffle the temper of the normally easygoing Captain Murray, and he swore that the *Calypso* would not escape so easily if he ever encountered her again.

Captain Bertrand spent just enough time at Brest to repair the minor damage done to the *Calypso;* then set out again in pursuit of glory, with Jacques proving to be a very capable first mate. Unfortunately, the disaster of Waterloo brought about a second abdication and, after that, peace. Bertrand watched the prisoner of Europe, the unlucky emperor himself, pass by aboard the *Bellérophon* en route to St. Helena, a prison from which there would be no escape as there had been from Elba. After that, prospects for privateers were increasingly bleak. The captain knew he would have to look elsewhere for his fortune. As the master of a swift, tightly run brigantine manned by a loyal and efficient crew, it was only natural that his thoughts should turn in the direction of the slave trade.

Slavery had been a booming business, indeed, before an avalanche of altruistic proclamations had all but buried the trade. Still, there was a great fortune to be made if a man was enterprising and resourceful. War, which comes and goes in Europe, rages eternally on the African continent. The natives' thirst for blood is matched only by their thirst for brandy, and in those days one had only to venture into Senegambia, Congo, Mozambique, or Zanzibar with a bottle or two of cognac to return with a black under each arm. If a tribe did not have prisoners to dispose of, mothers would sell their children for a glass of liquor. True, youngsters did not fetch much of a price, but there were large numbers of them, and they added up neatly in the end.

Captain Bertrand plied this trade honorably and profitably until 1820, and would have done so for much longer had an unforeseen event not put a premature end to his life. During a stop on Africa's western coast, after traveling up the rivière des Poissons to meet with a Hottentot chief who had promised to sell him a group of Grands Namaquois, for which he already had orders in Guadeloupe and Martinique, in return for two kegs of rum, Bertrand happened to step on the tail of a coiled rattlesnake, which reared up and bit him on the hand. The Hottentot shook his head at the captain's cry of pain. "Man bitten, man dead," he said gravely.

"I *know* that!" cried the captain. "That's why I screamed!" Bertrand seized the snake and strangled it to death, both for his personal satisfaction and to make sure it bit no one else, but no sooner had he done this than he collapsed on the ground. Everything had happened so quickly that by the time Jacques—who had been barely twenty-five paces behind his captain—reached his side, it was all but over. Bertrand gasped out a few words, his skin green as a lizard's, and expired. Within ten minutes his body was completely covered in black and yellow blotches, like a poisoned mushroom.

The swiftly decomposing corpse was so riddled with poison that it could not be returned to the *Calypso*. Jacques and twelve of his fellow sailors dug a grave on the spot, laid the body of their captain in it, and piled up a rough cairn of stones to mark Bertrand's final resting place and, hopefully, to ensure that it would be safe from hyenas and jackals. One of the men kept the rattlesnake for his pharmacist uncle in Brest, who had never seen a rattlesnake and yearned to display one in his shop window, between a bottle of red water and a bottle of blue.

There is an old adage that states, "Business comes first." Accordingly, despite his shock and horror, Jacques roused himself to complete the transaction with the Hottentot chief. Fifty Grands Namaquois slaves were duly exchanged for two kegs of rum; the two men who had completed the transaction, enchanted with each other, promised to continue their business relationship in the future; and the *Calypso* set off once more.

That evening Jacques assembled the entire crew on deck and extolled the virtues of the late Captain Bertrand before offering the men a choice of two scenarios. The first was that they would deliver their cargo to Martinique and Guadeloupe as promised and then sell the *Calypso,* dividing the profits equally and scattering to seek their individual fortunes as they chose. The second scenario was that they would elect a new captain and continue to deal in slaves under the name *Calypso et Compagnie.* The verdict was unanimous: The crew chose the second option without hesitation and named Jacques as their commander.

Jacques's first action as captain was to name as his first mate a brave Breton from Lorient popularly known as Master Tête-de-Fer— Ironhead—due to the remarkable hardness of his skull.

The *Calypso,* more forgetful than the nymph from whom she had taken her name, set sail for the West Indies that very evening. Her crew was saddened by the loss of Captain Bertrand, their Ulysses, but they had certainly found just as able a leader in Jacques. Bertrand had been one of those tough sea wolves who do everything by the book, never allowing himself simply to be inspired by the moment. Jacques, by contrast, was a child of impulse. He had a real genius for the sea, and could command his ship in storm or in battle as capably as the most experienced admiral—but neither had he forgotten how to tie a knot as well as the lowest deckhand. His energy seemed limitless; every day he came up with some new shipboard improvement to be made. He loved the *Calypso* as a man loves his mistress; she responded brilliantly to his ministrations, and it soon became impossible to imagine one of them surviving without the other.

Jacques's happiness was nearly complete—only the occasional thought of his father and brother caused a shadow to cross his brow. He was neither greedy nor cruel; he was an honest merchant, dealing conscientiously and treating his human cargo with care. Not for

Jacques the conduct of some slave traders, who lose half of their profit by treating their blacks miserably, and for whom violence soon turns from a habit into a pleasure. These natives of the Plains of Cafres, these Hottentots, Senegambians, and Mozambicans, were treated almost as well as if they had been sacks of sugar, barrels of rice, or bales of cotton. They ate well, slept on clean straw, and walked the *Calypso's* decks twice a day to benefit from the fresh sea air. Chains were used only when necessary. He tried as often as he could to sell husbands with their wives and children with their mothers—an unheard-of bit of delicacy and tact. Jacques's Negroes almost always reached their destination in good spirits and excellent physical condition, which increased their market value considerably.

Perhaps unsurprisingly, Jacques never stopped in any port of call long enough to form a serious romantic attachment. His wealth made him quite attractive to many young maidens in Jamaica, Guadeloupe, and Cuba; and their fathers—unaware that he was a mulatto—offered him their hands in marriage more than once. Jacques, though, had his own ideas about love. He was well acquainted with mythology and history; with the stories of Hercules and Omphale, and Samson and Delilah. He declared that he would have no other bride than the *Calypso*. This is not to say that he wasn't a man of Creole sensuality; on the contrary, he had mistresses aplenty, and in every color: black, red, yellow, and brown, depending on whether he was in the Congo or in Florida, Bengal, or Madagascar. To these physical joys he added a host of other pleasures. Nature was extremely pleasant for him, but instead of affecting his soul, it touched his senses. He loved wide-open spaces—not because they made him think of God, but because they gave him more room to move and breathe. He loved the stars—not because he believed they might be other worlds spinning in the heavens, but because he enjoyed the idea of having an azure canopy studded with diamonds over his head. He loved towering forests—not because their depths were full of mysterious and lyrical voices, but because their dense greenery threw shadows that not even the sun could pierce.

As for his view of the trade he practiced, he saw it as a perfectly legal business. He had witnessed blacks being bought and sold all his life; it was, he believed, the natural state of things—what they were made for. He never worried about whether it was arrogant to traffic in human beings; once he had paid for a Negro, he viewed him as his property, and saw himself as completely within his rights to sell him to someone else. He was a businessman; he bought and sold, and it was his business alone.

Unlike some of his fellow slave traders, Jacques never hunted for blacks on his own account. He found the thought of forcibly taking possession of a free man, and then making him a slave, repugnant. But, he reasoned, if a man was a slave already—well, he had no control over that, and there was no reason to refrain from doing business with the owner.

All in all Jacques's life was a decidedly pleasant one. There were minor skirmishes here and there; the slave trade had been officially abolished by a congress of governments in the days of Captain Bertrand, and once in a while some ship's commander would decide to investigate just what the *Calypso* was doing off the Senegalese or Indian coasts. Jacques often amused himself by sporting with these curious devils, hoisting one flag after another, and finally displaying his own standard, which consisted of three black heads. He would then dart away, and the chase was on.

Besides the twenty guns decorating her sides, the *Calypso* possessed two rear-facing, long-range cannons capable of firing thirty-six-pound balls. Jacques liked to hoist just enough sail to keep the pursuing ship in range of these, and at the first sign of enemy shot he would use all his old gunnery skills to wreak havoc on the opposing vessel. He would keep going in this way until the game of skittles, as he cheerfully referred to it, grew tiresome. Then, deeming his battered pursuer to be sufficiently punished, he would order all sails hoisted and, with a parting shot or two in farewell, skim away over the waves like a giant seabird.

Escapades such as these earned Jacques and the *Calypso* a reputation that made them rather unwelcome in many ports. The sly captain became a master of deception, disguising his ship and giving her an innocent name such as *Belle Jenny* or *Jeune Olympe*. They had come from loading tea at Canton, he would claim, or coffee at Mocha, or spices at

Ceylon. He would display samples of these cargoes, take orders for more, and advertise berths for passengers. Dressed in a long waistcoat and broad-brimmed hat, Jacques was the very image of an honest sailor from Bretagne. At other times the *Calypso* would be transformed into a French military vessel: the *Sphynx,* perhaps, or the *Léonidas.* The crew donned uniforms, and the ship sailed graciously into port, flying the white flag and firing courteous salutes that were returned in kind. On these days Jacques would dress in his predecessor's clothes and assume the character of a crotchety old sea dog, swearing and grumbling, or, if the mood struck him, that of a dashing young officer fresh from the academy. He called himself M. de Kergouran as the old man and M. de Champ-Fleury as the young one; he mumbled and squinted and limped. The act would have been seen through immediately in a French or English port, but it was wonderfully successful in Cuba, or Martinique and Guadeloupe, or Java.

Jacques cared nothing for speculations or schemes; he spent his profits on luxuries in Visapour and Guzarato and became almost as good a judge of diamonds as he was of Negroes. He wore a pouch full of gems at his belt, and if he ran out of ready money he simply withdrew a glittering stone as big as a hazelnut and sold it to some Jewish trader at the market price. Often, like Cleopatra, who ate and drank the pearls and diamonds given to her by Antony, he consumed a very expensive meal. It was not uncommon for him to be carrying two or three million francs' worth of jewels on his person at any given time, and his unorthodox way of saving allowed him to store a good deal more with ease. He had learned much during his career, and he knew that his was a profession frowned upon by many—and that ill fortune might befall him at any moment.

In the meantime it was, as I have said, a very enjoyable life, and Jacques would not have exchanged his place with that of a king. He would have been perfectly happy—were it not for thoughts of his father, and of Georges. One bright morning he could resist temptation no longer. After picking up a shipment of Negroes in Senegambia and the Congo and moving down the coast to pick up cargo from Mozambique and Zanzibar, he decided to make a visit to île de France to see if his father was still there and if his brother had returned. As he approached the coast, he had made the signals usually used by slave ships, and had received the expected signals in return. The incredible part of it was that these signals had been exchanged between father and son. By that evening he found himself not only back on the shores of his native land, but—better yet—in the arms of those he had come to seek.

PANDORA'S BOX

The happiness of the Munier family at being unexpectedly reunited after such a long separation may be imagined. Naturally, Georges's European-educated heart had given a lurch of regret when he learned that his brother was a trader in human flesh, but this quickly gave way to the simple joy of seeing Jacques again. As for Pierre Munier, an islander born and bred, he did not give his elder son's profession a second thought. He had both of his boys with him again; that was all that mattered.

Jacques returned to Moka for the night with his father and brother as if it were nothing, and the little family talked late into the night, sharing their most intimate feelings with one another. Pierre Munier was so happy to be back together with his sons that he could speak of nothing else; Jacques spun tales of the exotic adventures and pleasures of the life he had carved for himself. Georges, though, talked only of his love.

Pierre Munier was so shocked at his younger son's words that he shook from head to foot. His boy, a mulatto—the *son* of a mulatto—in love with a white woman? And so sure that he would win her, too! It was unspeakable, unheard-of audacity; nothing like it had ever happened on île de France. Pierre Munier felt horribly certain that no good could come of the matter. Georges was inviting all the wrath of heaven and earth down upon his own head.

As for Jacques, he saw no reason why his brother shouldn't love a white woman—though he preferred black ones himself, and laid out his reasons for this most eloquently indeed. Still, Jacques was the sort of fellow who understood that every man had his own taste; moreover, he thought his brother—handsome, wealthy, and cultivated—worthy of aspiring to the hand of any white woman he chose, even if she were Aline, queen of Golconda! Accordingly, he told Georges that if M. de Malmédie refused to bestow Sara upon him as a bride he would carry her off himself, aboard the *Calypso*, and take her to some remote spot where she and Georges could live in untroubled marital bliss. Georges thanked his brother, smiling, but he had another plan in mind.

The next day all three Muniers were up before sunrise, so anxious were they to meet and resume their conversation, telling one another the things they had forgotten to say the night before. Around eleven o'clock Jacques decided he wanted to visit some favorite places from his childhood, and suggested that his father and brother accompany him on a stroll around the estate. Pierre Munier agreed, but Georges begged off. He was waiting for news from town, as we know, and he had an appointment to keep with Miko-Miko at the house.

At the agreed-upon time, Georges saw his visitor approaching the house. The Chinese man carried his bamboo rod and baskets, just as if he was on an errand of business—indeed, businessman that he was, he *had* hoped he might encounter a willing buyer along the way to the plantation. Heart pounding, the young mulatto opened the door at Miko-Miko's knock. The man had just come from seeing Sara—surely he would have news of her!

Everything had happened exactly as planned. Miko-Miko had been granted immediate entry into M. de Malmédie's house where the servant Bijou, who had watched Sara purchase the ivory fan from him a few days earlier, had conducted him at once to mademoiselle's room. Sara had given a slight start at the sight of the peddler; he naturally stirred up memories of her first glimpse of Georges. She received Miko-Miko graciously, though to her dismay she was obliged to rely on hand signals and nods of her head to communicate with him. When he produced Georges's calling card, her cheeks flushed crimson. Clearly her lover, unable to come to her in person, was using this bit of paper to tell her she was in his thoughts. Without bothering to bargain with the Chinese merchant, she bought every one of the items Georges had written down. As for the card itself, Miko-Miko did not ask for it back—and Sara was all too happy to keep it.

As he left Sara's apartments, Miko-Miko had been waylaid by Henri, who took him aside to examine his collection of trinkets. He bought nothing for the moment, but made it clear to the Chinaman that as mademoiselle was to be his bride, he would soon have need of all the charming frippery the peddler could provide.

Miko-Miko was delighted, not only at the promise of future business but because his encounters with Sara and Henri had allowed him to observe their house in great detail. His bald cranium concealed a remarkable brain, and he now had a perfect architectural plan of the home imprinted on his memory.

The Malmédie town house had three entrances. The principal door, as we have already seen, opened onto the small footbridge that connected the home with its magnificent gardens. Another, on the opposite side of the house, led to a small, tree-lined path that led in turn to the bustling rue du Gouvernement. The third door was a side entrance, and opened directly onto rue de la Comédie. Entering the mansion through the main door, visitors found themselves in a large, square courtyard, planted with mango trees and Chinese lilacs whose leaves shaded the inner door of the sprawling home. The Negro servants' quarters were to the right of the courtyard; the stables to the left. Still farther to the right was a large pavilion guarded by a magnificent sculpted dragon, and facing it was another suite of small rooms also intended for use by the slaves. On the far left was the side door that opened onto rue de la Comédie, and to the right of that was a passage leading to a little staircase and a tree-lined terrace, affording a view of the stone façade of the theater.

The sharp-eyed reader will note that the dragon pavilion was separated from the main body of the house by the passageway containing the staircase. The pavilion was, as it happens, Sara's habitual retreat. It had four sides, one of which was connected to the slave quarters; the three others faced the fragrant courtyard, the passageway with the staircase, and a large and nearly empty shipyard, respectively. This shipyard faced the river on one side and a windbreak of trees on the other, which rose about a dozen feet above the floor of the yard itself. Two or three houses were built against the other side of the alley, their slanted roofs offering—to anyone who might wish it—easy and secret access into the shipyard. The pavilion also had three windows; one opened near the door of the house, another on the passage, and the third on the shipyard.

As Miko-Miko recited these details, Georges smiled three times— once when the Chinaman told him Sara had kept his calling card; once when Sara's forthcoming marriage to Henri was mentioned; and once when told he could easily enter the pavilion unseen, through the window that opened onto the shipyard. Giving Miko-Miko a sheet of paper and a pencil, he asked the peddler to draw the Malmédie house exactly as he had just described it. Then, taking another sheet of paper and a pen, he sat down and wrote a letter. When it was finished, he went to his room and brought back a little jewel box worthy of Mme de Pompadour herself. Placing the letter inside, he closed and locked the box and handed it and the key to Miko-Miko. After receiving a few final words of instruction from Georges, the Chinaman hefted his bamboo pole and baskets and went away as he had come, disappearing down the tree-lined avenue that connected the Munier plantation with the Moka road.

Just then Jacques and Pierre Munier returned, entering the house through a rear door. Georges, who had been preparing to set off in search of them, stopped in surprise. There were clouds gathering in the sky that warned of a storm, Jacques explained. As much as he trusted Master Tête-de-Fer, he loved the *Calypso* too dearly to leave her in anyone else's care, even his lieutenant's, under such circumstances. Climbing to the top of Mont Pouce, he had seen his ship standing barely two leagues off the coast; he had signaled Ironhead from there, and the first mate was sending a skiff to retrieve his captain. Jacques had returned home merely to bid his brother farewell.

Pierre Munier, understandably upset, pleaded with his elder son not to go. "I must, Father," said Jacques, gently yet firmly enough that his father immediately understood that there was no point in arguing further.

As for Georges, he identified with his brother's single-minded determination so completely that he didn't even attempt to dissuade him from returning to the *Calypso*. He and Pierre would accompany Jacques as far as the opposite slope of Mont Pieterboot, he said. From there they would be able to watch his skiff as it was rowed toward the *Calypso,* and thus be sure he made it back to his ship safely.

The three Muniers set out directly, taking little-known back roads to the mouth of the rivière des Calebasses. There Jacques took his leave of the cherished father and brother with whom his visit had been all too brief. He would come back, he promised, as soon as he possibly could. An hour later his skiff pushed away from shore, carrying him back to the ship he loved so fiercely that he was bound to protect her, or die in the attempt.

Georges and Pierre Munier watched as the little boat reached the *Calypso* and her captain climbed aboard. Almost immediately the sails were hoisted and the ship rounded île de Sable and bore away northward at top speed. Jacques was gone. Meanwhile the sea and the sky grew more and more threatening. Waves dashed violently against the shore, and the water rose rapidly even though it was hours away from full tide. The skies darkened and filled with heaving masses of dark clouds, and the wind howled in gusts toward the east and south. To anyone but a sailor, all of this meant nothing except that an ordinary storm was on the way, of the kind that threatened île de France several times each year. By the time Georges and Pierre Munier reached home, however, the barometer had fallen below twenty-eight degrees, and they were obliged to acknowledge Jacques's sharp eye.

Pierre Munier quickly gave orders for all the manioc stalks to be cut away, so that the roots at least might be saved, while Georges instructed his manservant to have Antrim saddled at eight o'clock that evening. "Why on earth do you need to saddle your horse, Georges?" Pierre Munier asked in some alarm.

"I have an appointment in the city at ten o'clock that I must keep, Father."

"Impossible!" cried Pierre Munier.

"I must, Father," said Georges quietly, in a resolute tone that echoed the one Jacques had used earlier. Pierre Munier's shoulders drooped in resignation, and he said no more.

———

During all this time Miko-Miko had been carrying out the task Georges had given him. Immediately upon his arrival in Port Louis, he went to the home of M. de Malmédie. On his way into town he had seen the well-to-do father and son down at the docks, watching the captains doubling the moorings of the ships lying at anchor there in preparation for the coming storm. The peddler was confident, therefore, that he would be able to enter the Malmédie residence without arousing suspicion. The servant Bijou, who had already seen Miko-Miko doing business with both Mademoiselle Sara and Monsieur Henri that day, led him unhesitatingly to the future mistress of the house—who was, as usual, seated in the pavilion.

As Georges had foreseen, the young beauty's attention was immediately drawn to the charming Boule jewel box Miko-Miko offered her. Taking it into her hands, she turned it over and over, admiring the exterior, and then tried to open it so that she could see the inside. Finding it locked, she asked the peddler for the key. He made a great show of searching his pockets for it, finally indicating by means of hand gestures that he did not have it. Signaling that he would return in ten minutes with the key, he left the box with Sara and disappeared.

Instead of going home, though, once inside the Malmédie house Miko-Miko gave the key—which had been in his pocket all the time—to Bijou, who went out to the pavilion with it just as Sara was examining the jewel box for the hundredth time. Asking no questions, she took the key eagerly from the servant—who then hurried to close all the shutters in the house against the winds of the oncoming hurricane. Child-like in her eagerness, Sara wasted no time in unlocking the box. It contained only a single slip of paper, folded twice.

She hesitated for an instant, but there could be no doubt who had sent the mysterious note. Curiosity, and love, got the better of her. Cheeks flushed and heart pounding, Sara unfolded the paper and read these words:

Sara,

There is no need for me to tell you I love you; you must know that already. I have dreamed my whole life of meeting someone like you. Sometimes, in this world, there are moments of supreme importance—when everything we know about society must crumble in the face of awesome and absolute necessity.

Sara, do you love me?

Think of what your life will be with M. de Malmédie, and weigh it carefully against the life you would have with me.

With him, you will want for nothing.

With me, you must share the burden of the prejudices I face.

But I will tell you again—I love you, more than any other man ever has, or ever will.

I know that M. de Malmédie is anxious to make you his bride; there is no time to waste. You are free, Sara. Look into your heart, and decide between Monsieur Henri and me.

I will regard your decision as sacred. Tonight, at ten o'clock, I will come to the pavilion to receive it.

Georges

Sara glanced around, terrified. It seemed that Georges might appear at any moment. Just then the door opened—revealing not the young mulatto, but Henri de Malmédie. Hastily the girl concealed Georges's letter in her bosom.

Henri was usually rather luckless in his advances toward Sara, and this was no exception, as he now happened upon her at a moment when her head was reeling with thoughts of another. "I beg your pardon for intruding upon you this way, my dear Sara," he said. "But after all, in a fortnight we will be husband and wife! I daresay it's all right for me to take a liberty or two! I've come to tell you that if there are any pretty flowers in the garden especially dear to you, you should get them to shelter as quickly as you can."

"Why?" murmured Sara, distractedly.

"Don't you know there's a hurricane coming? No living thing will be safe outdoors tonight."

"What?" Sara cried, thinking immediately of Georges. "You think it will be dangerous?"

"Well, not for people safely behind solid walls," said Henri. "But the poor devils living in huts or traveling the roads will have something to worry about. I wouldn't trade places with them; that's certain."

"Do you—do you really think it will be so bad, Henri?"

"Lord, yes! Don't you hear the filao trees in the garden? The wind is howling through them like a banshee—a sure sign that a storm is on the way—and look at that sky! You'd better bring your flowers inside, Sara, and quickly. I'm going to see about my dogs." With that, Henri left her alone.

Darkness fell rapidly, as heavy black clouds gathered in the sky. From time to time, violent gusts of wind shook the building and then passed, leaving an ominous, deep silence. Sara gazed out the pavilion window into the courtyard, where the mango trees trembled as if in terror of the awful battle about to take place among wind, earth, and sky, and the Chinese lilacs—trees indigenous to the colonies, which are placed on tombs instead of the cypresses we employ—drooped mournfully toward the ground. The girl felt a profound sense of terror and clasped her hands together, murmuring, "Please, Lord, protect him!"

"Sara?" It was M. de Malmédie, calling for her.

She opened the door.

"There you are, my child," M. de Malmédie said. "Come into the house; you're not safe out here in the pavilion."

"Yes, Uncle," Sara said. She stepped outside and closed and locked the pavilion door, slipping the key into her pocket. She followed M. de Malmédie into the house, but instead of joining him and Henri in the drawing room she went straight to her chamber. When her uncle came looking for her a moment later, he found her on her knees before the small crucifix that hung at the foot of her bed.

"Sara," he said, "whatever are you doing here, instead of coming to take tea with Henri and me?"

"I was praying, Uncle," said the girl. "For—for all the travelers."

"I wouldn't worry, my dear," M. de Malmédie said genially. "I doubt there's any fool crazy enough to be on the road tonight."

"I pray you're right, Uncle," said Sara—but she did not rise from the crucifix.

There could no longer be any doubt that a hurricane, that terror of the colonies, was approaching île de France; Jacques's sailor's intuition had been spot-on. Night had fallen with frightening speed, but flashes of lightning illuminated the sky so brilliantly and so often that the island was flooded with an eerie bluish light, which gave everything the cadaverous color of the bygone worlds Byron had visited on Cain, under the direction of Satan himself. Thunder crashed and growled in accompaniment to the incessant lightning, rolling down the hillsides to rumble, as loudly as if the mountains were being reborn, through Port Louis and out to be lost in the depths of the horizon. Powerful gusts of wind rattled windows and walls, bending even the strongest trees nearly double as easily as if they were baguettes, dying away only to begin again even stronger than before.

It was at the center of the island, especially in Moka and on the Williams Plains, that the storm had freest rein and raged most spectacularly. This only served to increase Pierre Munier's alarm when first Jacques, then Georges insisted on leaving the shelter of home; but of course he could do nothing, and backed down—as he always did—when faced with a will stronger than his own. Georges, however, felt no fear. Where his father turned pale at each clap of thunder, he drew himself up. Where Pierre started at each flash of lightning, his son only smiled. Georges had spent his adult life fighting other men; the hour had come for him to fight God himself.

It was time to depart. With the unshakable resolve that marked his character—something he had not learned in school, but instilled in himself—Georges moved toward Pierre Munier. Clasping his father's trembling hand without seeming to understand why the old man quivered as he did, he strode to the front door with an expression as calm and untroubled as if he were simply going out on an ordinary day. Ali, with the passive obedience typical of Orientals, was waiting at the door with Antrim. The horse seemed to hear the whispering of the simoom wind or the roaring of the khamsin as if he were back in the desert. He whinnied nervously, but Georges's voice calmed him, and his wide eyes and flaring nostrils relaxed a bit. Georges slapped his flank lightly, and with an impossibly graceful motion the young man leapt unaided into the saddle. He whispered a few words in Arabic to his steed—Ali let go of the bridle—and they were off like a shot. Georges had not turned back to look at Pierre Munier, who stood in the doorway and watched his son until he disappeared at the end of the avenue leading to the Port Louis road.

Georges rode nobly and fearlessly, seeming to move as quickly as the storm itself. He was Faust, riding his hellish steed to the Brocken. Disorder reigned all around him; tempest-ravaged tree boughs could be heard cracking and crashing, and stalks of sugarcane and manioc, ripped violently from the earth, whirled through the air. Birds, caught slumbering and lifted into the sky by forces they could not control, swooped around Georges's head, shrieking sharply. Here and there a deer bolted across the path like an arrow launched from a hunter's bow. Despite the chaos, the young man was happy. His heart swelled with pride; he alone was calm in the midst of the confusion, and he pushed onward relentlessly through the destruction swirling around him. Nothing could make him swerve from his path. Nothing possessed that much power.

Still, the journey was slow and difficult. It took Georges nearly an hour to reach the foot of Mont Signaux; the way was choked with broken tree trunks, streams swollen to muddy torrents, and huge boulders uprooted from the ground and flung down the hillsides. The sea foamed and thrashed, enormous green waves bursting against the shore with a deafening roar, as if God himself could no longer restrain the ocean's fury. Georges urged his steed onward, crossing the pont Bourgeois and turning right on the rue de la Côte-d'Or. He rode along the ramparts and down the rue de la Rampe, through the municipal gardens and deserted, debris-filled city streets until, finally, he reached the rue du Gouvernement. Turning into the narrow passageway there, he tied up his horse and vaulted easily over the gate separating the passage from the lane overlooking the Malmédie house. It was a simple matter to slide down the tiled roofs of the little houses built there into the shipyard, onto which opened the windows of Sara's pavilion.

During all this time Sara had kept to her chamber, listening to the howling of the wind and praying ceaselessly. She hoped the storm might have dissuaded Georges from coming to her, but she already knew his firm and determined character too well to believe it. Death alone, she was sure, would prevent her lover from keeping his rendezvous with her. In her mind's eye she pictured him, crushed and bleeding beneath a fallen tree or boulder or drowned in some raging river, and at the sensation of horror that filled her she knew it was useless to resist her love for him. However much she might struggle, Georges already possessed her heart completely.

As the hour of their meeting drew near, Sara's agitation increased. She could not tear her eyes from the clock; every swing of the pendulum, she thought, brought Georges closer to her. Nine o'clock . . . nine-thirty . . . quarter to ten . . . and with every moment that passed, the storm outside grew worse. The house trembled and shook as if it were being torn from its foundations. The wind screamed in the filao branches, and mournful cries could be heard from the direction of the Negroes' huts, which were none too solidly built and crumpled like houses of playing cards in the gale. From time to time the melancholy sound of a merchant ship's distress call echoed distantly from the churning sea, signaling uselessly for help no human hand could provide.

Then, above all these noises of devastation and chaos, Sara heard the faint whinny of a horse.

She stood, her mind made up. This man had come to her despite impossible dangers, when the island's bravest were trembling in their houses. He had come through uprooted forest, rushing rivers, crumbling precipices—and all that just to say to her *I love you, Sara. Do you love me?* Here was a man truly worthy of her love. He had saved her life. She was his, just as he was hers. It was no longer a decision she made of her own free will; it was the hand of God guiding her. She could not possibly resist. It was destiny, determined long ago. She no longer controlled her own fate; she simply submitted to it.

Leaving her room, Sara crept down the hall and then the little outside staircase that quivered beneath her feet. Moving slowly, stumbling over bits of brick and wood, clinging to the side of the pavilion to keep from being caught by the wind, she reached the door. As she placed the key in the lock, a vivid flash of lightning illuminated the courtyard, showing her the uprooted mango trees and the torn and scattered flowers. For a shuddering moment everything seemed uncertain; she thought she might have waited in vain; Georges would not come—not because he was afraid, but because he was dead. All else vanished in the wake of this terrible idea. Turning the key in its lock, she entered the pavilion.

"I thank you, Sara," Georges's voice murmured, and she trembled all over. "Oh, I was not wrong—you do love me!"

His hand grasped hers in the dark; his heart beat against her own; their breaths mingled together. A strange sensation swept over her, overwhelming and devouring, and she sank like a flower bent on its stem, breathless, dizzy, and exhausted from the two hours she had just endured, against his strong shoulder. "Georges," she murmured with the last of her strength. "Oh, Georges, have pity on me . . ."

He understood what she was asking of him: It was the appeal of fragility to strength, of a young girl to her lover. He knew, in every fiber of his being, that Sara was his. He would love this virginal maiden as his wife. He shivered with love, desire, happiness; moving so that they were in the faint light of the window, he bent his face closer to hers. "You are mine, Sara, aren't you? Mine, for life?"

"Oh, yes, Georges, yes! For life," she whispered.

"And nothing but death shall part us?"

"No, Georges, nothing but death."

"Do you swear it, Sara?"

"Yes—on the memory of my mother, dearest Georges."

"Well then," murmured the young man, quivering with joy and pride. "From this moment on, Sara, you are my wife, and God have mercy on anyone who tries to take you away from me!"

He pressed his lips to hers. Then, fearful of losing what remained of his self-control in the face of so much love, so much beauty, he wrenched himself away. Moving swiftly to the open window, he climbed through it and was gone.

A peal of thunder crashed violently, and Sara fell to her knees. Just then, the pavilion's door was flung open, revealing M. de Malmédie and Henri.

XVI

THE PROPOSAL

The hurricane ended during the night, and next morning the residents of île de France ventured outside to assess the aftermath.

Many of the ships in the harbor had sustained considerable damage. Some had been smashed against others by the wind; nearly all of them had lost their masts, which now lay like fallen logs on the surface of the water. Two or three, dragging their anchors, had been driven ashore on île des Tonneliers, and one—a merchant vessel—had foundered and gone down with all hands lost.

The devastation on the island was just as brutal. Only a few houses had emerged from the storm unscathed. Roofs of slate, tile, shingles, copper, and tin had been ripped off and carried away—only the argamasses, roofs built in the terraced style of India, had been able to resist the winds and remain intact. The streets were filled with debris; some buildings remained upright only because they had been braced with poles. On the parade grounds at champ de Mars, the stands erected for the forthcoming races had been completely leveled. Two enormous cannons mounted near the Grande-Rivière had spun 180 degrees in the gale.

Farther inland, the damage was extensive as well. It was fortunate that most of the harvest had already been gathered and brought indoors; what remained had been entirely blown away. In several areas whole groves of trees had been flattened like ripe wheat cut by an immense sickle. No freestanding tree had been able to resist the hurricane's power. Even the tamarind trees, strong and flexible—and, until now, regarded as indestructible—had been ravaged and broken by the fury of the storm.

The Malmédie house, one of the tallest on the island, had been severely damaged. There had been a moment the night before when the walls rattled so violently that M. de Malmédie and his son had decided to seek refuge in the pavilion, which, one story high, built of stone, and sheltered from the wind by the terrace, seemed the safest possible place. Henri had gone to Sara's chamber and found it empty; he assumed that she, terrified by the storm, had fled to the pavilion already. He and his father had gone down together and, indeed, they found that the girl had preceded them—but naturally they questioned neither her presence nor the terror she displayed at their arrival. Never, even for a moment, did M. de Malmédie or Henri suspect the real reason for Sara's actions.

The storm had finally abated, as I have said, around daybreak. No one in Port Louis had slept that night; they dared not sleep now. Every man was occupied in taking stock of his possessions to determine how much he had lost. The new governor was out in the streets at a very early hour; he ordered the garrison's troops to provide assistance wherever it was needed, and by that evening some of the disorder had already been put to rights.

If the citizens of Port Louis seemed especially anxious to erase all traces of the hurricane and return the town to its former appearance as quickly as possible, it was because they had a very special motive for wanting to do so. The festival of Yamsé, one of the most important annual events on the island, was rapidly drawing near. This festival, which is unknown in Europe, will play an important role in our story—so I must, I think, explain a bit about it.

As everyone knows, the great religion of Islam is divided into two sects, so different from each other as to be enemies: the Sunnis and the Shiites. The former group, which includes Arabians and Turks, recognizes Abu Bekr, Omar, and Osman as the legitimate successors of the Prophet Muhammad. The latter group, made up of the Persians and the Indian Muslims, regards these three caliphs as usurpers and claims that only Ali, son-in-law of the Prophet, was his true heir. During the many long wars fought between the Sunnis and the Shiites, Ali's son Hussein and sixty of his relatives were massacred by Omar's troops near the city of Kerbela, fighting bravely but vainly for their lives. It is the anniversary of this dreadful event that the Indian Muslims mark each year with a solemn festival they call Yamsé—a corruption of the cries of *"Ai, Hussein!"* chanted by the Persians. The festival is more than a religious celebration; it has come to include many native Indian customs and ceremonies born of other faiths, now long dead.

It was on the Monday following the storm, the day of the full moon, that the Lascars—representing the Shiite sect on île de France—had planned to bring the strange spectacle of the Yamsé festival to life once again. This year, the festival had been anticipated with even more curiosity and eagerness than it normally was. The Lascars, you see, are divided into two groups—those of the sea, and those of the land. The Lascars of the sea wear green robes, and the Lascars of the land wear white. Usually, each group celebrates the festival in its own way, with each seeking to outdo the other in pomp and show. Very often, this rivalry causes dispute. The Lascars of the sea, poorer but more courageous than the Lascars of the land, frequently use sticks and even sword blows to vent their anger and resentment—and on these occasions the police are obliged to intervene, in order to prevent an outbreak of mortal combat. This year, however, thanks to the efforts of some unknown mediator and no doubt to religious zeal, the two groups had agreed to put aside their animosity and unite for a single, concerted Yamsé celebration. The colony was abuzz with rumors that this year's festival would be both more peaceable and more lavish than it had been in a long time.

In a place as isolated as île de France, such an event as the Yamsé festival is awaited with impatience, even by those who have seen it every year of their lives. Even three months before the festival, it is a universal topic of conversation. Of particular interest is the gouhn, the central ornament of the celebration. Now that I have described the festival for you, I will describe the gouhn. It is a type of pagoda, three stories tall and built of bamboo, with each story becoming smaller the higher it is off the ground. The entire structure is covered in brilliantly colored paper, and each story is constructed separately and then bound to the others with strong ropes. The Lascars often spend months scouring the colony for its most skilled workmen: Indians, Chinese, free blacks, slaves—all may be called upon, though of course the slaves' wages are paid not to them but to their masters.

So it was with a feeling of universal happiness that the dejected inhabitants of storm-battered Port Louis learned that the hut containing the completed gouhn, sheltered by the bulk of Mont Pouce, had weathered the hurricane entirely damage-free. The Yamsé celebration would take place after all, in undiminished glory. Furthermore, the governor—both to mark his arrival and as a sign of goodwill—had arranged for horse racing to be added to the festivities. He announced that he would bestow the prizes himself, on the gentlemanly condition that horses must be ridden only by the men who owned them, according to English custom.

With the prospect of so much pleasure before them, the men and women of île de France banded together to clean away every trace of storm damage in short order. Scarcely a day had passed before the terror of the hurricane was replaced with the excitement of preparations for the Yamsé festival. Only Sara de Malmédie, absorbed in her own secret thoughts, appeared to have no interest in the event—which had always been a source of great anticipation for her in the past. It was customary for the island's entire aristocracy to attend both the Yamsé festival and the races that accompanied it, seated either in stands erected expressly for them or in their own elegant carriages; for the pretty Creole girls, it was a perfect opportunity to display themselves in all their finery. Naturally Sara's friends and family were shocked when the girl, who usually loved nothing more than to immerse herself in the social whirl, and for whom the announcement of a ball or any sort of spectacle was normally a cause for joyful excitement, seemed all but oblivious to the activity bustling around her. Even dear Henriette, who had raised Sara and could usually read her as clearly as if she were made of crystal, could not penetrate the mystery.

Let me hasten to assure you that Henriette, whose return to Port Louis I neglected to mention in the midst of the all the serious events I have been recounting, had been so terrified during the night of the hurricane that, despite still being shaken from the encounter with the shark, she had left the rivière Noire as soon as the wind had died down and had arrived in the city that day. Once she was reunited with Sara, the girl's unusual preoccupation had begun to worry her very seriously indeed.

It is true that, during the last three days, a great change had taken place in Sara's life. From the moment she had first laid eyes on Georges, his face and voice had been forever etched on her heart. Since that day she had heaved more than one involuntary sigh at the thought of her forthcoming marriage to Henri, a marriage that for ten years she had considered her unshakable destiny, and to which she had given her tacit consent—never dreaming that circumstances could ever arise that would turn the union into an obligation she could not fulfill. Now, though, and especially since the night of the governor's ball, she knew that to take Henri as her husband would condemn her to a life of misery. Most importantly, as we have seen, she had solemnly committed herself to Georges and promised that she would belong to no one but him. All this would have weighed heavily on any woman's heart, let alone a girl of sixteen. Little wonder, then, that everything that had seemed to be the most important things in her life before—dances, and parties, and fêtes—now appeared totally inconsequential.

The previous five or six days had not been free of anxiety for M. de Malmédie and his son, either. Sara's refusal to dance with Henri—or with any man, once she was told she could not dance with Georges—at the governor's ball; her early departure from that same ball; her obstinate silence whenever the subject of her marriage to Henri was brought up—all these things seemed strange, and father and son agreed that the rest of the preparations for the wedding should be made without the bride's participation. They would tell her what she needed to know when everything was ready. It was easier to conduct the matter this way, since no exact date had ever been set for the marriage ceremony itself. Sara was sixteen, they reasoned; old enough, after all, to fulfill the destiny M. de Malmédie had always had in mind for her.

With each resident preoccupied in his or her own way, the atmosphere in the Malmédie house was a frosty one. It was their habit to gather four times a day: for breakfast in the morning, dinner at two o'clock, tea at five, and supper at nine. For the last three days, Sara had asked for and received permission to have breakfast in her own room. This spared her one hour of discomfort, but it could not save her from the other three. The girl knew she could not plead indisposition at every meal, and she was forced to endure dinner, tea, and supper in the usual manner.

At around five o'clock on the day following the aftermath of the storm, Sara sat near the drawing room window working on a piece of embroidery—an activity that gave her the opportunity to keep her eyes down—while Henriette prepared the tea with all the attention English ladies usually devote to this activity. M. de Malmédie and Henri stood before the fire, speaking in low voices. All at once the door opened and the servant Bijou announced the arrival of Lord William Murray and M. Georges Munier.

This double announcement produced a variety of strange reactions from the occupants of the drawing room. The messieurs de Malmédie, astonished and sure that they must have misheard Bijou, requested that the servant repeat himself. Sara, flushing scarlet, kept her eyes resolutely fixed on her embroidery. Henriette, gazing distractedly at everyone by turns, overfilled the teapot so that boiling water spilled on the table and dripped on the floor.

Bijou repeated the names of the new arrivals, smiling widely as he did so. M. de Malmédie and Henri stared at each other in consternation for a moment more before the father pulled himself together enough to stammer, "Show them in."

Lord Murray and Georges entered the drawing room. Both were dressed formally in black, indicating a visit of some importance. M. de Malmédie moved forward to greet his guests; Sara, her cheeks still scarlet, managed to rise and nod before sinking back into her chair. Henriette, coming to herself, began to clean up the tea table.

At a signal from his master, Bijou brought in two more chairs—but

Georges, bowing, indicated that he wished to remain standing. Lord Murray spoke first, breaking the awkward silence. "Sir," he said to M. de Malmédie, "my friend, Monsieur Georges Munier, has asked me to accompany him to your home, to show my support for a proposal he wishes to make to you. It is my pleasure to see you again, and to express my sincere hopes that you will accept his request."

The governor followed these words with a graceful bow, which was returned by both father and son. "We owe a great deal to Monsieur Munier, of course," M. de Malmédie said. "We would be most pleased to be of service to him in any way we can."

Now Georges spoke. "If you are alluding to my rescue of Mademoiselle de Malmédie from the shark, please permit me to say that only God deserves your thanks for that; it was he who led me to her. Any man in my place would have done the same. Besides," he added, smiling, "you will soon see that my motives were not entirely unselfish."

Henri stepped forward. "Pardon me, sir, but I don't understand you."

"I'm about to explain myself, monsieur; do not worry."

"Should I leave, Uncle?" Sara asked, rising.

Georges bowed in her direction. "I hope, mademoiselle," he said, "that if a desire of mine can have any influence on you, you will do me the pleasure of remaining."

Sara sat down again. There was a moment of silence; then M. de Malmédie indicated, somewhat impatiently, that he was waiting for Georges to continue.

"Monsieur de Malmédie," Georges began, his voice perfectly calm, "you know who I am. You are acquainted with my family and my fortune—nearly two million francs at present. I beg your pardon for going into such detail, but I believe it is necessary."

"Monsieur," interrupted Henri, "I fail to see why any of this can possibly interest us."

"Ah, but you see, sir, I am not speaking to *you*, but to your father," said Georges serenely.

The muscles in Henri's jaw tightened. "I don't see why my father needs to know these things any more than I do."

"I am about to enlighten you," replied Georges coldly. He turned back to M. de Malmédie. "I have come to request the hand of your niece, Mademoiselle Sara de Malmédie."

M. de Malmédie looked stunned. "For whom, monsieur?"

"For myself."

"For *you?*" exclaimed Henri. He started forward convulsively, but a look from Georges halted him in his tracks. Sara turned pale.

M. de Malmédie still appeared utterly baffled. "For . . . for *you?*"

"As I said, monsieur," replied Georges, bowing.

"But—but surely you must be aware, monsieur, that my niece is intended to be my son's bride!"

"Yes, monsieur," said Georges, "but by whom?"

"By whom? By *whom?* Why, by *me,* of course!" spluttered M. de Malmédie.

"Allow me to remind you, sir," said Georges imperturbably, "that Mademoiselle Sara is your niece, not your daughter; she does not owe you a daughter's obedience in such matters."

M. de Malmédie seemed almost unable to speak. "I must say, sir," he managed, "that this discussion appears to me to be *quite* . . . extraordinary."

"I disagree with you," said Georges. "It is perfectly natural. I love Mademoiselle Sara, and I believe it is both my destiny and my duty to make her happy."

"But my cousin does not love you, sir!" cried Henri shrilly.

"Once again, you are mistaken, sir," said Georges. "Mademoiselle herself has authorized me to tell you that she does indeed love me in return."

"Impossible!" cried M. de Malmédie.

"No, Uncle," said Sara, rising. "Monsieur Munier has spoken the truth."

"*What?* How *dare* you—" His face white, Henri lunged in Sara's direction as if he would strike her. Georges moved instinctively to intervene, but Lord Murray restrained him.

Sara looked at Henri with frank disdain. "I am not afraid to say it," she said. "The life Monsieur Georges so bravely saved now belongs to him alone. I have sworn, and I swear again now, that I will never marry anyone but him." With the utmost grace and dignity, she held out her hand to Georges. With a deep bow, he pressed a kiss upon her fingers.

"Really, this is too much!" Henri cried. He seized a walking stick and brandished it menacingly, but Lord Murray now took his arm, just as he had taken Georges's a moment earlier.

Throwing a glance of complete scorn at Henri, Georges offered his arm to Sara and conducted her to the door, where he bowed low and she curtsied. Indicating that Henriette should follow her, Sara left the room.

"You see now how it is, monsieur," Georges said to M. de Malmédie, rejoining the other men. "You cannot possibly doubt Mademoiselle Sara's feelings for me. I ask you again for your response to my proposal."

"My response?" stammered M. de Malmédie, finding his voice at last. "My *response*? You—you have the audacity to hope that I will give you any response—other than the one you deserve, that is?"

"Whatever your answer may be, I await it, monsieur," said Georges calmly.

"I hope you expect nothing other than a refusal!" Henri cried.

"I am addressing your father, not you," said Georges coldly. "Let Monsieur de Malmédie give me his answer, and then you and I can speak of what concerns the two of us."

"Well!" huffed M. de Malmédie. "My answer, Monsieur Munier, is most definitely a negative one, you may be sure!"

"Very well," said Georges, inclining his head. "It is the reply I expected. Still, I have done my duty in formally asking you for Mademoiselle Sara's hand." He saluted M. de Malmédie as politely as if nothing untoward had passed between them, and then turned to Henri. "Now, sir," he said, "we must settle our difference. This is the second time you have raised a hand against me, as you might remember, even though it has been fourteen years since the first. Then you used a saber"—here he swept back his hair with one hand to show the scar that still marked his forehead—"and today a cane." He pointed to the walking stick Henri still held in his hand.

"Well?" demanded Henri.

"I demand satisfaction for both of these insults, sir," Georges said coolly. "You are not a coward, I know, and I trust you will behave in this matter as a gentleman should."

"I care nothing for your opinion of my conduct," sneered Henri. "My reply to you is a simple one."

"And what is this reply?"

"That I do not fight with mulattoes."

Georges turned white. A strange smile hovered about his lips. "And that is your final answer?"

"It is."

"Very well," Georges said again. "I know what my course must be."

Bowing to the Malmédies, he turned on his heel and departed, Lord Murray at his side.

"I see that I predicted rightly, I'm sorry to say," said the governor once the two men were out in the street once more.

"Yes—but you predicted nothing I didn't foresee myself," replied Georges. "However, the fact is that I returned to île de France to fulfill my destiny, and I must see it through to the end. I have a prejudice to fight. Either it must destroy me, or I it. In the meantime, milord, please accept my sincere thanks." He shook Lord Murray's hand warmly and, bowing, walked away.

Lord Murray watched until Georges disappeared around the corner of the rue de la Rampe, then shook his head. "Doomed, to be sure," he murmured to himself. "A great pity, really; such a waste of a noble heart."

XVII

THE RACES

The Yamsé festival was set to begin on the Saturday following the storm, and by then the people of Port Louis had worked so energetically that it was impossible to tell that, only six days before, the city had barely escaped destruction.

Early in the morning the Lascars of both sea and land set out from the Malabar camp outside Port Louis, located between the stream of Pucelles and the Fanfaron creek. Accompanied by a chorus of tambourines, flutes, and mouth organs, they filed down the road to town in pursuit of what they call "the quest." The two chiefs walked side by side at the head of the procession, dressed in their respective colors of green and white, each carrying an unsheathed saber with an orange impaled upon its point. Behind the chiefs marched two mullahs, bearing platters of sugar covered with Chinese rose petals, and behind them came the rest of the Indian phalanx.

Their quest began as soon as they reached the first dwelling on the outskirts of the city. The festival of Yamsé costs a great deal of money to produce, and it is customary for the revelers to stop at every house, whether large or small, and ask for a contribution to help defray the costs these poor people take upon themselves in order to render the ceremony as impressive as possible. Far from demeaning themselves, the "questors" conduct themselves with Oriental pride and touching dignity on these occasions. First the chiefs—who are always granted ready access to any dwelling—greet the master of the house by symbolically lowering the points of their sabers. Then the mullahs step forward to offer their dishes of sugar and rose petals, while other Indians pass plates to collect any money the home's inhabitants are willing to give. Finally the questors withdraw, murmuring *"Salaam"* again and again, leaving the impression that, rather than begging for alms, they have allowed strangers the honor of participating in the sacred ritual of the festival of Yamsé.

On île de France it is customary for the quest to include not just the houses in Port Louis but the vessels in the harbor as well. This task falls, naturally, to the Lascars of the sea. On this occasion, however, very little was asked of the beleaguered ship captains. The hurricane had inflicted horrific damages on them, and they were more in need of assistance than able to give it themselves.

Just as the Lascars reached the port, a new vessel that had signaled its arrival that morning arrived in the harbor between Labourdonnaie and Fort Blanc, flying the Dutch flag and firing a respectful salute, which the fort returned, as she glided across the water as gracefully as if guided by the hand of a goddess. It was immediately obvious that the ship had come from some location so far-flung that she had not been touched by the recent storm; not a sheet or a sail was out of place. With the aid of spyglasses, those on shore could see that the ship's entire crew was assembled on deck, and all wore full-dress uniforms in the colors of the Dutch king William; indeed, it seemed as if they were arriving for the express purpose of attending some splendid ceremony. Unsurprisingly, perhaps, they drew the immediate and complete attention of the Lascar chiefs. The ship had scarcely dropped anchor when the chief of the Lascars of the sea, accompanied by his plate bearers, pushed off toward her in a skiff.

Up close, the foreign ship was even more impressive. The beautiful brigantine seemed a floating temple to the renowned Dutch cleanliness; her deck was scrubbed as white as snow, and would not have disgraced even the finest drawing room. Her copper fittings shone like gold, and the gleaming companionway ladders, carved from the finest Indian woods, were so lovely that they appeared to be more decorative than useful. The same was true of her showpiece guns; if they had not been mounted aboard a warship, they might have graced a museum of artillery somewhere.

Captain Van den Broek, for so the commander of this fine vessel called himself, now appeared on deck. When he caught sight of the Lascars approaching in the skiff, he immediately grasped their purpose. Stepping forward, he graciously received the chief on board and, having exchanged a few words with the man in his native tongue— proof that he was no newcomer to the Indian seas—he presented him with the astonishing gift of a diamond worth at least a hundred louis. He had no other money on his person just now, he explained, and he hoped the Lascars would be content with this small offering.

Such a prize, which both exceeded the hopes of the worthy Muslims and completely belied the reputation for parsimony held by countrymen of Jean de With, so shocked the Lascar chief that he stood in silence for a moment, wondering if this display of generosity could possibly be genuine. It was only after Captain Van den Broek had assured him several times that the diamond was indeed intended to enrich the coffers of the Shiites, in whose welfare he took a lively interest, that the chief roused himself enough to show his thanks by proffering the dish of sugar and rose petals with his own hands. The Dutch captain took a decorous amount of the sweet on his fingertips and pretended to eat it with relish, to the great appreciation of the Indians, who then disembarked from the ship with many enthusiastic *salaam*s. Such a triumph induced them to make the rounds of the other vessels in the harbor—but they did so, as might be expected, with much less success.

———

The races were to be held the next morning. Races were always an important event on île de France, but this year, coinciding as they did with both the festival of Yamsé and the arrival of a new governor, they were sure to be spectacular indeed. As always, the parade grounds at champ de Mars were the designated site; every bit of public space was crowded with spectators by dawn. The day's principal attraction was to be the gentlemen's race, but it was by no means the only one. There were several other races that, since the common people were allowed to participate, often proved even more popular; these included a pig chase, a sack race, and a pony race. For each of these, just as for the main event, the governor handed out the prizes. The winner of the pony race received a magnificent double-barreled Menton hunting rifle, and the winner of the sack race a handsome umbrella; as for the winner of the pig chase, he was allowed to keep the animal itself as a trophy. The prize for the gentlemen's race was a beautiful silver-gilt cup of surpassingly fine workmanship.

At ten o'clock in the morning the members of île de France's fashionable set began to arrive at the parade grounds. As in London and Paris, stands had been erected for the wealthier spectators, but it was also customary for many of the belles of Port Louis to remain seated in their open carriages, so that they might best display themselves directly across from the gentlemen sitting in the governor's box. Most of the young men were on horseback, preparing to ride alongside those racing on the inner track, while the members of the Port Louis Jockey Club circulated on the lawn, making and accepting bets with careless Creole prodigality.

By ten thirty all of Port Louis was assembled at champ de Mars. In the most elegant carriages sat Mademoiselle Couder and Mademoiselle Cypris de Gersigny, still one of the loveliest women in île de France, whose magnificent raven-black hair has become legendary even in the salons of Paris. There were the six Druhn sisters, so fair, fresh, and delicate that the carriage in which they usually rode together was known as "the Basket of Roses." Still, on this day, the occupants of the governor's box might have claimed the grand prize for loveliness. If you have not visited the colonies, especially île de France, you cannot imagine the charm and grace of the Creole women—most of them with velvet-dark eyes and ebony tresses, but a few English lasses with the gleaming golden hair, slender necks, and translucent skin of the North. In the eyes of the young men, the bouquets these beauties held in their slender hands were worth more than all the Odiot cups, Menton rifles, and Verdier umbrellas that the governor, even with his boundless generosity, could ever bestow.

In the front row of Lord Murray's box that morning, between her uncle and the governess Henriette, sat Sara de Malmédie. Henri strolled the grounds, taking all bets offered against his winning of the gentlemen's race—which were few, considering that Henri, besides being well known as an excellent rider, owned a horse that was reputed to be the fastest on île de France.

At eleven o'clock the band played to signal the first race—which was, as I have said, a pig chase. I imagine that most of my readers are acquainted with this odd pastime, since it is still common in many villages in both France and England. A pig, his rear end well greased, is set free upon the track, and the competitors must attempt to seize him by the tail. The man who catches the pig is declared the winner. This particular race was open to the public; the names of the contestants were not even written down.

Two Negroes duly led in the animal. He was a magnificent hog, enormous in size, already greased up and ready to be chased. The crowd roared at the sight of him, and the pursuers—Negro, Indian, Malay, Malagasy, and native-born islander—crashed through the barriers separating them from the track and hurled themselves toward the animal.

The pig, terrified, took flight—but measures had been taken to ensure that he would not escape, and his forelegs had been loosely tied to his hind ones as one would bind a horse to keep it from breaking into a run. He was thus able to run only at a moderate trot; the mob soon overtook him, and the usual frustrations ensued.

As you may imagine, in such a game, chance is not usually with those who lead at the start. A freshly greased pig's tail is nearly impossible to seize, and the animal escapes easily from its pursuers at first. But as successive attempts rub off more and more of the lard, the hog realizes that the intentions of those hoping to seize him are not so ridiculous after all. He begins to emit squeals that alternate with frightened shrieks. From time to time, when the attack is too aggressive, he may turn against the men chasing him—who, according to their courage, either continue their pursuit or drop out of the race. Finally the moment comes when the tail, now bare of grease and returned to its natural state, no longer slides out of the hands that grasp it, and finally its owner is vanquished.

This race followed the ordinary progression. The unfortunate pig escaped easily from his early pursuers and, though bothered by the cords on his legs, attempted to gain on the racers. However, a dozen of the best and fastest runners grabbed at the ropes and then the tail of the poor animal so quickly that he had no time to react. Capture was inevitable for the hog, no matter how bravely he tried to escape. Eventually, though, five or six of the contestants grew winded and dropped out of the race—but, as the number of racers diminished, the chances of those who persisted increased. They redoubled their efforts accordingly, urged on by the shouts of the spectators.

Among the men still in the race were two of our old acquaintances, Antonio the Malay and Miko-Miko, the Chinese merchant. Both had stayed close on the pig's heels from the beginning; his tail had slipped through their fingers a hundred times, but each was determined to catch his prey. A few moments more, and they were the only ones left in the chase. Now the event became truly interesting. The crowd roared, and extravagant bets were freely exchanged.

As it turned out, there were only ten minutes left in the chase. The pig, grunting and lunging backward without intimidating his enemies—who, like Virgil's shepherds, took turns seizing his tail—in the least, and having by now made almost a complete circuit of the parade grounds, was tiring. Antonio managed to grab him, and for an instant he was believed to be the winner, but the animal used the last of his strength to jerk his tail from the Malay's fingers once again. Miko-Miko immediately saw his chance and threw himself at the prize, clinging with both hands and allowing himself to be dragged along the dusty ground as he tugged at the tail with all his might. Antonio followed, scowling, sure that he had lost the game but keeping ready nonetheless, just in case his rival lost his grip. After towing the Chinese peddler a considerable distance, the pig slowed and stopped, too weakened to run any farther but still resisting Miko-Miko, who, also exhausted, continued to yank in the opposite direction. The crowd howled with laughter as man and pig writhed together on the ground—then, suddenly and violently, flew apart! The animal rolled forward and Miko-Miko tumbled backward. Antonio lunged, elated and certain that he had another chance for victory—but his joy was short-lived. He found himself unable to seize the pig's tail, and for very good reason—it was no longer attached to the unfortunate pig, but was still clutched in Miko-Miko's hands. The peddler rose from the ground, holding his trophy aloft. This was a new case for the judges. They deliberated for a few minutes and then decided by a majority vote of three to two that, since Miko-Miko would surely have captured the entire animal if it had remained attached to its tail, he should be declared the winner. The Chinese merchant triumphantly claimed his prize, grasping the pig's hind legs and walking him from the grounds as if he were a wheelbarrow; Antonio the Malay withdrew, grumbling, into the crowd—which treated him with the sort of honor one might expect a rowdy mob to reserve for a man who has just lost a contest.

Now the spectators rose, buzzing about the pig chase, but they soon settled back into their seats once the sack race was announced.

The contestants were to race from the starting post to the governor's box, a distance of about 150 feet. At the signal, the racers— around fifty of them—emerged from the small hut they had been assigned as a dressing room, approached the starting line, and arranged themselves in a row.

This may seem a rather large number of men willing to compete for an umbrella, no matter how magnificent it may be, but the reader should know that umbrellas are, mysteriously, highly sought-after in the colonies, especially among the Negroes of île de France. Lord Murray had been well advised in choosing that particular item as the sack race trophy.

I'm quite sure that most of my readers have witnessed a sack race at least once in their lives. Each competitor is enclosed in a sack that covers his arms and legs and is tied about his neck, so that he cannot run, but is forced to make a series of hops instead. It is always very funny; this particular race was even more so because of the strange variety of heads popping out of their respective sacks—as in the pig chase, a large number of Negroes and Indians of all colors had chosen to take part.

Foremost among the competitors were the black servants Télémaque and Bijou. Having assumed the rivalry that existed between their respective masters, the two rarely met without exchanging insults that often degenerated into fisticuffs. Now, since their hands and feet were hidden inside the sacks and three or four other racers stood between them, they had to be content with glaring ferociously at each other.

Just before the starting gun was fired, a new competitor bounded from the dressing room hut and took his place among the racers. It was none other than the recently disgraced Antonio the Malay.

At the sound of the opening shot, all of the sack racers began hopping like kangaroos; they bumped heavily against each other, fell backward, tripped forward, and scrambled with difficulty to their feet only to bump, fall, and trip again. For the first sixty feet of the race, it was impossible to predict the winner. Several of the contestants were clumped together so closely as to be indistinguishable, and the standings changed so often due to falls that in an instant the first racer might be last, and the last first. Still, even amid the chaos, three racers could be distinguished as slightly ahead of the pack: Télémaque, Bijou, and Antonio the Malay. By the time they reached the hundred-foot mark, it was clear that one of these three would emerge from the race victorious.

Antonio, with his usual wiliness, had immediately noticed the palpable hatred that existed between Bijou and Télémaque and decided to use it to his own advantage. He had started out between the two rivals, but a well-calculated fall allowed him to move to one side so they were next to each other. Sure enough, they bounded ever closer to each other, scowling and muttering invective, and the movements of their fists beneath the cloth sacks made it obvious to all that, had they not been restrained, they would soon have been trading punches. During all of this, Antonio—stealthily but steadily—gained ground.

The Malay was five or six feet ahead of Bijou and Télémaque before they noticed him; calling a momentary truce, both of them tried with gigantic hops to regain their lost advantage. Some progress had been made, particularly by Télémaque, when Antonio had a timely stumble and the Muniers' servant was able to pass him. The finish line was by now only ten feet away. Bijou gave a yell of rage and, jumping desperately, drew near his rival—but Télémaque was not about to relinquish his lead without a fight, and he hopped so impressively that everyone was sure the prize umbrella would soon be his. The next moment, though, he took a false step. He wavered briefly while the crowd roared, then fell in a heap. Still, he found a way to use the tumble to honor his house—by falling directly in Bijou's path. The Malmédie servant, unable to swerve in time, tripped inelegantly over Télémaque's prostrate form and went sprawling in his turn.

At that instant, as they lay with limbs tangled in the dust, the same idea occurred to both of the archenemies at once—that it was better to let a third party win the race than to cede victory to the hated rival house. Both of them struggled to their feet, but to the astonishment of the crowd, rather than continuing the race they rushed at each other as aggressively as the sacks trapping their hands and feet would allow. Scuffling and wrestling, they allowed Antonio to reach the finish line unimpeded. The grinning Malay collected his prize and held it aloft before the envious eyes of the black onlookers, while Bijou and Télémaque continued to fight until they were finally dragged apart—the former minus a small piece of his nose, and the latter with a badly mangled ear.

The spectacle of the sack race over, the ponies were brought out. Thirty stout, handsome little animals from Timor and Pégu, ridden by Indian, Malagasy, and Malay jockeys, trotted from the holding area to a burst of enthusiastic applause; this event was especially popular with the island's black population. These ponies, only marginally tamed, generally provided a much more interesting contest than the sleek, well-trained racehorses. The crowd cheered as the jockeys were obliged to use every bit of their strength and skill to restrain their impatient mounts. Lord Murray now gave the predetermined signal, and the race was on.

The ponies shot away from the starting line like a flock of birds, their feet hardly seeming to touch the ground. Predictably, they had gone only a short distance before a number of them bolted. Fully half disappeared into the woods surrounding the parade grounds, despite the desperate efforts of their riders to keep them on the track. When they reached the bridge, a third of the remaining animals shied and refused to cross—so that already only seven or eight ponies were left, a few of which ran aimlessly, having thrown their riders.

This race consisted of two complete circuits of the parade grounds, so the contestants crossed the finish line in a cloud of dust and continued on their way. Turning the first corner, they vanished. Loud shouts reached the straining ears of the crowd, followed first by hoots of laughter, then a moment of dead silence. It eventually became clear that only one horse remained on the track—all the others had now bolted into the Château-d'Eau woods or the creeks, or under the bridge.

Ten minutes went by; then a single pony appeared at the top of the hill—but with no rider. The animal had apparently galloped through the town, passed the church, and reentered the parade grounds by instinct alone. Now other horses and riders could be seen returning from various directions, but it was too late. In the blink of an eye the riderless pony crossed the finish line and came to a stop, seemingly aware that he had won the race. The handsome double-barreled Menton rifle was duly awarded to the intelligent animal's owner, a colonist by the name of Saunders. The other ponies returned, one by one, to the holding area—except for those that had bolted so completely, their owners did not recover them for a day, or even two. Thus the pony race was concluded.

A thirty-minute intermission was now held, during which programs were distributed and final wagers placed. Among the highest bettors was Captain Van den Broek. Immediately upon stepping ashore, he had gone straight to the shop of M. Vigier, the town's premier goldsmith and jeweler, and exchanged a hundred thousand francs' worth of diamonds for banknotes and gold. Now, to everyone's surprise, he staked all of it on a horse whose name was unknown on the island—one Antrim.

There were four steeds entered in the race:

Restoration, ridden by Colonel Draper;

Virginia, ridden by Monsieur Rondeau de Courcy;

Jester, ridden by Monsieur Henri de Malmédie; and

Antrim, ridden by Monsieur (here the program listed two asterisks, but no name).

The favorites were Jester and Restoration, who had won last year's event. Even more was expected from them this year, ridden as they were by their owners, who both had reputations as highly skilled horsemen. Virginia, on the other hand, was at a disadvantage since she was running her very first race.

Captain Van den Broek continued to back Antrim, despite the multitude of charitable warnings that he was acting like a veritable fool; the spectators' curiosity about this strange horse and rider only grew as a result.

Since the horses were to be ridden by their owners, there was no weighing-in of the jockeys. It was no great surprise, then, when neither Antrim nor the rider who, instead of giving his name, used a hieroglyphic symbol to represent himself, appeared in the tent where the mounts were saddled and bridled; it was simply assumed that the mysterious duo would simply appear at the starting line when it was time for the race to begin.

In due course the competitors emerged from the tent—and at that moment the unknown fourth rider who had been the source of so much curiosity could be seen approaching from the direction of the Malabar camp. His appearance, rather than solving the mystery that swirled around him, served only to increase it. He was dressed in an Egyptian style that revealed lavish embroidery beneath the burnoose that concealed half of his face, and he was mounted in the short-stirruped manner of an Arab rider. His horse's trappings, moreover, were Turkish. As for Antrim, once they had seen him no one doubted that he was to be the stranger's mount. His sleek lines and obvious rapport with his master seemed to justify the confidence shown in advance by Captain Van den Broek.

No one recognized the stallion or his rider but, since he had entered the race under the governor's auspices and must therefore be a friend of Lord Murray, the crowd respected his wish to remain incognito. Only one person in the governor's box, perhaps, guessed the stranger's identity and leaned forward, cheeks crimson, to be sure she was correct. This, of course, was Sara.

The competitors now took their places in a row at the starting line. Since there were only four gentlemen racing, and since it was expected to be mainly a contest between Jester and Restoration, whose reputations had frightened away most of the other potential contenders, the judges had decided to draw out the spectacle a bit and give the watchers an especial treat by having the riders make two circuits of the track instead of the single one that was customary in a gentlemen's race. It was a total distance of three miles—one league—which would give the advantage to the horses that led out of the starting gate.

The signal was given, and the race was on. As we have seen, in such circumstances the beginning is often meaningless. Halfway through the first turn, Virginia—who, as I have said, was racing for the first time—had a lead of nearly thirty paces. Antrim was nearly alongside her, while Restoration and Jester, visibly restrained by their riders, brought up the rear. By the time they reached the top of the hill about two-thirds of the way around the track, Antrim had gained half a length, while Restoration and Jester were now ten paces closer. The second round of the race had begun. The audience leaned forward in their seats as the racers passed the governor's box, clapping their hands and shouting encouragement to the riders, and Sara—by intention or chance—let her posy of flowers drop to the track. The mysterious rider saw the blossoms fall; with magnificent grace and without breaking stride, he leaned down, perilously close to the horse's belly, as Arabian riders do when they play djerid, and swept up the bouquet. Saluting the flowers' fair owner he resumed his course, having lost barely ten paces and seemingly unconcerned with regaining them.

In the middle of the second pass around the track Virginia was neck and neck with Restoration, while Jester was only one length behind them. Antrim still trailed by seven or eight paces, but as his rider used neither whip nor spurs the crowd assumed that he was only waiting for the right moment to make up the distance.

Just as they reached the bridge, Restoration stepped on a pebble. Horse and rider went tumbling to the ground; Colonel Draper, still in the stirrups, urged his mount to stand, and the animal half rose with a great effort, then fell once more. The noble creature had broken a leg.

The three remaining competitors continued to race. Jester had taken the lead, with Virginia two lengths behind him and Antrim alongside her. Virginia began to lose ground as the hill grew steeper, while Jester retained the lead and Antrim, without any visible effort, began to gain on him. By the time they reached the Dreaper mark

Antrim was only one length behind his rival. Henri de Malmédie, already feeling that victory was his, broke out the whip. The crowd, twenty-five thousand strong, began to cheer enthusiastically, waving their handkerchiefs and shouting encouragement to the racers.

The stranger, leaning over his stallion's neck, seemed to whisper a few words in Arabic—and suddenly Antrim, as if he had understood, redoubled his speed. They were a scant twenty-five paces from the finish line, just passing the first set of stands. Jester was barely a head in front of Antrim, and it was only now that the mysterious rider, seeing that he had no time to lose, lightly touched his spurs to Antrim's flanks. Rising in the stirrups, he threw back the hood of his burnoose.

"Monsieur Henri de Malmédie!" he shouted to his rival. "I return one insult for the two you have dealt me—but I trust you will find this one is worth both of yours!" With that, Georges—for indeed it was he—raised his arm and bloodied Henri de Malmédie's face with a lash of his whip.

Then, digging his spurs into Antrim's flanks, he surged across the finish line, winning the race by a full two lengths. Instead of stopping to claim his prize, however, he continued at a gallop and, to the amazement of the crowd, disappeared into the woods surrounding the Malartic tomb.

Georges was right: In exchange for the two insults dealt him by M. de Malmédie, he had just returned a single—but public, terrible, and bloody—insult of his own. It would decide his entire future, for it was not only the provocation of a rival; it was a declaration of war against all whites.

Georges found himself inexorably and irresistibly drawn to face the prejudice that he had come so far to seek, and they would fight man-to-man, like two mortal enemies.

XVIII

LAÏZA

Georges had returned to his father's house in Moka and was in the room he had had furnished for himself, contemplating the position he had now put himself in, when a servant knocked and said a black man was asking to see him. Thinking, naturally, that Henri de Malmédie had sent a message, he requested that the visitor be admitted.

At his first sight of the new arrival, Georges knew he had been mistaken—he had a vague recollection of having met this man somewhere before, but he could not say where.

"You don't recognize me, monsieur?" asked the Negro, after a moment.

"No," admitted Georges, "but we have met already, haven't we?"

The man nodded. "Twice."

"But where?"

"First at the rivière Noire, when you saved the young woman. The second time was—"

"Yes," interrupted Georges, "now I remember! And the second time?"

"The second time," continued the black man, "was when you gave us our freedom. My name is Laïza, and my brother is called Nazim."

"Where is your brother now?"

"During our slavery, his only desire was to return home to Anjouan. Now that he is free, thanks to you, he has gotten his wish. He has left île de France and should be with our father even now. Let me thank you again, on his behalf."

"And you?" asked Georges. "You remain here, even though you are a free man? Strange."

The Negro smiled. "You will soon understand my reasons for that."

"Well?" Georges asked, interested despite himself.

"I am the son of a chief," Laïza began. "Half Zanzibarian, half Arab. I was not born to be a slave."

Georges smiled involuntarily at the other man's pride, seemingly unconscious of the fact that it was younger brother to his own.

"A Querimbo chief took me prisoner in battle, and sold me to a slave trader," Laïza continued, without appearing to notice Georges's expression. "It was he who sold me to Monsieur de Malmédie. I offered to buy back my freedom for twenty pounds' worth of gold dust, but they would not believe a Negro could have that much, and refused. I tried to convince them at first, but after a while"—he shrugged—"something changed in my life, and I no longer thought of leaving."

"Perhaps Monsieur de Malmédie treated you well, as you deserved?" suggested Georges.

Laïza shook his head. "No, it was not that. My brother Nazim was captured three years after me, and by a stroke of good fortune he was sold to the same master. But he lacked my reasons for wanting to stay; from the first moment he wanted only to escape. You know the rest, for it was you who saved him. I loved my brother as if he were my own child, monsieur. And you"—he crossed his palms on his chest and made a slight bow—"now I love you as a father. So! Let me explain the state of things; I think you will find it quite as interesting as we do. On this island, you see, there are eighty thousand men of color, and only twenty thousand whites."

"Yes—I've counted them already, myself," said Georges, smiling.

"I had wondered about that," admitted Laïza. "Now, of these eighty thousand colored men, at least twenty thousand are capable of bearing arms, whereas the whites—even including the eight hundred English troops in the garrison—have four thousand men at most."

"I'm aware of that as well," Georges said.

"Surely you can guess the rest!"

"Please explain it to me."

"We have resolved to be rid of the whites, monsieur. We have suffered enough! We have earned the right to avenge ourselves."

"And?" Georges prompted.

"Everything is ready, except—" Laïza paused, then met Georges's inquiring gaze. "We still need a leader, monsieur. Two men have been suggested, but neither of them is truly fit for such an undertaking."

"And who are these men?"

"The first is Antonio the Malay."

A scornful smile flashed across Georges's lips. "And the second?"

Laïza inclined his head. "It is I."

"You?" Georges gazed steadily into the eyes of the other man, who was setting such a strange example of modesty for the whites by recognizing that he was not worthy of the position to which he had been elevated.

"Yes," the Negro replied. "But our venture requires only one leader, not two."

"Ah," said Georges, nodding, and assuming that Laïza desired all of the power to himself.

"One supreme and absolute commander, whose worth will never be called into question," continued Laïza.

"Well; and where will you find such a man?"

"He has been found already," said Laïza, fixing his eyes on Georges. "The question is whether or not he will accept the post."

"He would be risking his neck," observed Georges.

"No more than the rest of us!" Laïza exclaimed.

"But what guarantee would you give him?"

"The same one he will give us—the end of persecution and slavery; vengeance; and a future of liberty!"

"What is your plan, then?"

"Tomorrow, after the Yamsé festival, when the whites are tired from the day's pleasures and, after watching the burning of the gouhn, have gone home, the Lascars will remain alone on the riverbanks. Then the rest of us will join them—Africans, Malays, Malagasies, Malabars, Indians; everyone who has agreed to take part in the uprising. We will elect our leader then, and he will direct our movements after that." He paused. "Simply say the word, monsieur, and you will be that leader."

"Who sent you here, to make this proposal?" Georges demanded.

"No one, monsieur."

"It was your own idea to come?"

"Yes."

"And what gave you this idea?"

"You, yourself, monsieur."

"What do you mean?"

"It seems to me," said Laïza, "that you cannot fulfill your own desires without helping us."

"My own desires?" Georges repeated. "What do you think I desire?"

"To wed the Rose of the rivière Noire," Laïza said simply. "What is more, you want to destroy Monsieur Henri de Malmédie. You wish to possess the one, and revenge yourself on the other—and we alone can offer you the means to do both of these things. They will never give her to you as a bride of their own accord, monsieur; nor will they allow young Monsieur de Malmédie to stand against you in a duel."

"Who told you I loved Sara?" Georges demanded.

"I could see it, monsieur."

"You mistake yourself."

"No." Laïza shook his head sadly. "One may deceive the eyes, but never the heart."

A faint smirk crossed Georges's lips. "Ah. Are you to be my rival, then?"

"No," Laïza said again. "Only a man who has the hope of being loved himself can be a rival, and the Rose of the rivière Noire will never love the Lion of Anjouan."

"Are you not jealous?'

"You saved her life, and it belongs to you. It is only right. I, alas, will not have the happiness of dying for her." Laïza's eyes met Georges's. "But you must admit, monsieur, that I proved myself worthy of such an honor."

"Certainly, you are very brave," murmured Georges. "But can we count on the others?"

"I can only speak for myself," said Laïza. "You will find me unfailingly constant, courageous, and loyal."

"You will obey me without question?"

"Yes—in all things, monsieur."

"Even in what touches—" Georges stopped.

"The Rose of the rivière Noire. Yes." Laïza completed the sentence.

"Where do you come by such devotion to me?" Georges asked, a bit wonderingly.

"The Stag of Anjouan—my brother—would have died under the lash if you had not purchased his life," replied Laïza simply. "And I— the Lion of Anjouan—would have spent the rest of my life in chains if you had not freed me. The lion is the strongest of animals, but also the most generous; and I am strong and generous as well. That is why I am called the Lion of Anjouan." Crossing his arms on his chest, he met Georges's gaze proudly.

"Well." Georges extended his hand to Laïza. "Give me one day, to make my decision."

"May I ask, monsieur, what will influence you to say yes or no?"

Georges looked at him. "Today I insulted Henri de Malmédie. Grievously, unforgivably—and publicly."

"I know it. I was there."

"If he will consent to a duel with me, I need have no further dealings with you."

Laïza smiled. "And if he refuses to fight?"

"Then I am at your disposal. Henri de Malmédie is known to be brave, though. He has fought two duels already, against other whites, of course; and he killed one of his opponents. He will have added a third insult to those he has already inflicted on me if he refuses to fight, and the die will thus be cast."

"Then you will surely be our leader," said Laïza, "for Henri de Malmédie may be brave, but he will never fight a mulatto."

Georges frowned; Laïza had voiced his own hidden thoughts. "And yet," he said, "how can a white man bear to live with the shame of having a mulatto's scar on his face?"

Just then Télémaque entered the room, clutching the ear Bijou had injured at the races. "Excuse me, sir, but that Dutch captain is here and wishing to speak with you."

"Captain Van den Broek?" Georges inquired.

"Yes, sir."

"Very well," said Georges. He turned back to Laïza. "Wait for me here. I will return shortly—in fact, I may have an answer for you more quickly than I anticipated."

Leaving his chamber, he entered the drawing room and strode toward the waiting visitor with open arms.

"Oho, my brother, so you recognize me!" said Jacques, clapping him warmly on the back.

"Of course—and I'm delighted to see you, I must say; especially just now."

Jacques grinned. "You came awfully close to missing out on that particular pleasure this time, my dear fellow!"

"Why?'

"I must be off, and quickly. The new governor is too much of an old sea fox for my taste."

"Not a fox, my brother. A wolf, perhaps, or even a tiger!" said Georges. "He is none other than the famous Commodore William Murray, who used to command the *Leicester*."

"The *Leicester*, eh? I should have known!" exclaimed Jacques. "In that case, we have an old score to settle. Yes, I understand it perfectly now."

"What has happened?"

"The governor came up to me after the races and complimented me on the beauty of my schooner. Very gracious, he was; nothing peculiar about it. But then he asked if he might have the honor of paying me a visit tomorrow."

"You think he suspects something?" Georges asked.

"Yes, and I—like a fool—suspected nothing. I asked him on board for breakfast tomorrow, and he accepted."

"And?"

"As I was ashore ordering supplies for breakfast, I noticed signals coming from Mont Découverte. I thought, just maybe, they might have a little something to do with me. I climbed the hill myself, armed with my trusty spyglass, and—sure enough, there was a ship responding to those signals, about twenty miles out."

"It was the *Leicester*?"

"No doubt about it. They're hoping to trap me, but as you know, Jacques wasn't born yesterday! The wind is in the southeast just now; the *Leicester* can't enter the Port Louis harbor without hugging the coastline. At that rate, it will take twelve hours at least to reach île des Tonneliers. I'm going to use that time to escape—and I've come looking for you in the hope that I can persuade you to come with me."

"I! Why should I leave île de France?"

"What the devil gave you the idea to slash that handsome fellow's face with a whip? That wasn't very polite of you, Georges."

"Didn't you recognize him?"

"Of course I did! Why do you think I bet a thousand louis against him? Fine stallion you've got there in Antrim, by the way."

"Jacques, it was Henri de Malmédie who, fourteen years ago, on the day of the battle"—Georges pushed the hair off his forehead, revealing his scar—"gave me this; don't you remember?"

"Blazes, I'd forgotten all about that! You *do* hold a grudge, my dear fellow! But, now, if I remember rightly, he paid dearly for that little piece of nastiness—a blow in the face in return for his saber cut."

"Yes," said Georges. "True enough; and so I was prepared to forget, if not forgive, that offense—but then he dealt me a second."

"Which was?"

"He refused to give me his cousin Sara's hand in marriage."

Jacques burst out laughing. "You *are* a prize, my brother! A father and son raise an heiress for fourteen years, just like a chick in a coop, in order to make her fit for marriage to the boy. Then, at the very moment when she is plump and ready for slaughter, here you come like a poacher to snatch her for yourself! Come now! How could they do anything but refuse you—you and I mulattoes into the bargain!"

"It was not simply that he refused to grant me Sara's hand. He also threatened me with his cane."

"Ah! Well, there he was certainly wrong. Did you knock him down for it?"

"No," said Georges, laughing at this remark, so typical of his brother. "I demanded satisfaction."

"And he refused? Of course he would; we are mulattoes. We may fight the whites, but they never fight us," mused Jacques.

"I promised him that I would make him fight me."

"And that is why, at the racetrack, in full view of a thousand spectators—*coram populo,* as we used to say at the Collège Napoleon— you gave him a lash in the face with your whip. Well played, my brother. You almost succeeded."

"Almost! What do you mean, almost?"

"I am sure he would have agreed to a duel then and there, but his friends talked him out of it. They said it was impossible—not one of them would agree to act as his second."

"Well, he may keep the mark of my whip on his face, then," said Georges, scornfully, "and he is welcome to it."

"I'm afraid it isn't as simple as that, Georges. They are planning something for you."

Georges knitted his brow. "Are they? And what might that be?"

"Henri de Malmédie was so keen to fight you that, to calm him down, they had to promise him that they would arrange for eight or ten men to ambush you one day soon, on your way home from Port Louis, and stretch you on a ladder, and give you twenty-five lashes with a whip."

"The blackguards! That is a Negro's punishment!"

"And what are we mulattoes, my brother? White Negroes, nothing more."

"So Henri's friends promised to punish me, eh? You're sure of it?"

"Yes, I was there," said Jacques. "They took me for a brave and thoroughbred Dutchman; didn't suspect me in the least."

Georges was silent for a moment. "Then my fate is decided," he said at last.

"So you'll come away with me?"

"No. I stay here."

Jacques took his brother by the shoulder. "Listen to me, Georges," he said. "Take an old sea dog's advice and leave with me today."

"It is impossible," said Georges. "It would look as if I were running away. And there is something else—I love Sara."

"You love Sara!" Jacques exclaimed. "What does this mean, 'I love Sara'?"

"It means that I must possess the woman or die."

"You're making a mistake," said Jacques, shaking his head. "It's true that I have never been in love, myself; but I would wager that one woman from the Comoros Islands is worth four of these Creole girls. You will agree with me, once you have tried them. I have six of them on my ship even now, and you can have any of them you like. I haul anchor at midnight. Come with me, and by daybreak we'll be twenty-five leagues from here, laughing at every fool white man on Mauritius—and I can promise you that if we should meet up with any of Henri's friends between now and then, a few of my strongest sailors will give them the punishment they had in mind for you."

"I thank you, but it is impossible," repeated Georges, firmly. "I cannot leave île de France."

"All right; I won't say anything more," Jacques said with a sigh. "You are a man, and when a man's mind is made up, it cannot be changed. I shall sail tonight, without you."

"Yes, go—but not too far," said Georges. "Otherwise you might miss a spectacular sight."

"Like what—an eclipse of the moon?"

"You will see a volcano erupting from the passe de Descorne to the peak of Brabant, and from Port Louis to Mahebourg—one that is well worthy of île de France."

"Ah, so you're planning some sort of pyrotechnical display? Come on, then, tell me more!"

"I will say only that in a week's time, these whites who despise and threaten me, who seek to treat me like a runaway slave, will be cowering at my feet."

"A revolt, then! Such a thing might work, if there were two thousand men on île de France to equal my hundred and fifty Lascars. I only call them Lascars out of habit; they're a brilliant lot—good Bretons, brave Americans, pureblood Dutchmen, and Spaniards—the pick of each nation's crop. But who have you got here, to carry off a coup d'état?"

"Ten thousand slaves, all of them weary of obeying, and ready to give the orders in their turn."

"Blacks, bah!" exclaimed Jacques, curling his lip scornfully. "Listen to me, Georges. I know these fellows well; I deal in them as my trade. They bear the heat well; they can live on a few bananas, and they work hard. They have many good qualities, no doubt about it. But they make poor soldiers; you can take my word for it. In fact, I was speaking to the governor about the blacks even today, when he asked what I think of them."

"What? How did that come about?"

" 'Captain Van den Broek,' he said to me, 'you have traveled widely and seem to have excellent powers of observation. Suppose there should be a slave revolt on an island of which you were governor. What would you do?' "

"And what did you say?"

"I told him I would simply set out barrels of rum in the streets through which the Negroes were planning to pass, lock my door, and then go to bed without a care in the world."

Georges bit his lip until the blood came.

"I ask you once more, will you come away with me?"

"My answer is the same. It is impossible."

"Then," said Jacques, "there is nothing more to be said. Shake hands, my brother!"

"Adieu, Jacques."

"Adieu, brother. Take my advice—do not trust the blacks too much."

"You are really leaving?"

"Blazes, yes! I'm not as proud as all that; I know how to flee, when the occasion calls for it, over the open sea. And if the *Leicester* wishes to follow me there for a game of skittles, I will be happy to oblige. But to stay here in the port, within range of Fort Blanc's guns and the Redoute Labourdonnaie? No, thank you! Now, let me ask you just once more. Will you come away with me?"

"No."

"All right, then. Good-bye."

"Good-bye."

The two brothers embraced one last time, then Jacques went to the bedroom where Pierre Munier slept, blissfully unaware of what was to come. Georges returned to his chamber, where Laïza awaited him.

"Well?" asked the Negro.

"You may tell the rebels that they have a leader."

Laïza crossed his hands on his chest, nodded his head once, and departed without another word.

XIX

THE YAMSÉ

The races, as I told you, had been only a part of the second day's entertainment. At around three o'clock in the afternoon, much of the vast and many-colored crowd that had covered champ de Mars began to move toward the plaine Verte. The fashionable set went home for dinner in carriages and on horseback, returning after the meal in time to be present at the Lascars' games.

These games consist of a series of symbolic races, dances, and fights, all accompanied by chanting and strange music. Mingling with these exotic sounds are the cries of "Bananas! Bananas!" "Sugarcane! Sugarcane!" and "Curds! Curds!" or "Kalou! Good kalou!" The criers are Negroes, who roam the crowds selling sugarcane, bananas, and curds and whey for their own profit or that of their masters. The Lascars' games last until six o'clock in the evening, when the lesser procession—so called to distinguish it from the first day's grand procession—begins.

The Lascars proceed between two rows of spectators. Some of them are half hidden under a sort of miniature pointed pagoda called an aïdoré, made to resemble the gouhn. Others are armed with sticks and broken swords; still others are half naked, clad only in rags. At a predetermined signal, all the Lascars rush forward. The men with the aïdorés begin to dance, spinning in wild circles. Those bearing sticks and swords begin to fight, thrusting and parrying their weapons with marvelous agility. Finally the men in rags beat their chests and roll on the ground in simulated despair, crying *"Yamsé! Yamli! Oh, Hussein! Oh, Ali!"* Meanwhile other Lascars circulate among the crowd, offering boiled rice and aromatic herbs to all.

This spectacle lasts until midnight, when the Lascars return to the Malabar camp in the same order by which they left it, and remain there until the following morning.

The next day the scene changes and becomes even more dazzling. After proceeding through the city once again, the Lascars return to their camp at nightfall to fetch the gouhn. This year in île de France, since it was a joint production by both groups of Lascars, the gouhn was larger and more splendid than it had ever been before. Covered with rich paper, brilliant and sparkling, lit from within by masses of blazing lamps, the outside hung with countless multicolored paper lanterns, the sides of the gouhn shimmered with ever-changing gleams of light. The structure was borne slowly forward, with crowds of men both inside and outside supporting its weight, singing a sort of dolorous, monotone hymn as they walked. Other men marched in front of the gouhn, carrying lanterns, torches, and various artistically wrought lamps. The dance of the aïdorés and the mock fighting resumed, yet more vigorously than before. The men in ragged clothes again beat their breasts and gave their mournful cries, and all the Lascars wailed *"Yamsé! Yamli! Oh, Hussein! Oh, Ali!"* even louder and more heartrendingly than they had the previous day.

The gouhn was intended to represent both the city of Kerbela, near which Hussein had perished, and the martyr's tomb. A naked man also marched in the procession, his body painted to resemble a tiger's hide, in order to commemorate the legendary beast that had guarded the imam's remains for several days after his death. From time to time he made a dash at the spectators, growling as if he meant to devour them, but his "keeper," walking behind him, restrained him with a rope, and a mullah at his side calmed him with mysterious words and gestures.

The gouhn was promenaded for several hours through and around

Port Louis; then its bearers proceeded toward the rivière des La-taniers, followed by the entire population of the town. The festival was nearing its end; the gouhn was now to be ceremonially burned, and everyone wanted to witness this final spectacle.

The men supporting the gouhn halted at the river's edge, and precisely at the stroke of midnight four men, all holding lighted torches, approached and set fire to each of its four corners. At the same instant the bearers let their burden drop into the water—but because the rivière des Lataniers is a small stream and only the base of the gouhn was submerged, the flames were not immediately doused. Rather, they rapidly climbed the pagoda's three stories, spiraling upward and leaping in the night air. It was a strange and fantastic moment. The crowd of nearly thirty thousand spectators stood in the flickering light, cheering and shouting in every conceivable language, waving their handkerchiefs and their hats. People thronged the riverbank and perched on nearby rocks and cliffs, looking like inky black spots as they grew closer to the shadows cast by the surrounding forests. The wealthy sat in palanquins and carriages or on horseback to complete the enormous circle. For an instant the water reflected the ruddy glare of the burning gouhn, and the multitude of people roared like the ocean; the trees stood out of the shadows like awakening giants. The sky could be seen only through a haze of crimson smoke that made each passing cloud resemble a wave of blood.

Soon, though, the light began to fade away. The faces in the crowd blended together, and the trees were again lost in the darkness. The sky paled, bit by bit reassuming its leaden hue, and the clouds grew shadowy and black once more. The gouhn continued to flicker weakly, unburned sections flaring up from time to time then fading to render the blackness even denser than before. The framework of the structure collapsed slowly into fragments; the water hissed and steamed. Finally the last sparks died away. The sky was now thickly filled with clouds, and the crowd found itself engulfed in darkness, which seemed all the more profound in contrast to the brilliant light that had preceded it.

Then, as always happens at the end of a public spectacle, especially after light shows or fireworks, a hum of voices rose to fill the silence, and the onlookers laughed, joked, and chatted as they made for home as fast as they could. The carriages departed with their horses at full gallop, and the palanquins with their Negroes at a full trot. As for those on foot, they walked rapidly in chattering groups.

Whether out of livelier curiosity or the love of gossip natural to their race, the Negroes and other colored men were the last to leave—but finally they did so, some taking the road to the Malabar camp, others disappearing upriver into the depths of the forest, and the rest following the line of the seashore. Very soon the site was completely deserted.

Fifteen minutes elapsed during which, save for the murmuring of the stream, the silence was absolute. The darkness, too, was nearly impenetrable; in the dim rays of moonlight that filtered through the passing clouds, a few enormous bats glided over the river—as if to smother the smoldering embers of the abandoned gouhn with their wings—and then vanished into the woods.

Suddenly there was a soft rustling sound, and two men approached the river from opposite directions—one coming from the direction of the Dumas battery, the other from Mont Longue. When they had reached the banks of the river, one of the men clapped his hands three times, while the other gave the same number of low whistles. At this obviously prearranged signal, an immense number of Negroes and Indians emerged from their hiding places among the trees and rocks. A moment before, they had been so well concealed that no one would have suspected their presence for an instant.

The crowd soon divided itself into two distinct groups. All of the Indians grouped themselves around one of the men standing on the riverbank; this was an olive-skinned individual who spoke in a Malay dialect. The Negroes gathered near the other man, who was black like them, and spoke in a mixture of the dialects of Madagascar and Mozambique.

The first man paced rapidly among the crowd, declaiming and gesticulating in the manner of a pretentious but ambitious lowborn man; a coarse intriguer. It was Antonio the Malay.

In contrast, the other man stood, calm and sober, nearly silent; he seemed to attract the gazes of his followers with no effort at all. He embodied the strength and brilliance of a born commander. This was Laïza, the Lion of Anjouan. He and Antonio were the chosen leaders of the slave revolt, and the men who crowded around them—the conspirators—were ten thousand strong.

Antonio was the first to speak.

"There was once," he began, "an island governed by apes, and inhabited by elephants, lions, tigers, panthers, and serpents. The number of those who were governed was ten times greater than the number of those who governed them. But the rulers were cunning baboons, and they had the talent to divide their subjects among themselves, so that the elephants lived at odds with the lions, and the tigers with the panthers, and the serpents with all. The result of all this was that whenever the elephants so much as raised their trunks, the apes caused all the other animals to march against them; and as strong as the elephants were, they were always defeated. If it was the lions that roared out, the apes again made all the other creatures fight them, and despite all their courage they were invariably enchained once more. The same was true for the tigers and the panthers, and the serpents, clever as they were, had it worst of all. If they so much as hissed, the apes caused the elephants, the lions, the tigers, and the panthers to march against them in their turn, and the serpents, no matter what they tried, ended up defeated. So it was that whenever there was talk of a revolt, the apes only laughed behind their hands. They knew they could use the same tactics that had been successful a hundred times before.

"Things went on in this way for a long time; yes, a very long time, indeed. But then one day a serpent even more cunning than the others had an idea. This serpent, you see, understood the rules of arithmetic. He calculated the number of apes, and saw that the rest of the animals outnumbered them eight to one. He waited until a great festival was held, and on that day he called a meeting of the elephants, lions, tigers, panthers, and serpents. 'Now,' he said to them. 'How many of you are on this island?' All the animals counted themselves, and found that they numbered eighty thousand. 'Very good,' said the serpent. 'Now count your masters, the apes. How many are they? Tell me, would it not be foolish if you failed to unite and rid yourselves of them? After all, there are ten of you for every single ape!'

"So the animals united, and they overthrew the apes. Then they were masters of the island. They enjoyed the best fruits, the most fertile fields, and the richest forests. They lived in fine mansions, and the apes became their slaves—and the apes' daughters, their mistresses. Do you understand what I am trying to say, my friends?" Antonio shouted.

Loud cries of *"Hurrah!"* and *"Bravo!"* erupted in response. Antonio's fable had made him a veritable Menenius.

Laïza waited patiently until the outburst of enthusiasm had died away. Then, holding his hand up for silence, he uttered these simple words: "There was once an island where the slaves wanted to be free. They rose up in one body, and fought and won their liberty. This island used to be called Saint-Domingue; it is now the Republic of Haiti. My friends, let us follow their lead—and like them, we shall be free."

Laïza's speech, though it received its share of applause and hurrahs, was too simple to move its listeners as Antonio's had. Noticing this, the Malay seized his chance. He motioned that he wished to speak again, and absolute silence fell.

"Yes," he said, "yes, Laïza has spoken the truth. I have heard tales of another island as well, far away, even beyond Africa, on which all black men are kings. But on the island of the animals, and on Laïza's island of Haiti, too, there was only one man chosen to be chief."

"That is true," said Laïza. "Antonio is right; power shared is power weakened. I agree that we must elect a leader, and only one."

"But who shall be this leader?" Antonio demanded.

"Those who are assembled here must decide that for themselves," Laïza replied.

"Our chief must be able to oppose the enemy stratagem to stratagem, strength to strength, courage to courage," said Antonio.

"Yes, that is so," agreed Laïza.

"He must have lived among both whites and blacks," Antonio continued. "He must hold blood allegiance to both. He must be a man who, though free, is prepared to sacrifice that liberty—indeed, to sacrifice all he has. Only a man such as this is worthy to be our leader."

"That is so," Laïza said again.

"I know of only one man who has all these qualities," said Antonio.

"As do I."

"Do you claim to be such a man?" Antonio demanded, indignantly.

"No." Laïza shook his head.

"Then you admit I am that man!" cried the Malay triumphantly.

"No, you are not," Laïza corrected him, "any more than I."

"Who is it, then?" challenged Antonio. Voices cried out, echoing him, Indians and Negroes alike, demanding to see this paragon of whom Laïza spoke.

The black man clapped his hands three times. The pounding of a horse's hooves was heard. Turning, the multitude saw a stranger riding toward them out of the forest, in the faint light of early dawn. The mysterious cavalier galloped at full speed straight into the center of the throng, and then reined in his mount so suddenly that the animal reared back on its haunches.

Laïza extended his hand toward the newcomer with an air of immeasurable dignity. "There he is!" he cried. "Behold your leader!"

There was a moment of stunned silence, then ten thousand voices cried out the name as one: "Georges Munier!"

"Yes, Georges Munier!" Laïza exclaimed. "You have asked for a worthy chief, one who can meet the enemy as an equal, who is willing to risk his wealth, his liberty, all he has, for your sake! Where will you find another such man?"

Antonio was speechless with shock. All eyes were upon Georges. The throng buzzed with murmurs.

Georges had known what would appeal to the men he was dealing with: He was dressed to satisfy their love of show, in a magnificent gold-embroidered burnoose over the caftan of honor he had been given by Ibrahim Pasha. The crosses of the Légion d'honneur and Charles III shone on his breast. His mighty stallion Antrim, trapped in scarlet cloth, stood restless and proud beneath him.

"But who will make the case for him?" Antonio cried, looking disgruntled.

"I will," said Laïza.

"Has he lived among us? Does he know our needs, our desires?"

"He has not lived among us," admitted Laïza, "but he has lived with the whites, and studied them closely. And yes, he knows our needs and desires—we have only one, do we not? Freedom, and nothing more."

"Let him begin by freeing his own three hundred slaves, then!" said Antonio, scornfully.

Georges answered him. "It has already been done, this very morning."

"Yes, yes!" shouted several men in the crowd. "We free now; M'sieur Georges has freed us!"

Antonio persisted. "He is too attached to the whites."

Georges shook his head. "Those ties were severed this morning as well, in full view of most of you."

"But," said Antonio stubbornly, "he loves a white woman!"

"Ah," said Georges, "there is another victory for men of color, for the white woman loves me, too."

"He will betray us," Antonio warned the crowd, "the moment the whites offer her to him as a wife."

"If they did offer her, I would refuse," rejoined Georges coolly. "I wish to have her by her own free will alone. I want no one to give her to me."

Antonio opened his mouth to protest again, but cries of "*Vive* Georges! Hurrah for our leader!" erupted, drowning his voice completely. Georges now signaled that he wished to speak, and the crowd grew quiet.

"My friends," he said, "the day is breaking, and it is time for us to part. Thursday is a holiday, and on that day you shall all celebrate as free men. I shall be here on that day, on this very spot, at eight o'clock in the evening. I shall put myself at your head, and we will march on Port Louis."

"Yes! Yes!" all the voices cried.

"One word more," Georges continued. "If we should discover a proven traitor among us, let us resolve now that he shall be speedily put to death. Do you agree to this arrangement?"

"Yes! Yes!" roared the crowd. "Death to traitors!"

"Good," said Georges. He turned to Laïza. "How many men do we have?"

"We are ten thousand strong."

"I have directed my men to give each of you four piastres," said Georges, addressing the crowd again, "so that you may each buy a weapon before Thursday evening. Until then!" Saluting the multitude, he left the same way he had come. His three hundred former slaves each opened a sack of gold and began to distribute the promised sums among the men.

The display had cost Georges Munier two hundred thousand francs, but he was a millionaire several times over; and, besides, he would have sacrificed his entire fortune to ensure the success of the project he had desired for so long. Finally, it was about to begin. The gauntlet had been thrown down at last.

THE RENDEZVOUS

Georges returned home in a surprisingly tranquil mood. He was one of those men whom inaction kills, and whom struggle only makes stronger. He occupied himself by planning what he would do in case of an ambush, mapping out an escape route through the Great Woods in which he had spent so much time as a young boy, and whose murmur and immensity, combined with the murmur and immensity of the sea, had made him the dreamy child we first met.

The unexpectedness and danger of the situation sat heaviest on the shoulders of poor Pierre Munier. For fourteen years the sole desire of his heart had been to see his children once more, and now that wish had been fulfilled. But their coming had turned his predictable life into an unending nightmare of worry: One son was the captain of a slave ship, forever at odds with both the elements and the law; the other, an ideological dreamer, struggling with prejudice and mankind as a whole—both of them fighting against the strongest forces in the world, and either liable at any moment to be crushed in the tempest. Chained by a lifetime habit of passive obedience, he now watched his sons march toward the abyss, powerless to hold them back. His only consolation lay in the words he repeated to himself, over and over: "At least I may be certain of one thing—that I shall die along with them."

Georges's fate would be determined very soon; only two days separated him from the catastrophic event that would make him another Toussaint L'Ouverture—or another Pétion. The young man's only regret during this time was that he had had no way to communicate with Sara for two full days, but it would have been imprudent to send to town for his regular messenger, Miko-Miko. Nevertheless, he was reassured by the conviction that she was as certain of his love as he was of hers. There are some souls who need only exchange one glance— one word—to understand each other completely, and to know that they may trust the other absolutely.

From time to time Georges would smile to himself at the thought of the great act of vengeance he was preparing to wreak on the society of île de France, and of the magnificent reward that would finally be his. He imagined what he would say at his next meeting with Sara: *I have not seen you in eight days, but in that brief time the face of the island has been changed as irrevocably as if a volcano had erupted. God himself tried to destroy everything with a hurricane, and he failed. I, on the other hand, desired to sweep away men, laws, and prejudice, all in one violent storm—and it seems that I am more powerful than God, for I have succeeded.*

Socially and politically dangerous situations, such as the one to which Georges was now exposing himself, hold a certain feeling of intoxication that will always draw conspirators and fuel their conspiracies. It cannot be denied that man's strongest motivation is pride. We are human beings—sons of original sin—and what greater thrill can we seek than the renewal of the struggle between Satan and God, between Jupiter and the Titans? True, Satan was defeated and cast out of heaven, and the Titan Enceladus was buried forever beneath Mount Etna. But it is also true that whenever Enceladus turns in his grave, he moves a mountain, and that Satan, exiled, became the king of hell.

Such thoughts as these could never be understood by poor Pierre Munier. Where Georges was able to sleep deeply and peacefully with his window half open, his pistol hanging from the headboard and his naked saber underneath his pillow, Pierre Munier could not rest at all. He armed five or six trustworthy Negroes and posted them all around the house while he himself stood guard on the Moka road, protecting his beloved son from any possible surprise attack.

The night passed quietly; blacks, when they hatch a plot, are known to be scrupulous secret keepers. They are not civilized enough, poor devils, to know the full extent of what their treason might mean.

The next day passed just as the previous night had, and that night it was the same. Nothing occurred that might lead Georges to believe that he had been betrayed. Only a few hours, now, separated him from his goal.

Laïza came at nine o'clock the next morning, and Georges immediately asked that he be admitted so they could speak privately. In general, nothing was altered. The rebels' feelings had not changed; if anything, they had intensified as a result of Georges's generosity. The plan was set; all ten thousand conspirators would gather, armed and ready, on the Lataniers riverbank at nine o'clock that night. At ten o'clock the insurrection would begin.

While Georges was still conferring with Laïza about the attitude of the men and their chances of success in the perilous enterprise they were about to undertake, he happened to glance out the window and see the distant figure of Miko-Miko approaching the house, his bamboo baskets slung over his shoulders as always. Hoping he might carry some message from Sara, whom Georges had not seen since the day of the races, the young man could not restrain himself from opening the window and signaling the honest Chinese merchant to quicken his pace. Laïza moved to withdraw, but Georges asked him to stay; there was still more they needed to discuss.

As Georges had thought, Miko-Miko had not come to Moka of his own accord. Immediately upon being ushered into the room, he drew from his pocket a daintily folded note, addressed in a beautiful hand with the single name "Georges." The young man's heart beat violently at the mere sight of the letter; he took it from Miko-Miko's hand, and retired to the relative privacy near the window to peruse its contents. The note was, of course, from Sara, and it read as follows:

My dearest friend,
     Go to Lord William Murray's house at two o'clock this afternoon, and
you will learn things that I dare not tell you, for they make me so happy.
After you leave him, come to me. I will wait for you in our pavilion.

Your Sara

Georges reread the letter twice. He was quite confused as to what
this double rendezvous might mean. What could Lord Murray possibly have to tell him that could make Sara so happy? And how could he
hope to present himself at the house of M. de Malmédie, in the broad
daylight of three o'clock and in plain sight of everyone?

Miko-Miko might have a few answers. Calling the merchant to his
side, Georges asked him to explain the letter—but as it turned out, he
knew nothing except that Mademoiselle Sara had sent Bijou to fetch
him (he had not recognized him at first; as it transpired, during his
fight with Télémaque the poor devil had lost a part of his nose, which
was already very flat); that he had followed Bijou to the Malmédie
pavilion where Sara waited, and that she had given him a piece of gold
and asked him to carry a note to Georges.

Still, the young man peppered him with questions. Had Sara written the letter in Miko-Miko's presence, or had she done it alone? Had
she appeared sad or joyful? Yes, was the answer; she had written it
while he stood in front of her. No, there had been no one else in the
room. And her face, as far as he could tell, had expressed nothing but
the most perfect serenity and happiness.

As Georges continued to question the peddler, a horse could be heard
approaching the house at full gallop. The rider turned out to be a messenger clad in the governor's livery. He was ushered to Georges's chamber directly and handed over a letter from Lord Murray, which read:

My dear fellow traveler,
     Since I last saw you, I have been very much occupied on your behalf; I
flatter myself that I have had a bit of success in the arrangement of your
little business.

Please be so good as to meet me at my home this afternoon at two o'clock, when I shall, I hope, have some good news for you.

> Your friend,
> Lord W. Murray.

The two letters coincided perfectly. Despite the risk, Georges resolved that he must keep the double rendezvous with Lord Murray and Sara—that it would be an act of near-cowardice not to—despite the danger he would no doubt invite by venturing into Port Louis, and especially by going to the governor's house. The young man's pride was at stake; furthermore, it was all the more important that he go, since Sara and Lord William were the only two people on the island upon whom he felt he could completely depend: the one for love, and the other for friendship.

Turning to the governor's messenger, he sent his respects to milord and said that he would meet him at the appointed time. This done, he sat down and began a letter to Sara. Let us peer over his shoulder, now, and see what he wrote:

Dearest Sara,

Let me first bless you for your sweet letter! It is the first I have received from you and, though it is brief, it tells me everything I need to know—that you have not forgotten me; that you still love me; and that you are mine, just as I am yours. I will go to Lord Murray's house at the time you have instructed me. Will you be there, too? You have not said so. Alas, my dear, the only truly happy news I can imagine would come from your lips, and it would be that I am to be your husband. Everything I have done, and everything I will do, shall be solely to make this desire a reality.

Stay faithful and strong, my dear Sara, as I shall. Our mutual happiness may seem very near to you, but I fear we must still endure terrible trials before we reach that sacred day.

Still, I believe in my heart that there is nothing in this world that can overcome the combined strength of fierce determination and deep, devoted love.

Trust in my love, Sara. I promise you, I will not disappoint you.

> Your Georges.

Georges folded the note and gave it to Miko-Miko along with the sort of generous remuneration that such a faithful servant deserved. The merchant slung his baskets across his shoulders again and set out for Port Louis, leaving the young man alone with Laïza—who had heard almost all, and understood everything—once more.

"You are going into town, then?" asked the Negro.

"Yes."

"It is unwise," said Laïza.

"I know, but I must go all the same. I would be a coward in my own eyes if I did not."

Laïza nodded. "Go, then. But if you are not at the rivère des Lataniers at ten o'clock—"

"Then you may assume that I am a prisoner, or dead. You shall march either to set me free, or to avenge my death."

"Yes," said Laïza. "You may count on us."

The two men, who instinctively understood each other so well that a gesture or a handshake was all they needed to communicate, now parted without exchanging another word.

It was ten o'clock, and a servant knocked on the door to ask if Georges would be joining his father for breakfast. The young man went to the table as calmly as if nothing out of the ordinary had happened. Pierre Munier looked at him with fatherly concern, but the untroubled expression on Georges's face reassured him.

"Well, my dear boy," Pierre said. "Seeing so many messengers come to you, I feared they brought you some evil news—but you are so at ease, I believe I was mistaken—God be praised."

"Quite so, Father," Georges said. "All is well. The revolt is still set for this evening at ten o'clock. The messengers you saw brought me two letters—one from the governor, who wishes to see me this afternoon, and the other from my dearest Sara, assuring me of her love."

Pierre Munier sat in astonished silence. This was the first time Georges had spoken to him either of the planned Negro insurrection or his friendship with the governor. He had heard whispers of both, though, and it shook him deeply to receive confirmation that his beloved son was treading so dangerous a path. He opened his mouth to speak, but Georges stopped him.

"Father," he said, smiling, "surely you remember the day fourteen years ago, when you performed with such valor, coming to the rescue of the volunteers and capturing the enemy flag, only to have it torn from your hands by Monsieur de Malmédie. That day you were heroic in the face of danger—great, noble, sublime—as indeed you always are. I swore then that one day I would make the world more just. The time has now come, and I will not renounce that oath. God shall judge who is to be the slave, and who the master; he will decide between the weak and the strong, between the martyrs and those who execute them. There is no turning back now."

Pierre Munier, powerless in the face of such determination, could voice no objection. He seemed to shrink in on himself, as if the weight of the entire world had settled on his shoulders. Georges ordered the servant Ali to saddle his horse, then quietly finished his breakfast. Finally he stood to go. Pierre Munier rose from his chair, holding his arms out to his son. Georges stepped close to him, and took the old man's head gently between his hands. His face, usually so inscrutable, bore an expression of filial love and tenderness he had never before allowed himself to show. He pressed his father's venerable head to his brow, and kissed the white hair.

"Oh, my son, my son!" murmured Pierre Munier.

"Dear father!" Georges said. "You shall be respected in your old age, or I shall go to an early grave. Adieu!"

He strode quickly out of the room. With a groan of anguish, Pierre Munier sank back into his chair.

XXI

THE REFUSAL

Georges had ridden about two leagues from his father's house when he overtook Miko-Miko, who was returning to Port Louis. Reining in his horse and signaling for the peddler to approach, he whispered a few words in the other man's ear. Miko-Miko nodded in understanding and continued on his way.

As he reached the foot of Mont Découverte, Georges began to encounter a few townspeople. He searched their faces, but detected nothing that might indicate that word of the planned revolt had leaked out. Satisfied, he rode on, crossing through the Negro camp and entering the city.

Port Louis was calm, the men in the streets preoccupied with their own affairs and seemingly free of worry. Merchant vessels lay quietly at anchor in the still waters of the harbor. The usual bunch of ne'er-do-wells idled at Pointe-aux-Blagueurs, and an American ship, arriving from Calcutta, had just dropped anchor in front of Chien-de-Plomb.

Still, Georges's presence seemed to create a certain sensation—but he attributed it to the incident that had occurred at the races, and to the audacity he had shown, as a mulatto, in striking a white man. Sev-

eral times groups of people stopped talking at his approach and stared
at him as he passed, murmuring their astonishment that he had had
the nerve to reappear in town. Georges's only reply was to return their
looks with one of his own so supremely disdainful that no one was
able to hold his searing gaze—or, indeed, to ignore the carved handles
of his double-barreled pistols, protruding from the holsters at his
sides.

Georges paid particular attention to the soldiers and officers he encountered as he rode through the town—but their faces reflected only
the tranquil boredom common to military men four thousand leagues
from home. If they had been aware of the events planned for that
evening, they would no doubt have worn airs of importance, even of
anticipation—but they did not, and Georges's mind was easy as he
continued on his way.

Finally he arrived at the governor's residence. Dismounting, he
handed Antrim's reins to Ali and instructed the servant to remain exactly where he was. Lord Murray had apparently ordered his doorman
to admit M. Munier as soon as he arrived, and Georges was immediately ushered into the parlor.

Waiting for him there were Lord Murray, M. de Malmédie, and
Sara. To the girl's surprise, Georges's face reflected dismay, rather
than happiness, when he saw her. He frowned slightly, and a small, almost bitter smile flashed across his lips. Sara, who had risen to her feet
on her lover's entrance, felt her knees grow weak, and sank slowly
back into her chair. M. de Malmédie, who had also risen, was as still as
a statue. A slight nod was his only greeting to Georges.

Lord Murray stepped forward and shook Georges's hand. "Well,
my friend," he said, "I am very happy to be able to give you a piece of
good news, which I hope will fulfill all your desires. Monsieur de
Malmédie here, wishing to put an end to the rivalries of color and
caste that have been the bane of île de France—indeed, of all the
colonies—for two centuries now, has agreed to give you the hand of
his niece, Sara, in marriage."

Sara, blushing, lifted her gaze to meet that of her lover—who, to
the astonishment of Lord Murray and M. de Malmédie, merely
sketched a silent bow.

The governor smiled. "My dear Monsieur de Malmédie," he said, "I see that my word alone is not enough to convince our young friend of his good fortune. Please, tell him yourself that you are ready to grant his request, and that it is your wish to bury forever all feelings of animosity between your families."

M. de Malmédie gave a somewhat forced nod; he was clearly struggling to control himself. "It is true, monsieur," he said at last. "Lord Murray has described my intentions rightly. If you still hold a grudge for something that took place fourteen years ago, at the surrender of Port Louis, I hope you will forget it—as my son has promised me he will forget your recent insult to him, which, after all, was much more grievous. As for your marriage to my niece, Lord Murray spoke the truth there, as well. I give my consent to the union, unless you wish to refuse it today."

"Oh, Georges!" Sara burst out, giving in for an instant to the strength of her emotions.

"Please, Sara," said the young man. "Do not judge me too hastily for the answer I am about to give. Believe me, I do only what is necessary. Since our meeting in the pavilion—since the night of the ball—indeed, since the moment I first saw you, you have been my wife. No other woman shall ever bear that title, which you have accepted despite the abasement that comes with it. Trust me when I tell you that what I say now is dictated by form and time alone."

He turned to Lord Murray. "I thank you, milord, a thousand times. I know that what has just happened is due in large part to your generosity and friendship. But from the moment Monsieur de Malmédie first refused me Sara's hand, and his son Henri insulted me for the second time, I believed it my duty to inflict a public, unforgivable punishment. That being done, I have severed all connection with the whites. There can be no further dealings between us. Monsieur de Malmédie may well have resolved to settle his differences with me, for whatever reasons of his own, but I can never do the same. If Mademoiselle Sara loves me, she must decide for herself what her path will be. She can only raise herself in my eyes by descending to my station; it is not for me to lower myself by attempting to ascend to hers."

"But, Georges!" Sara cried. "You know that I—"

"I know, Sara, that you are a noble young woman with a devoted heart and a pure soul. I know you would be mine despite all obstacles, all entreaties, all prejudice. I know I have only to wait, and one day you will be at my side—and I know that, in your sweet and generous heart, you have already decided to make this great sacrifice for me. But"—he turned to M. de Malmédie—"as for you, sir, and your son, who has doubtless consented to forgo a duel with me on the condition that I am ambushed and whipped by his friends, ours is a lasting enmity. Understand me well: Nothing will cool my hatred, except bloodshed."

"Monsieur le Gouverneur," said M. de Malmédie, turning to Lord Murray and speaking with more dignity than one might have expected of him, "you see that I have done my part. I have sacrificed my pride and agreed to forget offenses both old and new. I can do no more. But surely you must agree that I cannot ignore the declaration of war this gentleman has just made against me. We will wait for the attack, and we will be prepared to defend ourselves. Now, Sara"—here he looked at his niece—"as Monsieur Munier says, you are free to do as you please with your heart, your hand, and your fortune. Act as you like. Stay with Monsieur Munier, or follow me."

"Uncle," said Sara in a low tone, "it is my duty to go with you, and so I shall. Georges, adieu! I cannot claim to understand your motives for acting as you have done today—but you must do what you think is right." Curtseying to the governor with cool dignity, she followed M. de Malmédie out of the room.

Lord Murray accompanied his visitors to the door, then returned to meet Georges's steady gaze. A moment's silence passed between these two men who, despite their very different upbringings, understood each other so well.

"So you have refused," said the governor at last.

"I believed it to be my duty, milord."

"I don't mean to be too inquisitive, but may I ask why?"

"Dignity required it of me," said Georges.

"Dignity—is that all?"

"If there is anything else, milord, it must remain my secret."

"Georges, listen to me," said Lord Murray suddenly, with an impulsiveness that was all the more charming since it was so obviously foreign to his cool and restrained nature. "You must listen. Since I first met you aboard the *Leicester,* I saw in you the high and noble qualities that set you apart from other men. From that moment it has been my earnest desire to make you the link that would reunite this island's two castes, so long opposed to each other. When you entrusted me with the secret of your love affair, I agreed without hesitation to act as your sponsor and negotiate on your behalf—" He paused, for Georges had lowered his head. "—and for this, my young friend, you owe me no thanks. You acted in accordance with my wishes; you supported my plans for conciliation; you smoothed the path for my political endeavors. Because of all this, I was happy to go with you to the house of Monsieur de Malmédie, and to support your request for Sara's hand in marriage with all the influence my name and position afforded me."

"I know, milord; and I thank you. But you have seen for yourself that even your honorable presence did not spare me the pain of being refused."

"Yes, and I suffered for you as much as you did yourself, Georges. I admired your calm in the face of it, but I also believed you were preparing some sort of terrible vengeance—and, indeed, I was proven right on the day of the races. I have known, since then, that I must abandon my cherished hopes of conciliation between the races."

"I warned you of that, milord," said Georges, in a level tone.

"I know you did. But even so, I refused to accept defeat. I went to Monsieur de Malmédie's house yesterday and pleaded with him, cajoled him—indeed, I nearly went so far as to abuse the power of my station—and finally I obtained his word that he would forget his old feud with your father. Henri, too, promised not to take any action against you; and both of them consented to your marriage with Mademoiselle Sara."

"Sara is a free woman, milord," Georges interrupted him. "She needs no one's consent to become my wife, God be praised."

"That is true," agreed Lord Murray. "But think of the difference in the eyes of the world, between secretly taking a girl from the home of her guardian, and receiving her hand publicly from her family! Search your pride, Monsieur Munier, and tell me I did not obtain for you a triumph you had not even hoped for!"

"Yes," said Georges, "that you did. Unfortunately, though, the consent has come too late."

"What? Too late? Why?" Lord Murray demanded.

"I am sorry, milord, but that is my secret."

"Is it? Shall *I* tell *you* this secret, which you are so reluctant to tell me?"

Georges could not conceal an incredulous smile.

"A very well-kept secret, indeed," continued Lord Murray, "entrusted to ten thousand select individuals!"

Georges's smile disappeared.

"Listen to me," the governor said again. "You have willfully sought your own ruin. I wanted to save you; I went to Sara's uncle, and said to him, 'You are underestimating Monsieur Georges Munier. You have offended him openly and driven him to cut himself off from us, and you were wrong to do it. Georges Munier is a distinguished man, with a noble heart and a brave soul. You should not have scorned a man such as him, for now he holds our very lives in his hands. He has agreed to lead a vast rebellion, and tomorrow night at ten o'clock'—it was yesterday that I visited the Malmédie house—'he will march on Port Louis with ten thousand blacks following him. We have only eighteen hundred men to defend ourselves, and unless Fate blesses me with a stroke of genius we are all lost. The truth is, monsieur, that on the day after tomorrow you may very well be enslaved yourself by a man you have long despised as the descendant of slaves—and he may not consider you worthy to serve him in turn!

" 'You can prevent all of this,' I said to Monsieur de Malmédie. 'You have the power to save the colony. Forget the past, and give Georges Munier your niece's hand in marriage. If he accepts it, you will have preserved not only your own life, liberty, and fortune, but those of us all!' At last, he consented to act as I urged him. But alas, what I feared has come to pass. You have already committed yourself, and you can no longer turn back."

Georges had listened to this speech in mute astonishment, but retained his calm. "So," he said, when Lord Murray had finished. "You know everything."

"I should think so. Or have I left something out?"

"No," replied Georges, smiling. "Your spies are well informed. I must compliment you on the efficiency of your police force."

"Well then," said the governor. "Now that you are acquainted with my motives, there is still time to accept Sara's hand. Do so, and be reconciled with her family. Renounce these senseless plans of yours, and I promise you I will forget everything I have learned."

"It is impossible," said Georges.

"Think, for a moment, of the sort of men you are joining with!"

"You forget, milord, that these men of whom you speak with such disdain are my brothers, who have chosen me to lead them out of slavery. When they entrusted their lives to me, I vowed to sacrifice my own for them."

"You refuse, then?"

"I refuse."

"Despite everything I have said?"

"I beg your pardon, milord, but I cannot heed you."

"Despite your love for Sara, and hers for you?"

"Despite everything," said Georges resolutely.

Lord Murray sighed. "Then let me ask you just one more question." Georges nodded. "Of course."

"If I were in your place, and you were in mine, what would you do?"

"What do you mean, milord?"

"Imagine for a moment that I am Georges Munier, leader of a slave revolt, and you are Lord William Murray, governor of île de France. If you held me in your grasp as surely as I now hold you in mine, I ask you again—what would you do?"

Georges was silent for a moment. "What I would do," he said at last, "is release the man who came to me because I asked him to; the man who came under the impression that he was being summoned by a friend, not lured into a trap. Then, when the time for revolt came, if I believed myself to be in the right I would appeal to God, who alone can choose between us."

Lord Murray snapped, "Then you would be wrong! If I were you,

you would not be able to save me. From the moment I agreed to lead a rebellion, it would have been your duty to quench the flames with my blood. Once I had drawn my sword, there could have been no reprieve from you. No! I cannot allow you to perish on the scaffold like a common criminal! I will not see your name dragged through the mud! I must save you from yourself, my friend. Monsieur, I arrest you!"

"Milord!" Georges exclaimed, his eyes darting around the room in search of a weapon he might use to defend himself.

"Guards!" Lord Murray cried. "Come, and take this gentleman into custody!" Four soldiers entered the room and surrounded Georges. "Take Monsieur Munier to the guardhouse," the governor directed. "Put him in the room I had prepared this morning, and watch him carefully. Take care that you—and anyone else who may come to see him—give him the respect due a man of his rank." With these words, the governor bowed and Georges was taken from the room.

XXII

THE REVOLT

Georges's arrest happened so quickly and unexpectedly that he did not have time even to resist. His self-control remained infallible, however, and he hid the many emotions that assaulted him beneath his usual smile of disdain. His guards escorted him by a back entrance out of the governor's residence and into one of Lord Murray's carriages. As Georges stepped up into the equipage, Miko-Miko—whether by chance or otherwise—passed by its open door. The men exchanged a glance.

As Lord Murray had ordered, Georges was taken to a large building known as the guardhouse, located on rue du Gouvernement, and into the room that had been prepared for him there. It was evident that pains had been taken to make the chamber as pleasing as possible: The furniture was comfortable, and the bed very nearly elegant. Nothing about the place suggested that it was a prison, except the iron bars at the windows.

The moment Georges's door closed behind his guards and he found himself alone, he went directly to one of the windows. It was about twenty feet off the ground, directly facing the open window of a room in the Hôtel Coignet. From where he stood, he could see directly into this opposing chamber. Georges crossed the room and listened attentively at the door until he heard the guards leave a single sentry and depart; he then returned to the window and opened it.

There was no guard stationed in the street below his chamber; evidently, the iron bars were considered safekeeping enough—indeed, they were thick and extremely strong. Georges knew he would have no way of escaping without some help from the outside.

Serene and confident that such help would come, he waited. Leaving the window open, he kept his eyes fixed on the room opposite his, in the Hôtel Coignet—which, as I have said, stands directly opposite the guardhouse. Sure enough, scarcely an hour had gone by before Miko-Miko appeared, his bamboo pole across his shoulders, escorted by a concierge. The merchant exchanged only the briefest of glances with Georges as he passed the window, but it was enough. Georges's brow relaxed, and his face grew peaceful.

From that moment onward Georges appeared almost as calm as if he had been in his own room at Moka. Still, from time to time an attentive observer might have noticed that he knitted his brows and passed a hand over his forehead. The truth was that, beneath his untroubled appearance, a thousand ideas teemed in his mind like a rising sea that seemed to batter his brain with each surge and recession.

The hours dragged by, and Georges could hear nothing to indicate that preparations for the revolt were being made in the city. Neither the roll of a drum nor the clash of weapons could be discerned. Here and there the young man heard sounds that caused him to dash to the window—but they invariably turned out to be nothing more than the rumble of a passing cart laden with barrels.

Night fell, and Georges paced from the door of his room to the window and back again. A lone guard could still be heard keeping watch in the corridor; the street below was empty. Georges's face remained as impassive as ever, but the occasional, compulsive movements of his hand to his heart and the slight creasing of his brow betrayed his growing anxiety. Even the bravest of men cannot remain altogether unmoved in circumstances that may decide the course of his entire future life. Georges thought of his father, who was unaware of the peril he faced, and of Sara, who had been its unwitting cause. As for Lord Murray, Georges now felt for him the cold, intense fury of a gambler who has lost the game. Still, he could not deny that the governor had, on this occasion as on all others, shown him the courtesy of a true gentleman: He had not summoned his guards until Georges had refused every escape route he had the power to offer. Finally, though, he had had no choice but to arrest the young mulatto, and on the most serious of charges: high treason.

The darkness grew thicker. Georges looked at his watch; it was half past eight. In another hour and a half the revolt would begin. He fixed his eyes again on the Hôtel Coignet. Suddenly a dark shape appeared in the open window and signaled to him. Georges moved to one side of the window as a packet was thrown into his room, passing between the bars and landing on the floor. He picked it up; it contained a rope and a file. Freedom now lay within his grasp—freedom he wanted for no other reason than to be at liberty when the hour of decision came.

Night had fallen completely, and the room was absolutely dark. Hiding the rope under the mattress of his bed, Georges began to file away at one of the window bars. They were spaced widely enough apart that the removal of a single one of them would allow him to squeeze through. The guards had brought supper earlier in the evening, and Georges felt fairly certain that he could now work undisturbed.

It was a slow, laborious process. Nine o'clock struck; then half past nine, then ten. As Georges sawed patiently at the bar, he thought he saw a bright light shine from the direction of the port, at the far end of the rue du Gouvernement near the rue de la Comédie. Still, the streets remained empty and quiet. No patrols walked the city; not a soldier made for the barracks. Georges could not understand Lord Murray's apparent indifference to an uprising he knew was coming, but he was too well acquainted with the governor to believe that he had not taken every precaution against it. Still, the city seemed defenseless, almost abandoned.

At ten o'clock, however, Georges thought he discerned a faint murmur coming from the direction of the Malabar camp. It was from here, remember, that the rebels were supposed to stream as they made for their rendezvous on the bank of the rivière des Lataniers. He filed away as fast as he could at the iron bar. Its base had been completely sawed through; he now concentrated his efforts at the top.

The noise outside began to grow, and there was no longer any doubt of its source: It was the mingled voices of several thousand men. Laïza had kept his word. A smile of joy came to Georges's lips, and he flushed with excitement and pride. The battle was close at hand! They could not be certain of victory but, by God, they would fight for it!

And their leader would be with them for the battle. The bar now held by a thread. Heart pounding, Georges strained his ears to listen. The noise was growing nearer and nearer, and the light he had noticed earlier shone more and more brilliantly. Could Port Louis be on fire already? No; it was impossible—there were no cries of distress.

Even more confusing, the rumble of shouting voices sounded joyous rather than threatening. No gunfire could be heard, not a single shot; the street on which the guardhouse stood remained deserted and perfectly silent. He waited fifteen more minutes, hoping to hear a gunshot or some sound that would dispel his uncertainty about whether the revolt had begun—but the same strange hum of voices went on, a low buzz unmarked by shouts or screams.

Georges decided that the time had come for his escape. One strong tug, and the bar gave way. Fetching the rope, he tied it securely to the broken base, dropped the sawed-off bar into the street below so that he might take it to use as a weapon, and, squeezing through the opening he had created, lowered himself smoothly to freedom.

Immediately he picked up the iron bar and moved in the direction from which the noise had come. As he approached the rue de Paris, which traversed the entire northern quarter of the town, he saw the light again—even stronger this time, and accompanied by the ever-growing rumble of voices. Finally he reached a brightly lit corner, and the mystery was explained.

Every street leading toward the Malabar camp was illuminated as if in preparation for some great festival. In front of each house was an uncorked barrel of brandy, rum, or eau-de-vie, obviously free and there for the taking.

The rebels had set out for Port Louis with vengeance in their hearts, shouting the battle cry, but when they arrived in town they had been confronted with glowing bonfires and the inviting barrels. Despite Laïza's commands to keep moving and their own fears that the alcohol might be poisoned, the temptation had been too great. Both fear and discipline had been overthrown by their natural urges. A few men broke ranks to taste the spirits, and their exclamations of approval had moved the rest to follow suit. In an instant the entire multitude, which could have overwhelmed Port Louis's defenders with ease, scattered. The city was safe. Groups of men surrounded the barrels, happily availing themselves of the brandy and rum, that eternal poison of the black races, so irresistible for the average Negro that he will sell his father, mother, children, and very frequently himself for a drink of it.

This, then, was the source of the strangely joyful shouts Georges had been unable to comprehend. The governor had obviously heeded the advice given to him by Jacques Munier, which had turned out to be sound indeed. The flames of the insurrection had already been dampened before the rebels even reached the town center or crossed the quarter stretching from Petite-Montagne to Trou-Fanfaron, and within a hundred yards of Government House they had been extinguished altogether.

As he stood alone, watching the spectacle, Georges knew that his hopes had been dashed. He remembered the prediction Jacques had made the day before, and was flooded with shame and rage. The men he had expected to lead in an uprising that would shake the island to its very foundations, that would avenge two centuries of slavery and pave the way for a free and victorious future, now reeled drunkenly before him, singing and dancing, laughing and staggering—and thoroughly disarmed. A few hundred soldiers would now have no trouble in driving all ten thousand of them back home to their masters.

In that instant Georges realized that all his long and painful labor had been wasted. All the time he had devoted to the study and improvement of his own heart, his strength, his worth: It had been in vain. The superiority of character that God had given him and that he had built upon with education and self-discipline had now been brought to nothing by the primitive instincts of men who loved their drink more than their liberty.

Georges felt his ambition and his pride, which had carried him briefly to the highest mountaintop and shown him the whole world lying at his feet, crumble and fall away. It was all gone, like a dream. He found himself standing alone where his false pride had led him.

He gripped the iron bar in his fist, seized with a ferocious desire to plunge into the crowd of revelers and crush the heads that had not had enough sense to resist temptation.

Several curious passersby, who did not understand why the governor had arranged for île de France's slaves to be fêted in such a manner, had stopped to gape in astonishment at the scene. Georges dashed from group to scurvy group, gazing down the long and brightly lit streets filled with drunken Negroes and buzzing with the noise of their revelry. All he wanted now was to find the only man he knew he could still trust in the midst of this madness—Laïza.

Suddenly there was a loud noise from the direction of the guardhouse, followed by a few gunshots—some sharp and precise, as if fired by trained marksmen; others irregular. Somewhere the two sides were actually fighting! Georges ran toward the sounds, and in five minutes he was back on rue du Gouvernement.

A small force was indeed battling there, led by Laïza—who had been informed that Georges was a prisoner, and had handpicked four hundred men to march on the guardhouse and free him.

It appeared that Lord Murray had anticipated this, for as soon as the band of rescuers appeared, it had been set upon by British troops. Laïza had also expected a struggle—but he had counted on the main body of rebels to provide a sufficient diversion, and that, as I have told you, had failed to materialize for the reasons we now know all too well.

Georges now launched himself into the midst of the fighting, calling Laïza's name as loudly as he could. He had, at last, found a black who was truly worthy of being called a man, and who had a strength of character equal to his own.

The two men met in the center of the clashing throng and, heedless of the commotion and the bullets whizzing past them, exchanged a few of those short and shouted words called for in such extreme situations. Georges told Laïza of the rebels' desertion; the other man shook his head and said merely, "All is lost."

Georges, wanting to revive his friend's spirits, suggested that maybe the drunken men could be roused to action once again—but Laïza replied with a smile of supreme disdain. "No," he said, "they will keep drinking until there is no more brandy, and the governor has supplied them all too well. We cannot hope to win."

With Georges free, the reason for the fighting at Government House vanished. There was nothing to do but regret the dozen lives already lost and give the signal to retreat. However, it soon became clear that they could not escape via the rue du Gouvernement. Another British troop, which had been lying in wait at the powder magazine, had blocked off the end of the street while Laïza and Georges were occupied, and they could not leave the same way they had come. They could only plunge into the maze of side streets surrounding the Palais de Justice and make a dash for the Malabar camp.

It took only two hundred steps to put them back in the quarter where the barrels of rum and brandy had been set out. The scene had degenerated even further; by now the blacks there were thoroughly intoxicated. At the ends of the streets English troops stood at the ready, their bayonets gleaming faintly in the light from the bonfires.

Georges and Laïza looked at each other and smiled briefly, the sort of hard, fierce expression a man wears when there is nothing more to be done, when he is resigned to his own death and his only desire is to die honorably. The two men moved into the middle of the main street, calling for the drunken insurgents to rally behind them. Their cries were all but lost in the din; the few who did hear them roared out slurred drinking songs and danced around on wobbly legs. Most of them, now drunk to the point of incapacitation, simply rolled about on the ground. Laïza, seizing a whip, tried vainly to lash the wretches to their senses, while Georges simply leaned on the iron bar he still held and looked on with the utmost contempt, silent and motionless as the statue of Disdain.

After a few moments it became clear to both Georges and Laïza that the situation was hopeless. Every minute now lost might represent a year of their lives. Spurred on by the conduct of the rest and lured by the scent of brandy, some of the men in Laïza's own troop now broke ranks in search of their share of the drink. They had already wasted too much time; they needed to cut their losses and retreat. Already, they had lost too much.

Georges and Laïza reassembled the small number of men who remained sober and loyal to them; it amounted to barely three hundred. Positioning themselves in the front rank, they marched resolutely toward the end of the street, which, as I have said, was guarded by a wall of British troops. Moving closer, they could see that the soldiers' muskets were aimed straight at them. A flash of light ran along the line of guns, and a hail of bullets fell on the rebels. A dozen men fell immediately, but the two leaders remained unhurt. Their joint cry of *"Forward!"* rang out, and they continued their advance; now a second burst of bullets killed even more blacks than the first—but now the distance between the two groups had closed, and hand-to-hand combat began.

It was a dreadful mêlée. British soldiers are well known for their tenacity, and they were fully prepared to die where they stood rather than giving way. However, they were now dealing with desperate rebels who, quite aware that execution would be their fate if captured, were determined to die as free men.

Georges and Laïza displayed miraculous courage; Laïza with a captured musket, which he held by the barrel and used like a club, and Georges with the iron bar he had taken from his prison window. Their men supported them wonderfully well, rushing on the British with bayonets in hand, while their wounded companions slashed away at the enemy with their knives.

After ten minutes of furious and bloody fighting, neither side had a marked advantage—but at last discouragement overcame discipline, and the English ranks broke like a ruptured dike, giving way to the flood of surviving rebels who surged away and fled into the woods and fields outside the town.

Georges and Laïza stayed at the rear of the group to ensure the retreat. When they reached the foot of Petite-Montagne, a spot too steep and thickly forested for the English soldiers to follow them, they finally called a halt. They stood with the remaining rebels, trying to catch their breath. There were but twenty men left with them; the others had either scattered or been killed in the battle. It was no longer a question of fighting, but only of finding a safe place in the woods to hide. Georges named Moka, the quarter in which his father's house was located, as the rendezvous point for anyone who wished to join him. He would, he announced, leave the following morning at dawn for the area of Grand Port, home of the densest woods in île de France.

As he gave these final instructions to the pathetic remains of the troop with which he had, for a glorious moment, dreamed of conquering the island, the moon gleamed briefly down on them as it passed between the clouds. All at once, the flash and crack of musket fire echoed from a thicket about forty feet away from where Georges stood. A bullet struck him in the side, and he fell at Laïza's feet. At the same instant the shadowy figure of a man could be seen fleeing from the bushes clutching a still-smoking rifle, disappearing into a small ravine behind them, and emerging to join the British soldiers grouped on the bank of the Pucelles stream.

Quick as the assassin had been, Laïza had been able to recognize him. As Georges slipped into unconsciousness, he heard Laïza murmur, with cold hatred, the name of Antonio the Malay.

XXIII

A Father's Heart

During the various events at Port Louis that I have just recounted, Pierre Munier waited anxiously at Moka for news of the terrible destiny he had let his son go to meet. Accustomed to the whites' eternal supremacy, as I have said, he considered this supremacy not only an acquired right, but a natural one as well. As much as he trusted Georges, he did not think it possible that the young man could overcome the insurmountable obstacles in his way.

From the moment Georges had departed, he had been in a state of despondence, his heart and mind so overcome with emotion that he appeared all but insensible to what was going on around him. Once or twice he even considered going to Port Louis himself, so that he might see what was happening there with his own eyes, but to march against such dreadful certitude requires a strength of will the poor father did not possess. If it had simply been a question of facing danger, Pierre Munier would have run to confront it.

The day dragged by with agonizing slowness, all the more painful because of his mental anguish and the fact that he dared tell no one, not even the faithful Télémaque, of the reasons for his despair. From time to time he rose from his chair and walked to the open window, gazing in the direction of the city and listening attentively—but he was invariably greeted with blank silence, and returned, sighing and vacant-eyed, to his seat.

The dinner hour came, and Télémaque set the table and served the food, but Pierre Munier seemed oblivious. The servant waited fifteen minutes, then approached his master and touched him lightly on the shoulder. Pierre Munier gave a great start and, rising from his chair, exclaimed, "What? Is there news?" Télémaque pointed to the table; the old man heaved a great sigh, smiled sadly, and returned to his reverie. It was obvious to the Negro that something extraordinary must be going on—the master had been behaving strangely all day— but he did not dare ask for an explanation. He rolled his big white-rimmed eyes around the room, but everything seemed calm and orderly. All he knew was that something dreadful had befallen the Munier household.

The rest of the day progressed in this manner.

Télémaque left the food on the table, hoping that hunger would assert itself, but Pierre Munier did not eat. Once, seeing drops of perspiration on the old man's forehead, Télémaque thought his master must be too warm, and offered him a glass of watered wine. Pierre Munier took it, but set it aside immediately and asked again if the servant had heard any news. Télémaque could only shake his head and gaze in confusion at the ceiling and the floor. Finally—since neither yielded any answers—he departed in search of the other blacks who served as the household staff—perhaps they would understand the cause of the master's uneasiness better than he.

To Télémaque's utter astonishment, however, except for himself there was not a single Negro to be found in the house. The barn, where the berloque habitually took place, was likewise deserted; the slave cabins were occupied only by women and children, who told him that as soon as the day's work was over the men had taken up weapons in lieu of resting, and had set off in groups toward the rivière des Lataniers.

Télémaque returned to the house in consternation. When he closed the door behind him, Pierre Munier turned quickly at the sound.

"Well?" he demanded. The servant relayed what he had been told of the other Negroes' actions, and the old man groaned. "Yes; alas!"

There could no longer be any doubt. The poor father knew his son's fate would be decided very soon—if, indeed, it had not been already. Ever since Georges's return, Pierre Munier had bound up his life so closely with that of his son, so handsome and brave, so self-confident, so full of the past and sure of the future, that he had come to feel almost as if they shared a life. He knew that he could not survive without his boy.

How bitterly the old man reproached himself for letting Georges go that morning without asking questions and learning his deepest thoughts, without determining exactly how much danger the young man would be in! How he regretted not insisting on going with him! But the idea of his son doing open battle with the whites, who had always been so invincible, had rendered him morally powerless. It was, as I have said, in the nature of this naïve soul to cower in the face of all but physical danger.

Night fell. The hours ticked by without any news of Georges. Ten o'clock struck; eleven o'clock; midnight. The darkness outside was impenetrable, yet Pierre Munier did not cease his endless trips from the armchair to the window, and all the lamps in the house remained brightly lit. Télémaque, now really concerned, had resolved to keep his master company—but his devotion could not overcome his fatigue, and he finally fell asleep in his chair, leaning against the wall where his silhouette was outlined like a charcoal drawing.

At two o'clock the watchdog who normally prowled the grounds at night but had been chained in view of the situation let out a low and plaintive howl. Pierre Munier started and rose from his seat, trembling. Among blacks, the howl of a dog is considered the harbinger of dreadful misfortune. The old man felt his strength desert him. He clung to the edge of a table to keep from falling.

Five minutes later the dog howled again, and in another five minutes he did yet again—each time louder, longer, and more mournful than the last. Pierre Munier stood, speechless and paralyzed with fear. His face was white, and drops of perspiration shone on his forehead.

He stared at the door, knowing it might open at any moment and dreading the bad news he feared would arrive when it did.

Only a few moments had passed before the footsteps of a large number of people could be heard approaching the door. To the poor father, the steps seemed horribly slow and measured, as if they might be following a bier. The next instant the foyer was filled with people—though they were oddly quiet. In the midst of this thick silence Pierre Munier heard a faint moan, and thought he recognized the voice of his son.

"Georges!" he cried. "In the name of heaven, my son, are you here? Speak to me!"

"It is I, Father," replied a voice that was weak but calm. "It is I."

Pierre Munier turned and saw Georges leaning against the door frame, so pale that for an instant the father thought he was looking at his son's ghost. He took an involuntary, frightened step backward. "In the name of heaven," he murmured again, "what has happened to you?"

"A serious wound—but rest assured, Father, not a fatal one. As you see, I can walk and stand—but not for very long." Then, in a whisper, "Help me, Laïza. My strength is quite gone."

He sank back into the Negro's arms. Pierre Munier darted to his son's side, but Georges had already fainted. With typical bravery, the young man had been determined that his father would see him on his feet, even as he weakened almost to the point of death. It was not mere pride that had propelled him; his love for Pierre Munier was so great that he had feared the sight of him prostrate might kill the old man—so, despite Laïza's protests, as he and his comrades neared the Munier house he had risen from the litter on which he had been carried all the way from Petite-Montagne and, with a superhuman effort, walked to meet his father. As he had wished, Pierre Munier had been calmed by seeing him upright; but the show had entirely drained Georges's remaining strength.

The father's grief at his son's loss of consciousness was terrible to see. It was too deep for words, too deep for tears; silent and despairing. They laid Georges on a sofa, and the old man knelt beside him, supporting his head and holding his hand, his eyes fixed on the young man's closed lids, his breathlessness echoing his son's. He asked nothing about the revolt or the exact cause of Georges's injuries; all that mattered now was that his boy had been seriously hurt—that he lay here wounded, bleeding, unconscious—and that he might not survive. What else could possibly matter in the face of such a grim truth?

Laïza stood at a corner of the sideboard, leaning on his musket and looking out the window for the first signs of daylight. The other Negroes, who had respectfully withdrawn from the room after placing Georges on his couch, huddled in the adjoining chamber or outside near the window, looking in from time to time on their fallen leader. Many bore wounds of their own, some of them serious, but they seemed ignorant of these in their concern for Georges.

More and more Negroes arrived at the plantation as the hours went by; the rebels, after scattering in the woods to avoid being captured or killed, had been drawn to the Munier house like a flock of sheep to the fold. By four o'clock that morning there were nearly two hundred men on the grounds.

Georges eventually regained consciousness and tried to reassure his father with a few murmured words, but his voice was so weak that Pierre Munier, anxiously imploring him to keep still despite his desperate desire to hear the young man's voice, could no longer refrain from asking about the nature of the wound his son had received, and the name of the doctor who had dressed it. With a smile and a feeble motion, Georges pointed to Laïza.

In the colonies, as we know, there are many Negroes who are such skillful surgeons that even the whites prefer their services to those of conventional physicians. These primitive men who pose such a challenge even to trained doctors, similar to our shepherds, spending as much time as they do outdoors, invariably stumble upon secrets of nature that are unknown to other men. Laïza was such a man, known throughout the island as a capable surgeon. His fellow Negroes attributed his skill to magic; the whites trusted his knowledge of the medicinal properties of herbs and plants. Pierre Munier was a little easier in his mind when he found out that it was Laïza who had tended to Georges's wound.

Daybreak was drawing near, and Laïza appeared more and more

anxious. Finally he could suppress his impatience no longer. He went to Georges and, under the pretext of taking his pulse, spoke to him in whispers. Pierre Munier looked at him. "Is there something you need, my friend?"

"He is afraid I will fall into the hands of the whites, Father," replied Georges. "He wants to know if I feel strong enough to be taken to the Great Woods."

"The Great Woods?" Pierre Munier exclaimed. "And you as weak as you are? No, it is impossible!"

"I am afraid there is no choice, Father, unless you wish to see me arrested before your eyes."

"And if they arrested you, what would happen to you?" Pierre Munier inquired nervously.

"They would seek immediate revenge upon the wretched mulatto who has dared to oppose them," Georges replied, "and who—for a moment—has made them afraid." He smiled weakly. "I imagine they would give me the mild punishment of cutting off my head on the plaine Verte."

The old man turned white and shook visibly. "Take you away, my Georges, and cut off your head? All because you are more handsome, more brave, more learned than they? No! Let them come and try it!"

With an energy he would not have been thought capable of five minutes earlier, he seized the rifle he had not fired in sixteen years. "Yes, let them come! We shall see what happens then! The whites have taken everything from me! They robbed me of my self-respect, and I let them do it. They might have killed me and I would not have reproached them with my dying breath. But to take my son, to imprison him, torture him, execute him? Never! I have half a century's offenses to avenge! It is time to settle accounts!"

Georges raised himself up on his elbow, a feverish gleam in his eye. "Father! Once again, you have become the man I always knew you to be!"

"Let us all go to the Great Woods," said Pierre Munier, "and we shall see if they dare follow us there. Come, my son! The woods are much preferable to the town—for there we are under the eye of God, and may he watch over us and judge our cause." He turned to the waiting Negroes. "As for you, my children, have I not always been a good master to you?"

"Yes, yes!" they cried.

"Have you not said a hundred times that I am less a master than a father to you?"

"Oh, yes!"

"Then it is time to prove your devotion!" Pierre Munier cried.

"Only command us, master," the blacks roared. "We will obey!"

"Come in, all of you," commanded Georges's father.

The room quickly filled with blacks.

"Look," the old man continued, "gaze upon my son, who has laid down his life to make you free men! You see how he has been rewarded! Now the whites seek to tear him away from me, wounded and defenseless! Will you protect him? Will you swear to die for him, and with him, if you must?"

"Yes, yes!" every voice cried.

"To the Great Woods, then!" Pierre Munier commanded.

"To the Great Woods!" echoed the blacks. Several of them hastened to fetch the bamboo litter and placed Georges gently upon it. With Laïza in the lead, they set out, Pierre Munier bringing up the rear. The house was left open, completely abandoned of all human creatures.

In a single body the Negroes marched, nearly two hundred of them, down the road from Port Louis to Grand Port and toward the foot of Mont le Milieu, at the mouth of the rivière des Créoles.

As they approached le Milieu, Pierre Munier lagged behind a moment to climb a low hill and gaze one last time at the rich, gracious home he had left. His gaze swept up the fertile plains planted with sugarcane, manioc, and corn; the groves of grapefruit, jambosa, and takamaka trees, and the solid, majestic wall of the mountains that surrounded his property. He thought of the three generations of honest, industrious men who had worked to make his plantation the glory of the island, and he could not hold back a tear, and a sigh. Then, turning back with a determined smile on his lips, he strode to catch up with the litter bearing his wounded son, for whom he had now given up everything else.

XXIV

THE GREAT WOODS

Just as the band of fugitives reached the source of the rivière des Créoles, dawn broke and the rays of the eastern sun shone on the rocky peak of le Milieu. Every creature in the forest appeared to awaken at the same moment; with every step the Negroes took, tenrecs leapt from their hiding places and then back again; monkeys sprang chattering to the farthest leafy branches of one vacoa tree, then swung by their prehensile tails to cover great distances and land with marvelous accuracy in the safety of another tree. Woodcocks rose noisily into the air, and gray parrots uttered their harsh cries. Flamered cardinals shot through the air, sparkling like rubies. Nature, serene, carefree, eternally young and exploding with life, seemed to mock the transitory pains and agitations of mankind.

After three or four hours of walking, the group halted on a plateau at the foot of a nameless mountain that tapered away into the riverbank. Hunger began to gnaw at them; fortunately, they had had ample opportunity to hunt during their trek through the woods. Some had used their sticks to club the mouse-like tenrecs, considered a delicacy by the blacks; others had killed monkeys or woodcocks—and Laïza had wounded a stag, which four men pursued and brought down in less than an hour. There would be plenty of food for everyone.

Laïza now took advantage of the pause to change the dressing on Georges's wound. As the group passed through the woods, he had gathered precious medicinal herbs and plants—the properties of which he alone understood—which he now crushed together with a rounded stone in the hollow of a rock. Soaking a linen cloth in the juices, he applied this to the wound. Fortunately, the bullet had not lodged in Georges's flesh—it had entered his body on the left side just below the rib cage and passed out slightly above the hip.

Pierre Munier watched Laïza's ministrations with deep anxiety. The wound was serious, to be sure, but not mortal. By all appearances, no internal organs had been damaged. In fact, it might even heal faster here than it would have in the city, under a licensed physician's care. Still, the poor father could not help but feel agony at the sight of his son injured, and in pain. Georges, on the other hand, endured Laïza's attentions without flinching; the hand his father held did not clench in pain even once.

The dressing changed and the meal finished, the party set out again. Bearing Georges on his litter made their progress slow and laborious, and their footsteps left a path easy to detect on the uneven ground.

They walked for almost an hour, following the bank of the rivière des Créoles, and, turning left, finally reached the edge of the Great Woods. Enormous mimosas and leafy ferns grew tall and thick between the trees, pushing even above the treetops here and there, and creeper vines hung draped like enormous serpents from the topmost boughs of the takamakas.

The bamboo grew thicker and thicker and proved increasingly hard to pass through, especially for the men carrying the litter. Tree trunks seemed to form walls, and creeper vines entwined together to form barriers across the path. Georges, aware of the difficulty, protested that he could walk on his own, but his father pleaded with him—and Laïza ordered him—to lie back. In order to satisfy the devotion of one and the tenderness of the other, the sick man resumed his position on the litter. From time to time he asked again to be allowed to walk, but his voice grew weaker and weaker, and finally he fell silent.

Difficult as it was for the band of Negroes to penetrate the forest, they did not complain, for the density of the woods also provided a measure of security. They were quite used to negotiating wildernesses such as this, whereas the soldiers pursuing them were British, accustomed to performing their maneuvers at champ de Mars and champ de Lort.

Eventually, though, the rebels came to a dense wall of foliage through which even they could not pass. They contemplated hacking their way through it with an ax, but to do so would allow their pursuers to follow them more easily, so they decided against it.

As they searched for a way through the barrier, they came upon a small, crude hut called an ajoupa, commonly built by hunters needing overnight shelter. Inside, the remains of a fire were still smoldering; evidently, other runaway slaves had been in the area quite recently. They could not be far away now.

Laïza set out to follow their trail. We know how easy it is for savages to hunt the traces left by friend or foe across huge, lonely spaces. With single-minded determination, doubled over as he walked, he followed the bent blades of grass, overturned stones, and broken branches marking the path the earlier fugitives had taken—but all at once he came to a place where the traces vanished suddenly and completely. On one side of him was a stream that tumbled down the mountainside and emptied into the rivière des Créoles; on the other was a solid wall of rocks, stones, and brush, at the top of which the forest seemed denser than ever. Laïza crossed the rivulet and searched on the other side for the traces he had followed to its banks, but in vain. The blacks—for there were several of them—could not have gone much farther.

Laïza tried again to scale the wall and succeeded to a point—but when he reached the top, he realized that it would be impossible for his group, some of whom were wounded, to follow him. He climbed back down and, convinced that the party he was searching for must be close by, called out the code names commonly used by runaway slaves to recognize one another.

In a few moments he thought he could hear a slight rustling coming from the thickest part of the brush. The rocks that made up the barrier seemed to quiver. If Laïza had not been quite accustomed to solitude and the sounds of nature, he might have assumed that the wind was responsible for this slight movement of the undergrowth—but he knew otherwise. He gazed fixedly at the thicket in question and eventually discerned two eyes, which were staring back at him warily. He repeated the words he had called out a moment before, and the next instant a man slid noiselessly as a snake from his hiding place. It was, indeed, a runaway black.

The two men spoke briefly, and then Laïza rejoined his companions. The group, in their turn, followed him along the path to the place where the runaway had been hidden. He was able to lead them to a particular spot in the wall of rocks, a few of which had been loosened for easy removal. The cavernous passage thus revealed led to a large clearing, and the rebels now moved, two by two, into this highly defensible space.

When the last of them had entered, the runaway stranger replaced the stones in the wall exactly as they were before, so that not a trace of the entrance was visible. Then, clinging to the brush and protruding edges of the rocks, he scaled the wall and disappeared once again into the depths of the forest, leaving the two hundred fugitives so completely swallowed up in the belly of the forest that only the alertest of eyes would have had any chance of discovering them.

Whether by one of those accidents of nature that occurs occasionally without man having any hand in the effect produced, or as a result of the long and diligent work of runaway blacks, the summit of the mountain now concealing the band of rebels was protected on one side by a wall of rock that served as a rampart and on the other by the wall of tree trunks, vines, and brush that had earlier been an insurmountable obstacle. The only navigable entrance was the one I have just described, and this was a cavern, entirely hidden by stones and brush. It was so well hidden, in fact, that neither armed colonists acting on their own behalf nor English soldiers acting on that of the government would have noticed it had they passed by it a hundred times. It was a refuge known only to fugitive slaves.

On this side of the grotto and its impassable wall, the terrain was completely different. There were still towering trees and thickets, but these were not so dense that a path could not be forced through them. All the necessities of life were to be found here, despite the remoteness of the place; a waterfall tumbled sixty feet from the mountain's peak to explode in clouds of spray upon the rocks, flowing away in rivulets and disappearing into the ground only to bubble up again outside the walls of the enclosure. Stags, boars, deer, monkeys, and tenrecs were plentiful; in the places where sunlight penetrated the foliage there were heavily laden grapefruit trees and cabbage palms whose fruit, when ripe, drops to the ground at the slightest breeze or shake of its trunk. If the fugitives could remain undiscovered, they would have everything they needed to survive until Georges was well and could determine their next move. Whatever he might decide, the remaining rebels had pledged themselves to remain with him to the last.

Severely wounded as he was, Georges retained his customary calm. He had examined their hiding place thoroughly and taken note of every advantage it offered. Once on the other side of the enclosure he called Laïza to his side, and they discussed how the grotto and the entrance cavern could be defended both inside and out by means of trenches, as well as booby-trapped with mines made from the gunpowder they had brought with them from Moka. Work on this project began immediately under Pierre Munier's supervision, for Georges knew that his enemies would search relentlessly until they found him, and that they would not rest until he was bound hand and foot, and completely in their power.

Thus the men set to work on the defensive measures they had planned, with Georges presiding passively and Pierre Munier actively over them.

Meanwhile Laïza made an exhaustive tour of the mountain. It was almost entirely defended by steep and rugged rock formations; there was only one place where these might be scaled, and even then it would require ladders at least fifteen feet high. The path that led to the mountain was bordered by a sheer cliff, and would have been easily defensible if the rebels had numbered more than two hundred. As it was, they would have to confine themselves to protecting their natural fortress and the entrance into it.

Dusk had fallen, and Laïza stationed ten guards at the entry and went to make his report to Georges, whom he found resting in a crude shelter that had been hastily built from tree branches. Work on the trenches was proceeding steadily despite the advancing darkness; twenty-five men stood sentinel around the enclosure, to be relieved every two hours during the night. Pierre Munier remained at his post in the cavern, and Laïza went to keep his own watch after changing the dressing on Georges's wound.

Thus the night passed anxiously, as everyone awaited whatever might happen next.

XXV

JUDGE AND EXECUTIONER

In a war of surprise such as the one in which the rebels and their adversaries were now embroiled, night, with its increased risk of ambush, was a time of particular anxiety. This night was clear and calm, though the moon was waning and did not rise until almost eleven o'clock.

For men less preoccupied with danger than our heroes, and for those less accustomed to the beauty of the islands, the gradual fading-away of the sun so deep in the vast and silent forest would have been a majestic spectacle indeed. The shadows seemed to rise from the horizon like a tide, washing over the tree trunks and the faces of the rocks and engulfing the rugged peaks. Daylight lingered at the very summits of the mountains for an instant, illuminating the crags so they seemed briefly like flaming volcanoes, then slipped finally into darkness.

Still, for eyes used to the tropical night, the darkness was not complete; nor, for ears accustomed to solitude, was the silence absolute. Life is never completely still in the wilderness; as the sounds of the day fade away, they are replaced by those of the night. The murmurs of rustling leaves and rushing water mingle with the voices of a multitude of nocturnal animals. The sounds are plaintive and mysterious, and inspire in even the stoutest hearts an intangible emotion that reason can never quite banish.

Not a single one of these sounds went unnoticed by Laïza's well-trained ear. A wild hunter and therefore a man of solitude, long familiar with the night, he saw and heard every nuance of the wilderness around him. He recognized the scratching noise of the tenrecs gnawing on the exposed roots of the trees, and the soft footfalls of the deer coming to drink at the stream; he heard the fluttering of bats' wings as they soared through the clearing, and he remained perfectly immobile.

Strangely enough, it was here, where two hundred men hid themselves, that the silence was deepest and the solitude most complete. The ten Negroes whom Laïza had stationed at the entrance to the clearing lay facedown on the ground, unmoving and scarcely visible in the darkness. Some were awake and some slept, but it seemed that even the breathing of the sleepers was carefully controlled and quiet. Laïza leaned against an enormous tamarind tree, whose slender branches extended over the rocky path and past the edge of the precipice beyond it. Thanks to the blackness of night and the dark hue of his skin, he was all but indistinguishable from the tree trunk itself.

Laïza had stood in silent immobility for nearly an hour when he heard the footsteps of several men behind him, crunching softly on ground covered with pebbles and dead branches. Though quiet, the approaching individuals did not seem to be trying to conceal their movements, and Laïza turned toward them, untroubled. Indeed, his eyes were accustomed to the darkness, and he was soon able to make out the forms of six or eight men; among them—recognizable due to his great height and the fine cut of his clothes—was Pierre Munier.

Laïza detached himself from the tree he had been leaning against and went to meet him. "Well," he said, "have the men you sent to take stock of our situation returned yet?"

"Yes," Pierre Munier replied. "The British soldiers are searching for us."

"Where are they?"

"An hour ago they were camped between le Milieu and the mouth of the rivière des Créoles."

"They are following our trail, then," said Laïza.

"Yes. We shall probably hear from them tomorrow."

Laïza shook his head. "Sooner than that, I think."

"Why?"

"We have already sent out our scouts. They must have done the same."

"And?"

"Some of their men are already nearby."

Pierre Munier frowned. "What makes you think so? Have you heard voices, or footsteps?"

"No," said Laïza, "but the stag I shot was in such a fright that someone must have startled him badly."

"You think we are being tracked, then."

"I am sure of it," said Laïza. He raised his finger suddenly to his lips. "Quiet!"

"What is it?"

"Listen." They waited.

"Yes, I hear something," whispered Pierre Munier.

"It is a woodcock in flight. Around two hundred feet away, I should think." Laïza pointed toward a clump of trees whose topmost branches just barely showed above the edge of the ravine. "You see? It has landed now, only thirty feet away, just on the other side of the path beneath that great rock."

"And you think it was startled by a man?"

"One man, or several. I cannot tell."

"That is not what I meant," Pierre Munier said. "I mean, are you absolutely certain it was a human that frightened the bird?"

"Yes; animals know by instinct the sounds made by other animals," replied Laïza. "It is only human noises that terrify them. Someone is coming, I am sure of it." He lapsed into alert silence.

"What do you hear?" Pierre Munier whispered after a moment.

"The sound of a dry branch, breaking under a man's foot," murmured Laïza. "Keep very still; they are close enough to make out our voices. Hide yourself behind the trunk of the tamarind tree, monsieur." He resumed his former position while the others concealed themselves in the shadows. They waited, silent and motionless as statues.

Only a few seconds had passed before they heard the noise of a rock that, kicked loose from its resting place, clattered down the steep slope of the precipice. Laïza felt Pierre Munier's breath quicken against his cheek, and the old man would have spoken if the Negro had not seized him firmly by the arm so that he kept silent. At the same instant, the woodcock flew up again, shrieking loudly, and soared over the tamarind tree to safety farther up the mountain. The spy was no more than twenty feet from them—he was following their trail! Laïza and Pierre Munier could not breathe, and the other blacks stood frozen in their tracks.

Just then a faint, silvery light gleamed on the distant peaks of the mountains ringing the horizon. A few moments afterward the moon appeared behind the peak of Mont Créole and began its nightly voyage across the sky. Unlike the darkness, which had begun at ground level and risen upward, the moon's rays illuminated the heavens from the top down. But the light penetrated only into areas that were not too thickly clustered with trees; the rest of the forest, except for stray bits of ground here and there, remained in deep shadow.

There was a barely perceptible movement in a bush on the edge of the path. The bush rose to the top of the bank, concealing, remember, the perilous drop on the other side. The branches parted, and a man's head could be seen. Despite the darkness, Laïza and Pierre Munier saw this at the same moment. They grasped each other's hands in an instinctive motion. The stranger remained motionless for a second, then leaned a little farther out of the bush, his gaze sweeping the area and his ears straining into the silence until he was apparently satisfied that there was no one else around. He raised himself to his knees, then got to his feet. Laïza squeezed Pierre Munier's hand, wordlessly urging him to be utterly silent. There could be no doubt that this man, whoever he was, was looking for them.

This night spy now moved onto the path itself and bent down, evidently examining the ground for footprints. He ran the palm of his hand over the grass to see if it had been crushed and felt the stones with his fingertips to determine if they had been kicked out of their original positions. Finally, as if the very air had preserved traces of the men he sought, he raised his head and looked directly at the tamarind tree concealing Laïza and Pierre Munier. At that moment, a beam of moonlight shone between the branches and illuminated the spy's face.

With a movement quick as lightning, Laïza pulled his right hand from Pierre Munier's and leapt forward. Seizing the end of a long bough in one hand and the stranger's belt by the other, he plunged like a swooping eagle to the foot of the rock and pulled himself and his prey up to safety. Landing near the tree trunk again, he tightened his grip on the prisoner, who was now slashing vainly at him with a knife as the snake tries vainly to bite the hawk that has taken it from the depths of the marshes unexpectedly to the sky.

The stranger's identity now became as clear to Pierre Munier and the other half a dozen blacks as it had immediately been to Laïza. It was Antonio the Malay. He had been captured so quickly that he had not even had time to yell.

Finally Laïza's mortal enemy was in his power. He would now be able to punish the man who was both traitor and assassin. He pushed Antonio facedown on the ground and held him there with one knee, looking at him with the terrible ferocity of a conqueror who gives the vanquished no reason to hope for life—and then the distant barking of a dog broke the stillness. Without relaxing his iron grip on Antonio, Laïza raised his head and cocked his ear in the direction of the noise.

Antonio shuddered beneath him.

"All in good time," Laïza murmured, as if speaking to himself. Then, raising his voice, he addressed the Negroes who stood nearby. "Tie this man to a tree. I must speak to Monsieur Munier."

Seizing Antonio by the hands and feet, the blacks bound him to the trunk of a takamaka tree using strong vines. Laïza checked to ensure that the Malay would not be able to escape, then he led Pierre Munier a few steps away. "Did you hear a dog barking?" he asked.

"What?"

"The barking of a dog."

"No," the old man said.

"Listen; it is getting closer."

"Yes," said Pierre Munier after a moment's silence. "I do hear it now."

"They are hunting us like deer."

"You think it is the soldiers?"

"Who else?"

"An escaped dog, perhaps, hunting on its own."

"No," murmured Laïza. "Listen again." They waited for a moment; the barking resumed, even nearer this time than before. "It is us they seek."

"How can you be sure?" asked the old man.

"That is not the bark of a hunting dog. It is the howl of a lost animal in search of its master. The devils must have found a dog chained in some Negro's hut and taken him along as a guide. If that Negro is among us, we are lost."

Pierre Munier was shaking. "It is the voice of my Fidèle," he whispered.

Laïza turned pale. "Yes," he murmured. "I recognize it now. The same dog howled last night, when we brought Georges home to Moka."

"I forgot to bring him with us when we left the plantation," Pierre Munier said. "But wait—it seems to me that if it is Fidèle, he would be running faster. The bark is approaching so slowly!"

"They must have him on a leash," said Laïza, "so they can follow him more easily. He may have an entire regiment on his heels! It is no use getting angry at the poor animal," the Lion of Anjouan added with a hollow laugh. "He may not be able to go very fast, but believe me, he will get here."

"What must we do?" Pierre Munier asked.

"If you had a ship lying in wait at Grand Port, we would have a very good chance of reaching it. We are not more than eight or ten leagues away from the harbor. I don't suppose there is such a ship?"

"No; none."

"Then we must defend ourselves," said Laïza grimly, "or die in the attempt."

"Come, then!" said Pierre Munier, who always recovered his courage when faced with the choice between battle and death. "My dog may lead them to the entrance of our hiding place, but they will have a difficult time going any farther than that!"

"Yes." Laïza nodded. "Go now to the trenches."

"You are not coming with me?"

Laïza shook his head. "I must remain here a few moments longer."

"But you will join us soon?"

"Rest assured, when the first shot is fired, I shall be at your side."

The old man clasped Laïza's hand; then, slinging his rifle over his shoulder, he and the other blacks walked rapidly toward the entrance of the grotto. Laïza watched his retreating figure until it was swallowed by the shadows, then returned to the bound figure of Antonio the Malay. "Now," he said, "it is time to conclude our business."

"Business?" repeated Antonio in a trembling voice. "What does Laïza want of his friend and brother?"

"I want him to remember what was said on the banks of the rivière des Lataniers, the night of the Yamsé festival," said Laïza sternly.

"Many things were said that night," quavered Antonio. "My brother Laïza was eloquent indeed, for he brought everyone around to his way of thinking."

"Do you remember what was said about the sentence to be carried out on all traitors?"

Antonio trembled from head to foot and, despite the coppery hue of his skin, turned visibly paler in the moonlight.

"It would appear that your memory is faulty, *brother*," Laïza continued, his voice heavy with irony. "Let me refresh it. It was said that, if a proven traitor was discovered among us, he should be put to death on the spot by whatever means we chose—quick or slow, gentle or painful. Do you remember now?"

"Yes," whispered Antonio faintly.

"Now you must answer the questions I am about to ask you."

"What right do you have to question me?" Antonio cried shrilly. "You are not my judge!"

"Then I shall leave others to ask the questions," said Laïza calmly. He gestured to the twelve Negroes who were still lying, facedown and silent, on the ground around him. "Rise, men, and do your duty!" The blacks obeyed, standing and forming a semicircle around the tree to which Antonio was tied.

"But these are slaves!" the Malay cried indignantly. "I ought not to be judged by slaves; I am not black! I am a free man, and it is for a court of law to pass sentence on me—if indeed I have committed a crime—not for you!"

"Enough!" interrupted Laïza. "We will try you first, here and now. Afterward you may appeal the decision before any court you like."

Antonio fell silent. In the pause that followed, the barking of the approaching dog could be heard, nearer than before.

"It seems that the accused has nothing to say," Laïza said to the Negroes surrounding Antonio. "You, men, must reply on his behalf. Who was it, I ask you, that informed the governor of our plan, out of spite that he had not been chosen to lead the revolt?"

"Antonio the Malay," answered the blacks in a voice that was heavy but united.

"That is not true!" the prisoner cried. "I swear it!"

"Silence!" Laïza commanded. "Who was it," he continued, addressing the blacks again, "that fired upon our leader with a rifle at the foot of Petite-Montagne, seriously wounding him?"

"Antonio the Malay," repeated the Negroes.

"Who saw me do anything of the sort?" Antonio shrieked. "Who dares accuse me? Who can tell one man from another in the dark of night?"

"Silence!" Laïza said again. He paused, then continued, his voice carefully controlled. "Finally, I ask you, who is it that—after betraying us to the governor, after attempting to murder our chief—has come again in the night, slithering like a serpent around our retreat, searching for an opening by which the English soldiers might enter it?"

"Antonio the Malay," said the blacks for the third time, in tones of firm conviction that did not waver once.

"I came to join my brothers!" Antonio protested. "To share their lot, whatever it might be! I swear it!"

"Do you believe him?" Laïza asked the blacks.

"No! No! No!" they cried.

"My good friends, my dear friends!" pleaded Antonio. "Listen to me, I beg you!"

"Silence!" thundered Laïza. Then, reassuming the attitude of calm he had retained throughout the proceedings, obviously aware of the import of his words, he continued: "Antonio has been shown to be a traitor—not in one instance, but in three. If he could, he should by rights die three times. Antonio, prepare yourself. You are about to meet the Great Spirit."

"This is murder!" shrieked Antonio. "You have no right to murder a free man! The English cannot be very far away—I will call to them! Help me! Murder! Help me!" He broke off, for Laïza had seized him by the throat.

"Bring me a rope," the Negro said to his comrades. When he heard these words and understood what they implied, Antonio struggled so violently that he broke some of the vines binding him to the tree—but he was unable to escape from Laïza's iron grip. After a moment Laïza realized that if his prisoner continued to writhe in this way, the rope would not be necessary. He relaxed his hold slightly, and Antonio's head sagged. "I will give you ten minutes to prepare yourself to meet your maker," Laïza told him.

Antonio tried to speak, but his voice had deserted him. The dog's bark sounded again; it grew nearer every minute.

"Where is the rope?" Laïza asked.

"Here," said a Negro, handing him a length of cord.

"Good." With the single word, Laïza changed from judge to executioner. Seizing one of the stoutest limbs of the tamarind tree, he drew it down and knotted one end of the rope securely to it; he fashioned the other end into a noose, which he slipped around Antonio's neck. Directing two of his men to hold the branch and checking once more to make sure that the prisoner could not escape, he repeated his statement that the Malay must prepare himself for death.

Antonio had by now recovered his powers of speech, but he did not use them to implore God for mercy; rather, he made a final appeal to the pity of his judges.

"Well!" he said. "Ah—yes, yes, my friends, it's true, I am guilty. You are right to condemn me as you have. But surely you will pardon me, your old acquaintance! Surely you will take pity on Antonio, who has made you laugh on so many evenings, who has told you so many fantastic stories and sung you so many merry songs? What will you do without Antonio? Who will entertain you; who will drive away your sadness and make you forget the troubles of the day? Mercy, my friends, for poor Antonio! Life, my friends! I beg you, on my knees, for life!"

"Turn your thoughts to the Creator, Antonio," said Laïza implacably. "You have only five minutes left to live."

"Give me five years, not five minutes, good Laïza," wheedled Antonio. "I will be your slave—I will be at your command—you can whip me as much as you like; beat me, I won't complain. I will sing your praises wherever I go! Life, dear Laïza, is all I ask."

"Listen, Antonio," Laïza said. "Do you hear the howling of that dog?"

"Yes. Do you think it was I who advised the soldiers to unleash it? I didn't; I swear it!"

"Antonio," said Laïza imperturbably, "a white man would never think of using a dog to pursue its own master. This idea, too, came from you."

The Malay let out a pathetic groan. Then, obviously hoping to soften Laïza with humility, he spoke. "Well—yes, it *was* my idea. The Great Spirit had abandoned me, and I was crazed with the desire for revenge. Pity me as a madman, Laïza. In the name of your brother Nazim, spare me!"

Laïza's eyes flared. "But who was it that denounced Nazim in the first place? Who made him so desperate to flee? You made a grave mistake, Antonio, in speaking my brother's name. Your five minutes are up. It is time to die."

"No! No! Oh, no! Don't kill me!" Antonio screamed. "Have mercy, Laïza, please! Have mercy, my friends!"

His cries and supplications went unheeded. Laïza drew out his knife and, with one slash, severed the vines still binding Antonio to the tree. At his nod, the two men holding the branch to which the noose was attached released their grip. It sprang upward to its former position, carrying the miserable Malay with it.

A last wretched, choking cry, terrible and full of despair, rang out and died away, vanishing into the depths of the abyss. The deed was finished, and Antonio's body hung lifeless, swinging to and fro gently above the precipice. Laïza stood motionless, watching the rope as it quivered and grew still. Then, cocking his ear, he listened again to the barking dog, now barely five hundred feet from their hiding place. Shouldering his gun, he turned to the other Negroes.

"Come, my friends," he said. "We have had our revenge; now we can die in peace." With firm and rapid steps, he and the others headed in the direction of the trenches.

XXVI

THE HUNT FOR THE NEGROES

As Laïza had predicted, the dog Fidèle, following his master's scent, had led the English soldiers directly to the entrance of the grotto where Pierre Munier and the others were hiding. The animal plunged immediately into the underbrush and began anxiously pawing a section of stones there. The British now came forward with picks and shovels and set to work, and within moments an opening had been created that was large enough for a man to pass through.

One soldier raised himself up to peer through the gap, and as soon as he did so a rifle shot rang out. He fell to the ground, a bullet having pierced his heart. A second soldier followed the first and met the same fate; then a third. It was clear that the rebels had decided on a desperate course of action.

The attackers now took the proper precautions, sheltering themselves as much as they could while working to enlarge the breach in the stone wall to accommodate more than one man. The drums rolled ominously and the foot soldiers advanced, bayonets at the ready. But it was soon evident that the advantage lay with the defenders: The breach piled up rapidly with corpses, and the British were obliged to spend precious time clearing away the bodies of their slain comrades in preparation for a fresh assault.

On the second try they were able to penetrate as far as the middle of the cavern, but this resulted in an even greater number of dead. Crouching in the trenches Georges had ordered them to dig, the Negroes, under the direction of Laïza and Pierre Munier, kept up an unceasing barrage of gunfire on their enemies.

Meanwhile Georges, still confined to his litter in the crude hut, cursed his own weakness and the inactivity it had forced upon him. The scent of the powder smoke swirling in the air and the cracking of musket fire in his ears left him frantic to join his comrades in the fray. His anxiety to fight was made even greater by the fact that this was no foreign cause for which they battled, no king whose honor they defended, no nation whose borders they protected. It was Georges these brave blacks were fighting for, and now he, strong of heart and ambitious of spirit, could not join them on the field of combat, or even counsel them in their strategy of defense. Georges gritted his teeth as he lay there on the rough mattress. Finally he wept tears of rage.

The next attack brought the British soldiers as far as the middle of the clearing, and they fired a few shots on the trenches. Georges's hut was directly behind the fortifications, and two or three musket balls whistled between the leaves and branches of its walls. Such a close call would have terrified a normal man, but Georges was pleased—even comforted—by it. He was grateful that he could share his comrades' peril, and consoled by the thought that if he could not deal out death himself, he could at least die in the line of fire.

The English troops now ceased fire momentarily, but it was clear that they were preparing for a fresh assault. The constant clinking of the pickaxes outside the enclosure told the rebels that it was only a matter of time before their refuge was completely breached; indeed, a large portion of the grotto's outer wall had already been torn down. The drums rolled again, and in the pale moonlight the soldiers' bayonets could be seen gleaming at the entrance cavern. Pierre Munier and Laïza exchanged glances; this, the third skirmish, promised to be the bloodiest yet.

"What is our last resort?" Laïza asked Pierre Munier.

"We've booby-trapped the grotto," replied the old man.

"In that case," said Laïza, "we still have a chance of winning. When the moment of truth comes, do what I tell you or we are all lost. With Georges wounded, there will be no possibility of retreat."

"Then I shall die by my son's side," Pierre Munier said.

"It would be better," said Laïza, "if both of you were safe."

"Both of us?"

"Yes, or either of you. What difference does it make?"

"You know, Laïza, that I will never leave my son."

"You will, if it is the only way to ensure his safety."

Pierre Munier frowned. "What do you mean?"

"I will explain later." Laïza turned to the waiting blacks. "Now, my men, the hour of decision has arrived! Fire upon the redcoats, and do not waste a single shot! In another hour, powder and bullets will be scarce indeed."

The Negroes fired. In general, they are a race of excellent marksmen, and several gaps were made in the British ranks—though it must be owned that these were filled again with admirable efficiency, and that the soldiers' forward advance, though slowed a bit by the rough terrain of the cavern, barely missed a step. The hail of bullets raining down on the rebels had ceased; it appeared that the enemy was now determined to take the trenches by bayonet.

The situation, grave as it was for everyone involved, was doubly perilous for Georges. He had raised himself upon his elbow, then struggled to his knees, and finally came shakily to his feet. But his weakness was so great that the earth seemed to rock beneath his feet, and he had to cling to the branches surrounding him with both hands. Well aware of the unswerving courage of the men who had pledged themselves to him until the end, he could not help regarding the cool bravery of the English troops with nearly equal admiration. They moved forward as smartly as if they were on parade, though rebel bullets felled a few of them and they were obliged to reform their ranks with every step they took. He felt sure that they would never consider retreat; despite the ongoing fire of the blacks, they would likely overwhelm the trenches within five minutes.

Suddenly a realization hit Georges like a thunderbolt. For him, *him,* a useless and wounded man unable to participate in the battle raging around him, all these men were going to lose their lives. Remorse washed over him. He tried to take a step, to throw himself into the midst of the fray as a sacrifice so that the carnage might cease—after all, it was in all probability him alone that the pursuers were seeking—but he knew he would not be able to walk even a third of the distance that separated him from the English troops. He shouted to the rebels to cease their fire, and to the attackers to stop their advance; he wished to surrender himself. But his weak voice was lost in the noise of battle.

Just then he saw his father draw himself up to his full height—which placed his entire upper body above the safety of the trench—holding a flaming fir branch aloft. Moving a few steps toward the enemy, Pierre Munier touched his torch to the ground. A trail of fire ignited, ran a short distance along the dirt, and buried itself in the earth. An instant later the ground on which the English soldiers were standing crumbled under their feet. A terrible explosion was heard, and the roof of the cavern blew apart. An enormous crater now yawned beneath the enemy's feet. Boulders and shards of rock tumbled into the crater, and the cries of the troops on the other side of the entrance were drowned out as the passage imploded with a rumbling crash.

"Now," cried Laïza above the din, "there is not a moment to lose!"

"Tell us, what must we do?" shouted Pierre Munier.

"Go to Grand Port. Try to find asylum aboard a French vessel. I will take care of Georges."

Pierre Munier shook his head. "I have already said I will not leave my son."

"And *I* have said you will, because for you to remain would mean his certain death!"

"But how?"

"Your dog is still tracking you, monsieur," Laïza reminded the old man. "They will follow you anywhere you go—into the deepest woods or the darkest caverns. Georges is wounded; he cannot move very fast, and they will catch him easily. But if you run, they will assume your son is with you and leave the rest of us alone. I can use the darkness—I will take four loyal men and carry Georges in a direction opposite of yours. If we can reach Mont Bambou, we can hide in the forest there. Get to île des Oiseaux and light a signal fire, if you are able. We will take to Grande-Rivière on a raft, and you can fetch us in a skiff at its source. Then we can all flee together."

Pierre Munier gazed at Laïza as he listened, barely breathing, grasping the Negro's hands in his own. Then, as the other man finished his speech, he grasped him in a fierce hug. "Yes," he cried, "yes! I understand now; there are no longer any other means open to us. Let the English come after me, and in the meantime look after my Georges!"

"I will save him, or die with him," Laïza vowed. "I promise you that."

"I know you will keep your promise," said Pierre Munier. "Let me embrace my son just once more, and then I will go."

"No!" said Laïza. "If you see him, you may lose the will to leave—if he sees you, if he learns that you are risking your life to save his, he will not allow it! Go, now!" He turned to the rest of the blacks. "Follow Monsieur Munier, all of you! I need only four men, the strongest and most loyal among you, to remain with me." Twelve men stepped forward, volunteering themselves, and Laïza chose the stoutest among them. Then, seeing that Pierre Munier still hesitated, he urged him again to run. "The English will be upon us in an instant," he warned.

"I will see you at the mouth of Grande-Rivière," said the old man.

"Yes—if we are not killed, or taken prisoner."

"Adieu, Georges! Adieu, my son!" Pierre Munier cried. Followed by the surviving Negroes, he turned and dashed in the direction of Mont Créole.

In his hut Georges heard Pierre Munier's shouted farewell. "Father!" he cried. "What are you doing—where are you going? Why do you not remain, to die with your son? Father, I am here! Wait for me!" But Pierre was already far away, and Georges's words were uttered in a voice so weak that the old man could not possibly hear them.

Laïza went to the wounded man; he found Georges on his knees. "Father . . . ," the young man murmured, and sank to the ground, unconscious.

Laïza moved quickly; indeed, Georges had fainted at a very opportune moment. He knew that if the mulatto had been in full possession of his faculties he would have fought to the death, regarding retreat as an act of cowardice. But in his weakened state, he was entirely in Laïza's power. The Negro now laid his prostrate form back on the litter, and the other four blacks each seized a handle and hoisted it to their shoulders. The party moved toward the area known as Trois-Ilots, from where they hoped to reach Mont Bambou by following the winding course of the Grande-Rivière.

They had not gone more than a quarter of a league when they heard the barking of a dog. They stopped in their tracks. Georges was still unconscious, or at least so weak that he seemed unaware of what was going on around him. Laïza had predicted correctly once again. The English had scaled the rubble created by the gunpowder blast and were again following Fidèle, who was hot on the fugitives' trail.

There was a moment of terrible suspense while Laïza listened to the howling of the dog. For a few moments the sound remained stationary; Fidèle had evidently reached the spot where the fighting had taken place. Then the barking drew nearer once again. The dog moved from the deserted trenches to the hut in which Georges had lain, and where his father had come several times to see him. Then the howling moved south—the direction Pierre Munier had taken when he fled with the rebels. Laïza's ruse had worked. The hunters now unknowingly pursued the father instead of the son.

Still, the situation in which Laïza, Georges, and the four litter bearers now found themselves was hardly a safe one. The first rays of dawn had appeared in the sky, and the sheltering shadows of the forest began to fade away. If Georges had been unhurt the party would have been in an advantageous position, for his cunning and skill, as well as Laïza's, easily matched those of the pursuers. But the young mulatto's injury made the field an unequal one, and Laïza could not deny the fact that they were in grave peril.

One thing was especially worrisome: The English had most likely enlisted the services of slaves trained in the pursuit of runaways, promising them some lofty reward—such as their liberty—if they were able to capture Georges Munier. If this was indeed the case, Laïza would lose part of his advantage by facing other men used to nature and equally skilled in navigating the wilderness and the blackness of the forest at night. There was, he concluded, no time to lose. Deducing the direction from which the pursuers were coming, he led the others decisively eastward.

The woods felt strange here, as if all the animals shared the refugees' anxiety. The night's unceasing musket fire had frightened the birds from their nests, the wild pigs from their dens, and the deer from their hiding places among the trees. Everything seemed to be moving, fleeing in fear. It was almost as if a sort of terrified dizziness had seized every living creature.

Two hours had passed when it became necessary for them to halt. They had fought all night and eaten nothing since four o'clock the previous afternoon. Laïza stopped beneath the ruins of an ajoupa that had obviously served as a refuge for other runaways that very night; it contained a fire that still smoldered beneath its bed of ashes. Three of the men now set off in search of some tenrecs while the fourth busied himself rekindling the fire. Laïza went out in search of the medicinal herbs he needed to refresh the dressing on Georges's wound.

As strong in both spirit and body as Georges was, on this occasion matter had triumphed over mind. He was feverish and delirious, unaware of what was happening around him and completely unable to take any active part in it. The cleansing and rebandaging of his wound seemed to give him some comfort, though; as for Laïza, he seemed to have risen above any consideration of the flesh. He had not slept in sixty hours, or eaten in twenty, yet he appeared neither tired nor hungry.

The hunters eventually returned to camp bringing half a dozen tenrecs, which they set to roast on the bonfire their companion had built. The smoke from the fire made Laïza slightly uneasy, but he comforted himself with the knowledge that they had left no tracks behind them and must now be at least two leagues from the grotto where the fighting had taken place. Even if their pursuers noticed the smoke, they would be so far away that the fugitives would have time to flee before they reached them.

The meal was ready, and the blacks called Laïza from his seat at Georges's side. As he joined them, he noticed that one of the men had a gash in his thigh, which was still bleeding. In an instant his sense of security was gone. The British would be able to follow the trail of blood drops, just as if they were tracking a wounded deer—and they would certainly do so; not because they believed Georges was at the other end of the trail, but because any prisoner would be of great importance to them. A prisoner would be able to give them information, and the English would use any means necessary to extract it from him.

The realization hit Laïza like a thunderbolt. Just as he opened his mouth to order the others to prepare to start moving again immediately, a small, dense clump of trees nearby—which he had eyed uneasily more than once—flared with light. A staccato series of shots rang out, and bullets whistled through the air. Five or six of them whizzed past Laïza. One of the Negroes collapsed face-first into the fire. The others ran, but not quickly enough. Another man fell, then another ten paces away. Only the fourth remained untouched; he disappeared into the surrounding woods.

At the sight of the smoke and the sound of the gunshots, Laïza had leapt with one enormous bound to Georges's side. Lifting the wounded man as if he were a child, he dashed into the trees. Almost at the same moment eight or ten British soldiers accompanied by half a dozen Negroes emerged from the thicket and ran in pursuit of the fugitives. They had followed the trail of blood, just as Laïza feared. One of them had recognized Georges's prone form, and seen that he was wounded. The ambush had gone off without a hitch; out of Georges and Laïza's party of six, only three remained.

A desperate race now began; it was clear that despite Laïza's agility and strength, his pursuers would soon overtake him. His only chance was to lose them in the depths of the forest, but that option held its own dangers. If he sought out the area where the trees and foliage were thickest, he would probably come up against a barrier he could not pass; on the other hand, if he stayed in the open glades, his enemies could see him much more easily.

Despite its perils, he decided upon the latter course. Even carrying Georges, Laïza was able to move fast enough to be almost out of range of the English guns; if the soldiers had been on their own in this unknown territory, he could have escaped them easily. But the Negro slaves were there, too; however regretfully, however propelled forward by the points of bayonets, they chased their human prey out of not zeal but fear.

The hunters fired a few shots whenever they caught a glimpse of Laïza among the trees; the bullets sliced through the leaves around his head or tore up the earth at his feet but, as if by magic, none of them penetrated his body. Indeed, his speed seemed to increase along with the danger he faced.

Finally they reached the edge of a clearing that was steep and almost bare of foliage, crowned with trees only at its summit. If Laïza could reach the top of the hill, he might hide behind some boulder or drop down into the shelter of a ravine, thus concealing him from his pursuers; but the fact remained that he would be an easy target during the climb. There was no time to decide; he thought fast. If he went to the right or the left he would lose precious ground.

Fortune had been kind to the fugitives thus far; perhaps their luck would hold. Laïza darted forward into the open glade. His pursuers, seeing that they had a good chance of bringing him down, redoubled their fire. They came to the edge of the clearing when Laïza was about 150 feet up the slope. Halting and raising their rifles, they fired. Their quarry did not fall, but continued his desperate race to the summit.

Hurriedly, before they lost sight of him, the soldiers reloaded. Laïza took advantage of the momentary pause to gain as much ground as he could. He was barely 25 feet away from the edge of the thicket now; his pursuers were fully 150 feet behind him. If he could manage to evade the second round of English fire as successfully as he had the first, he would reach the woods safe and sound. Everything seemed in his favor. Suddenly he disappeared into a small crevasse—but unfortunately he did not slide immediately to the right or the left. He followed its curves as best he could, trying to lose the enemy, but when he reached the end of the ravine he had no choice but to scramble up the bank that had momentarily protected him and reappear in view of the English soldiers.

A dozen shots rang out at once.

It seemed to the man hunters that they had won. Laïza staggered a few more steps, and fell to first one, then both knees. Gently, carefully, he placed the still-unconscious Georges on the ground. Then he rose to his feet and, drawing himself to his full height, turned toward the English soldiers. He threw out his hands to them in a final gesture of pride and supreme malediction—then, drawing a knife from his belt, he buried it up to the hilt in his breast.

The soldiers rushed forward, whooping as joyfully as if they had brought down a prize stag, as hunters do when they celebrate a kill.

For a few seconds more, Laïza stood erect. Then all at once he fell like an uprooted tree.

When the English soldiers reached the prone forms of the two fugitives, they found Laïza dead and Georges nearly so. The mulatto, determined not to fall into enemy hands alive, had used the last of his strength to rip the bandage off his wound. Blood flowed from it in thick streams and soaked the dark earth.

The knife had pierced Laïza's heart. One bullet had struck him in the thigh. Another, passing through his back, had gone cleanly through his chest.

XXVII

THE REHEARSAL

Georges barely remembered the two or three days following the catastrophe I have just related. In his delirium he remembered only vague, disjointed images, and was unaware of time or space. Suddenly, finally, he awoke as if from a nightmare-filled sleep to the bright light of morning—and found himself in prison. The surgeon of the Port Louis military garrison was at his bedside.

Georges struggled to collect his thoughts. Memories came to him like lakes, mountains, and forests seen through thick fog. He could remember everything up to the moment when he had been shot, but his return to Moka and the departure with his father were a complete blank. His recollections of the time after his arrival in the Great Woods were vague and indistinct, like a dream.

The only clear, incontrovertible fact was that he had, somehow, fallen into his enemies' hands.

Georges's pride would not allow him to ask any questions or request any favor of his captors, so he would be obliged to remain ignorant— but deep in his soul, two questions raged. Was his father safe? Did Sara still love him? These thoughts consumed him, filled his whole being to overflowing. When one of them left his mind, the other took its place.

They were like two tides, incessantly beating upon his heart. But as always, his pale face was as cool and inscrutable as a marble statue's whether he was in view of visitors to the prison or alone.

Once the surgeon had determined that his patient was well enough to be questioned, he lost no time in informing the authorities. The next day an examining magistrate and a clerk came into Georges's room. The young man was not yet able to leave his bed but, greeting the men with dignified patience, he raised himself on one elbow and declared that he would reply to any questions the magistrate wished to ask.

By now my readers are too well acquainted with Georges's character to imagine that he would, for an instant, consider denying any of the charges brought against him. He replied to every one of the magistrate's questions with complete truthfulness, and even offered to dictate a detailed account of the entire conspiracy the next day, when a little more of his strength had returned—an offer much too handsome to be refused.

Of course, the motives behind Georges's willingness to cooperate were twofold. First, he wished to hasten the process of his trial. Second, he was determined to take sole responsibility for the entire revolt.

The two officials returned to his sickroom the next morning, and Georges gave them the narrative he had promised. It was indeed complete, except for one thing—he did not mention the proposals Laïza had made to him. The omission did not go unnoticed by the magistrate, who informed Georges that it was not necessary to leave out anything in order to protect Laïza; since the Negro had been killed by British soldiers, his crimes were no longer imputable to anyone.

This was how Georges found out that his friend was dead, and learned the circumstances of his demise for, as I have said, his memory of that time was cloaked in darkness.

He was careful not to utter the name of Pierre Munier, and the officials did not bring it up; neither, for even more profound reasons, did he mention Sara. When he had finished relating the details of the conspiracy, there was no point in questioning him further. Except for the doctor, no one disturbed his solitude again.

One morning, when the physician came in to check on his patient, he found Georges out of bed. "Monsieur!" he exclaimed. "You must not stand for a few days yet—you are still much too weak!"

"Sir," Georges said, "you do me a dishonor if you imagine that I am like an ordinary criminal, desperate to defer the day of my trial as long as I can. On the contrary, I am quite eager for this entire matter to be over. Besides, if we are being frank, what is the purpose in making sure that I am healthy enough to die? It seems to me that as long as I have enough strength to mount the scaffold, no man can demand more of me—nor I of God."

"But who told you that you will be condemned to death?" asked the doctor.

"My conscience has told me," Georges replied. "I played a game in which my very life was at stake, and I lost. I am ready to pay the price. That is all."

"Whatever the case," said the doctor, "I believe you still need a few days more of rest and care before facing the difficulties of a trial—and the anxieties of a verdict."

But Georges wrote that very day to the examining magistrate to inform him that he was entirely recovered and at the disposal of the law. The trial began the next morning.

When he entered the courtroom, Georges's first act was to look around anxiously—and he saw, with relief, that he was the sole defendant. He gazed, confidently now, around the chamber. It seemed that the whole population of île de France had turned out for his trial—with the notable exceptions of M. de Malmédie and Sara. A few of the spectators' faces displayed pity for the accused, but most of them bore only hatred and satisfaction.

Georges, as ever, was calm; even haughty. He wore his usual attire of a beautifully cut black frock coat and cravat, with white waistcoat and trousers. The double ribbon of honor given to him by the king of France was knotted in his buttonhole.

The court had appointed an attorney to defend him, for he had refused to choose one of his own. He firmly believed that none should even attempt to plead his cause.

When the time came for Georges to testify on his own behalf, what he said could not be considered an attempt to defend himself. Rather, it was the story of his life. He did not try to hide the fact that he had returned to île de France with the sole purpose of fighting, by whatever means necessary, the prejudice against men of color that had existed there for so long. On the subject of the specific events that had precipitated the revolt, he said nothing at all. When the judge put questions to him regarding M. de Malmédie, Georges asked permission to remain silent.

Despite the defendant's cooperativeness, the attorneys' fondness for their own voices, a trait common to lawyers everywhere, stretched the trial for three full days. The leading prosecutor spoke for no less than four hours, haranguing Georges endlessly. The young man listened coolly, attentively, nodding from time to time in confession to charges that were leveled at him. When the barrage of words had finally ended, the presiding judge asked Georges if he had anything to say.

"No," Georges said. "The prosecutor has spoken very eloquently."

The prosecutor sketched a bow.

The magistrate now announced that the trial was over, and Georges was taken back to his prison cell. The verdict would be determined privately, and the accused notified later.

Upon his return to the prison cell Georges asked for paper and ink, to write his will. English verdicts did not extend to confiscation of property, so he could dispose of his fortune as he pleased.

He left the surgeon who had attended him one thousand pounds sterling, and five hundred pounds to the warden. The prison guards received one thousand piastres each. For all of them, it was a fortune.

To Sara, he bequeathed a gold ring that had belonged to his mother.

Just as he was about to sign his name at the bottom of the document, a court clerk entered the room. Georges stood, still holding the pen, as the verdict was read.

As he had predicted, he was condemned to death.

Bowing to the clerk, he sat down again and signed his name to the will. His handwriting remained as smooth and steady as it had been before he heard the death sentence. Then, rising again, Georges went to the mirror and looked at his face—it was as pale, calm, and inscrutable as ever. Satisfied, he smiled to himself, murmuring: "I did think that hearing oneself condemned to death would be more emotional than this."

At length the doctor returned to check on his patient, routinely asking him how he felt. "Very well," Georges replied. "You have treated me remarkably well. How frustrating it must be that you will not have time to complete the cure. Tell me, monsieur: Is the British method of execution here the same that was used by the French?"

It was. Georges was pleased; he would suffer neither the indignity of the London gallows nor the horror of the Parisian guillotine. In Port Louis executions were conducted so as to be almost poetic, even picturesque—a fact that soothed Georges's pride. A black man—a slave-executioner—would strike off his head with an ax. Thus had Charles I, Mary Stuart, the marquis de Cinq-Mars, and François-Auguste de Thou met their deaths. It would be a fitting end for Georges Munier.

Calmly, almost indifferently, he engaged the surgeon in a discussion about whether one might continue to feel physical pain after decapitation. While the doctor insisted that death would be instantaneous, Georges was not so sure. Once, in Egypt, he had witnessed the execution of a slave. The victim had knelt down, and the swordsman had taken off his head in a single blow. The head had rolled several feet away, but the body had climbed to its feet and taken two or three clumsy steps, beating the air with its fists, before falling again—still in apparent agony; not absolutely dead. On another occasion in the same country, curiosity had led him to pick up the head of that day's victim immediately after it had been severed from the body. Holding by the hair, close to his face, he had asked it in Arabic: "Are you suffering?" At the question, the eyes had opened and the lips moved, seemingly attempting to voice a reply. For Georges, this was certain proof that life did continue for some moments after decapitation—and the doctor ended by agreeing with him, for he had in truth believed the same thing all along, and had only wished to console the young man with the promise of an easy and painless death.

The rest of the day passed for Georges just as the previous ones. He wrote to his father and his brother; once he picked up the pen to write to Sara, but before committing a single word to paper he let the pen drop and buried his head in his hands. He remained that way for a considerable time, and if anyone had been there to watch him raise his head, which he did with the haughty movement so habitual for him, they would have seen that his eyes were reddened, and that a single tear still trembled at the ends of his long black lashes. Since the day he had refused Sara's hand in Lord Murray's elegant parlor he had not seen her, or even heard her name mentioned—yet he would not, could not, believe that she had forgotten him so easily.

Night fell, and Georges went to bed at his usual hour. He slept as soundly as he always had, and the next morning he asked to see the warden. "Monsieur," he said when the man had arrived, "I have something to ask of you."

"Yes, what is it?"

"I should like to have a word with the executioner."

The warden frowned. "That will require the permission of His Excellency, the governor."

"Oh," said Georges, smiling, "then please do ask it of him. Lord Murray is a true gentleman, and I am sure he will not refuse to grant this favor to an old friend."

The warden withdrew, promising to do as Georges asked, and as he left a priest entered the cell.

Georges harbored the sort of religious ideas that many men have these days: They neglect the outer trappings of faith but remain at the bottom of their hearts profoundly affected by sacred objects. Thus it is that a somber church, a lonely cemetery, a passing casket make a far deeper impression on their souls than any of the coarser aspects of life to which they are so often exposed.

The priest was a venerable old man, the sort who does not waste time trying to convert others but speaks with all the authority and force of true conviction. He had been brought up amid the majesty of nature, and believed that the Lord could be found in every aspect of its glorious scenery. His serene and godly nature attracted those who were suffering or downtrodden, consoling them and holding them up by selflessly sharing their burdens. Georges had an immediate rapport with the old man, and they impulsively clasped hands.

The conversation that followed was intimate and friendly, with nothing in it of a confession. Georges was humbled by the priest's gentleness. The young man reproached himself for his pride, feeling that—like Satan—it was the only sin he was guilty of, and that it alone had caused his downfall. Yet it was pride that, even now, sustained him, gave him strength, and made him great in the eyes of all who saw him—though grandeur is not the same thing to men as it is to God.

He was tempted again and again to speak of Sara, but he stopped himself. His heart was a dark pit of emotion and his face, like a sheet of ice, concealed the depths of his soul.

As the priest and the condemned man talked, the door opened and the warden appeared. "The man you asked for is outside," he said. "He will wait until you are ready to see him."

Georges paled. A nearly imperceptible shudder ran through him. "Let him come in." The priest made to leave the room, but Georges stopped him. "Please, stay," he said. "What I have to say to this man is nothing you may not also hear." Perhaps, in his pride, he needed a witness to help him keep his strength.

A tall Negro of Herculean proportions entered the room. He was nude except for his red loincloth, and his large, expressionless eyes were devoid of intelligence. He turned to the warden, who had escorted him to the cell, and jerked his head at Georges and the priest. "Which one?" he asked.

"The young man," the warden replied and withdrew from the room.

"You are the executioner," stated Georges, impassively.

"Yes."

"Good. Come, my friend, and answer a few questions." The big Negro moved a few steps closer to Georges. "You are aware that you are to execute me tomorrow morning?"

"Yes," responded the black, "at seven o'clock."

"Seven o'clock, eh? Thank you for telling me; the warden would not when I asked him. That, however, was not my main question."

The priest's heart sank.

"I have never witnessed an execution here in Port Louis," Georges continued. "I am anxious that everything should be conducted with decorum. That is why I wanted to see you—so that we could rehearse, as they say in the theater."

The executioner looked confused. Georges repeated what he wanted, slowly and clearly. The Negro, when he finally understood, fetched a stool from the corner of the room; it would serve as the "block." He led Georges to it and had him kneel down, positioning him so that, he promised, the ax would strike off his head in one blow.

The priest, distressed, rose to leave the room. He could not endure this macabre rehearsal in which the two actors remained so emotionless—the one thanks to his primitive spirit, the other to his strength of character. But the old man's knees trembled as he stood, and he sank back into his chair.

The instructions for death given and received, Georges took a diamond ring from his finger. "I have no money here," he said to the Negro. "But take this, so that you will not have entirely wasted your time."

"I am forbidden to accept any gifts from condemned prisoners," replied the black man. "But I can inherit things from them. Leave the ring on your finger, and I will remove it after you are dead."

"Very well." Nodding calmly, Georges returned the ring to his hand. The Negro departed. Georges now turned to the priest, who sat in his chair, his face deathly pale.

"My son," the old man murmured, "never yet have I met with a soul as firm as yours. I must tell you that tomorrow will be the first time I have accompanied a condemned man as he walks to the scaffold; I fear I will lose my nerve. You will hold me up if I do, will you not?"

"You may be sure of it, Father," Georges replied. The old priest was gratified. His small church lay along the route to the scaffold, and it was there that the condemned men usually stopped to hear a final mass. The church was called Saint-Sauveur.

Promising to return later in the evening, the priest departed. Georges was left alone.

What passed through Georges's mind and over his face during the hours of solitude, no one could know. Perhaps all his years of self-discipline failed him and nature, pitiless nature, overcame him, and he became as weak as he had formerly been strong. Perhaps, once the curtain had fallen and he was no longer obliged to act stoic for the benefit of others, his tranquility gave way to real agony. But it is probable that none of this happened—for when the key to his door turned and a guard appeared with his dinner, he found Georges rolling a small cigar as calmly as if he were a fashionable vacationer on the Puerta del Sol in Madrid or the boulevard de Gand in Paris.

Georges ate with his usual good appetite, then called the guard and asked to be awakened at half past five, and for a bath to be drawn by six o'clock.

In his prodigious reading over the years, Georges had perused many accounts of the awakening of condemned men and women on the mornings of their executions, and wondered if those unfortunate individuals had really been able to sleep. The time had now come for him to learn the truth firsthand.

The priest returned at nine o'clock as he had promised. Georges lay in bed, reading. What was the book he was reading to prepare himself for death, the old man inquired: perhaps *Phaedo,* or the Bible? Georges handed it to him. It was Bernardin de Saint-Pierre's *Paul et Virginie,* the famous novel set on île de France. How strange it was, thought the priest, that on this terrible night the young man had chosen to read a story of such poetry and peace!

The clergyman stayed until eleven o'clock. Georges spoke nearly the entire time, sharing his perception of God and his theories about the immortality of the soul. The young man had always been eloquent, but now, during this last evening of his life, he was sublime! Tonight, he—a condemned man—was the teacher. It was the priest who listened, and learned.

At eleven o'clock Georges rose and announced that he must retire. He would need strength, he said, for what was to come. As the old man went to the door, though, Georges suddenly called him back—a painful conflict appeared to be raging in his heart.

But no sooner had the old man returned to his side than the young man, controlling himself with a visible effort, again told him to go. "It is nothing, Father," he said, "nothing at all." He was lying, of course; it was Sara's name that had risen once more to his lips. But still he held back, and the priest finally bade him farewell and departed none the wiser.

At half past five the next morning the guard entered and found Georges sleeping soundly. "Ah, so it is true," the young man said as he awoke. "A condemned man can pass his final hours at rest." But how long had he stayed awake the night before to achieve that result? It is impossible to say.

They brought in his bath.

The surgeon entered. "You see," Georges said to him, "how I keep to the customs of antiquity. The Athenians always bathed before going into battle."

The doctor was at a loss for words. Finally he fell back on the empty phrases always used by physicians when there is nothing else to say: "How do you feel?"

"Very well," said Georges, smiling. "I am beginning to think that my wound will not kill me after all." He placed his will, folded and sealed, in the doctor's hands. "I have named you as my executor," he said. "A few lines in this document concern you, as well; I wished to leave you something in remembrance."

The physician dashed away a tear and murmured a few words of thanks. Georges got into the bath.

"Tell me," he said after a short silence. "Under normal circumstances, how many times does a healthy man's heart beat in one minute?"

"Between sixty-four and sixty-six," said the doctor.

"Take my pulse, please," said Georges. "I would like to feel how my body is reacting as death grows closer."

Pulling out his watch, the physician took Georges's wrist. "Sixty-eight," he said after a minute.

"Good; I am well pleased!" Georges exclaimed. "What do you think, monsieur?"

"It is a miracle," said the surgeon. "You must be made of iron."

Georges smiled with pride. "The whites are in quite a hurry to see me die," he said. "Well, I will give them a good show—and a lesson in courage, besides!"

The jailer entered the cell and announced that it was almost six o'clock. "My dear doctor," said Georges, "may I have a moment of privacy to dress myself? Please, do not go far. I should like to shake hands with you before I depart."

The surgeon left the room. Georges got out of the bath and donned his white trousers, polished boots, and cambric shirt—the collar of which he carefully turned down. Standing before the mirror, he combed his jet-black hair, mustache, and beard with as much care as if he were preparing for a ball. Then, going to the door, he knocked to indicate that he was ready. The priest, who had just arrived, looked at him in wonder. The young man had never been more handsome. His eyes shone, and his face glowed.

"Oh, my son!" cried the priest, involuntarily. "Beware of pride! Already it has cost you your life; do not let it destroy your soul!"

"But you have promised to pray for me, Father," Georges reminded him. "Surely God will not ignore the prayers of a man as holy as you."

At that moment he became aware of the executioner, standing half hidden in the shadows by the doorway. The Negro was wrapped in a billowing cloak beneath which, Georges knew, the ax hung concealed. "Good morning, my friend," he said. "I trust your ax is well sharpened?"

"It is," replied the Negro. "You may rest easy on that score."

"Good," said Georges. He noticed the executioner's eyes moving to his hand, looking at the diamond ring he had been promised the evening before. The ring had turned and the stone, now facing inward, was hidden. "Do not worry," he said, turning the ring so the diamond was visible again. "You shall have your reward. Indeed, let me make sure you will have no trouble getting it." Taking off the jewel, he handed it to the priest with instructions that, when he was dead, it should go to the big Negro.

Now he went to the desk and, opening it, removed two letters. One was addressed to his father; the other, to his brother. He gave them to the priest as well. Then, again, he hesitated. Placing his hand on the old man's shoulder, he gazed at him and opened his mouth as if to speak—but, once more, his will was stronger than his emotions, and the name he yearned to say died away on his lips. Six o'clock struck.

"It is time; let us go," Georges said. He strode out of the cell, followed by the priest and the executioner. The physician waited at the bottom of the steps to bid him a last farewell. Georges grasped his hand and leaned over to whisper a single phrase in his ear: "I commend my body to you."

Then, shoulders squared, he walked to the courtyard.

THE CHURCH OF SAINT-SAUVEUR

As may be imagined, the prison gate was thronged with curious spectators. Spectacles are rare in Port Louis, and everyone wanted to watch the condemned man—if not as he met his end, at least as he made his way to the scaffold. As a last act of kindness, the warden had asked Georges how he wished to go to his death, and Georges had requested—and obtained—permission to go on foot. It was a final gesture of friendship on the part of the governor.

Eight mounted artillery soldiers waited at the gate. The streets through which Georges would walk were lined with soldiers, both to guard the prisoner and to keep the populace under control. As the condemned man passed, a hum of murmurs arose—but contrary to what Georges had expected, most of the voices did not sound hostile, only interested, and pitying. The simple fact was that the sight of a proud and handsome man going to his death held, as it always does, a powerful fascination.

Georges walked with a firm step, his head held high and his features impassive—but inside, his heart was twisted with grief and despair. He thought only of Sara, who had not even attempted to see him in prison. Sara, who had not written a single word or sent a single remembrance of their passion. Sara, in whom he had believed completely, and because of whom he now suffered his final disappointment. If he had been sure of her love, Georges would have felt much more regret at dying—but her indifference had left him drained of emotion. His lover had betrayed him; his pride had deluded him. He had failed at everything. All his superiority of character and education, his long struggle, had led him nowhere but to the steps of the scaffold, alone. He would be remembered as nothing but a madman.

As he walked, looking at the crowd, a faint smile crossed his lips. It was an expression that concealed pure bitterness. Still, at every corner, every window, he looked for Sara. Surely she, who had dropped her bouquet at his feet when he raced Antrim to victory in the Yamsé festival, would spare a tear for him as he trod the path to the scaffold!

But she was nowhere to be found.

Coming to the end of the rue de Paris, he turned right toward the Church of Saint-Sauveur. It was draped in black, as if for a funeral—and indeed, what is a condemned man en route to the scaffold but a living corpse? As he approached the church door, Georges started in surprise. The good priest was there, waiting for him, and at his side was a woman dressed in black, her face covered by a long veil. Why was she there? For whom did she wait?

Despite himself, Georges walked more quickly. He could not tear his gaze away from the woman in black. As he approached her, his heart beat wildly in his chest. He, who had been so calm in the face of his imminent death, now grew feverish. As he mounted the first step to the church door, she moved forward to meet him. Georges leapt the remaining four steps in a single bound, threw back her veil, and fell to his knees with a cry.

It was Sara.

She extended a hand slowly and solemnly, and silence fell over the enormous crowd.

"Listen to me; all of you," she said. "Here, on the threshold of this holy place about to serve as Georges Munier's tomb, I ask you to bear witness. Before all of you—before God—I, Sara de Malmédie, ask this man to do me the honor of taking me as his bride."

Georges burst into tears.

"Oh, Sara," he murmured. "You are the noblest, most gracious, most generous of women!" He stood, drawing himself up to his full height, and enfolded her in his arms, holding her tightly as if he were afraid she would disappear. "Come, then, my widow," he said. They entered the church.

In an instant everything had changed for Georges. Defeated the moment before, now he was triumphant beyond measure. With a few words Sara had raised him far above the crowd that had watched him pass. No longer was he a madman, stymied in all he had attempted and dying in disgrace; now he was the victor, about to fall at the height of his triumph. He was Epaminondas, mortally wounded on the field of battle but able to watch his enemies flee as he died.

By his will alone, by the power of his character, he, a mulatto, had won the love of a white woman. He had not pursued her; he had not tried to influence her with letters or words or signals; yet she had come, draped in black, to wait for him on his way to the scaffold—had, in front of the entire population of Port Louis, taken the unprecedented action of choosing him for her husband.

Now, Georges felt, he could die. His long struggle had paid off. He had fought prejudice with his bare hands, and—though he had been mortally wounded in the process—he had vanquished it after all.

These thoughts made Georges radiant as he led Sara into the church. He was no longer the condemned man about to climb the scaffold. Now he was a martyr, surely, joyfully, on his way to heaven.

Twenty soldiers flanked the main aisle of the church, and four more guarded the choir. Georges passed by them without noticing, and knelt with Sara at the altar. The priest began the nuptial mass, but the young man was deaf to the words he spoke. He held Sara's hand in his own, turning now and then to throw the crowd a look of supreme disdain. He gazed at Sara, who was pale as death, and felt her hand tremble in his. His eyes shone down at her, full of gratitude and love, and he fought down the rising sorrow in his breast. What a life he could have had, with such a woman at his side! It would have been heavenly indeed—but after all, heaven is not for the living.

The mass was proceeding apace when Georges caught sight of Miko-Miko, gesturing and trying frantically to break through the ranks of soldiers and get to his master's side. He must have come as a final act of allegiance, hoping to meet Georges's eye once more, to shake his hand one last time. Georges murmured a few words to the commanding officer, asking permission for the Chinese man to be allowed to approach him. This was a harmless favor to grant the condemned man, and the soldiers drew aside to let Miko-Miko into the choir.

We have seen how the poor merchant had been devoted to Georges from their first meeting. Miko-Miko had risked his own life to save the mulatto when he had been held prisoner at the guardhouse; now he did so once again, in the very shadow of the scaffold. He threw himself on his knees in front of Georges, who held out his hand. The Chinese man took it, and pressed it to his lips—and at the same moment, Georges felt the peddler slip a small piece of paper into his hand. The young man felt a jolt of surprise. Miko-Miko rose silently and left the choir. He had not uttered a single word. Georges grasped the bit of paper in his hand, frowning. What could this mean? It must be important, but he dared not look at it. He turned his attention back to the wedding ceremony.

Sara was so beautiful, so devoted, so far beyond all earthly love, that a feeling of deep anguish gripped Georges's heart like an iron fist as he looked at her. The prospect of so much happiness with her as his wife had renewed his desire to live. He had prepared his soul for the flight to heaven, but his heart was firmly bound to earth.

For the first time, he felt afraid to die.

The slip of paper seemed to burn his hand. He could not possibly read it now and risk the soldiers seeing it, but what if it contained some message to give him hope? It was madness even to think such a thing, he knew, in the present situation. Impatience and curiosity raged within him, but with his usual self-control he kept his face perfectly impassive. Only the hand that held the note was clenched so tightly that the fingernails pressed into the flesh.

Sara was still kneeling, lost in prayer. They had now come to the administration of the sacred Host. The priest held the offering aloft, and at the sound of the chorister's bell everyone in the church dropped to his knees. Georges knelt as well, and took advantage of the moment to look at the note in his hand. It contained a single line: "We are here. Be ready."

The first sentence was in his brother Jacques's handwriting; the second in Pierre Munier's.

Georges, astonished and alone in the midst of the kneeling crowd, raised his head and looked around. At that instant the church doors burst open. Eight sturdy sailors rushed toward the altar, seizing the four soldiers guarding the choir and holding them immobile at dagger point. Now Jacques and Pierre Munier appeared; the former scooped Sara into his arms, while the latter seized Georges by the hand. They dashed toward the sacristy; the eight sailors holding the stunned British troops at bay and using their four captives as human shields. Jacques and Pierre slammed the sacristy door. Beyond the outer doors of the church there was open countryside. Two horses stood ready, saddled and bridled. One of them was a stallion named Yambo. The other was Antrim.

"Now mount up, you and Sara! Make like the wind for the Bay of Tombeau!" Jacques shouted.

"What about you and Father?" Georges cried.

"Bah! Let them come and try to take us, with my men protecting us!" Jacques placed Sara on her horse, while Pierre Munier hoisted his son onto Antrim. "Come to us, my fine Lascars!" Jacques bellowed. A hundred and twenty men, armed to the teeth, burst from among the trees at the base of Mont Longue and came toward them.

"Flee, now!" Jacques commanded Sara. "Take Georges away— make sure he is safe!"

"And you?" Sara asked.

"Don't worry; we will soon follow!"

"Georges!" cried Sara. "In the name of heaven, come with me!" The girl rode off at full gallop.

"Father, Father!" cried Georges again.

"I promise you, I will protect him with my life!" Jacques vowed. He struck Antrim's rump with the flat of his sword, and the stallion flew away like the wind. In less than ten minutes Georges and Sara had disappeared beyond the Malabar camp. Jacques and Pierre Munier and their men followed so rapidly that the English soldiers did not even have time to rouse themselves from their astonishment before the little band was on the other side of the Pucelles stream, and out of the range of their guns.

THE *LEICESTER*

By five o'clock that evening the brigantine *Calypso* was heading east-northeast at full sail, embracing the wind that, as is customary in those waters, blew from the east. In addition to her trusty crew and Master Tête-de-Fer, the first mate, whom my readers know by reputation if not by sight, the ship carried three passengers: Pierre Munier, Georges, and Sara. The old man paced the deck from mizzenmast to great mast and back again, Jacques at his side. The newlyweds sat together in the stern, holding hands. Sara gazed at the sky, and Georges gazed at Sara.

Without personal experience of the sort of dreadful situation the two lovers had just escaped, it would be impossible to imagine the sensations of supreme happiness and infinite joy they felt at finding themselves free on the immense ocean, sailing farther away at every moment from the country that had given them both life, it is true, but which, like a cruel mother, had alternated periodic persecution with habitual neglect. From time to time one of them would sigh so painfully as to make the other tremble; hearts long accustomed to torture do not regain trust in joy very quickly.

The truth was, though, that they *were* free. There was nothing above them but the blue vault of the sky; nothing below them but the emerald depths of the sea; and their swift ship was bearing them rapidly away from île de France, which had so nearly proved fatal to both of them.

Jacques and Pierre Munier conversed at length; Georges and Sara were all but silent, each murmuring the name of the other from time to time. Occasionally the father would pause to gaze at the lovers with an expression of indescribable contentment. The old man had suffered so much, and for so long, that he wondered if he would be able to bear such happiness.

Jacques, less sentimental by nature, also cast glances in the direction of the stern—but it was not the tender tableau I have just described that attracted his gaze. Rather, he looked over the heads of Georges and Sara at the open sea, gauging the distance between the *Calypso* and Port Louis. It was obvious that he did not quite share the general happiness, even that he was worried; he often dashed a hand across his brow, as if trying to chase away a storm cloud.

As for Tête-de-Fer, the first mate, he remained quietly stationed near the ship's wheel, chatting with the pilot. The brave Breton could be fearsome if one of the crew proved reluctant to follow his orders, but he was otherwise very down-to-earth, always ready with a handshake and a kind word. The rest of the crew was cheerful and carefree once more, as they always were after a dangerous engagement or the perils of a storm. The men on duty stood on deck; the others were in the battery below.

Pierre Munier, distracted as he was by the pleasure of witnessing his younger son's happiness, did not fail to notice his elder son's disquiet. Several times he followed Jacques's gaze, but saw nothing in that direction except a few immense clouds gathered around the setting sun. Perhaps the *Calypso*'s captain was worried about a storm, he thought.

"Does the weather seem threatening?" he inquired when Jacques cast one of his aforementioned worried glances toward the horizon.

Jacques shook his head. "No, no. If it were only a storm, the *Calypso* would be as threatened by that as she would by a mere seagull. Something altogether worse is menacing us, I'm afraid."

Pierre Munier's voice was worried. "What? I thought we were beyond danger as soon as we set foot on the *Calypso*."

Jacques smiled. "Our chances are certainly better now than they were twelve hours ago, when we were hiding in the woods of Petite-Montagne waiting for Georges to finish making his confession in the Church of Saint-Sauveur! I don't want to worry you, Father, but it is true—our heads aren't completely safe on our shoulders just yet." He raised his voice and shouted to no one in particular, "Aloft to the masthead!"

Three sailors jumped into action, and in a few seconds one of them was perched in the crow's nest, the others returning to the deck.

"What is it that you fear, Jacques?" the old man persisted. "Do you think we will be pursued?"

"You've hit the nail on the head, Father," Jacques replied. "And this time you've touched upon a sensitive spot. There's a frigate in Port Louis called the *Leicester*—an old acquaintance of mine. I'm afraid they will not let us escape without a little game of skittles—one we won't be able to decline."

"But—we must have a twenty-five- or thirty-mile head start at least," protested Pierre Munier. "At this rate we shall soon be out of sight of the island altogether."

"Cast out the log!" Jacques cried. Three men hastened to perform this duty, closely watched by their captain. "How many knots?" he asked one of them after a few moments.

"Ten, sir."

"Not bad for a close-hauled brigantine, eh? There is, perhaps, only one frigate in the whole English navy capable of going even half a knot faster in an hour. Unfortunately, that frigate happens to be the one following us. It looks as if the governor has taken it into his head to chase us."

"Oh—if you are worried about Lord Murray coming after us, you need not be," said Pierre Munier. "The governor and Georges were close friends."

"I know it," said Jacques. "But that did not protect Georges from a death sentence."

"Lord Murray could not have acted otherwise without failing in his duty as governor."

"Ah, but this time, Father, it is not only his duty that is at stake—it is his pride, as well. I have no doubt that he would have pardoned Georges if it had been in his power to do so. Indeed, it would have been a credit to him! But now his prisoner has escaped, and just when the governor believed him to be most securely held. Georges one-upped him, you see. Lord Murray will want his revenge."

"Sail ahoy!" cried the crewman in the crow's nest.

Jacques nodded at his father, then raised his head. "Where?" he called.

"Under the wind and coming toward us!" the sailor replied.

"How high?" the captain asked.

"Almost as high as the île des Tonneliers," came the response.

"Can you tell where it is coming from?"

"Port Louis, I'd say!"

"There," Jacques said to Pierre Munier, "you see? I told you we weren't out of their clutches just yet."

Georges and Sara approached them. "Is something wrong?" Sara inquired.

"Nothing; just that we are being pursued," Georges answered for his brother.

"My God!" Sara cried. "Have you been restored to me so miraculously, only to be taken away again? No; it is impossible!"

Meanwhile Jacques drew out his spyglass and climbed to the top of the mainmast. He gazed attentively for a few moments in the direction the watchman had indicated; then, collapsing the instrument with the palm of his hand, he came down and, whistling, returned to his father's side.

"Well?" Pierre Munier asked.

"It's as I thought," replied Jacques. "Our good friends the English are hot on our heels." He looked at his watch. "Fortunately, though, it is only a couple of hours until nightfall, and the moon will not rise until around half past twelve."

"Do you think we will be able to outrun them?" asked the old man anxiously.

"We'll do our best, Father; count on it. I'm not a proud man; I see nothing to be gained by fighting when there are only injuries to be acquired. I'll not put all my precautions to waste, hang it all!"

"What?" Georges exclaimed. "You, Jacques? The intrepid, unde-feated captain—fleeing from the enemy?"

"My dear fellow," said Jacques, "I will always run from the devil when his pockets are empty and his horns two inches longer than my own! It would be a different story if his pockets were full! Then I might risk something; now it isn't worth it."

"You realize," warned Georges, "that they will say you are afraid."

"And I will agree with them, by God! If we rub up against those fel-lows and they take us, it's all over for us. They'll hang us all from the yardarm one by one as quick as you please. And if we take them, we'll have no choice but to sink their ship, and them with it."

"Sink them?" Georges exclaimed. "But why?"

"What else would we do with them? If they were black, we might sell them and make a tidy profit—but what can we do with a bunch of white sailors?"

"Jacques, my dear brother!" Sara put in. "Surely you would not wish to be responsible for the deaths of so many men!"

"Sister," replied Jacques, "we will do what we can. When—if—the time comes, we will put you belowdecks, in a charming little room where you'll be safe and unable to see any of what goes on. You can just imagine that nothing has happened." He returned to the rail and looked in the direction of the pursuing ship. "There she is—you can just see her sails! Look, Father, do you see?"

"What; that white smudge on the waves? Surely it is a seagull, noth-ing more!"

"Not a seagull, Father—a thirty-six-gun frigate. But still a bird, for all that! An eagle, though; not a mere swallow!"

"Might it be only a merchant ship?" asked Pierre Munier, hopefully.

"No; a merchant ship would not lean into the wind like that."

"But—*we* are leaning into the wind, are we not?"

"Oh," said Jacques, "that is another matter entirely! We could not pass by Port Louis; it would be like casting ourselves into a den of wolves! We had to take the nearest route."

"Can we increase our speed?" the old man asked.

"Not at the moment, Father. She's going as fast as she can. When the wind is behind us we can let out the sails a bit more, and perhaps gain a knot or two. The *Leicester* will do the same, though, and she must gain a mile or so on us, I'm afraid. I know her well."

"When do you think she will catch up?" Pierre Munier asked. "Tomorrow?"

"Yes; unless we can escape her during the night."

"Do you think we can?"

"That is in the opposing captain's hands."

"And if they overtake us?" the old man persisted anxiously.

"Then, Father, we will have no choice but to board her. It would be hopeless to engage a ship such as the *Leicester*—if indeed it is she—in running combat. I would bet a hundred Negroes to ten that she outguns us by twelve cannons, at least—and she can run to île de France or île Bourbon, or to Rodrigues for repairs if she must. We have only the open sea. Land is our enemy. We need our wings more than anything else."

"And if we board her?"

"Then the playing field becomes more level. We have howitzers—one of the privileges of being a pirate, you know; we grant them to ourselves, but they are not standard issue on a man-of-war. Also, fortunately, it is peacetime. The *Leicester* probably has a crew of no more than two hundred and seventy men. We have two hundred and sixty, so you see we are evenly matched, especially with such fine rascals as I command! Rest easy, Father! There is the dinner bell; please, do not let a little scrape like this ruin your appetite."

Indeed, the clock had struck seven, and the dinner bell had rung at its customary hour. Georges took Sara's arm and, with Pierre Munier following them, descended to the captain's cabin, which had been transformed into a miniature banquet hall in honor of the newlyweds. Jacques remained on deck a little longer to give a few instructions to his lieutenant.

The interior of the ship was an extraordinary thing to see by any standard. Just as a besotted man lavishes his mistress with jewels and silks, so the *Calypso*'s captain had fitted her out in luxury befitting a sea nymph. Her mahogany staircases shone like glass, and her copper ornaments—polished three times every day—were as bright as gold. Even the ship's weaponry—axes, cutlasses, and muskets—was so well maintained that it seemed more decorative than functional, ranged exquisitely on the decks and around the portholes where the cannons stretched their long bronze necks. Anyone would have thought it was the studio of a famous artist rather than the belowdecks of a ship.

The captain's cabin was especially remarkable in its luxury. Jacques Munier was, as I have said, a man of sensuality, and though he could live quite spartanly when necessity demanded it, under ordinary circumstances he enjoyed voluptuous richness to the utmost. His quarters, which served as parlor, bedchamber, and dining room all at once, were a thing of true beauty.

Two wide couches stood at the port and starboard sides of the cabin, with cannons cleverly concealed beneath them and only visible from the outside. One of these couches served as a bed, and the other as a sofa. Between the windows there was a beautiful Venetian mirror, its Rococo frame ornately carved with figures of cherubs, flowers, and fruits. A silver lamp of superb Renaissance workmanship—no doubt taken from a Madonna's rich altar somewhere—was suspended from the ceiling. The couches and inner walls were covered with magnificent Indian damask, its scarlet ground embroidered with flowers worked so exquisitely in gold thread that it seemed as if fairies had plied their needles to create them.

Jacques, with his customary gallantry, had given Georges and Sara the use of the cabin for their wedding night. But Sara, in view of the fact that their wedding ceremony had been interrupted by Georges's rescue from the church, was not entirely convinced that they were legally married—and Georges promised that he would enter only during the day and find somewhere else to sleep at night until they knew for certain.

The four people gathered around the captain's table that evening were flooded with a strange sort of happiness at finding themselves together when they had so recently despaired of ever seeing one another again. Savoring the present, loath to think of the future or the past, they lingered over dinner for two hours before going back up on deck.

Their first action was to look out to sea where they had last seen the pursuing frigate. There was a short silence.

"The ship seems to have disappeared," observed Pierre Munier, hopefully.

"No," said Jacques. "Her sails are merely in shadow because the sun is setting. Look carefully in this direction, Father."

"Ah!" said Pierre Munier. "I see her now."

"Yes," Georges agreed. "She has gained on us."

"A mile or two nearer, I'd say," mused Jacques. "Look, Georges—you can make out her lower sails now. She can't be more than fifteen miles from us."

The *Calypso* was, at this moment, just off the passe du Cap; they were heading away from the island now. The sun was sinking into a bed of clouds on the horizon, and night was falling with the rapidity peculiar to the tropical latitudes. Jacques beckoned his lieutenant, Ironhead, to his side. "Well, Master Tête-de-Fer!" he said. "What do you think of that ship?"

"I beg your pardon, sir!" said the lieutenant. "Surely you know more about it than I!"

"No matter; I'm asking for your opinion. Is she a merchant ship, do you think, or a man-of-war?"

Ironhead laughed heartily. "You must be joking, Captain! Why, there isn't a merchant ship in the world, even in the East India Company, that could keep pace with the *Calypso,* let alone overtake her!"

"True; and this ship has not only kept pace; she has gained on us. How much distance do you estimate she has gained in, say, the last three hours?"

"Surely you have a better idea than I, Captain."

"I want your opinion," Jacques said again. "Two heads are better than one, as they say!"

"Well," mused Ironhead, "it looks to me like she has gained about two miles."

"Yes," agreed Jacques. "Have you any idea who she is?"

"Surely you recognize her, sir."

"Perhaps, but I would hate to be wrong."

"You, wrong? Impossible!" said Tête-de-Fer, laughing again.

"No matter; tell me anyway."

"She is the *Leicester*, by God," said the lieutenant, without hesitation.

"What do you think she wants?"

"She's after the *Calypso*, no doubt about it. Has a bone to pick, I should say. If I recall correctly, we once cut her mizzenmast in half with a cannonball."

"Quite right," Jacques said, grinning. "I knew everything you've just told me, of course—but I'm glad to see that we are of the same mind. The guard is changing in five minutes; tell any crewmen who aren't on duty to turn in for the night. They'll need a good sleep to be ready for what is to come."

"You don't mean to try and lose her in the night, Captain?"

"Quiet, man!" Jacques bellowed. "We'll speak of that later! Go, carry out my orders."

The watch duly turned over five minutes later, and every crewman not required on deck disappeared below. Within ten minutes, the ship was silent—but no one really slept, though they tried valiantly to look as if they did, for the men were well aware that there was an enemy vessel in pursuit of the *Calypso*. Still, they trusted their captain completely, and they were not afraid.

The brigantine continued on its course—but the swells of the sea were growing larger, and she could not avoid losing speed. Georges, Sara, and Pierre Munier went below to get a bit of sleep; Jacques remained on deck, alone. Night had fallen, and the pursuing frigate was lost in the darkness. After half an hour Jacques summoned Ironhead once more, and the first mate sprang immediately to his side. "What is our position?" he asked the lieutenant.

"Just north of Coin-de-Mire."

"Tell me, do you think you would be able to steer us between Coin-de-Mire and île Plate, without running aground to either side?"

Ironhead grinned. "With my eyes shut, sir."

"Good! Prepare your men for the maneuver, then. We have no time to lose."

"Aye, sir!" The lieutenant shouted a few orders, and the men leapt to their stations.

"Ready about!" bellowed Jacques after a moment of silence.

"All ready, sir!" Ironhead replied.

"Forward helm!" the captain cried. The whistle blew, and the brigantine hesitated for a moment, like a stallion in full gallop suddenly pulled up short; then, slowly, she turned, nosing into the brisk wind, large waves beating against her hull.

"Helm to leeward!" ordered Jacques. The helmsman obeyed, and the ship leaned into the wind. "Raise the windwards—hard astern!"

The crew obeyed with the same speed and efficiency as before, and the *Calypso* changed direction. Her rear sails billowed, and she moved gracefully in the new direction the captain had chosen. "Now, Master Tête-de-Fer!" Jacques exclaimed, watching the movements of his vessel with satisfaction, as a horseman follows the movements of his prize stallion. "You must steer us around the island, taking advantage of every small change in the wind to bring you closer in to the wind, and run parallel to the reef of rocks that extends from the passe des Cornes to Flac Cove."

"Yes, sir!"

"Excellent! And now, I will bid you good night; wake me when the moon is up."

With that, Jacques went off to sleep the untroubled slumber of those who are accustomed to treading a fine line between life and death. Within ten minutes he was as deeply asleep as the lowliest of his crewmen.

THE BATTLE

Ironhead kept his word. He guided the *Calypso* safely through the channel made by the sea as it passes between Coin-de-Mire and île Plate and, rounding the passe des Cornes and the île d'Ambre, brought the ship as close as he could to the coast. At half past midnight, when the moon shone south of Rodrigues Island, he woke the captain as he had been instructed.

Immediately after coming on deck, Jacques swept the horizon with the piercing gaze that only sailors seem to possess. The wind was blowing fresh and brisk east-northeast, and Port Bourbon lay nine miles off the starboard side. There was no sign of the ship that had been pursuing them, either behind them, or to the port side, or ahead of them.

Jacques had played the game perfectly. If the frigate, which they appeared to have lost during the night, had continued sailing to the east, she would not be able to make up the time at daybreak and catch up to the *Calypso;* they would be safe. If, on the other hand, the pursuing captain had figured out Jacques's maneuver and followed them, they could still hide by skirting the coastline and shielding themselves in one of the many small coves that dotted it.

As Jacques peered at the horizon with his spyglass, he felt someone touch him lightly on the shoulder. He turned around; it was Georges. "Ah, so it's you!" he said, holding out his hand.

"What news, my brother?" the young man asked.

"None, at present," Jacques replied. "It is still too dark to see the *Leicester*, if she is out there behind us. We'll know a good deal more at daybreak." He broke off, cocking his head. "Ah!"

"What is it?" Georges asked.

"Nothing; merely a small shift in the wind."

"In our favor?"

"Yes, if indeed the frigate is still pursuing the same course as we are. If she isn't, the wind will benefit us both. In any case, we must take advantage of it!" He turned to the mate who had relieved Ironhead. "Hoist the studding-sails!" he cried.

"Hoist the studding-sails!" the sailor called.

Immediately five white sails unfurled and billowed out like clouds from the topsail, to be speedily tied to the port side of the mainsails. The brigantine seemed to leap forward. George noticed this and made an admiring remark to his brother.

"Yes," replied Jacques proudly, "she is a bit like your Antrim—sensitive and responsive to the bit, and she never requires a flogging to make her gallop. Simply give her enough sail, and she will run with swiftness and style."

"How many knots do you suppose we are going now?" Georges inquired.

"Cast out the log!" Jacques shouted to his men, and this was immediately done. "How many knots?"

"Eleven, Captain."

"Two knots faster than we were going before. We cannot ask any more from a beast of wood, canvas, and iron," Jacques said. "If we had any ship on our heels other than that demon of a *Leicester*, I would dearly love to lead her a merry chase as far as the Cape of Good Hope—and then say good night and leave her there."

Georges did not reply. The two brothers paced the deck in companionable silence. Jacques, though, continued to strain his eyes into the darkness aft of the *Calypso;* finally he stopped and leaned over the rail.

The night seemed to be lifting a bit, though the first streaks of daylight were still barely visible on the horizon. Even in this faint light, like a fog dissipating to make way for bluish dawn, Jacques fancied that he could make out the form of the frigate, about fifteen miles distant, following their exact course. He opened his mouth to tell Georges what he saw, but he was interrupted by the cry of the lookout in the crow's nest: "Sail astern!"

"Yes, yes," said Jacques, as if speaking to himself. "I see her. They have followed our track as surely as if we had left behind a trail of crumbs. Hmm . . . they must have gone between île Plate and île Ronde instead of passing between Coin-de-Mire and île Plate. It cost them two hours—but nevertheless, here they are. There is someone on board who knows the sea very well indeed."

"I see nothing," said Georges, standing at his brother's elbow.

"Look there," said Jacques, pointing. "You can just make out her lower sails. And when she rises on a swell—like that, by God!—her trimmings flash in the light of sunrise. She looks for all the world like a whale rising out of the water to breathe; do you see?"

"Ah," said Georges, nodding. "Yes. I see her now."

"What do you see?" asked a soft voice from behind Georges's shoulder. It was Sara.

"A beautiful sight, my love," he replied. "The sunrise. But as there is no pleasure in this world that is not marred at least a little by pain, I must tell you that there is also a ship. Despite our hopes and my brother's skill, we were not able to lose her in the night."

"My dearest Georges," said Sara calmly. "God, who has so miraculously preserved us thus far, will not desert us when we need him the most. Do not let the sight of our enemies shake your faith, my love. Watch the sun rise, instead. It is beautiful!"

Indeed, the rising sun was an awesome spectacle. The thick shadows of night gave way—reluctantly, it seemed—to a faint, blue-tinged gleam that spread upward from the horizon, gradually expanding and deepening from palest silver to soft rose, and then from deep rose to crimson. At length a violet cloud shot above the horizon like a monarch on his throne—the sun, king of the world, arriving to take possession of his vast and glorious empire.

It was the first time Sara had ever beheld a sunrise at sea. She stood as if paralyzed by the ecstasy of the moment, lost in a moment of spiritual faith, holding tightly to her husband's hand. Georges, who had traveled the oceans enough to witness many a daybreak, was the first to look away—and gaze anew at the object that demanded their immediate attention.

The pursuing frigate was now less visible, lost in the glaring eastern light. The *Calypso*, on the other hand, could easily be seen; there was no doubt of that.

"So," murmured Jacques, "he has seen us—there go his studding-sails." He leaned over to whisper in his brother's ear. "You might do well to prepare Sara, in some small way, for what is about to take place."

"What is Jacques saying?" inquired Sara.

Georges smiled. "He doubts your courage, my love. I was about to set him straight."

"When the moment comes, dearest husband, you have only to tell me what to do, and I will obey you."

"That infernal frigate is sailing so fast that she might as well have wings!" grumbled Jacques. "My dear sister-in-law, did you ever happen to hear, at Port Louis, the name of this ship's commander?"

"I saw him several times at my uncle's," the girl replied. "He is called George Paterson. But I do not think it is he who is captaining the *Leicester* now. Only two days ago I heard that he had fallen mortally ill."

"Well, if they do not promote the first mate to captain when this Paterson dies, they will have done him a grave injustice!" Jacques exclaimed. "I must say that there is a certain pleasure in dealing with such a clever fellow as this. Look how he handles his ship—like a skilled jockey on a prize racehorse, by God! If he can keep up that pace for five or six hours more, we will have quite a battle on our hands!"

"We will engage him, then!" exclaimed a new voice. It was Pierre

Munier, who had just come on deck. His eyes shone with the ardor that always filled his soul in times of danger. Jacques grinned.

"Good morning, Father! I'm delighted to see you in such a mood. In a few hours we shall have need of every able hand on board!"

Sara paled slightly, and Georges felt her grip his hand. He turned to her, smiling. "Now, my dear, are you beginning to doubt your faith in the Almighty, after having so much trust in him?"

"No, of course not," the girl replied. "Even when I hear the roaring of the cannons and the whistling of bullets, and even when I am tormented by the groans of the wounded, I will still be full of hope and faith, and certain that I will see my Georges once again, safe and sound. I cannot explain it, but there is something that tells me that we have already been forced to drink the bitterest dregs from our cup of unhappiness—and that, like shadows disappearing in sunlight, we will soon emerge from darkest night into the brilliance of day."

"Bravo!" Jacques exclaimed. "You have a way with words, my girl! A lovely speech, indeed! I don't see why we shouldn't pull alongside this frigate, by God, and spare him the trouble, and us the boredom, of prolonging the chase any further! What do you say, Georges? Are you ready for such an experience?"

"I am for it," Georges replied. "But tell me, are you not afraid that there is a British ship at anchor in Port Bourbon that might hear the cannons and come out to help her compatriot?"

"Blast it, Georges; you talk like Saint Jean Bouche d'Or! We will stay our course." He turned as his lieutenant approached. "Ah, Master Tête-de-Fer! Your timing is perfect. As you see, we are just off Mont Brabant. Keep us west-southwest of the peak, if you please, and in the meantime we will go down to breakfast. Nourishment is always necessary, especially when one is not sure if he will ever eat again!"

Offering his arm to Sara, Jacques led Georges and Pierre Munier down the cabin stairs. Hoping to distract his guests from the immediate danger, he prolonged the meal as much as possible. Nearly two hours passed before they returned to the deck.

Jacques's eyes went immediately to the *Leicester*. She was so close now that her gleaming guns were clearly visible. However, it appeared that Jacques had expected the enemy ship to be even nearer; his shoulders relaxed a bit. He looked aloft to make sure the sails were still in position, and motioned the first mate to his side. "Tell me, Master Tête-de-Fer," he said, "do I delude myself, or have we gained a little speed during the past two hours?"

"Yes, Captain, you might say that," the other man replied.

"What in blazes have you done to the ship, then?"

"Oh, a trifle or two. I changed our trim a bit, and ordered the men to the bow."

Jacques smiled. "You are a credit to the ship, my dear fellow. Now, how much have we gained?"

Ironhead frowned. "Only one poor knot, I'm afraid. We're at twelve now; I just cast the log. It will not serve us too well, I fear. They have increased their speed as well; we have a pretty clear view of their hull now. I daresay we're dealing with a crafty old sea wolf who will plague us greatly before we are done with him! It puts me in mind of the other time we were pursued by the *Leicester*—Lord William Murray was her captain then, as I recall."

A light seemed to go on in Jacques's head. "Ah!" he cried, striking himself on the forehead. "Ye gods! Why did I not see it before? I'd bet you a thousand louis to a hundred, brother," he said, turning to Georges, "that your mad governor himself is commanding that frigate. He is eager indeed to take his revenge!"

Georges looked thunderstruck. "Do you really think so?" he asked, rising and clutching his brother's arm. "I confess—I will be glad if that is the case. I, too, have an insult to avenge."

"Yes, by God," said Jacques. "It is him; I'm sure of it now. There is not another man who could have followed our trace as he has done, the scoundrel! Quite an honor for a simple slaver like me, to do business with a commodore in the Royal Navy! Thank you, my dear Georges; you have brought me good fortune indeed!" With a hearty laugh, Jacques shook his brother's hand.

Still, in the face of such a dangerous situation as an engagement with Lord William Murray, Jacques felt obliged to take additional precautions. He made a quick inspection of the brigantine. The hammocks had been neatly stowed; he now looked at his crew. They had instinctively divided themselves into groups, each gathered around the gun they would fire. Jacques was satisfied; his men obviously knew what to do as well as he did. No further instruction was necessary, after all. They all knew what was to come, and they were ready for it.

All of a sudden, the rolling of a drum was borne on a sea breeze from the *Leicester* to the *Calypso*. "Ah!" exclaimed Jacques. "No one could accuse them of tardiness! Come, men, let us follow their lead. The sailors of the Royal Navy are good examples indeed!" He took a deep breath and cried with all his strength, "Into the breach!" A second later the pounding of the *Calypso*'s own drum was heard, along with the piercing trill of a fife. The ship's little trio of musicians emerged from the stern, made a circuit of the deck, and disappeared into the fore hatch.

The effect of this little musical display was magical. The men leapt to their posts, armed with light weaponry. Sailors climbed the masts with rifles; muskets were stacked on the deck, and cannons were readied in their portholes. Grenades were piled anywhere they could be easily seized and thrown onto the enemy ship, and lastly the boatswain ordered the decks cleared and the boarding planks hoisted into place.

Belowdecks, the activity was no less frenetic. The powder kegs were pried open, the safety lanterns lit, and the spare wheel and spars readied. Bulkheads were pulled down, and the captain's cabin cleared of its furnishings; the two cannons it contained were rolled aft, ready for service.

Once the bustle had ceased, dead silence fell. Jacques moved around the ship swiftly and quietly, ensuring that everything was ready; every man was at his appointed post, and every piece of equipment placed precisely where it needed to be.

Still, Jacques knew deep in his bones that the engagement he was about to face would be one of the most serious of his life. His inspection was even more thorough than usual, and took a full thirty minutes. He scrutinized every detail, and spoke to every man.

By the time he returned to the bridge, the frigate had visibly gained on them. The two vessels were no more than a mile and a half apart. Another half an hour passed, during which barely a dozen words were exchanged aboard the *Calypso*. Her crew, officers, and passengers alike were enveloped in single-minded concentration. Each of our heroes' physiognomies reflected their characters: Jacques looked carefree; Georges proud. Pierre Munier displayed fatherly solicitude, and Sara pure devotion.

All at once, there was a slight puff of smoke from the frigate. The British flag was hoisted aloft, floating majestically on the breeze. There was no avoiding the battle now; even if the *Calypso* had wished to get away, it was clear that the *Leicester* had superior speed. Jacques ordered his men to lower their spyglasses and turned to Sara. "Come, little sister," he said. "You see that every man is at his post; now you must go to yours."

Sara blanched. "My God, it is time, then? The battle is at hand?"

"It will begin within fifteen minutes, I should say," said Jacques. "It should be quite a heated one, I wager, and anyone who is not absolutely crucial to the fight should retire now."

"Sara," Georges said to the girl. "Do not forget what you promised me."

"No, dearest, I am ready to obey you, of course. But—"

"My love, I know you would not ask me to be a passive observer of the battle, when it is for my sake alone that so many courageous men are risking their lives."

"No!" Sara shook her head. "I ask you only to think of me, my love, and to remember that if you die, I die with you." She kissed Pierre Munier on the cheek; then, turning to Jacques, pressed his hand. Georges took her elbow gently, and the two of them disappeared down the cabin stairs.

He returned fifteen minutes later, a cutlass in one hand and a pair of pistols tucked into his belt. Pierre Munier was armed with the beautifully inlaid rifle that had rendered him faithful service on so many occasions. Jacques, on the other side of the quarterdeck, held a speaking horn—the symbol of command. A saber and an iron helmet lay at his feet.

The two vessels continued to pursue their mirror course, the frigate close on the brigantine's heels. The ships were so near to each other that the sailors in the topmasts could easily watch what was happening on their counterparts' decks.

"Master Tête-de-Fer," said Jacques. "You have good eyes and sound judgment. Kindly climb to the foretop and tell me what is happening aboard the *Leicester*."

The lieutenant sprang to this duty, and within seconds he was perched high on the mast.

"Well?" asked the captain.

"All the men are at their stations, sir, and the gunners are manning the guns. There are marines on the gangways, and the captain is on the quarterdeck. They look ready for action, sir."

"Are there any troops on board besides the marines and the ship's crew?"

"I don't think so, sir, unless they're belowdecks. All the uniforms look the same to me."

"Good!" said Jacques. "It is an equal game, with a difference of only ten or fifteen men. That is all I needed to know, my man; you may descend."

"Wait!" Ironhead exclaimed. "The English captain has raised his speaking horn. If we're quiet, we may be able to catch what he says."

This was not too likely; despite the silence that reigned on the *Calypso*, not a sound from the frigate could be heard on the brigantine. As it turned out, there was no need to hear what the *Leicester*'s captain said. An instant after he lowered the speaking horn, two jets of smoke issued from the bow of the enemy ship and two cannonballs ricocheted along the water in the *Calypso*'s wake.

"Eighteen-pounders," said Jacques. "The same as we have. Good! The odds grow more and more equal! Come on down, Lieutenant," he said to his first mate. "You will be of more help to me down here than up there." Ironhead slid down the mast and stepped to his captain's side.

The frigate continued her advance but did not fire again. The experiment of a moment before had taught her that she was still too far away from the brigantine to fire with accuracy.

"Now, Master Tête-de-Fer," said Jacques, "to the battery. As long as we are in retreat, use only the cannons—but as soon as the frigate pulls alongside, switch to the howitzers, and only the howitzers. Understood?"

"Aye, sir." The lieutenant disappeared down the aft stairway.

Another thirty minutes passed without any further signs of hostility between the two vessels. Jacques, with his eye for distance, refused to waste good powder and shells on the sea and did not respond to the other ship's earlier provocations. But it was obvious, from the excited faces of the two crews and the attention with which the captain measured the space that separated the combatants, that the battle was close at hand; that, as they say, the monologue would become a dialogue very soon indeed.

Scarcely ten more minutes had gone by—ten minutes that seemed like a century to everyone involved—when the bow of the frigate flared with smoke once more, followed by the whistle of cannonballs passing through the *Calypso*'s rigging, punching holes through the foremost topsail and severing a few sheets.

Jacques sized up the damage with a practiced eye. Judging it to be slight, he ordered his men to return fire. "Come on, men!" he cried. "One good turn deserves another, eh? Fire!" A double blast echoed throughout the brigantine, and Jacques leaned over the rail to watch the cannonballs' progress. One of them tore away a portion of the frigate's bulwark, while the other buried itself in her bow.

"Voilà!" Jacques cried. "What will you do now? Give her a broadside! Aim at the rigging—let us clip this bird's wings and break her legs! Wood is more precious than flesh at the moment, is it not? Ha!" No sooner had he uttered these words, however, than two more enemy cannon shells tore through the rigging and sails of the *Calypso*. One merely grazed the mainyard, but the other carried the foremost mast clean away.

"Fire, by God, *fire!*" Jacques shouted. "Teach those rascals a lesson! Twenty-five louis to the first man who brings down a mast!"

The booming of the cannon nearly drowned out his final words, and the balls hurtled through the air toward the enemy ship's rigging. The action was answered immediately, and for nearly a quarter of an hour there was an uninterrupted volley of cannon fire. The breeze had disappeared, and the two vessels were running at barely four or five knots apiece. The space between them was full of black smoke, and the gunners fired blindly. The frigate continued to creep closer and closer to the side of the brigantine—which had the advantage of a rear wind and was sailing in clear air, only her topmasts visible through the smoke.

This was the moment Jacques had been waiting for. He had done everything he could to avoid a shipboard skirmish; now he had no choice but to turn on his pursuer like a wounded boar. The frigate was to starboard of the *Calypso*, firing with her forward guns. Jacques, seeing the advantage in his position, was determined to profit by it. "Bring the watch on deck!" he shouted.

The boatswain's whistle acknowledged his order, and it was carried out in an instant. The firing continued. Jacques's voice rang out again above the fracas. "Tighten the mainsail! Man the rear braces! Haul up the main sheet! Keep alongside her, now! Steady, men!"

These orders had hardly been carried out when the *Calypso*, obeying both her rudder and her rear sails, swung rapidly around to starboard, cutting off the frigate and coming to a stop, thanks to her captain's foresight in supporting the starboard foresails. The *Leicester*, damaged in sails and rigging and unable to halt her forward progress, surged helplessly through the clouds of smoke and the crashing waves, and ran directly into the *Calypso*. With a terrible noise, the frigate's forward mast crashed and tangled in the brigantine's mainsail.

Jacques's voice rose above the din again. "Fire!" he cried. "Fore and aft, men! Raze her like a pontoon! Don't leave a spar standing!"

Fourteen cannons, six loaded with grapeshot and eight with howitzer shells, roared to life. Balls hailed down on the frigate, cutting down thirty or forty men where they stood, and the foremast snapped at its base. At the same moment, a shower of grenades exploded on the frigate's forward deck. The *Leicester*'s only feeble reply was to fire from atop the mizzenmast, which was half enveloped by the ruined topsail.

Now using the *Leicester*'s ruined riggings, ropes, sheets, and spars as bridges, the pirates of the *Calypso* surged aboard the crippled frigate. The British marines tried to hold them off with their muskets, but they could not stem the tide. For every man who fell, another took his place; even those men who were wounded continued to crawl forward, tossing grenades and brandishing their cutlasses. Georges and Jacques were prepared to declare victory when, at the cry of "All hands on deck," the British sailors who had been stationed belowdecks came rushing up through the fore and aft hatchways. This reassured their comrades, who had begun to fold.

The *Leicester*'s captain now emerged at the head of his troops. Jacques had been right. It was Lord William Murray, who had resumed his old command so that he might take his revenge. He and Georges faced each other once again, but this time awash in blood and carnage, their swords in their hands—no longer friends, but mortal enemies.

They recognized each other immediately, and moved to begin hand-to-hand combat—but the commotion around them was so great that they could not reach each other.

The Munier brothers cut great swaths through the British ranks, fighting side by side with calm bravery. Once two sailors raised their axes over Georges's head; then they fell simultaneously, cut down by an unseen marksman. Several times the brothers were threatened with bayonets, and on every occasion their invisible savior shot the assailants dead. It was Pierre Munier, wielding his trusty carbine and protecting his sons like a guardian angel.

All of a sudden a terrible cry rang out over the booming of the grenades, the clash of the bayonets, and the screams of the wounded. The words struck terror into every heart:

"Fire! We're on fire!"

Dense smoke billowed from the aft hatchway and out of the portholes. A howitzer shell had exploded in the captain's cabin, and the frigate was ablaze. For a moment every man stood frozen. Then Jacques's clear and commanding voice made itself heard once more above the din: "Back to the *Calypso*, men!"

With the same speed they had shown in boarding the *Leicester*, the privateers abandoned her to scramble back aboard their own ship. Jacques and Georges, with a few trusty hands assisting them, covered the retreat.

Now Lord Murray appeared again, charging to the forefront of the assault in pursuit of the pirates, brandishing his sword and obviously hoping to reach the deck of the *Calypso*. Jacques's men darted up the masts to toss down a fresh hail of grenades, holding back the enemy while throwing down ropes and mooring lines to aid their comrades' return to the brigantine. By this time Jacques had regained his own deck.

Georges was still aboard the *Leicester.* The governor faced him; the young mulatto readied himself for the fight. Then all at once a hand seized Georges in an iron grip and pulled him to safety. It was Pierre Munier—who would not leave his son, and who had now saved him from certain death for the third time in this extraordinary day.

Jacques's voice rang out again. "Bring us 'round, men! Hoist the jib and haul down the main tack. Helm, hard to starboard!" His orders were obeyed with such swiftness that the English, fast as they were, were not able to lash the two ships together. The *Calypso,* with a great heave, pulled away from her enemy as if she understood the danger she was in.

The *Leicester,* now lacking her forward mast, moved slowly under the power of the sails remaining on the mainmast and the mizzenmast.

A terrible spectacle could now be seen on her bloody decks, witnessed with horror by those safely aboard the *Calypso.*

The fire, which had been allowed to spread unnoticed in the heat of combat, had spread too far to be controlled.

The famed British discipline was never more admirable than at this moment. In the midst of the choking smoke, Lord Murray mounted the quarterdeck and raised the speaking horn he still clutched in his left fist.

"Steady, men! Stay calm! I am in control!" The English sailors stopped in their tracks.

"To the boats!" the captain cried. The launch was swiftly lowered; then the jolly boat, and finally the two quarter boats. "The jolly boat and launch for the marines," ordered Lord Murray. "The two quarter boats for the crew!"

The *Calypso* widened the gap between herself and the frigate, and the rest of Lord Murray's commands were inaudible. From the brigantine's deck, the privateers could see the four boats filling with the remnants of the frigate's crew, while the wounded crawled on their knees, begging to be taken along.

Jacques, watching closely, realized that the *Leicester*'s escape boats could not possibly contain all the survivors. "Launch two lifeboats!" he shouted at once. Two empty launches were unlashed from the *Calypso*'s side and dropped to float lightly on the waves. Immediately the English sailors who had not been able to find a place in the other craft began swimming toward them.

Lord Murray had remained on board the *Leicester.*

His men had tried to persuade him to join them on the lifeboats, but he had refused. There were wounded men aboard his ship, and he was responsible for them. He would go down with them.

The churning sea was fearsome.

The four lifeboats pulled clear of the burning vessel, their occupants rowing desperately. The remaining sailors were still pulling themselves aboard the boats Jacques had ordered dropped.

The *Leicester* sat motionless in the smoke, burning, with her dying crewmen scattered on the decks and her commander standing erect among them.

It was a terrible spectacle. Aboard the *Calypso*, Georges felt Sara's trembling hand come to rest on his shoulder. He did not turn; he did not take his gaze from the flaming wreckage of the *Leicester.* Even the lifeboats, once they were at a safe distance, halted upon the waves. Every eye was fixed on the crippled frigate.

This, my friends, is what happened next:

The smoke from the *Leicester* grew thicker and thicker. Tongues of fire flickered out of her portholes; climbed her masts; devoured her sails. The loaded guns burst, one by one. Then, all at once, there was a deafening explosion. The body of the ship split, and a geyser of flame shot skyward. The observers watched fragments of masts and riggings hurtle through the air and plunge into the sea.

Of the *Leicester,* nothing remained but debris.

Sara's voice was quiet. "What of Lord Murray?"

"If it were not my fate to live on with you, Sara," Georges said, turning to face her, "on my honor, I would choose to die exactly as he has."

NOTES

CHAPTER I. L'ÎLE DE FRANCE

P. 3, chapter title. *L'île de France:* Better known as Mauritius, it is part of the Mascarene Islands in the southwest Indian Ocean. Known to Arab and Malay traders in the Middle Ages as Dina Mozare, it came under Dutch control from 1598 to 1710 and was named Mauritius in honor of the governor Prince Maurice of Nassau. Renamed île de France, the island was colonized by the French until 1810, and the sea battle represented at the beginning of *Georges* marked its end as a French colony. It then came under the rule of Great Britain, which renamed it Mauritius and abolished slavery in 1835. Mauritius remained a British colony until independent sovereignty in 1968.

P. 3, L. 16. *Walter Scott:* The Scottish novelist and poet (1771–1832) whose *Waverley* (1814)—followed by many other novels, from *The Antiquary* (1816), *Rob Roy* (1818), and *The Heart of Midlothian* (1818) to *Ivanhoe* (1819), *The Pirate* (1820), and *Redgauntlet* (1824)—initiated the vogue of historical fiction in European and American literature. Scott produced a massive œuvre at a very fast writing pace, and in his novels he let imaginary central figures ("Scott heroes") encounter documented historical characters and events, presenting memorably detailed settings as well as dramatic battle and travel scenes. In these aspects, Dumas's *Georges* follows the Scott tradition.

P. 4, L. 11. *modern Prometheus ... St. Helena ... martyr is gone:* Dumas is referring to Napoleon Bonaparte, who, after a series of military losses, abdicated as French emperor in April 1814. His English opponents insisted on his exile and sent him to the Mediterranean island of Elba. Nine months later Napoleon escaped and orchestrated his reinstallation, resulting in the famous battle of Waterloo on June 18, 1815, that signaled Napoleon's final defeat. (It also finalized the British rule over the former île de France.) In order to prevent another escape, the English had him exiled much farther away, to the barren South Atlantic Ocean island of St. Helena, where he died in 1821. Dumas was sympathetic to Napoleon, his father having distinguished himself in the French army and been allowed the opportunity to succeed despite his status as a mulatto.

P. 4, L. 13. *Joan of Arc:* (1412–31) a national heroine of France and a saint of the Roman Catholic Church. She claimed to have been directed by God to recover her homeland from the English occupiers in the latter part of the Hundred Years' War. Joan of Arc led troops to military victories against the English under the instructions of the uncrowned king Charles VII. She fell prisoner in battle and was convicted of heresy. Subsequently, the English regent John of Lancaster, first Duke of Bedford, had her burned at the stake.

P. 4, L. 13. *Mary Stuart:* (1542–87) Better known as Mary, Queen of Scots, she was the monarch of the Kingdom of Scotland (1542–67) and the queen consort of France (1559–60). Mary Stuart was forced by her Protestant lords to abdicate the Scottish throne to her infant son. She fled imprisonment and sought shelter in England, where instead she was held captive for nineteen years. In the wake of a series of Roman Catholic plots against Elizabeth, the queen's ministers demanded and put into action Mary Stuart's execution.

P. 4, L. 14. *Golgotha:* the hill on which Jesus was crucified.

P. 4, L. 20. The Lusiads: Portuguese epic, *Os Lusíadas* (1571) in the original, by the poet Luíz Vaz de Camões (1524–80), often called Camoens in English. A continuation of the tradition of Homer and Virgil, *The Lusiads* tells the story of the hero Lusus's coming to the part of the Iberian peninsula that was named Lusitania and is now Portugal. In the fifth canto of the poem, the giant Adamastor, descended from the *gigantes* of Greek myth, rules the Indian Ocean (where île de France lies) and represents the dangers Vasco da Gama has to overcome braving the Cape of Storms, turning it into the Cape of Good Hope.

P. 5, L. 20. *Cléofas:* Hero of the Spanish satire *El diablo cojuelo* (*The Limping Devil,*

1641) by Luis Vélez de Guevara and adapted by Alain-René Le Sage as *Le Diable boiteux* (1707). When the student Don Cléofas Leandro Pérez Zambullo frees the devil Asmodée from the bottle in which he is imprisoned, the devil takes Don Cléofas on his coattail to the steeple of San Salvador, above the city of Madrid, and lets him magically see through the roofs and walls, revealing a satiric panorama of many comically intimate scenes of human folly. By casting the reader as a new Cléofas, Dumas's narrator takes the part of the devil and invites the reader to the "Asmodeus ride" of a bird's-eye view of the island.

P. 6, L. 10. *Creoles:* a word of Spanish origin ("Criollo") referring to people born in European colonies, especially in the Americas. Whether it should be applied to people of both European and non-European descent is disputed. Dumas uses the term in the narrower sense of people of French origin born in the colonies, who were often believed to be particularly prejudiced.

P. 7, L. 31. *Paul and Virginie: Paul et Virginie* is a sentimental island romance published in 1787 by Jacques-Henri Bernardin de Saint-Pierre. Set on Île de France, it tells the story of two young people who fall in love completely according to nature's laws due to the isolation of their homeland from civilization. Their sad deaths at the end of the tale made the book one of the most popular novels of the eighteenth century.

CHAPTER II. LIONS AND LEOPARDS

P. 10, L. 1. *It began:* As Douglas Munro suggested in *Alexander Dumas, Père,* "Dumas' account of the battle was for a long time considered to be false in that it differed from the official account published in *Le Moniteur;* it has, however, since been proved that his description was the correct one, the official version having been distorted for political reasons" (pp. 60–61).

CHAPTER III. THREE CHILDREN

P. 17, L. 6. *caissons:* carriers of artillery ammunition. A large case rests on an axle, with a road wheel at each end, while poles connect the center of the axle to the harnessed horses. Commonly used to tow guns.

P. 18, L. 18. *cuirassier:* a member of the cavalry who wears a cuirass, a type of protective armor.

P. 18, L. 28. *Malgache dog:* a dog of the Coton de Tulear breed. The breed appeared at the pirate and slave-trading port of Tulear, Madagascar, during the seventeenth century. It was adopted by Madagascar's nobles as a companion dog and subsequently became known as The Royal Dog of Madagascar. A symbol of wealth, it was adopted by the conquering French colonists.

P. 23, L. 32. *the Dumas battery:* one of the two principal fortification batteries of Port Louis, capital of Mauritius, at the time.

CHAPTER IV. FOURTEEN YEARS LATER

P. 33, L. 33. *Sixtus Quintus:* Pope Sixtus V (1520–90), one of the founders of the Counter-Reformation.

CHAPTER V. THE PRODIGAL SON

P. 40, L. 7. *one of these ribbons:* the ribbons of Charles III and the Legion of Honor; see ch. 4, p. 34, l. 21.

P. 40, L. 13. *equerry:* a steward in a noble household who is responsible for the stables and horses.

CHAPTER VI. TRANSFIGURATION

P. 51, L. 3. *Antæus:* in classical mythology, the *gigante* son of Poseidon and Gæa, the gods of the sea and of earth. He forced travelers to wrestle with him but was crushed by Hercules.

P. 51, L. 3. *child Hannibal:* (247–183 BC) a Punic military leader and politician. His military accomplishments as commander in chief of the Carthaginian forces over Rome distinguished him as a superb tactician and commander. It is said that Hannibal's father, Hamilcar Barca, demanded him to swear allegiance to the Carthaginian cause against Rome.

P. 54, L. 9. *louis:* short for "Louis d'Or," a gold coin issued by the kings of France to replace the franc in 1640. By the time this tale takes place, the louis was valued as a twenty-franc piece.

P. 55, L. 13. *Lais . . . Montyon Prize:* The beautiful, high-priced hetæra Lais of Corinth lived during the Peloponnesian war and had many lovers, among them the philosopher Aristippus; Demosthenes considered her too expensive. She fell in love with Eubotas, who, after deceptively promising to take her to Cyrene with him, carried only her portrait along; she became addicted to drinking after that. Hans Holbein the Younger painted a *Lais of Corinth* (1526) who is separated from the viewer by a counter on which many gold coins have been deposited, though she holds out her hand for more. The book *Les Amours de Laïs* was published anonymously in 1765. (There was also a younger courtesan

Lais of Hyccara in Sicily who loved Hippolochus and followed him to Thessaly, where she was stoned to death by jealous women in a temple for Aphrodite.) The Montyon Prize had been given out by the Académie française since 1783 for the virtuous act of a poor person.

P. 55, L. 19. *Astarte:* ancient goddess of Tyre, Sidon, and Elat mentioned in the Bible (1 Kings 11:5).

P. 56, L. 17. *Chevalier de Saint-Georges:* Joseph de Boulogne (1745–99), the natural child of a French aristocratic settler and a young African slave in Guadeloupe, who was educated at an elite Paris academy, became a fencing champion, musician, and composer, and, during the French Revolution, commanded a mulatto unit in which Dumas's father, Thomas-Alexandre Dumas-Davy de la Pailleterie, served.

P. 60, L. 1. *modern Cato:* Cato the Elder (234–149 BC) was known for his striving for manly heroism and moral strictness.

P. 60, L. 15. *Muhammad Ali . . . Ibrahim Pasha:* Born in Ottoman Macedonia, Muhammad Ali (1769–1849) became a viceroy of Egypt who fought against the Napoleonic invasion in 1798, then industrialized Egypt, modernized the army, and conquered parts of Sudan and of the Arabian peninsula, transforming Egypt from a part of the Ottoman Empire into a modern dynasty. One of his sons, Ibrahim Pasha (1789–1848), fought against the Wahhabite rebels in Arabia in 1816–1818, becoming governor of Mecca and Medina. Asked by the Ottoman sultan to subdue the Greek independence movement, Ibrahim Pasha conquered the Peloponnese in 1824, though the Egyptians were ultimately forced out again. Invading Palestine in 1831–32 was a new military campaign against the Ottoman sultan, which led to the annexation of Syria and Adana.

P. 60, L. 33. *duke d'Angoulême:* Charles Philip (1757–1836) held the title between the years of 1773 and 1836 and reigned as Charles X, king of France and of Navarre; *Ferdinand VII:* (1784–1833), king of Spain from 1813 to 1833; *that of Charles III:* a Spanish decoration.

CHAPTER VII. THE BERLOQUE

P. 65, L. 29. *Francis I:* (1494–1547) Francis I reigned as king of France from 1515 to 1547; *Louis XIII:* (1601–43), Louis XIII was the French king from 1610 to 1643.

P. 66, L. 28–P. 67, L. 16. *I live . . . Carouba pipe:* a song written in a somewhat arbitrary mix of French and Creole. The original lyrics are as follows:

I

Moi resté dans un p'tit la caze,
Qu'il faust baissé moi pour entré;
Mon la tête touché son faitaze,
Quand mon li pié touché plancé.
Moi té n'a pas besoin lumière,
Le soir, quand moi voulé dormi;
Car, pour moi trouvé lune claire,
N'a pas manqué trous, Dié merci!

II

Mon lit est un p'tit natt' malgace,
Mon l'oreillé morceau bois blanc,
Mon gargoulette un' vié calbasse,
Où moi met l'arak, zour de l'an.
Quand mon femm' pour faire p'tit ménaze,
Sam'di comme ça vini soupé,
Moi fair' cuir, dans mon p'tit la caze,
Banane sous la cend' grillé.

III

A mon coffre n'a pas serrure,
Et jamais moi n'a fermé li.
Dans bambou comm' ça sans ferrure,
Qui va cherché mon langouti?
Mais dimanch' si gagné zournée,
Moi l'achète un morceau d'tabac,
Et tout la s'maine, mois fais fumée,
Dans grand pipe, à moi carouba.

P. 68, L. 8. *Anjouan:* part of the Comoros Islands, on the opposite side of Madagascar from île de France.

CHAPTER VIII. THE TOILETTE OF THE RUNAWAY SLAVE
P. 75, L. 9. *tenrecs:* members of a family of mammals, somewhat akin to a hedgehog; *Centetes ecaudatus.*
P. 80, L. 12. *Alcidamas:* an Athenian rhetorician (fourth century BC).
P. 80, L. 13. *Milo of Croton:* famous Greek wrestler (fifth century BC) who is believed to have carried an ox to the stadium at Olympia.
P. 80, L. 20. *Antæus:* See note for ch. 6, p. 51, l. 3.

CHAPTER IX. THE ROSE OF THE RIVIÈRE NOIRE

P. 86, L. 12. *English put a stop to the slave trade:* The British transatlantic slave trade of Africans was abolished in 1807, and France and Spain banned it in 1815, though there were many violations of these international agreements. Slavery was ended in France and England before it was in the United States; the French first abolished all slavery as of 1794, but reinstated it in 1802, terminating it only in 1848. In the British colonies slaves were generally emancipated in 1834. In Mauritius slavery was brought to an end in 1835.

CHAPTER X. THE BATH

P. 93, L. 26. *amaranth:* a type of plant that features beautiful clusters of small, brightly colored flowers.

P. 95, L. 12. Clarissa Harlowe: *Clarissa, or The History of a Young Lady* was an epistolary novel published by Samuel Richardson in 1747 or 1748. The sad story of its heroine's refusal to marry the rich Roger Solmes, her falling victim to the wicked Robert Lovelace, her entrapment, rape, and death made this very long novel a popular tale in its day and a foundational work in the rise of the sentimental tradition.

P. 95, L. 27. *Venus:* goddess of love and beauty; Roman counterpart of the Greek Aphrodite. According to myth she was born from the foam of the Aegean waves.

CHAPTER XII. THE BALL

P. 107, L. 33. *Juvenal called . . . "woven air":* Dumas may have confused two Roman satiric poets, Juvenal (c. 55–c. 127) and Petronius (c. 27–66). It was Gaius Petronius who used the phrase in his *Satyricon:* "Aequum est induere nuptam ventum texilem, / palam prostare nudam in nebula linea?" (Is't right the bride should wear the woven wind, / And stand exposed in garments thin as air? Transl. Alfred R. Allinson)

P. 117, L. 8. *Don Quixote:* the protagonist of Miguel de Cervantes Saavedra's early seventeenth-century novel, *Don Quixote de la Mancha.* Alonso Quixano, inspired by stories of chivalric bravery, believes he is a knight, renames himself Don Quixote de la Mancha, and embarks on a journey against injustice in the name of his beloved maiden. In a famous scene in the novel, Don Quixote tries to fight windmills, believing them to be giants.

CHAPTER XIII. THE SLAVE SHIP

P. 118, L. 7. *abolition of public slave trading:* See note for ch. 9, p. 86, l. 12.

P. 119, L. 24. *Cesare Borgia:* (1475–1507) a Spanish-Italian condottiere, lord, and cardinal. He was appointed commander of the papal armies and was sent by his father, Pope Alexander VI, to subdue the cities of Romagna in central Italy. The death of his father in 1503 ended his own career, for Borgia was captured by his political enemies and exiled to Spain. He later escaped to join his brother-in-law, King John III of Navarre, and died in his service.

CHAPTER XIV. THE SLAVE TRADER'S PHILOSOPHY

P. 127, L. 5. *the fabled donkey:* Dumas may be alluding to one of Aesop's donkey fables; in "The Man, the Boy and the Donkey," for example, the donkey drowns.

P. 127, L. 7. *East India Company:* a joint-stock company founded in 1600 that operated under an English Royal Charter granting it trade privileges in India. It effectively enjoyed a trade monopoly in the East Indies. In time, the Company wielded ruling power in India by virtue of its governmental and military activities. It was dissolved in 1858.

P. 129, LL. 10–11. Ran tan . . . allons rire!: lines from the military song "La Marche d'Austerlitz," written to commemorate Napoleon's decisive victory at the battle of Austerlitz in 1805. The first line cannot truly be translated, but the second may be rendered as "How we're going to laugh!"

P. 130, L. 34. *bulwark:* the woodwork above the deck that runs around the length of the ship.

P. 131, L. 22. *the disaster of Waterloo:* On June 18, 1815, Napoleon Bonaparte led his last battle at Waterloo. Having escaped from his exile in Elba, Napoleon reinstalled himself on the throne of France for a hundred days. In response, the English, Prussians, Germans, and Belgians joined forces against the French. After the costly defeat at Waterloo, Napoleon was deposed and banned to St. Helena.

P. 133, L. 20. *Ulysses:* the Latin name of Odysseus, the protagonist of Homer's epic, the *Odyssey,* and a character in the *Iliad.* Odysseus, king of Ithaca, spends ten years trying to return home after fighting in the Trojan War. During the sea journey, Zeus destroys Odysseus' ship, leaving Odysseus the only survivor. Odysseus is washed upon the shores of Ogygia, the nymph Calypso's island. Calypso confines him to be her lover for seven years, promising him immortality in return for his stay.

P. 134, L. 19. *Hercules and Omphale:* In Greek mythology, as penalty for his murder of Iphitus, the great hero Hercules was sold as a slave to Omphale. Hercules was forced to do women's work and wear women's clothing. Some accounts contend that Omphale later freed Hercules, married him, and gave birth to his children.

P. 134, L. 19. *Samson and Delilah:* In the Hebrew Bible's Book of Judges, Samson is a judge who performs superhuman feats and fights enemies. After Samson falls in love with Delilah, the Philistines beseech her to try to find the secret of Samson's strength. When he eventually discloses that he would lose his power if he were to lose his hair, Delilah instructs a servant to shave Samson's locks. For his lapse, Samson is abandoned by God and subsequently is captured by the Philistines. He is blinded, imprisoned and forced into labor. He later brings down the Philistine temple on the heads of his captors, sacrificing himself in the process.

CHAPTER XV. PANDORA'S BOX

P. 139, L. 10. *Aline, queen of Golconda:* a novel by French statesman and writer Stanislas-Jean de Boufflers (1738–1815). It was adapted as an opera by Gaetano Donizetti and performed in Paris in 1828. Aline, a humble shepherd girl, is abducted by pirates and brought to the kingdom of Golconda. When Golconda's king falls in love with her and marries her, she becomes queen. He subsequently dies and she is urged to choose a husband among her suitors.

P. 141, L. 20. *Mme de Pompadour:* born Jeanne-Antoinette Poisson (1721–64), she was the renowned mistress of King Louis XV of France. Louis XV installed her at Versailles, bought her the Pompadour residence, and made her a marquise. Poisson was known for her interest in fashion and art.

P. 146, L. 8. *Byron . . . Cain:* the poetic drama *Cain: A Mystery* (1821) by Lord Byron (1788–1824), a leading poet in the Romantic literary movement, and particularly known for his longer epic poems. Dumas is alluding to the scene in which Lucifer offers Cain to "fly with me o'er the gulf / Of space an equal flight, and I will show / What thou dar'st not deny,—the history / Of past—and present, and of future worlds."

P. 147, L. 8. *Faust:* an allusion to the "Walpurgisnacht" scene in the drama *Faust: Part One* (1808) by Johann Wolfgang von Goethe (1749–1832). In the night in which the witches congregate in the Harz mountains, the devil Mephistopheles takes Faust for an eerie ride over the assembled figures.

CHAPTER XVII. THE RACES

P. 162, L. 12. *louis:* See note for ch. 6, p. 54, l. 9.

P. 170, L. 20. *burnoose:* a long hooded cloak worn in desert climates to keep the rider cool and out of the sun.

P. 171, L. 20. *djerid:* a game played on horseback in which riders attempt to throw blunt spears at members of an opposing team.

CHAPTER XVIII. LAÏZA

P. 180, L. 7. coram populo: Latin for "before the eyes of the people": (from *cora*, "pupil of the eye," and *populus*, "people").

P. 182, L. 34. *the Redoute Labourdonnaie:* multisided, visible fortification for guns, named after Bertrand-François Mahé de la Bourdonnais (1699–1753), a French naval officer and, from 1735, governor of île de France and île Bourbon (Réunion).

CHAPTER XIX. THE YAMSÉ

P. 189, L. 11. *Menenius:* Menenius Agrippa, a Roman consul famous for conquering the Sabines in 503 BC. Dumas here refers to a famous speech that Menenius gave to members of the plebeian class who were involved in a labor stoppage, in which Roman society was likened to a human body that had to work in harmony in order to be effective.

P. 189, L. 16. *Saint-Domingue:* In 1791 the black population on the island colony of Saint-Domingue rose up against the ruling French plantation owners. At the end of a thirteen-year political revolution that destroyed slavery and the plantation system, the new black government changed the name of the island back to the precolonial *Haiti* ("land of mountains" in Arawak), and the Republic of Haiti declared its independence from France on January 1, 1804.

P. 189, L. 26. *only one man* . . . *:* Antonio could either be referring to Toussaint L'Ouverture (1743–1803), the leader of the rebel forces in Saint-Domingue, or the first official ruler of Haiti, Jean-Jacques Dessalines (1758–1806). Dessalines was murdered by co-conspirators only two years after the Haitian government was put in place, and the country was divided between Henri Christophe and Alexandre Pétion.

P. 190, L. 31. *burnoose:* See note for ch. 17, p. 170, l. 20.

P. 190, L. 31. *caftan:* a full-length tunic or robe, usually made of rich fabric, worn chiefly in eastern Mediterranean countries by men.

CHAPTER XX. THE RENDEZVOUS

P. 194, L. 5. *Pétion:* Alexandre Pétion (1770–1818) was a mulatto leader during the Haitian Revolution and, after the murder of Henri Dessalines, became president of the Republic of Haiti, controlling the south while the black ex-slave Henri Christophe ruled the north.

P. 194, L. 29. *Enceladus:* in Greek mythology, a *gigante,* a child of Gæa (Earth) who rebelled against the gods. He was wounded and thrown underneath Mount Etna in Sicily; thereafter, fire coming from the volcano was said to be his breath.

CHAPTER XXIV. THE GREAT WOODS

P. 224, L. 4. *tenrecs:* see note for ch. 8, p. 75, 1. 9.

CHAPTER XXVII. THE REHEARSAL

P. 255, L. 13. *Charles I . . . de Thou:* Charles I (1600–49) was king of England, famously beheaded for his religious and political differences with the British Parliament during the English Civil War (1642–51). Mary Stuart, queen of Scots (1542–87), was Charles's grandmother and was executed on suspicion of taking part in a plot against Elizabeth I, queen of England. The marquis de Cinq-Mars (1620–42) was a confidant of Louis XIII of France who tried to turn the king against his minister Cardinal Richelieu. Richelieu in turn had the marquis imprisoned and beheaded. François-Auguste de Thou (1607–42) was Cinq-Mars's friend and was likewise executed for not revealing the conspiracy.

P. 259, L. 19. Paul et Virginie: See note for ch. 1, p. 7, l. 31.

CHAPTER XXVIII. THE CHURCH OF SAINT-SAUVEUR

P. 265, L. 12. *Epaminondas:* a general (c. 418–362 BC) of the Greek city-state of Thebes who liberated Thebes from Spartan rule and changed the makeup and politics of Greece through his cunning political and military strategy.

P. 267, L. 13. *sacristy:* the section of a church that contains the vestments, chalices, and other church valuables.

CHAPTER XXIX. THE *LEICESTER*

P. 274, L. 17. *howitzer:* a type of field artillery that is relatively small—less than thirty caliber—and shoots at high angles to deliver artillery shells so that they plunge from above.

CHAPTER XXX. THE BATTLE

P. 283, L. 24. *Saint Jean Bouche d'Or:* a French translation—literally "golden mouth"—of the Greek surname of St. John Chrysostom (347–407), a church father known for his eloquent and commonsense preaching as well as his denunciation of decadent lifestyles.

FOR FURTHER READING

Michel Fabre. *From Harlem to Paris: Black American Writers in France, 1840–1890.* Urbana and Chicago: University of Illinois Press, 1991.

Léon-François Hoffmann. *Le Nègre romantique: Personnage littéraire et obsession collective.* Paris: Payot, 1973.

Léon-François Hoffmann, ed. Alexandre Dumas, *Georges.* Paris: Gallimard, 1974 (folio 567). With introduction on "Dumas et les Noirs" and a dossier including chronology, textual comment, documents, and annotations.

Douglas Munro. *Alexandre Dumas, Père: A Bibliography of Works Translated into English to 1910.* New York: Garland, 1978.

Scott Robert Russell. "Héroïsme et Bâtardise: Alexandre Dumas, *Georges.*" PhD dissertation, Brown University, 1992.

Daniel Zimmermann. *Alexandre Dumas le Grand: Biographie.* Paris: Juillard, 1993.

ACKNOWLEDGMENTS

I am indebted to my research assistant Cambridge Sena Ridley, who helped in many ways in the preparation of this edition. She assisted in background research, proofread an earlier version of the translation, commented on my introduction, and drafted many notes. Anastasia Artmyev Berg helped write additional notes, and Lawrence Rosenwald reviewed the translation of the song "Moi resté dans un p'tit la caze," written in a mix of French and Creole.

—W.S.

About the Translator

TINA A. KOVER was born and raised in Colorado and studied French at the University of Denver and the University of Lausanne in Switzerland. She has translated commercial and government documents in the United States and Europe for more than ten years. Her first literary translation, George Sand's *The Black City*, was published in 2004.

ABOUT THE EDITOR

WERNER SOLLORS teaches African American Studies, English, and Comparative Literature at Harvard University. The author of *Beyond Ethnicity: Consent and Descent in American Culture* and *Neither Black Nor White Yet Both: Thematic Explorations of Interracial Literature,* he edited *Theories of Ethnicity: A Classical Reader, The Life Stories of Undistinguished Americans,* and *An Anthology of Interracial Literature: Black-White Contacts in the Old World and the New.*